The Queen's Serpent

Venom Series

A.L. Maruga

Cover: Cady Verdiramo of Cruel Ink Design

Editing: Furious Editing

Contents

Author's Note   1

Dedication   3

Author's Quote   4

Fullpage Image   6

1. Diego   7

Fullpage Image   12

2. Issy   13

Fullpage Image   24

3. Diego   25

Fullpage Image   32

4. Issy   33

Fullpage Image   42

5. Diego   43

Fullpage Image   50

6. Issy   51

Fullpage Image   62

7. Diego   63

Fullpage Image   70

8. Diego   71

Fullpage Image	80
9. Issy	81
Fullpage Image	88
10. Diego	89
Fullpage Image	98
11. Issy	99
Fullpage Image	108
12. Diego	109
Fullpage Image	118
13. Issy	119
Fullpage Image	128
14. Issy	129
Fullpage Image	142
15. Diego	143
Fullpage Image	150
16. Issy	151
Fullpage Image	160
17. Diego	161
Fullpage Image	168
18. Issy	169
Fullpage Image	178
19. Diego	179
Fullpage Image	186
20. Issy	187
Fullpage Image	196
21. Diego	197

Fullpage Image 208

22. Diego 209

Fullpage Image 220

23. Issy 221

Fullpage Image 232

24. Diego 233

Fullpage Image 240

25. Issy 241

Fullpage Image 254

26. Diego 255

Fullpage Image 260

27. Issy 261

Fullpage Image 268

28. Santiago 269

Fullpage Image 274

29. Issy 275

Fullpage Image 284

30. Diego 285

Fullpage Image 292

31. Issy 293

Fullpage Image 298

32. Issy 299

Fullpage Image 306

33. Diego 307

Fullpage Image 312

34. Issy 313

Fullpage Image 35.   324

Issy   325

Acknowledgements   333

About the Author   336

Author's Note

For those of you who are looking for a *Cinderella & Prince Charming* love story. **Look elsewhere.** You won't find them in this book or really in anything I write, my mind is too dark and unhinged for that.

The characters in this book and series are unapologetically toxic on their own; together, they are uncontrollably depraved, unhinged, filled with flaws, and dangerous to themselves and others.

I rewrote this book three times, trying to soften their lines, but in the end, they demanded their story be told just how they wanted it. This is not a story for the faint of heart and the truth is a piece of me broke writing it.

No prince is coming to save the princess in this book; he would rather imprison her himself and selfishly keep her under lock and key. This is a story of obsession, destruction, and wickedness. This book is filled with darkness that will drag you down to the deep and lay waste to your soul.

Please heed my warning and read the T.W. before proceeding. If you have any issues or may be triggered by *drug addiction, addiction, relapse, and suicide,* **PLEASE** do not read this book.

I wrote this book with love for my own loved ones who struggle with addiction and for a special woman whom I've had the privilege to meet on this journey who suffered an unspeakable loss.

"Sometimes the smallest step in the right direction ends of being the biggest step of your life. Tiptoe if you must, but take the step." Naeem Callaway

This is a complete work of fiction and is not meant to target anyone, or any group. This book has spoilers for the Casbury Prep series. You may be a little lost if you have not read that series first. There are Spanish and Portuguese sentences in this work of fiction.

Please don't turn the page if you can't handle the level of *darkness* I bring to my characters. No return trip from hell will be available to you, and no refunds on your sanity.

There are so many **T.W.** and sensitive topics in this book that it would literally take up multiple pages to mention them all here. Please check them **here** or on my website.

For those of you who wish to go in blind, please remember this is a work of fiction, and I **DO NOT** condone or approve of any of the situations, actions, or behaviors of the characters.

This book will completely mess you up. **Guard your mental health.**
Don't say I didn't warn you.
xoxo

A.L. Maruga

Dedication

Sometimes you need to wake up with violence to show the villains who the
fuck you are.
Sometimes you need to be a *good girl* on your knees, and take it any way you
can.
To the ones out there who crave the dark,
but also like to fight back, with a hand wrapped around their throat.
Take it, baby,
take it nice and deep,
and swallow it like it's your favorite drug.

Author's Quote

Just when you think your very bones will shatter and break,
fragmenting along with your heart and soul,
that there is no way that you can continue
breathing, living, hoping.

That is when life will reflect back to you your true strength.
When you have nothing left to lose,
that is when you find yourself.
At the bottom of a deep,
dark hole, with only your demons for company,
a light grows and shines bright,
leading you out of the darkness.

Hold on, you were never truly alone.

A.L. Maruga

CHAPTER ONE

"Without obsession, life is nothing."

John Waters

Casbury, North Carolina

"**A**re we good?" Theo inquires, his dark blue eyes sliding from Carter to me. God, this motherfucker makes me want to shank him, but I have to restrain myself and play nice. I have too much to lose at the moment if I do, and let's face it, he's just not worth it.

We both nod back at him; humor fills me at the apprehensive look he had on his miserable, fucking face only moments ago, as he approached the dark Range Rover waiting next to us. The *fucking king of Casbury* was worried I would take off with his precious, vicious queen.

I'm not going to stand here and pretend I haven't thought about messing with the fucker, and just taking Mia Stratford and hiding her somewhere. Just to see what he would do and how full-blown psycho he would go. But time is not on my side if I am going to pull off one of the greatest heists in modern history. *Trust me*, not only am I going to attempt it, but I'm going to succeed in helping to steal not one crown jewel, but two of them, right from underneath Stella Stratford, AKA *the fucking Ice Queen's* snobby-ass nose.

"Bro, you know you're the shit, right? Still ugly as fuck, but you're alright."
Carter starts with his comically complicated handshake, and as usual, I go along
for the ride. I would never admit it out loud 'cause his already inflated *pretty-boy*
head would swell to an impossible size, but I'm going to miss the psychotic
fucker.

Who knew two unhinged, possessive psychopaths like us, could find common ground in falling in love with two dramatic, over-the-top privileged sisters,
and our insistent need to not just protect them, but to keep them for ourselves.
We are as thick as fucking thieves, pun fully intended, since we are both criminals
through and through.

While we don't share the same background and we live in two very different
worlds, he and I will always be brothers now. A bond that was forged, not only
through our own suffering, but through witnessing unspeakable horrors done
to those we care about. Horrors that will give me nightmares for years to come,
and I have no doubt disturb his sleep as well.

My eyes trail to my cousin, Mateo, who still walks with a slight limp and even
now shifts uncomfortably, whenever any male is too close to him. Then, over
to Finn, with his quiet strength, and then lastly, I meet the blue eyes of the man
who began as my rival and still undoubtedly hates me, but now knows I am not
his enemy. *Well, maybe not wholly his enemy; I still don't like the asshole.*

I lean forward, lowering my voice so only he can hear me. "I can still take
her away from you, fucker. You'll never find her if I do, little spoiled king
of Casbury; you had better fucking remember that. Watch your back, Theo
Saint-Lambert. I'll be watching every step you take."

He growls deep in his throat, a primal wolf ready to defend his mate from
any harm, and a grin crosses my face. *Gotcha, motherfucker.* "You watch your
back, *bitch*. Somebody is going to fuck you up one day, and I can't wait to watch
you lose your psychotic mind when they do." Theo's chest bumps mine, and it
almost causes the laugh I am trying to restrain from breaking free to burst from
my lips.

He moves away from me and gets into the front seat. I watch as Carter
and Mateo lift a drugged-out Mia Stratford in tandem, and lay her gently and

reverently across their laps, as if she were a precious piece of crystal instead of a bloodthirsty vixen. They ensure she's strapped to the seat by the belt, and their arms hold her tightly.

So fucking dramatic, like where is she going to go? Although, if she were to wake up right now, I have no doubt those two would never be able to procreate or walk straight again. That Stratford princess even fucking frightens me with her unhinged violence, and I am the number two at the head of a vicious cartel.

"Fucker... thank you for this. You know Stella is going to hunt you down for helping us, right?" Carter calls out the window, making a smirk lift the tips of my lips. The scar across the side of my face pulls up tightly, reminding me that I am just as damaged as these four fuckers, except some of my wounds are on the outside and visible. I give each of them a dark, sinister look; I wouldn't want to give the four of them the impression that I like them or something.

Shut up, fool, you know you like them. In a different place and time, you would have fit right in with them. After what I am about to do, the chances of meeting any of them alive again might be slim if Stella Stratford has her way.

"She can try. I plan to make her work for it." *Ain't that the fucking truth.* I'm about to not only make her work for it, but cause an all-out war to erupt between the powerful and mighty Stratfords and the Cabanos. I'm going to go out on a limb and say the *Ice Queen of Manhattan* is not going to be too pleased when she comes out of her drug-induced nap, and realizes that one of the heads of the most dangerous weapons cartel has kidnapped one of her precious granddaughters, and has zero intentions of giving her back.

Fuck her for thinking she's better than me and my family. I'll show her by knocking her granddaughter up again and again, until I populate her future line with nothing but my kids. Fuck, I'm getting a chub just thinking of Issy's perfect cunt stretching around my cock, and my cum filling her up until it drips out of her.

They put the car in drive, and my cousin Mateo lowers his window and calls out to me, as they start moving away. "*Gracias, primo.* Run far and fast before Stella wakes. I would hate for there to be one less Cabano in this world." Then they're gone, speeding away from the Casbury mansion and off with their own valuable jewel.

No worries, *little primo*; I plan to add many more Cabanos to the world shortly.

My man Santiago moves quickly across the yard towards me, and I can see the displeasure and anxiety across his features. He doesn't like this plan; in fact, he has repeatedly vocalized his concerns that this is a mistake, and that we will start a war. He's probably right, but the thing is, I don't honestly give a fuck. I'm not afraid of taking on Issy's grandmother, and I don't give a fuck how much power she has.

She's standing in the way of something I want with a desperation that I can taste, and no one stops me from getting what I want. Not some socialite playing queen, not my father, and certainly not one of my men. I want Isabella Stratford to be *mine*, regardless of her fucking wishes, and so she shall be.

"Everything set? Are we ready to get the fuck out of here?" I question, already moving back towards the interior of the spacious mansion made of glass.

"*Jefe*, are you sure about this? I beg you to reconsider. One woman is not worth all of our deaths." At the look I give him, which promises nothing but physical pain if he continues to utter words I don't want to hear, he sighs. "The guards are still passed out from the cookies those *psicópatas* fed them. I can't believe that shit even worked. *Idiotas!* They almost deserve us to slaughter them while they sleep."

He's not wrong; my men would have never fallen for something like drug-laced cookies, but I guess that's the difference between real-world criminals, and hired soldiers playing pretend. "Make sure that when they wake, they won't be able to move or raise the alarm for a while. We need time to put some distance between us and them."

"Yes, *jefe*."

I keep moving forward, entering through the door that leads in from the large pool area, heading in the direction of where I told Theo to leave my beautiful prize. I spy her dark hair sprawled along the sofa cushions until it almost meets the floor. She's so fucking beautiful; her pale porcelain skin seems to glow with an internal light. Her dark, full eyelashes rest upon her high cheekbones, disguising her beautiful sapphire eyes that always shine with emotion and heat when they glare up at me, and her lips pout with displeasure.

Fuck, I need a taste of her mouth, even though one taste will never be enough, I need to run my mouth all over her sweet, firm body, relishing in all her curves. I want to wrap her around me, burying myself in her heat until you can't tell where she begins and I end.

She's not only an obsession; she's a fucking addiction. One that strums through my veins every moment of the day and night. The need to have her overriding all my good sense and self-preservation, and making me an addict.

Fuck, she is perfection. I lean down and press my lips against hers, running the tip of my tongue between the seam of her soft pink lips until a small moan leaves her mouth, and gives me the opening that I need to slip inside and taste her. Sweet honey greets my senses, and a growl leaves my lips as I force myself to pull back from her. *Soon.* Soon, I will have her to myself, and then I can feast on her anytime I want.

My head turns and I spy Raegan asleep on the couch across from my Issy. She's a formidable opponent in a small package. You would never know, looking at her petite features and angel-like appearance, that she's a fucking violent banshee who chooses violence every chance she gets. I try to stifle a laugh. I wish whoever ends up with her a ton of good luck; that person will be dodging her angry little fists daily.

I slip my arms underneath my sleeping beauty and lift her, cradling her small, slight frame like you would a newborn. Issy is so delicate and beautiful; she looks like a perfect porcelain doll. My beautiful broken doll is flawless on the outside, but hides a mountain of cracks within.

Don't worry, baby. I'm going to fix you by tearing you apart and putting you back together.

I move towards the door and give this place one last look. The chances of us ever returning here are slim to non-existent. I will never allow Isabella Stratford to be parted from me, not in this life or the next.

She's fucking mine, and no one is ever going to take her from me.

Chapter Two

Issy

"If you ever looked at me once with what I know is in you, I would be your slave."

Emily Brontë, Wuthering Heights

My limbs feel so heavy, almost like they're weighed down, and my skin itches as beads of sweat make their way across my flesh. It's scorchingly hot, oppressive, and confining. A sensation starts at the base of my spine, rising and encompassing me, whirling within me until it feels as if it's taking me over with its electricity. My body bows off the firm surface I think I'm lying on, a moan being forcefully ripped from my lips and sounding deranged.

I crack one of my tired eyes open, trying to pull myself from the deep darkness that has me wrapped in its thick chains. I shift my hand to run it over my eyes to help push away the sleepiness that clings to me, refusing to release me from its firm depths, with limbs that don't seem to obey my commands. My arm refuses to lift from the surface I'm on. I try harder, willing it to rise, only to feel something tightening and pinching around my wrist, and forcing it back down. *What. The. Fuck.*

My heart starts thundering wildly in my chest, the feeling causing a lump of dread to form in my throat as some of the fog that has me trapped starts to dissipate, and noises around me accost my ears. It sounds like an animal is in the dark with me; low growls vibrate across the surface of my heated flesh, causing more goosebumps to form. I try to lift my head and pull on my arms and legs, only to come to the horrifying realization that I'm completely tied down.

"Nooo... whhaaaatt... the fuuuck?" My tongue feels thick and dry inside of my mouth, preventing the scream that is crawling its way up my throat, and desperately wanting to escape my lips. All my struggles manage to do is tighten the restraints holding me down, and cause shivers of fear to race across each of my limbs. *Fuck, fuck, fuck!* My mind races with terror about where I am, flashbacks of the last images I can remember flying across my vision and assuring me I'm not safe. *Where the fuck am I? Oh my God, where the fuck am I?*

My blood rushes in my veins, the sound so loud that it's almost deafening in my ears. A chilling, urgent sensation races through my body, an instinctive warning blaring through my thoughts like a siren in the dead of night, warning of danger, of consequences, and even of death.

Warm tears slide down the sides of my face and slip into my ears and hair, reassuring me that I'm very much alive. My numb lips mumble words in a strangled breath, pleading and begging for what, I don't know. The adrenaline and fear rushing through my system are making my head spin, and aiding in further disorienting me. *I can't fucking breathe, I can't breathe, where am I?*

Is something touching my legs? What the fuck is touching me? I feel pressure forcing my thighs apart, as my head spins faster and bile rises up the back of my throat. Something is skimming along my skin roughly, scratching, and feeling as if it's trying to push against me. *We*t. I feel wet down there. *Oh my fucking God*, is an animal trying to consume me? Am I bleeding? I'm going to die here, eaten by whatever has me restrained.

Get it together, weakling, an animal wouldn't be able to restrain you. Human. Focus, Issy. The words skate through my mind, and with them, I can finally get a breath inside my lungs. My heart is still pounding furiously in my chest, but at least now, I'm almost a hundred percent positive it's a human, and I'm trapped in a nightmare.

I force all my senses to focus, and I think I can feel someone's head in between my bound and spread legs, grazing, licking, and sucking on my most intimate areas. Their hair brushes against the side of my slickened thighs, and a rough and abrasive texture grazes my pussy lips. Scariest of all, I realize my core feels needy, swollen, and wet. My body is responding against my will.

I try to pull and shift my body away from the sensations, still not convinced that I'm not trapped in a nightmare. One that I need to wake myself from now, before my heart explodes out of my chest. "Noooo... waakke... up." I hear my slurred words, my voice sounding entirely out of it.

Loud groans and growls respond to my words, making the hairs on the back of my neck and arms stand on end. *Not a nightmare, it's not a nightmare! FUCK, FUCK, FUCK! I'm going to die.*

Various sensations are accosting me at the same time, making the panic that is enveloping me even worse and more horrifying. Whoever is touching me is taking what they want, and devouring me, as I lie helpless below them. The heat that soared across my skin just moments ago cools and turns to frigid ice, as my limbs try harder to fight against their restraints. I try in desperation to close my legs, and stop the conflicting sensations that are rising across my skin, but whatever or whoever is holding me captive prevents even that small mercy.

"Please!" The word leaves my lips with strength as I thrash my head on my neck against the hard surface; it's the only part of my anatomy available to me to move, even as my core tightens painfully, and my clit throbs against the invading force.

"Mine." A feral growl rents the air and has my chest tightening painfully, forcing the air to become trapped in my lungs. Scents are starting to accost me as I fully awaken into this nightmare I find myself in. The rich smell of musk, something earthy and spicy, and sweat meet my nostrils. Male. My mind provides the word as it stirs and awakens utterly, to claw through layers of obscurity and confusion currently engulfing me.

"No... stop!" A muddled scream leaves my lips as my heart gallops inside my chest. The beast between my legs ignores my request and thrashes, slipping their tongue further inside of my tight core, and causing the next scream to become trapped inside my throat. Rough, firm hands grip either side of my thighs without mercy, tightening their punishing hold and forcing them wider, while the shadowed beast eats me like they're starving. *No, fuck, no.*

My body and mind are becoming overwhelmed with all the confusing sensations. The fear and dread, mixed with the pleasure that is rising within me, are sending confused signals to my brain on whether to lean into the pleasure, or to fight to seek our escape. An electric current is running through my limbs and up my spine, signaling the approach of an orgasm I'm unable to stop from crashing over me. My body wants the release; it craves it, even while my mind screams in terror. My hands tighten into fists, my nails biting into the flesh of my palms, and even my toes scrunch as the sensations hit my body like a tsunami making landfall, and taking everything with it in its wake and causing chaos and destruction.

A guttural scream leaves my lips, ripping through my vocal cords and making the muscles in my neck strain and my ears ring, as all the breath escapes me in a whoosh, and my heart feels like it's going to explode in my chest. My whole body tightens as I pull on the restraints, my neck lifts from the surface I'm on, and my eyes roll to the back of my head. Still, whoever is between my legs doesn't stop or relent, continuing to push me over the edge of insanity, causing one mind-blowing and earth-shattering orgasm to roll quickly into another, until even my screams are stolen from me with my lack of oxygen.

The temperature in the room has become scorching, filled with humidity, and downright unbearable. My skin feels like it is blistering hot as moisture coats it further. My thick hair sticks to my scalp, shoulders, and back. I'm entirely naked before whoever is using me for their depraved pleasure. My nipples are sharp, hard points, standing at attention painfully, both wanting to be touched and pulled, and yet fearful and dreading whoever is touching me. Moisture pools from inside of me as my orgasm abates, soaking the surface below my asscheeks, and causing further horror at the knowledge of how wet I am.

FUCK! How could my body have come like that? I don't even know who this is ripping these sensations from me. *FIGHT, ISSY!* My brain shrieks, yet I'm still unable to move. Fight or flight has kicked in, and I can no longer get enough air inside my lungs. I try to suck in huge breaths but end up choking on air, and sobbing at the same time. Tears, snot, and saliva all coat my face and join the perspiration covering me.

I'm trapped. I'm subdued, and someone has me. Once again, I'm reminded I have no control over what happens to me and that, as usual, I am a doll to be played with. *Weak. We are weak*, my mind provides the word that I dread. The one that has described me all my life. *Who has me? Who is doing this to me? Was I captured by another of my grandmother's enemies? Fuck, has someone taken me like they did my sister?*

How am I going to get out of here? More tears slide down my face, and stifling sobs are swelling in my throat. Hopelessness mixes with fear, and I feel like I am drowning. I need someone to save me. Where is my sister and grandmother? Where is Diego?

Diego. The name slides through my mind, and I can feel my hope rising inside of me, like a beacon calling to a lost merchant out at sea. Could this be Diego? The more I think of his name, the slower the frantic rhythm of my heart beats. It has to be him, *fuck*, please let it be him touching me.

Where the hell am I? Am I still in my sister's house in Casbury? The last thing I remember was being with Raegan, my sister's best friend, on the sofa, watching a show on Netflix. Then Mateo was before us, offering us fresh cookies from the local bakery, but everything after that is a blank. *Where are my grandmother and sister? Are they trapped somewhere, too?*

Fear overwhelms me at the thought of my sister once again being taken, and both her and my grandmother being harmed. *NO! I won't allow it.* I won't allow Mia to suffer again; she's already been through so much. I won't allow anyone to harm my grandmother, Stella, either.

How are you going to protect them? My mind questions with snark, *you can't even stop orgasming for whoever has you. Besides, they are both strong women and warrior queens. They are nothing like you; pathetic, weak, useless.*

Another feral growl rents the air, and I feel my core spasm again against my will, as another orgasm threatens to rise and be pulled from me by force. My mind spirals with nothing but dark thoughts of what happened to my sister. I will never be able to endure and survive what she did. I hope whoever has me plans to kill me. *Gutless, frail, worthless*, my mind hisses at my thoughts.

"*Princesa.*"

The word is mumbled in pleasure, as a finger is slipped inside of my throbbing core and then another, slamming into me over and over, while my clit is circled and thrummed. *Diego!*

Fuck, it is the bastard who has me tied down. Some of my fear vanishes with the relief that it's him, as pleasure once again starts climbing within, but so does anger. How fucking dare he tie me down and force pleasure on me? I told the bastard that we were done, and that I wanted nothing more to do with his psychotic ass.

What the fuck does he think he's doing? Does the bastard believe this will make me change my mind? That he can put me in an orgasm coma, and I will relent and forget everything that has happened? Forget all of the shit he did, and how manipulative he is? *Fuck, no!* He can give me a *hundred orgasms*, and I won't forgive him.

"DIEGO! STOP!" My voice sounds hoarse to my ears. His fingers stop moving inside of me, and for a moment, I swallow the fear in my throat that he wouldn't listen. That he would do what he always does, and be the domineering psychopath that he is.

A low, menacing rumble, the sound laden with a cruel satisfaction that hints at wickedness and madness, greets my straining ears before I feel him pulling back from me. The sound crawls under my skin, sending a cold shudder through my body and the air, and signals danger and unpredictability. His strong fingers brush against my pussy lips, smearing my wetness before continuing across my stomach, then sliding between my breasts and wrapping around my throat, where they tighten, before I feel his body rising and hovering above me.

His grip is firm but isn't stopping air from flowing, at least not yet, but knowing the fucker, it won't be long before he does. "Oh, *Princesa*, you don't make demands here. You're not royalty now, just my favorite little whore to play with."

He leans forward, his lips brushing against mine, his fingers tightening on my throat and forcing my lips to open, to siphon in oxygen that he's quickly depriving me of. I can taste myself on his lips, my musky, sweet scent reaching my nose, and it has me swallowing a pitiful moan.

"Whhaat... have... you... done?" I get the words out before I have no air left, and his lips seal over mine, taking my ability to speak. He licks at the inside of my mouth like a ravenous wild beast who is starving, sucking on my tongue even as I struggle to breathe, and dizziness attacks me. In another moment or two, I will pass out into complete darkness, and he doesn't seem to care as he keeps taking from me without mercy.

I feel the head of his cock at my entrance; just as I'm about to pass out from the lack of air, he slams inside of me at the same time, and releases his brutal grip on my throat. The burn and stretch have me moaning and screaming at the same time, as he starts a thundering rhythm of slamming into me over and over again. The sound of flesh hitting flesh is so loud in the air around us that it supersedes the sound of my ragged breathing.

"Mine. You are mine now, Issy. Mine to do with what I fucking please. Mine to fuck. Mine to hurt. Mine to use, and no one is going to stop me. Not you, your sister, or your bitch of a grandmother. Here you're not a Stratford, Issy; you're just a hole I slip my cock into."

He thrusts one last time until his body is pressed flush against mine, and I feel his cock twitch inside of me as he fills me with his cum. His grip on my throat tightens once again, as he bites down on my chin and forces another scream past my lips. "I will never let you go, never."

He pulls back from me, slipping from inside my soaked pussy, and I feel his weight move off of me before wetness greets my lips. "Be a good whore now, and clean off the mess you made on my cock, *Princesa*."

He doesn't wait for my acknowledgment, or even give me a moment to prepare, before he shoves his wet cock past my lips, the taste of our combined cum hitting my tongue with a bitter, musky combination. The fucking savage that he is, he doesn't even give my throat a moment to adjust to his thick girth or long length, before he slams to the back of my throat, making me gag and tears race down my face, as his still hard cock begins roughly fucking my throat.

"That's it, my dirty, spoiled slut. Show me how good you can take a cock in that traitorous mouth. How well you deep-throat a hard dick, Issy. You were born to be a whore, my whore, weren't you, baby?"

I gag over and over, unable to breathe or stop him from brutalizing my throat and taking what he wants from me. My core tightens painfully, another orgasm beginning to rise to the surface with his cruel words, and the way he's using me for his own pleasure. Shame and desire war within me at the way he's getting me off with his violence and abuse. How, right now, I'm drenched between my legs, and my nipples are so painfully hard from his words and actions. As much as I want to deny his words, I'm the slut he names me. His slut, even though I don't want to be.

His other hand reaches out, and he slaps my right breast hard, the spark of pain shooting down my chest and straight between my legs like a bolt of electricity, before he delivers the same treatment to my other breast. My screams are muffled by his cock inside of my throat as he slaps me again, and then pulls on my hard nipple until the combination of the pain and throat fucking has me seeing stars before my eyes.

"What a dirty whore you are; look at how far you can swallow my cock, Issy. My balls are sitting on your chin. It's all the practice you had before me, wasn't it, baby? It made you a pro, didn't it? I bet you if I slip a couple of fingers inside of you, you'll explode again, won't you?"

He answers his own question by doing that exact thing and slipping three fingers inside of me, stretching me wide as he continues to fuck my face hard in tandem. I feel him stutter in his rhythm, and I know he's close to coming down my throat. His fingers pick up speed inside my cunt until my whole body is shaking, and trembles are making their way through my core. I know he can feel that the orgasm he's ripping from me is about to barrel through me. At the last moment, just as it's about to crest, he pulls his fingers out of the inside of me and rips his cock from my throat, splashing my face with his cum.

He cums all over my lips, nose, and cheeks and even spurts into my eyes and eyelashes, *the fucker*. A groan of satisfaction leaves his lips as he makes a fucking mess of me. I force my eyes to shut, the stinging burning my eyes, as I inhale his scent and feel the warm stickiness sliding on my skin. *Bastard*.

His fingers trail through the mess on my face, almost gently and reverently. I can't see him through the darkness, but I can picture his cruel face, the scar pulling along his skin, and his olive-green eyes filled with passion and hate. *Always hate*. Diego Cabano lives and breathes it. He knows no other emotion; it's as much a part of his overall being as that horrific scar on his face.

"Release me, Diego. This has gone too far. You have gone too fucking far! I told you we were done." I punctuate my words by pulling on my restraints forcefully. The fucker left me hanging, leaving me achy and needing release. A release that I know he will deny me. It's his way of punishing me, making me crave something only he can give me. Violence and pain mixed with hate and satisfaction, it's the story of us, after all.

I don't know which one of us is more fucked up in the head. Him; for knowingly putting me through shit like this and taking me by force, causing me to crave him more, or me; for never holding my ground, despite my words and intentions to have nothing further to do with him. We are completely toxic together. We both feed off of each other, our sick depravities and kinks, and have become unhealthily consumed with each other. He brings out the very worst in me, calling it forward and playing with my emotions, like a maestro does a symphony.

I know I have to stay away from him. I have to hold my ground and stop being the weak, pathetic bitch who drops all of her resolve, morals, and panties, every time he pulls out that fucking cock of his. He's not good for me. We are from two very different worlds. I know I can't and shouldn't be with him. I'm a Stratford heir, and he's just some lowlife manipulative criminal from the underworld. Our worlds were never meant to connect. I should have never given in to the urges and desire to have him to begin with.

Horror and shame fill me at the recognition that if my grandmother only knew how low I have let myself fall, she would instantly have me shipped back to

Manhattan, and locked up in the family compound. How dark my desires are, and how easily I allow him to make me his whore. *We want to be his whore; he makes us feel so fucking good. He makes the pain feel so good*, my mind whispers.

No, this time, we have to be strong. We have to pull back from the urges and the desires that he has awakened in us. We can't let him win. We can't ever let Diego Cabano own us; if he did, there would be no escape, *ever*.

Chapter Three

"There's treachery in her hips, rebellion in her heart & magic in her mind."

Curtis Tyrone Jones

I watch the fear, confusion, and anger cross her features in the barely visible light. My *Princesa*, my Stratford prize, my *captive*. She has no idea yet how much danger she is in right now. She believes she's still safe under her sister's roof, under her grandmother's thumb. She doesn't realize that I have taken everything from her. That when I am done, there will be nothing left of Isabella Stratford but a name once spoken of in high society. A memory of a privileged, spoiled girl who once looked like a porcelain doll. My own fairytale fucking Snow White for me to use and own.

No, Isabella Stratford will be forgotten, stolen away by a villain, ripped apart piece by tender piece, and buried in a deep, unmarked grave. The same grave she would have buried her feelings for me, and our relationship, in to save face with her grandmother. She would have left me behind as if I never mattered. As if I hadn't awoken parts of her she never knew existed, as if she didn't belong to me. *She fucking belongs to ME!*

"Release me, Diego. This has gone too far. You have gone too fucking far! I told you we were done."

Done? We were never done. We will never be done. Not while she has a breath still leaving those deceitful pouty lips. Not while that heart inside of her chest still beats. The same heart that was willing and ready, to walk away from me like I was nothing to her. No, *I say when we are done, and I never will.*

Not even when she truly is long gone from this fucking, miserable earth, and I am left here alone. I will follow where she goes, because Issy and I will never be parted again. Not in this lifetime or the next. She is mine, and I mean to have her always, with or without her agreement.

Does that make me insane, a stalker and a kidnapper? I like to think it's all part of my charm, along with the fact that I feel no regret for what I have done, and will do, to keep her.

I spread my warm cum along her beautiful ivory skin and stunning features, wanting it to be absorbed by her very pores. Every part of Issy will have me inside of her, coating her, tainting her. She needs to be covered in my scent and essence, as a reminder to herself that she belongs to me, and as a warning to others of who her master is. My brand will be plain to see.

My whore, my doll, my Princesa.

It's a lesson I plan to teach her every single day until she can't think of anything else. Until I tell her to crawl to me, and she falls to her hands and knees in obedience, and does it without a moment's hesitation. I will break Issy Stratford, and reassemble all her precious and privileged jagged pieces back together, in the image of a woman who knows she is mine. One who will never leave my side, no matter who comes for her or beckons her.

She will have no other family aside from me. No other safe harbor will be available to her. I will be her beginning and her end. I will be her everything, and she will be mine, and together, we will rule this new world that I plan on building. Issy Stratford will be my wife, the mother of my children, and my fucking queen, or she will die painfully and never see her family again.

"I would save your breath, Issy; your words mean nothing to me. You're in no position to make any demands. You are no longer within the Stratfords' reach, and they can't stop me from having you."

I move away from the bed I have her confined spread eagle to, and reach for the room-darkening curtains, pulling them back with a yank and letting the bright jungle sunlight penetrate through the dark, shuttered windows. I open them wide and take a deep breath of the humid, thick, earthy jungle air, and it helps to subdue some of the rage her words are causing to rise within me.

The gasp that leaves her lips is a soothing balm to my wrathful soul, and brings me so much pleasure that I turn back around and watch, as her eyes finally adjust to the light and make out what she's seeing. A sarcastic and cruel chuckle leaves my lips. *Sorry Dorothy, you're not in fucking Kansas anymore. You're now in the kingdom of Oz, or more like the Kingdom of Diego.*

No one will find her here, deep in the South American jungle. Even if her grandmother looks for her in my family's home in Columbia, she will never discover her thousands of miles away, in a completely different country, buried in the deep, treacherous, and uninhabitable jungle. No, no one is coming to save her; I made sure of it.

"Where the hell are we, Diego? What the fuck have you done?" She screams and thrashes against the thick mattress, making more of my precious cum escape her pretty, pink cunt. The desire to push my fingers back inside of her, and force the cum to stay within her, starts to ride me, but I force myself to stay where I am. I, too, will have to learn to control this obsessive need to touch her.

"Your new kingdom, Issy." I turn back around slowly, motioning to the thick wooden walls, and out through the window at the dense and high tree tops. "You're a jungle queen now, your *fucking majesty*."

"You kidnapped me? Are you fucking insane? Do you know what my grandmother will do to you?" She continues to scream as my cum dries on her pretty face. Those bright, sapphire blue eyes shine with malice and incredulity in my direction, pulling a massive grin from me that has me baring my teeth at her. *So fucking beautiful when she's angry.*

Her ivory skin is flushed with the heat and her rage, the marks I left already sprouting all over her body. My eyes trail down to her perky breasts, to see the red welts visible from the slaps I gave her, her pink nipples still hard and peaked, making my mouth salivate at the thought of another taste of her. *Fuck, I want her again right now.*

My eyes continue down her chest to her stomach, where I left a trail of my cum drying and flaking on her skin, to her pink, swollen pussy covered in my cum and spit. There are red marks from my facial scruff on her thick thighs, which are already blooming with my fingerprints from when I held her in my rough grip, while I ate her cunt to my satisfaction, and then fucked her raw. *Mine.*

My cock twitches once again with renewed need, and precum beads at the tip. Maybe I should take her ass too, so that I have my fill of all her holes? *Who am I kidding?* I will never get my fill of her. I could spend every waking moment for the next twenty years buried inside of Issy's holes, and it would still not even make a dent in my desire for her, the need that constantly courses through me to be near her, inside of her, and possess her.

"I took what was mine; a Stratford heir. You are fucking *mine*, Issy, and you thought your words would part us. That you could walk away from me like we were nothing, and like you didn't belong to me."

"SHE'S GOING TO KILL YOU, DIEGO! I don't fucking belong to you! When she finds me, and she will, asshole... you know she will tear the whole world apart to find me, especially after what happened to Mia. How could you do this?" A sob leaves her lips, and tears slide down her flushed face. They are so beautiful, like shining diamonds sliding down her skin, that I am momentarily mesmerized by them.

"She will never find you, Issy. The tracker she had embedded is gone. I removed it before you even left your sister's property. You were all drugged so those rich fuckers from Casbury could take Mia, and I seized the opportunity to take you. You've been gone already for four days, *Princesa*. You are so deep in the jungle that no one will ever find you."

I move forward again, reaching out and grabbing her chin and forcing her to stare deep into my eyes. I want her to see the madness that resides within me. The anger that she provokes to the surface, every time she denies that she belongs to me. The rage that festers, because she thought she could walk away from me. *No one fucking walks away from me!*

"No one will ever find you, Isabella. I made sure of it. You are as good as dead and reborn to this new world, where you will live here with me as my property, as my *fucking queen.*"

She tries to pull her face away from my grip, but I tighten my fingers until I know I am hurting her and probably bruising her soft, delicate skin. "You mean as your captive, Diego. I will never be anything else. I will never stop trying to leave you. I HATE YOU!"

Her words sting, making a tightness appear in my chest. Do I think she truly means them? I stare into that bottomless blue, and see the truth within their depths. She will never stop trying to leave me. *She will never succeed, not while breath is still in my body. I will never release her from her fate.*

Her words push me over the edge of the rage I was trying to leash. I quickly unclasp her legs from the restraints, and then her wrists. She immediately tries to fight me and scamper off the bed, but I wrap one hand around her throat and squeeze tightly, while fisting my other hand into her hair and forcing her to stop moving.

She is but a fly, fighting an angry bear. In no world will she ever win against me. In no world could Isabella Stratford be ruthless enough to defeat the villain, but it amuses me greatly to watch her try.

"Fight, *Princesa*. It fucking turns me on when you do." I push her in front of me towards the closed door by her neck and hair. "Open the door, Issy." I grit out between clenched teeth, and when she complies with a sharp cry, I push her through and down the corridor that leads to the small flight of stairs.

I drag her, kicking and fighting, screams and shrieks blaring in my eardrums, down the short grouping of stone stairs and past a few of my bewildered men, who avert their shocked gazes at the sight of us both naked and fighting. I can feel her starting to struggle to breathe, and it's making my dick throb. *Fuck.* Maybe I should just force her to the jungle floor right here and fuck the brattiness out of her? Naw, that won't work; she's a stubborn bitch, even though I have no doubt I would enjoy it immensely.

She wants to act like she hates me, but we both know that's not the full story. If she wants to behave like a captive, then I'll treat her how we would a captive. I drag her along the jungle floor, her body tripping and banging into everything in her path. I loosen my grip slightly on her neck to ensure she can get some air into her lungs, when we reach the deep pit I had my men dig twenty feet from our new home. I hold her tightly at arm's length, staring at her while she continues to try to fight me.

"I'm going to kill you, Diego! Release me, you piece of shit! You're a psychopath!"

Her words amuse me. Yeah, I know I am behaving like a psychopath. Do I fucking care, though? *No, I fucking don't.* She's a spoiled princess used to getting whatever she wants, and using her grandmother or sister to fight her battles. My queen needs to be strong. She needs to be able to stand on her own two feet, and fight her own battles. I will make Issy fucking strong so that she can survive the world I am bringing her into.

What if she fails? The thought whispers through my mind, bringing with it unease, as I stare at her frightened face. *If she fails, she dies.* It is the only mercy that I can provide her. Only the strong survive in my world.

With one last look at her, I push her over the edge of the pit and release my hold on her, and she goes screaming inside its twelve-foot sloped drop. I hear her bang down on the palm leaves-covered bottom, and look over the edge to see her naked body sprawled, and her dark, sweaty hair covering her face.

"Enjoy your stay in your new prison, my pretty captive. Maybe a few nights sleeping with the beasties of the jungle will improve your fucking attitude." With a final quick observation to ensure she didn't break anything in the fall, I start to walk away just as she jumps up and starts screaming, and trying to climb out of the pit.

Good luck with that; she's not getting out of there. It's the same style of pit my family has used for generations to deal with our enemies. If I want her to die out in that pit, she will. None of my men will dare defy me to help her. She wants to behave like my captive instead of my queen, well fucking let her then.

CHAPTER FOUR

Issy

"She had been defeated by herself alone, and the sadness of it left a dark shadow in her heart."

Yo Yo, Ghost Tide

I jump up and try to grab onto anything along the slicked and firm dirt-packed walls, in an attempt to climb out of this pit that fucker Diego threw me into, what feels like days ago. It's the same result every single time. I manage to make it no more than a foot or two off the ground before I'm sliding back down, and my feet are making contact with the thick palm leaves all around me.

My weakened and quickly dehydrating state isn't helping me get out of here. That motherfucking bastard, just wait till I get my hands on him; I'm going to rip off his balls and choke him with them. *Sure you are, princess,* my mind snickers with disbelief.

Sweat slickens every part of my itchy, bug-bitten, and dirt-covered body, as I let out another feral scream of frustration at my situation. The bright sunlight soars above me through the thick canopy of trees, bringing with it the oppressive heat and humidity. I drag my hands down my face as the throbbing in my temples intensifies. My right eye is twitching with the migraine that is refusing to leave me.

How many days has he left me trapped down here? One, two, maybe fucking three? I still can't believe the psychopath threw me into a hole in the ground, and left me here to die. *What. The. Fuck.*

Don't be so dramatic, you sniveling weakling. He didn't completely abandon you. One of his men brings you water, food, and the bucket twice daily. That's a lot more than most prisoners get. Besides, I'm sure by now some jungle creature would have eaten you, if they weren't out there protecting you from above.

My mind plays devil's advocate with me, calling me out for my continuous weakness even now while we are being held prisoner in a fucking hole. How can I try to rationalize what he has done? How can I continue to berate myself when he is the villain? *He is the villain, isn't he?* His sick and deranged need to own me, to control me, that makes him insane, doesn't it?

"*Señorita?*" A gruff male voice calls from above, sounding unsure and curious. Why does he even bother calling out and sounding like he's questioning my whereabouts? Where the fuck else would I be? I can't teleport the hell out of here, and they all know I can't climb out of this death trap, despite my pitiful attempts to do just that.

I am surrounded by lunatics, it seems, all of them answering to the devil, who goes by the name of Diego Cabano. "I'm here. Where else would I be?" I shout back up the hole, using my hands to block out the blinding sunlight.

"Please, miss, stand back so I can drop your water, food, and the bucket." He calls down, appearing at the edge of the hole, but refusing to actually stare down at me. I roll my eyes at the absurdity of his orders. He apparently has been ordered not to look directly at me by his boss, cause you know, the fucker threw me naked into a hole in the ground. *That motherfucker, I can't wait to kick him in the balls.* The orders are so absurd that poor Santiago hit me with a water bottle in the face yesterday, or was that the day before? *Fuck, how many days have I been trapped here?*

"Santiago, how many days have I been in this hole?" I question, my voice sounding raspy as I use the name he unwillingly provided me, after I begged and cried like the weakling I am. Poor Santiago seemed completely distressed at my predicament, and my breakdown. *Imagine how I feel, Santiago, just fucking imagine.*

"Today is the third. Watch out for the bucket!" He yells before he lowers the thin bungee cord attached to a metal bucket. The indignity of having to relieve myself twice a day into a damn bucket, which is then carted away, so I don't further soil my jungle prison. *At least Diego was willing to give you a bucket. I'm sure his other prisoners don't get that luxury*, my mind snarks, but I'm done with that bitch always trying to look on the bright side.

There is no bright side to being drugged and taken captive by a psychotic weapons-dealing warlord, dragged to the middle of the fucking jungle, fucked ruthlessly, filled with cum, and then thrown into a damn hole in the ground, when you demand that he release you. All because you tried to break up with his unstable and unreasonable ass.

I unhook the small clasp off the bucket handle and pull it aside, moving closer to the furthest wall of my round, earthy prison cell. My hands shake as I lower the bucket to the ground, giving Santiago my back and using my hair to give me an imagined sense of dignity, as I squat the best I can over the bucket, and relieve my aching bladder. When I'm done, I reach forward and grab a palm leaf from the top layer of my prison floor, grimacing as I use it to wipe myself.

The fucker didn't even provide me with toilet paper. When I questioned Santiago on why I was given a bucket but nothing to wipe with, I was told it was not good for the environment. *Can you believe this shit?* Someone call fucking *Greenpeace* or some shit, and give my captors a medal or something.

I attach the disgusting bucket back onto the hook and give it a tug, and Santiago carefully pulls it back up through the hole and out of sight. My eyes search the ground around me for the bottle of water, and pieces of fruit he threw down to me. Oh, look, I get a banana and what Santiago called an aguaje yesterday. Some round orange fruit that kind of looks like a cross between a persimmon and an apple, but actually tastes like a lemony tomato. I'd roll my eyes at the absurdity of that combination, but I don't have the energy to even do that anymore.

As I sit down in my prison with my knees tight against my chest, consuming my only source of nourishment, I once again wonder if my grandmother Stella is looking for me. She has to be so worried after my sister was taken not so long ago, and held prisoner by an unhinged psychopath. It appears that we Stratford women seem to be plagued by them, and I will be no exception.

Someone is always out to take, overpower, and hurt us. That is our legacy. The legacy of constantly being at war, and on the defense against the whole world that would do us harm. When will it ever be enough? When will we have peace?

I shake my head as the juices from the aguaje drip down my chin and make my hands sticky. I am nothing like my sister or grandmother. I am not a warrior, willing to fight off everyone who means our family harm. I don't have it in me to fight back, never mind to protect myself. Just look at the predicament I find myself in. *Trapped. Disheveled. Hopeless.*

As I lean my head back and close my eyes tightly, a memory accosts me, so vivid that I'm almost positive that my grandmother is here in this hole with me, her perfume making its way through my nose, and her presence causing my stomach to tighten painfully with anxiety.

Two little girls stand before a beautiful, regal woman with a mixture of dark tresses with threads of silver through her thick length. Her icy blue eyes narrow down on each of them, her face serious and stern, unwavering in her visible disappointment.

I watch as she purses her lips while she takes stock of the other dark-haired girl next to a younger version of me; my new sister, Mia. I want to step in front of her to protect her from our grandmother, but my knees shake, and my hands sweat. I can't bring myself to take the one little step needed. I can't even bring myself to speak. My tongue feels swollen and numb inside my mouth. Weakling, my mind provides the word that causes me further distress.

"What have you two done?" She questions with coldness in her tone. I love my grandmother, but I'm terrified of her most of the time. My grandfather Jaxon calls her his 'Little Viper' and swears that she has venom in her bite. Right now,

looking at her, I totally believe him. I wish he were here with us; Grandmother isn't so harsh when he's around. Besides, I'm his little doll, and he would protect me.

"Nooothinng..." my sister replies, her voice shaking but filled with defiance.

"Lies! You dare lie to me? Your grandmother?" My grandmother's tone drops another degree, and I feel my whole body starting to tremble.

"Isabella, what have you two done? Confess, child."

I squeeze my lips closed tightly, refusing to look up into her eyes and utter a word. She already knows what we have done; otherwise, she wouldn't be asking, and we wouldn't be standing here in her presence. I knew we shouldn't have done it. I told Mia that we needed to forget about it, but did she listen? No, of course she didn't, she's fearless.

"There will be punishments if you do not confess to your actions. Come clean, and I may reconsider donating all your precious electronics to charity, Mia." She turns her glare back in my direction, and a lump forms in my throat. "Isabella, would you like to lose your horse, Buttercup?"

Lose Buttercup? No! Oh my God, no, she can't take him away. He's the only thing that makes me feel alive and happy. He is the only thing that brings me a sense of calmness in the terrifying world that I live in. Buttercup is the only thing that doesn't scare me. When I'm riding him across the large fields, I'm no longer Isabella Stratford, some Manhattan princess. I'm free. A fairy riding through the wind that cannot be tamed. One who fears nothing and no one. I can't lose him.

"Don't do it, Issy. Be strong!" Mia whisper-shouts at me.

"What's it going to be, girls? Are you going to confess, or stick together and lie?" Grandmother Stella taps the toe of her pointy black shoe in a sign of impatience. I can't lose Buttercup, though. I can't go a day without seeing him, and I know she's not bluffing. She will give him away. She can be so mean, like one of those evil queens from the fairytales I used to love.

Tears slide down my cheeks, meeting my chin and finding their final destination in the front of my shirt. My hands clench at my sides, as I finally lift my eyes to meet my grandmother's cold glare, her jaw stiff and eyebrow raised in anticipation of my weakness. "We... we... ummm... we glued the door shut..."

"Issy! NO!" My sister screams, but it's no use. I'm not strong like her; I'm weak. I cave under pressure.

"Go on, child," my grandmother urges, with a further hint of disappointment in her voice.

I rub the back of my hand across my running nose, and stare into the coldest pair of blue eyes I've ever seen. Her beautiful face is filled with disappointment as she stares down at me.

"We glued the bathroom door shut and then pulled the fire alarm, after stealing all of Bethany's things, and making sure there was no toilet paper. Mia... had poured... lax... laxatives into her milk at lunch."

A hiccup leaves my lips and causes further mortification as I side-eye my sister, who is glaring at me. "Why did you do that to Bethany?" Grandmother Stella questions.

"Issy, stop," Mia demands without any fear. She's constantly in trouble with our grandmother.

She fears nothing and no one. If it wasn't for her, there is no way I would have done what I did today. I wouldn't have had the courage. Most days, I wish I was more like her. The fact that she's adopted but has more of the Stratford spirit than I do, the one born into this family, hasn't escaped me.

"She was... bull... bullying me and call... calling me names. She put... put garbage into my locker and threw dirty... mmm... underwear at me in the lunchroom, and everyone laughed and started... call... calling me names." I swallow the lump in my throat as my face heats, having to confess to my fearless grandmother what my peers are doing to me, how everyone in that school hates me and enjoys torturing me.

"What were they calling you, Isabella?"

I can't bring myself to utter the words, the horrible names. The humiliation and shame are too intense, and if I had my way, I would crawl into a hole and just die right now. I would never step foot into that school or see any of those girls again. I shake my head no and lower my eyes to the ground, as my whole body is wracked with ugly, loud sobs.

A frustrated groan leaves Mia's lips, and she pulls me by the arm behind her small body. She straightens her shoulders and faces my grandmother, while I sob behind her, taking the easy way out and letting her once again protect me. I'm a coward, and I always have been and always will be.

"They were calling her a dirty cunt. I managed to bust a couple of faces from uttering those disgusting words. I came up with the plan, grandmother. If you want to punish someone, punish me and leave Issy out of it. I wanted revenge; no one gets to hurt her." Mia shakes with rage, her small fists tight in front of me, as I peek from below my lashes at her.

A deep sigh escapes my grandmother. "Well done, Mia. No one is allowed to hurt either of you. You are Stratfords, girls. We are not afraid of anyone or anything. You should have done more to her. I would have set the bathroom on fire with her in it."

My grandmother huffs with agitation, and I watch as she clenches her fists tightly. My eyes open wide, and my jaw drops at her statement. I see a devious smirk crossing my sister's face at my grandmother's words. She really shouldn't be encouraging Mia to create more mayhem; she's perfectly capable of doing that all on her own.

"As for you, Isabella, Stratfords stick together, granddaughter. We don't ever rat each other out. You need to learn to be stronger, child. This world is a horrific place, and if you don't toughen up and become more like your sister, you will always be hiding from the bullies. Weakness is not in our Stratford blood, Isabella."

Stella reaches out and trails a red-tipped finger down my sister's face in tenderness, a tenderness that she doesn't usually show me. It pains me to watch, because I know I crave that touch and look on her face. How I would just like her to look at me once the same way she looks at Mia.

"It looks like I will have to go destroy Bethany's future, as well as her parents' legacy. How dare she have the audacity to come after a Stratford!"

My grandmother turns with one last appraising look at us, and starts to walk out of the room. "What about my horse?" I question with desperation.

"She was never going to take your horse, Issy. Come on, get it together and grow a pair. You ratted us out for nothing," Mia huffs with disdain, before following my grandmother out of the room without a backward look in my direction.

I snap out of the memory, releasing my hold on the remaining fruit in my grasp and watching, as it rolls to the palm leaves-strewn, dirt floor. My body shakes as I lean my head against my knees and try to stop the tears that are already trailing down my dirty and itchy face.

I was weak then, and I'm weak now. The difference is that I don't have my sister or grandmother to fight my battles. I'm utterly alone and powerless out here with my monsters now. I prayed for a hole to hide in, and it looks like fate decided to play some sick joke with me years later. Here I am now, trapped in the ground.

A Stratford never lets anyone hurt them; that's what my grandmother drilled into us all these years. That we need to fight and keep our heads held high. Yet once again, I prove that I am nothing but a defective Stratford, a waste of a name and body. Maybe I should just die in this hole after all. The world might be a better place without me in it. Who really would miss me? I'm a burden and a disappointment to everyone I know.

Not everyone. There was once someone who thought you were the best thing that ever happened to him. He thought you hung the stars and the moon, and would have done anything to stay with you. Glimmering bright blond hair and blue eyes try to rise within my mind, but I slam a door on the attempt. No, I won't allow my mind to go there; it will only lead to further madness.

Maybe I should let Diego keep me trapped in this hole. Be his captive for the rest of my life; at least I know he truly wants me.

Chapter Five

Diego

"Every man is guilty of all the good he did not do."

Voltaire

"*Jefe*," Santiago clears his throat as he fidgets from one foot to the other in front of me. The older man is so agitated that beads of sweat trail down the side of his face. It's strange because I have known him most of my life, and never given him a reason to fear me, at least not directly.

He has been one of my father's loyal men for as long as I can remember, but now he answers to me, out here in this dangerous jungle paradise rather than my father, who is back tending to our business affairs in the States. I wonder if he regrets agreeing to come out here with me?

"Speak," my eyes narrow on him as he continues to shift before me.

"Sir... it's the *señorita*... I... ummm... how long are we going to keep her in that hole?"

I lean back against my wooden desk with my ankles crossed in front of me, my eyes trailing over him as tension-filled seconds turn into minutes, while I assess why he might be asking me about my precious treasure stuck in the hole I placed her for safekeeping.

It's been four days since I fucked her raw, filled her with my cum, and then dragged her out of our new hidden jungle residence and threw her into a fucking hole in the ground, for her brattiness, disobedience, and inability to stop fucking fighting me. As if there was ever a chance of her escaping me once I set my sights on her.

"Has something happened?" A tinge of apprehension creeps up my spine with concern. Did something happen to her out in that hole? Has she gotten sick, perhaps from the oppressive heat she's not used to? *She is delicate, like a piece of the finest spun crystal, just waiting to shatter.* Has one of the predators of the jungle attacked her? *No, I am the only predator who can get close to her.* I made sure to station men around that hole to ensure no beasty gets their claws on my *Princesa*.

I've had to physically restrain myself from going out there daily to watch her, knowing full well that her tears and distress might have had me caving on my need to punish her. I need her to understand that I'm all that she has now. That she has belonged to me since that first moment I laid eyes on her back in that hospital in Casbury. I also need to ensure that I don't show weakness before my men. If they realize how important she truly is to me and her hold on me, how many of them would use it against me? How many of my enemies would try to take her from me? *I'll kill them all if they try.*

"No disrespect, *Jefe*, but she is too fragile to be out here like this. She... she stopped eating yesterday morning. I brought her the bucket and food again today, and she never stirred from her position against the wall of the hole. She hasn't eaten or drank anything today, her food from yesterday is lying at the bottom of the hole, and the bucket was not used." He rubs his large, meaty hand across his forehead, swiping away at the sweat, and his dark, penetrating eyes meet mine, filled with worry and confusion.

"Maybe she is sick? The heat is very strong during the day, and the bugs must be biting her down in that hole." For a moment, I watch as disapproval crosses his face before he wipes the sentiment away, and his features once again become neutral. He's been loyal to my family for years; would he betray me to save my girl from her current fate?

No, he knows what we do to traitors. His fate would be far worse than Issy's down in that hole. He wouldn't risk it to save some spoiled, wealthy princess from Manhattan, would he? Shadowed doubts start to plague my mind, and I have to stop myself from seeing betrayal in every corner. Santiago is loyal. The men I have out here with me were handpicked by me to be faithful, and follow through with my plans.

The thought nags at me that she might actually be sick, and as much as I want to break Issy and put her back together again, I don't want her ill, and I know she is not used to this type of environment. She's useless to me if she dies out there in that hole of dehydration or something worse.

It irritates me, though, to bend my will. I wanted her to beg me to release her. To promise me that she will never try to leave me again. I wanted her to break, her fragility and weakness left in that hole, and my strong queen to be reborn.

Maybe she will never be strong enough. The thought crosses my mind, but I refuse to let it sink its sharp claws any deeper into me. Isabella Stratford will become Isabella Cabano, my greatest possession, my wife, my fucking queen, and for that, she cannot waste away, but she also can't be weak.

I straighten and move away from the desk, not bothering to utter a word to a worried Santiago about my intentions as I stride out of my den, down the stairs, and out of my jungle compound. As I approach the hole, my men nod in restrained greeting, each placed strategically around the compound, and the hole, to prevent any unwelcome visitors, both of the animal and human variety from making their way inside.

No sounds are heard around us other than those native to the jungle. The wind rustles the thick leaves, birds call to each other, and far in the distance, the sound of water can barely be heard over all the other noises. I lean forward, staring into the twelve-foot hole and my captive queen. She's filthy and ragged, her skin covered in angry red bumps, and all scrunched in on herself up against the furthest wall of the hole. Her arms are tightly wrapped around her raised knees, her head is braced against them, and her thick, sweat-matted hair covers most of her body. *My prize.*

She looks utterly defeated, broken, even. Is it a facade, or have I truly managed in four days to bring her to the realization that she is mine, and no one is coming to save her? I know her grandmother is out there frantically tearing the world apart, searching for her. I'm aware the bounty placed on my head right now would help fund a small third-world country for years. That doesn't frighten me, even though it should. That knowledge won't deter me from my plans. No one is going to find us unless I want them to.

"Get the ladder," I order my men, and Juan scrambles to grab the rope ladder and throw it over the hole's edge. He makes a move to start climbing down, but a feral growl leaves my throat. No one is going to fucking touch Issy. Not him or any of my other men. I will be the one to grab her and hold her naked body in my arms. Her flesh is mine to touch, bruise, and leave my imprint on.

He steps back immediately with his hands raised as if to ward off an attack, as I move closer to the ladder, preparing myself to climb down and rescue my precious captive. "Grab a sheet from inside of the house, Santiago, and have it ready."

I start to climb down without another word to my men, knowing that my orders will be immediately obeyed, or they will be receiving a bullet to their brains. As I reach the last rung on the ladder, my eyes trail over the interior of the hole I've had her restrained in. The heat is more oppressive and stifling down here in the hole. The smell of stale leaves, sweat, dirt, and rotting vegetation accosts my senses, and has me wrinkling my nose.

Fuck, maybe this was a terrible idea; I shouldn't have left her down here so many days.

I slowly move away from the ladder and closer to her, anticipating her attack, but she doesn't stir or even acknowledge my presence. Her body is so still, and her beautiful blue eyes are unfocused, staring in front of her as if she has completely shut down, and her mind has escaped the predicament she is in.

My eyes trace over her porcelain skin covered in bug bites, welts, and a red, angry-looking heat rash. Her beautiful face is swollen and even paler than usual. Her stunning sapphire eyes are lifeless and dull; the deep purple shadows underneath them tell me she hasn't slept in days. Her beautiful rose-colored lips are all dry, chapped, and bleeding from dehydration, no doubt, and her biting on them.

She's a mess. Fuck, what have I done?

I crouch down and allow my hand to reach out, trailing over the crown of her thick hair. The strands are sweat-slickened, greasy, and a tangled mess. She doesn't stir at my touch, her eyes never flickering from the place she's staring at, lost in her own mind.

The desire to grab a fistful, and demand that she stare at me and obey me fills me, but I force myself to remain gentle with her. She has already been through so much in a short period of time.

"Issy..." I call out softly, wanting her to look at me but afraid of frightening her further. My heart thuds painfully in my chest, and bile rises at the back of my throat.

Nothing. I get absolutely no reaction to calling her name or to my touch. There is not even a flicker of recognition in her features, or a response in her body to my contact. *Dammit.* I can't have broken her. I refuse even to consider it. She's stronger than this; she has to be.

I lower myself to my knees until I'm entirely in front of her, blocking her sightline of the wall she is staring at. I reach out and allow my trembling fingers to run over her forehead, and down the side of her face. My fingertips grace her soft, dirty skin, and a tinge of electricity races back up my arm. My body craves her, even like this, even completely broken. I will always want my *Princesa.*

Real fear is now filling me with the knowledge that I may have genuinely broken her, that her mind might have fractured while confined, all alone in this dark hole in the ground. A prison of my own making, one that I firmly believed limiting her to would get me what I wanted. *Her.*

I reach forward and grab both her forearms, pulling her towards me and into my arms, where I cradle her slick and feverish skin against my own. *Fuck, is she burning up?* She doesn't fight my hold, and instead goes limp in my grasp. I stand up with her in my arms, her weight not doing anything to stop me from regaining my feet, and move towards the ladder.

It will be tricky getting her out of here. I didn't really count on her being incapacitated when I released her from captivity. I also didn't count on leaving her stubborn ass in that hole for four fucking days. I brace her against my body, and she goes limp like a rag doll as I throw her over one of my shoulders in a fireman's hold. Her head and upper body hang down my back, bouncing with my movements, as I grasp onto the rope ladder and commence climbing.

I grit my teeth, and a growl leaves my lips as I sway on the ladder. Her light body shifting against my back muscles, and a tiny whimper escaping her lips, as her head bangs against my lower back. When I'm closer to the top, I call out to Santiago. I'm not afraid of dropping her, but I want her covered, the minute she's out of the hole. I don't want my men's eyes on her in this vulnerable state, a state that I have fucking caused with my angry, psychotic actions.

Regret swims inside my blood, an emotion I'm not accustomed to feeling for anything or anyone, but right now, it's suffocating me. I did this; I caused the fragile creature in my arms to suffer, all for the sake of my fucking pride, and my need to control her every waking moment. I'm a fucking monster.

"Santiago, grab her and wrap her," I grunt through my teeth, knowing that he has to touch her feverish skin to do it. We reach the top of the hole, and Santiago pulls her away from me, cradling her body in the sheet like that of a small, wounded animal he was tending to. His disapproval is evident on his age-lined face, as his eyes trace over Issy's features.

Rage and jealousy fill my body as I reach forward and take her from his grasp. *MINE!* Even in her broken and fragile state, she is mine. I cannot release her. Even after witnessing the damage I've already caused her, I know I will never let her go.

"*Jefe*, she needs the medic. She's *no buena*." The sound of desperation in his voice instantly irritates me. Does he think I can't fucking see with my own two eyes that she's not alright?

I take her into my arms, her slight weight not even causing my muscles to strain, as my six-foot-two frame towers over the man who held her. What would I do if he had refused to release her to me?

Dead, he would be dead before he took his next breath. I take my precious captive and stroll quickly back inside the compound. "Get the fucking medic."

Fuck, let's hope I haven't completely destroyed the woman I crave more than anything. *We should release her, and send her back to her family,* the rational side of my brain argues, but my hackles rise with just the thought.

Even though I know that is the right thing to do, after everything I've already put her through, I know I will never follow through with it. I can't let her go, not now, not ever.

CHAPTER SIX

Issy

"Some old wounds never truly heal, and bleed again at the slightest word."

George R R Martin, A Game Of Thrones

Warm air moves over my irritated and feverish skin, as my head is turned from side to side, and my sweaty strands are shifted away from my neck. My eyes close of their own volition, wanting to avoid looking at anything and anyone. I can feel strong, rough hands on my body, lifting my limbs, maneuvering me this way and that way, so that someone can wash me with a wet cloth. I swallow the pained but relieved moan that tries to leave my lips. *Shhh, now try not to show your weakness; it will be used against you.*

The feeling of the abrasive material, and cold water, across the surface of my inflamed skin is both a soothing balm and an irritation. Why can't they just leave me alone? Why can't they let me die, so all of this could be over quickly? Of course, *he* wouldn't allow me even that small mercy. *Unhinged bastard.*

"Diego, sir, you need to step back so that I can examine her," a soft, hesitant voice calls out.

The grip on my arm tightens momentarily, causing me to have to bite the inside of my cheek and stiffen my limbs, before a cursed-filled grumble rents the air and the cloth is moved away from my body. My arm is lifted, and pressure is placed on my wrist. Then, a cold object is pressed against my chest, a vicious animalistic growl loud in the air accompanying its touch.

"Sir, please. I have to... check her... thoroughly," the soft-spoken, hesitant voice utters with fear evident in his tone. So his men are afraid of him, too. It doesn't really surprise me since he's the fucking devil incarnate.

I wish I had the energy or desire to fuck with him. I would grab onto this poor sucker's hand and place it right over my breast, making sure to fucking moan like a whore. I hope that would hurt him like he's fucking hurt me. The problem is I don't have the energy, or the desire, to hurt an innocent. *Is anyone really innocent if they are helping him keep you captive here?* My mind questions with resentfulness.

"Miss, I need to check your eyes and the inside of your mouth. Could you please allow me to assess and help you?" The voice questions. *Help me?* This man wants to help me, but there is only one way he could help me right now. *You are so weak, always looking for the easy way out of everything,* my mind scalds me with bitterness.

A deep sigh leaves my lips, my chest rattling with the sensation, and my body feeling like it wants to cave in on itself. "*Die.* You... want to... help. Kill... me." There's no point in begging for him to help release me. I know he won't do that, but maybe if there is even a small amount of mercy and decency in this stranger, he could help me escape this world permanently.

"WHAT THE FUCK, ISSY!" The growled words are like deep shards of glass embedding in my skin. The anger in them is unmistakable, *fucking good.* I'm angry, too, but the difference is I have no power in this situation. He's made sure to take it all away from me, the bastard.

The soft hands keep checking over my limbs, listening to my chest, forcing my eyes and mouth open, so he can assess the damage that his caveman of a boss has caused, all while ignoring my plea for death. So *much for helping me.*

"Sir, she is extremely dehydrated, and suffering from heat exposure. Her bug bites are all infected, and so are the cuts and rash she has across her body. I believe she might be suffering from a chest infection; that is where the wheezing and the fever are coming from."

"Will she recover?" The question is demanded in a deep tone, and I swear I almost heard fear in its depth. Of course, the bastard wouldn't want to lose his precious prize after all he has done to obtain it.

A sense of curiosity to see his face, and his expression, has me opening my sore and tired eyes and staring at him. His large olive-green eyes stare down at me, while his face remains impassive and tense. His rugged jaw is clenched, and a tic is evident on its side, jumping away as his thick lips remain in a straight line without mercy. No, there is no mercy inside of this man. What did I ever see in him that made me desire him the way I did? *He's death walking, ready to steal your fucking soul; too bad for him, mine is already broken and useless.*

Why does he still have to look incredibly handsome, even while committing the most heinous of acts? *The devil sends his most tempting evil in beautiful packages. He is a demon straight from hell, urged to climb out of its deep, fiery depths and brought here to destroy me.*

"Yes, with proper rest, medicine, and nourishment, she should." What a fucking pity that he doesn't tell him that I'm going to die. I would have loved to see the expression on his face at the knowledge that he would lose me to his own psychotic actions; it would serve him right after all he has put me through.

"Good, treat her and get the fuck out of the room." Diego turns away from me, refusing to hold my stare. "Santiago, I want two men stationed outside of that door twenty-four hours a day. She is not to leave the room, and only you and the medic are allowed inside *together*. She is never to be alone with either of you, *am I understood*?"

"Yes, *Jefe*."

"Yeess, Sir."

Anger soars through my limbs, giving me a moment of energy even though every part of me is on fire, and in pain. How fucking dare he?! How dare he take me from one prison only to place me in another under lock and key?

"*Bastard,*" the word sounds slurred, leaving my dry lips. I'm almost sure that he hasn't even heard my insult, until he turns that malicious glare back down on me, searing me with its hostility. I notice out of the corner of my eye both the young male doctor and Santiago taking some subtle steps back, and away from me. *Fucking cowards.*

"There's that serpent tongue of yours, my *Princesa*. If you can still call me fucking names, Issy, then maybe you're not as ill as the medic says you are? Shall we find out, my beauty? Shall I make you crawl back to your hole?" His dark eyebrow rises questioningly, and I can see the desire to punish me in his eyes. He wants me to continue to talk back, so he has a reason to hurt me further.

I turn my head away from his menacing glare, and stare at the furthest wooden wall, taking shallow breaths, as my blood continues to race loudly in my ears. The desire to run, to fight and get away from here, is all-encompassing, but my body and mind know that I wouldn't make it two steps before I face-planted, never mind my inability to fight off Diego Cabano. He has me at his mercy, and he knows it, as if I need any further reminders of how weak I truly am, both of body and mind.

One day, I won't be weak. One day soon, I will be strong like my grandmother, sister, and all the other Stratford women who have come before me. Then he'll experience my vengeance for what he has done. At least, that's what I repeat to myself as darkness once again claims me, as the medic injects something into my arm. One day, I will be strong or *die* trying to be.

I pace back and forth from one wall to the next, one bare foot in front of the other, filled with restless, unsteady energy. My skin feels too tight, as if insects are crawling all over it. I scratch down my arms with my broken, jagged nails, causing my flesh to bleed. It's not enough; I want to rip my skin from my bones, and watch myself bleed out on the floor. The morbid, deranged thought should scare me, but it's made itself at home with the rest of the darkness that inhabits my mind.

How could he have done this to me? How could he have hurt me in this way? The thought keeps circling round and round in my mind, keeping me in a manic state. Of all the shitty things to do to me, including throwing me in a fucking hole, this might be the worst of them.

I release a pent-up scream as I once again do a circuit of the room. Visions and sounds keep trying to accost me, but I know they're not truly here with me in this stifling room, and in this unforgiving jungle. It's all in my head. I repeatedly slap both palms against my skull to stop their sounds.

The medic hasn't been by in hours, and I need another hit of pain relief. I need something to numb all these sensations that I'm feeling. I don't want to feel anything; I desire the nothingness that the drugs provide. They temporarily bring quietness to my head, so that I don't have to hear how I'm worthless, over and over in my loved ones' voices.

Why are you afraid of the truth being spoken, Isabella? My mind plays tricks and asks the question in a voice that sounds suspiciously like my grandmother's.

It's been two days since Diego removed me from my earthy hole-in-the-ground prison, and placed me in this new confined prison of four sturdy walls. At least the view is slightly better, and I have a more comfortable bed to sleep on. Regardless of the better accommodations, one fact remains: *I am still a prisoner.*

Is my grandmother out there looking for me? She has to be, right? She has to be tearing the world apart, searching for me. How come she hasn't found me yet? It's been more than a week since that lunatic drugged and kidnapped me. She should have found me by now.

Unless she's given up searching. I was never as valuable to her as my sister, Mia. Constantly disappointing her with my inability to behave like a Stratford heir should. Always causing embarrassment to the Stratford name. Perhaps she has finally realized that she can be rid of me now.

How convenient for her that Diego has provided her with this opportunity. She won't have to watch me self-destruct with drugs, men, or having my face splashed across the tabloids and social media. I'm the constant bane of her existence, one that she has to continuously save, and hide my misdeeds in dark places.

She has the Stratford heir she always dreamed of; I was just a spare heir. The one she had to love because I was part of her bloodline. Her beloved son's child. The one she felt sorry for because I was a weak orphan.

Defective. Useless. A disappointment.

I stare once again at the bed linens, and wonder if I can rip them apart with my bare hands and use them somehow to escape. I know there is no way out through the barred window, and no way out through the bedroom door undetected; Diego made sure of that. Could I somehow use them to take my own life? Therefore depriving Diego of the satisfaction of watching me beg for my wretched life and freedom? A freedom that I know he will never grant.

I drag my hands down my face, knowing that it's hopeless; even if I could rip the linens apart, how would I use them to take my life? There is nothing to hang them off of, even if I could form them into a noose. No, I need to provoke Diego into killing me in a fit of rage. I know he's capable of it. He's a merciless killer. A weapons dealer with no remorse for who he has to hurt to get what he wants.

One problem with that thought: he hasn't been back to see me since he placed me under lock and key in this room. I guess he only remembers me when he wants a place to shove his cock into, *the bastard.*

My only options are to try to bribe one of the guards stationed outside of the room, or the medic. There is no point in even trying with Santiago; the man is loyal to his cockroach of a boss. *Can I seduce the medic, Raphael?* He's such a timid creature, so unsuited to this criminal gangster life out here in the jungle. Is he perhaps a prisoner, too?

My thoughts are interrupted by the light tapping on the thick wooden door, and the knob turning. At least he has some manners, unlike the rest of these heathens, constantly barging in here without warning. My blood hums with anticipation of the morphine I hope he has with him, and my hands tense as sweat breaks out across my neck.

Act normal, bitch, or he will know something is wrong with you. The words are a whispered hiss in my mind, as I try not to jump out of my skin.

"Señorita?" A throat clearing from the doorway greets my ears. "I have come to give you your meds, and check on your bites."

Raphael moves quietly into the room carrying a metal tray, his soulful brown eyes darting to me before a gentle smile appears, and then quickly disappears off his face. Santiago, his constant shadow, steps into the room behind him and closes the door, before leaning his large body against it. His face is passive and watchful.

"*Buen día, señorita,*" Santiago nods respectfully in my direction. His dark gaze trails over my healing form before his eyes divert to looking elsewhere, as Raphael approaches me and starts his inspection of my bites.

At least I am no longer naked, or wrapped in a sheet. I was so grateful when Santiago brought me a few loose, white, sleeveless linen sundresses to wear. No fucking undergarments, but at least the dresses all go down past my knees, so I'm not flashing anyone my vagina. *Small mercies, I guess.*

I nod, but my eyes keep coming back to the clear vial of morphine on Raphael's tray. The craving for oblivion calls to me like a sweet, seductive mistress, begging for me to end our pain. Need courses through my veins, as I try my best to remain still under Raphael's inspection.

My mouth waters at just the thought of how good the feeling is when he gives me that shot. It feels like I'm soaring outside of my body; my limbs feel weightless, and euphoria explodes through my brain. It's better than any orgasm I've ever had, even the ones Diego has given me. It makes every part of me light up and sing. *I want it. I fucking need it.*

I guess the all-knowing Diego didn't do his research on his captive. The fucker either doesn't realize that I'm a recovering addict, or perhaps he doesn't care as long as the drugs make me docile, and help him keep me here.

Either way, all that hard work of getting clean, all those months in rehab, and going through withdrawals, have gone out the window, and I'm right back to where I was before I ever stepped foot in Casbury, North Carolina, and met Diego Cabano.

Weak, my mind hisses, but I ignore it. I no longer care. *Yes, I'm weak; yes, I'm an addict and a whore.* There is no pride left in me. I know what I'm capable of for a hit of oblivion. It's not like I haven't traded my self-respect and body before.

A handsome face filled with an expression of pain and loss fills my vision; he calls out to me, begging that I take back what I have done, who I am, and the crimes I committed against his love, but I can't undo what I have done. As much as we crave absolution, one can never go back to the past. More of those memories try to rise within the confines of my mind, but I shut them down with a slam of a thick metal door. No, now is not the time to wallow or self-reflect; now is the time to ensure we get what we need. Oblivion, painless oblivion, is what we crave and would do anything for.

"Isabella, your bites are healing very well, and the rash is starting to subside with the antibiotics. How is the pain in your chest today?"

Raphael's sympathetic chocolate eyes meet mine, and I see genuine concern in their depths. *Fuck, can he tell how on edge I am? How much I need that hit of the drug he's brought with him?*

"Everything hurts. My chest feels tight and on fire. My body aches, I... I can't sleep. The insect bites are still so painful." I bite down on my lip and try to look at him demurely through my lashes as I stroke a finger across his hand, which is still holding on to my arm. I watch as his eyes trace my face and center on my lips, before flicking back up to meet my eyes. A slight pink blush crosses his cheekbones before he ducks his head, removes his hand, and swipes at the sweat on the side of his neck.

Gotcha. Santiago clears his throat loudly, dissolving the moment, and the sound has Raphael taking a step away from me. *Fuck.* I might have a chance if Santiago just left the room for a moment. One little moment is all I need, and he would be putty in my hands, like all the other men before him with whom I have used the same tricks.

A chance to do what? To suck his cock on your knees like a drugged-out whore? My mind questions. *Diego will kill him, and probably you, too. You do realize that, right?*

"Let's... ummm... check your... breathing, and then I can give you the antibiotic, which should help with your chest."

"What about the pain? You're going to give me something for the pain, aren't you?" My voice sounds a little desperate even to my ears, and I observe as Raphael raises a dark eyebrow in concern.

FUCK, FUCK, FUCK! I need to tone it down.

He's staring at me more intensely now, his medically trained eye cataloging what he sees. Can he tell that I'm an addict? Can he sense that I need that hit of drugs more than I need my next breath? That if I had my way, I would take so much of the drug he has and never wake again. My body feels slick with sweat as I nervously fidget with my fingers, and sway back and forth on my feet.

I need it; I fucking need it. Just one hit... please, just one hit. Just so the pain can stop, so all the voices can stop. I need the silence, please.

My eyes keep traveling back towards the tray, even though I am trying desperately not to look in that direction, not to give myself away. Shit will be so much worse for me here if he stops giving me the pain meds. I won't be able to handle it at all. Not the captivity, not the knowledge that my family has probably abandoned me, and that I'm only a hole for Diego to fuck when he feels like it. That none of it was real between us. I'm a prize that he wanted to win, and now he has, and he's realized I'm actually worthless.

Raphael moves closer to me, his eyes trailing across my face as he brings his stethoscope up to my chest. "Breathe slowly through your nose, hold for a count of five, and then release the breath through your mouth, please."

His body shields me from Santiago's prying eyes as I do what he has requested, taking deep breaths in and holding them. "Isabella, we should stop the pain meds; you seem to be getting attached to them," he whispers.

Panic seizes me at his words, and my breath falters. *No!* No, I can't allow him to stop. Desperation fills me as I stare into his eyes. From this close of a distance, I can see the honey flecks in his pupils. "Please, no, it hurts. I can't bear it. I can't keep going. I... I'll do anything you want... anything."

My hand reaches up and grabs his wrist, tightening before I soothe it with a slight touch. His eyes focus on mine, and his breathing quickens. "Please," I whisper.

"I can't save you," he whispers back.

"Then help me at least... bear it," I whisper as a tear trails down my face.

He moves the scope back and forth across my chest, his eyes lingering on mine as more tears slip from my eyes, and make their way down my face. I can see the moment he makes up his mind on whether he will help me or not. His jaw tenses, and he tears his gaze from mine. He refuses to meet my eyes again as he steps back away from me. *NO! Please no!*

"I'm going to give you the antibiotic now. Your chest sounds much better, and your skin is healing from the bites and rash." I hear what he refuses to say out loud. He won't help me escape into oblivion. He's not going to give me the morphine.

Rage fills me like it never has before. How fucking dare he deny me the one comfort that he can provide in this awful place? This fucking hell that I'm trapped in. He thinks he's helping me by healing me with antibiotics, so his psychotic boss can keep me alive and trapped here forever. FUCK HIM! Fuck all of them. I would rather die.

My hand lashes out before I can even process what I have done, and strikes across his face so hard that it makes it turn to the side. The loud sound makes my ears ring, and I can sense Santiago moving closer to us, but I can't seem to contain myself. I launch myself at Raphael, biting, slapping, and snarling, hitting him anywhere and everywhere my limbs can reach, even as he cries out in shock.

"You bastard! You're just like them! Give me what I want. What I need!" I try to get around him, to the tray on the table holding what I desire more than anything in this world. I need it! If I can just get to it, maybe I can take the whole bottle, and it will kill me.

"Señorita!" Santiago's voice is loud in the room, as he grasps my arms and hauls me back roughly away from Raphael, stopping my attempt to reach the bottle.

"NO! I need it! I fucking hate all of you! I need it, please!" I scream even as he throws me on the bed roughly, and I bounce, falling over to the other side.

"Get out of the room, hurry now!" Santiago instructs Raphael, and I watch as he snatches the morphine vial, before they both move towards the door. Panic races through my body, my blood rushing in my ears, and I race around the bed towards them but reach them just as the door slams, and the sound of the lock is engaged.

I fall to my knees, a scream leaving my lips. I failed! I once again failed, even this small task I couldn't accomplish. They will never give me the drugs now that I have played my hand. Now they know how desperate I am. I truly am weak and useless; I can't even help myself.

I know now that I'm never getting out of here. *I will never be free.*

CHAPTER SEVEN

Diego

"The loneliest moment in someone's life is when they are watching their whole world fall apart, and all they can do is stare blankly."

F. Scott Fitzgerald

I'm trying hard to concentrate on what my father's telling me through the phone, but the words he's uttering all seem to string along into background noise. I know I should be paying attention; he's relaying important information about Stella Stratford's hunt for Issy and me, but some part of me just doesn't care.

It's been two agonizing days since I last saw her. Since I dragged her up out of that deep hole in the earth, covered in dirt, filth, and insect bites. Her small body was so sweaty and feverish to my touch, and her beautiful sapphire eyes were dull and lost. She was sick down there because of me, because of my irrational actions.

I fucking hurt her. She could have died if Santiago hadn't approached me with his concerns. I was prepared to leave her down there for a few more days until I broke her will to leave me, her desire to continue to deny that she belongs with me. I could have killed her. The thought races over and over in my mind on repeat. I could have killed the one woman I yearn for above all else.

"*Hijo*, are you even listening to me?" My father's annoyed voice penetrates the thoughts that continuously circle my mind on a never-ending, chastising loop.

"Yeah, I'm listening," I reply with aggravation.

"I don't think you are, Diego. You have made an enemy of a very powerful, furious woman. One who could destroy our organization, and wipe our bloodline off the face of the earth. She will not stop until she has her granddaughter returned to her, and you cannot hide in the jungle forever, *mi hijo*. She has hired an army of the best mercenaries to find you; it's just a matter of time before they do, and they have orders to kill you on sight."

My eyes close as I drag my hand down my face, my palm rubbing against the rough skin of the scar along the surface of my cheek. A scar another enemy graced me with when they, too, tried to kill me, and I survived. I'll survive Stella Stratford's attempts to kill me, too.

It's not that I believe myself invincible; quite the opposite. It's the fact that I don't fear death or meeting the devil. I've seen what evil walks amongst the earth disguised as humans. There are no monsters that are more frightening.

It's also because I know I'm like the great and mighty serpents that have survived since the world first began to turn; one way or another, I will shed my skin and evolve, but never truly die. My plans are to ensure that my name lives forever, and in order to do that, I need that little dark-haired broken doll under lock and key.

A knock on the door has me turning towards it. "I got to go, *papá*. I'll be in touch soon." I don't wait for his objection before disconnecting the satellite phone, and bracing my body against the solid wood desk in the room. I need a distraction to take my mind off what I have done to the beauty confined to yet another prison of my making.

We should let her go. The thought whispers through my mind, but I shut it down immediately. Any guilt that I'm feeling, I need to put aside and think of the big picture. All the sacrifices that I've made to have her. I can't turn back now.

"Enter," I command, and seconds later, a disheveled Santiago and red-faced Raphael enter the room. *Oh goody, this should be good.* It looks like my *Princesa's* spirit has finally woken up from its slumber. I was wondering how long it would take before she stopped playing the meek and broken victim, and showed the world the vicious, formidable creature that I know hides inside of her, the one I have all intentions of provoking to the surface.

I watch them approach, giving each of them my coldest, most brutal glare. The look that makes mens' knees shake, and pray to a benevolent being, because they know I'm about to rip their hearts right out of their chests with no regard for their humanity.

"Sir, I... it's... *la mierda*," a frustrated and frightened Raphael utters as he meets my gaze. His face is all red on one side, and I can clearly see the imprint of Issy's fingers on his olive-toned skin. Looks like she got him good. An irrational sense of pride fills me at the sight of the damage my girl has caused.

Raphael takes a deep breath and tries once again to get his words out, as he shifts nervously on his feet. His dark eyes meet and hold mine, even though I can see fear across his face and in his demeanor. "*Jefe*, with respect, sir... I... the *señorita* Isabella... there is a problem."

"A problem? *Estás bromeando?* I'll say there is a problem; she just attacked him because he wouldn't give her the drugs he has," Santiago lets loose with an irritated snark, his large body tense.

A feeling of trepidation crawls up my back as I move closer to Raphael. What the fuck is he blabbering about? Drugs? What fucking drugs? "You have thirty seconds to tell me what the fuck is going on, before I have both your heads ripped from your fucking bodies, and put on spikes in the jungle."

My heart is thundering so loudly in my ears that it's starting to drown out all the other sounds. A wash of heat cascades down my back as I repeat Santiago's words in my mind. *No, he has to be fucking wrong. Not my Issy, not my perfect broken doll.* Rage starts to rise within me, from the soles of my feet and crawling up my limbs with licks of pure fire. They are lying, slandering my Issy. I'll fucking kill them both.

"*Dios perdoname*. Isabella... is... an addict... or at least is addicted to the morphine I have been giving her. She tried to get me to give her a shot today, begged in fact, then tried to... to seduce me, and when I wouldn't, she attacked me and tried to take the vial herself." His words tumble from his lips in a high-pitched voice filled with terror.

He should be fucking terrified, because his words trigger my anger further. The desire to snap his neck for calling her an addict makes quick work of my steps, as I wrap my fist around his neck and tighten, until his breath gasps out of him. He tries to fight my hold, clawing at my hand in a useless attempt to remove my grip, while his eyes widen dramatically with the realization that I will end his fucking life right here. I lift him by his nape from the ground, and he makes a choking sound as the air is cut from his lungs.

"You lie," I seethe through clenched teeth. "She must be in pain; she wouldn't beg if she weren't."

"He's not lying, *Jefe*. Please, Diego! She attacked him for the drugs, and not because she is in pain... at least not that type of pain you speak of. *Joder*, she did try to seduce him into giving them to her, knowing that I was in the room watching, and... it didn't work. She was desperate, *Jefe*. She has all the signs of a person with an addiction." Santiago drags his scarred hand roughly through his short hair, as my attention shifts to him instead of the man being deprived of oxygen in front of me.

She tried to seduce him? My fucking Issy? My prize, with this piece of shit, all while another man watched. Does she crave death so badly that she knows her actions would cause me to strangle the life from her? She doesn't want to be mine, but would she use this as an opportunity to leave me permanently? Is death preferable to spending a life with me?

Deep in my soul, I hear the confirmation of my fears. She has already tried to leave me, back in Casbury, and would not have agreed to come to this jungle and be with me, unless under force. She doesn't want to be mine, and death for her at my hands or through some vile fucking drug, would be preferable to life with me.

"She couldn't even keep her eyes off of the bottle, and she was behaving erratically, like... *mierda*... like an addict coming down from a fix." Santiago's words have me pausing my tightening grip on Raphael's neck, who is quickly turning an alarming shade of puce.

Raphael struggles in my grip, and I push him away, releasing my brutal grasp and sending him crashing to his knees. "Explain, fucking now," I demand. "Leave nothing out, or I will crush your fucking skull with my bare hands."

Raphael attempts to clear his throat while getting to his feet unsteadily, and recovering his breath. "I... I don't..." he coughs and tries again. "I don't think she became addicted here. I... she has all the signs of being a recovering addict, one who has fallen off the wagon. If I had known, I wouldn't have given her anything for the pain."

A rough, sarcastic laugh leaves my lips, "You think Isabella Stratford is an addict?" I take a menacing step forward as he takes one back, "that her grand-mother, the powerful Stella Stratford, would have allowed that to happen?"

He swallows the lump in his throat and takes another step back from me. *Smart man*, I'm sure he can see I am moments away from murdering him, here in my den, for accusing Issy. Could there be even a morsel of truth behind his words? Doubt begins to slither through my mind, a snake just waiting patiently and silently to attack.

"Diego... whether her *abuela* knew or didn't, she has issues with addiction. Right now, she is coming off the high from the powerful shot I gave her a few hours ago, a shot that should have lasted longer than it has before she stopped feeling it. I had noticed yesterday that the dosage wasn't having the effect it should. That's because she's conditioned her body to... need more of it."

Raphael waves his hands warily in front of me as if he could ward me off with them, if I decide to end his fucking life right now. "Kill me if you must, Diego, but it won't change the fact that she has a substance use disorder. She will get worse as she comes down, more violent and desperate. She will get sick as her body goes through withdrawal."

Doubt clouds my mind, even though I hear the belief of truth in Raphael's words. He believes she is an addict. He believes that she tried to seduce him for the drugs, not because she was interested in him. That helps to fight back the monster who is trying to claw its way out of me and rip him to shreds. She doesn't want him. She isn't trying to replace me, just to fucking leave me.

"*Jefe*, please, Raphael is not lying. Look at his face; she attacked him because he wouldn't give them to her. She tried to take them from him without thinking of the consequences; she's unstable." Santiago approaches me, his face filled with worry and sincerity.

"Is she still locked in the room, or did she manage to get past you two fuckers?" I question with a nervous energy soaring through my body.

How could this be? How could my Issy be an addict like these two are claiming? I would have seen the signs before this. I was with her for weeks, locked in her sister's mansion. Wouldn't I have noticed if she had a problem?

How? Her grandmother had everyone under lock and key. She couldn't escape to procure drugs, and no one was getting into the property under Stella's army's watch. What if she is a recovering addict? Then she would have been managing it before we started pumping her with fucking morphine here in the jungle. Just one hit would have been enough to push her back over the edge. To make her crave her next hit.

FUCK! God fucking dammit, what if I did this? What if she was in recovery before I kidnapped and brought her here, and now she's spiraling? I never truly wanted to hurt her; I just wanted to make her stronger, so she could survive a life with me that is filled with danger.

I didn't want to be what ended up killing her. *We should let her go. We should send her back to her grandmother, where she can get the help she needs, and the support to fight off the cravings that we have reintroduced,* my mind begs with rational thought.

NO! I will never fucking let her go. Not even when her last breath leaves her body. Not even if she is a fucking addict. She is mine, and she will always be mine. She wants to crave something, let it be fucking me. I won't allow her to desire anything else; she wants a drug, here the fuck I am.

"Give me the morphine," I demand with my hand outstretched, my glare meeting the shocked faces of the two men before me.

"Sir, please, you can't give it to her," Raphael begs as he removes the glass bottle from his pant pocket.

I disregard his words even though they burn through my veins, causing me to want to bloody him for telling me what I can't do with *my prize, my Princesa, my whore*. No one will make decisions for Issy Stratford but me. Santiago's words tumble back through my mind that she tried to seduce Raphael into giving her the drugs.

My little *Princesa* wants to behave like a drugged-out whore, selling herself for the next fix. I'm about to fucking show her what that life looks like, and it won't be pretty. The only person my little whore will ever beg is me.

CHAPTER EIGHT

Diego

"Humans are obsessed with pain. We fall in love, we prolong our own depressions, and we ask to be let down by having hopes and expectations."

Soft Grung

I move towards the room Issy is confined to, and even before I make it through the door, I can hear the destruction she's in there causing. The sound of items slamming against walls and the floor, and her high-pitched screams vibrate through the solid wood door.

I take deep, fortifying breaths to prepare myself for what I'm about to see, and to help control the anger racing through my veins like hot lava. The way I'm feeling right now, I could do some serious damage to her if she pushes me with her vicious viper tongue.

I unlock the door and storm into the room, prepared to have to subdue her, but the sight that greets me has my eyebrows meeting my hairline. *What. The. Fuck.* Utter destruction and chaos are all over the room. The little psycho has even managed to flip the king-size mattress off the solid wood four-poster bed, and it's now haphazardly thrown on the floor. All the bed linens are strewn across the floor, and shards of glass are everywhere from the items she has thrown in her tantrum.

Dark sapphire eyes filled with malice meet mine from across the room; her face is flushed, and her long, dark hair a rat's nest. She looks like one of those Greek goddesses of destruction they write about in fables, possessed with power. *Erinys* in her divinity. Fuck, just looking at her staring back at me with wrath and defiance makes me want to throw her to the floor, and fuck the anger and fight right out of her.

My cock begins to harden at the possibility of doing just that. Maybe I'll wrap my fingers around her delicate throat and choke the fucking life out of her, while I'm filling her with my cum, for her insolence and the daring move she just tried.

"YOU FUCKING BASTARD!" She screams at me, before rushing across the room and lunging at me. Her nails manage to slice down the side of my neck, before I restrain both her hands behind her back, and hold her at arm's length. That doesn't stop her attempts to get at me, though. The little tempest tries her best to kick and knee me in the balls.

Her attempts are amusing, and if it wasn't for the disturbing fucking reason I'm actually here in the room, I might actually let her play for a bit to see how far she could take it before she exhausts herself. I take a good look at her, and I see the signs that Raphael and Santiago mentioned. Ones I've missed because I couldn't bear to look at her, knowing I caused her harm. I've been a coward, hiding in other parts of the compound instead of at her side.

Her pupils are large, her skin clammy, and her pulse is beating rapidly in her neck, like a trapped hummingbird. She can't hold my stare or hold still at all. Her body vibrates with a sickening energy that seems unnatural to the woman I know.

The little she-devil is practically foaming at the mouth like a rabid dog, one that needs to be put down, except I won't end her, not ever. My grip on her tightens, and I shake her like a rag doll. Her bottom lip trembles as she tries to avoid my glare, her beautiful eyes darting to desperately look around the room for an escape. She can look all she wants, but there will never be an escape from me.

"Are you an addict, Issy? My men tell me that you are." I grip her tighter until a wince leaves her pouty lips. "That, in fact, you are a drugged-out whore, one who would do anything for a hit of morphine. One who would attempt to seduce them, and offer herself up in exchange for drugs."

The rage that is infiltrating every part of me beckons me to force her to her knees until she begs for my mercy, but the problem with that is that once I have her down there, there is a good chance I am going to stop her from breathing, maybe even permanently. "Is that fucking true, *Princesa*? Would you do anything for another taste?" I release her, and she stumbles backward, falling to her ass with a pained cry.

I pull the glass bottle from my pants pocket and hold it between my fingers, her eyes immediately narrowing on it and her breath picking up. A small moan escapes her lips as she tries to scramble back to her feet.

"You were willing to seduce Raphael to get another taste of this, weren't you, my little slut?" I wave it back and forth, and her eyes track the movement, like a dog with a treat being offered to it; she's practically salivating.

"Or maybe I should be calling you my drug whore? That's what you are, isn't it, Issy? That's what you have always been? I was just too blinded by your beauty and wealth to see it." I take a step closer to her and her eyes widen dramatically. "Those whispered stories your grandmother did her best to squash, about you fucking dealers for coke were true, weren't they?"

I had heard about the gossip surrounding her when I researched her sister, Mia. One must know everything they can use to conquer an enemy and claim a prize, and at the time, I thought her sister was to be my prize, my wife, whether she wanted to be or not. Of course, I assumed the rumors were just malicious gossip about an entitled Manhattan princess, maybe one who partied a little too hard, and had made enemies along the way. Never in a million fucking years would I have believed that they were, in fact, true.

Yet here I am, watching her lose her shit, not the heir to one of the world's largest fortunes, not a sophisticated and well-bred billionaire princess, but a girl ready to sell her soul and body for the oblivion a drug can temporarily give her.

Weak. Wasteful. Disappointing.

I want to be disgusted by her. I want to throw her back in that fucking hole to die, but I can't, because a substantial irrational part of me can't be away from her. I can't give her up, even though everything is telling me she will never survive my world. This behavior, this fucking weakness, her having an addiction is a huge complication, one I never imagined having to plan for.

How the fuck does one plan for the girl they want to own every single delectable inch of, to marry one day and breed so she pops out spawn after spawn, to be an addict and willing to give herself away, like she's worth nothing instead of priceless?

"Please... please, Diego." Her voice is so small, and she sounds so beaten and fragile, begging me for what she perceives as oblivion. Doesn't she know that one hit will never be enough, that she will be begging for more for the rest of her life? The drugs will consume her until there is nothing left of her, and then they will eventually take her away from me. I can't let that happen, not now, not ever.

Fury and disappointment at the situation and her weakness fill me, and I dangle the bottle before her, watching as beads of sweat appear on the side of her face, and trail down skin I long to mar with my touch.

"Remove your clothes, Issy," I hiss the words at her with venom in my tone, and she momentarily stares back at me, a lone tear sliding down her pretty face before she swipes at it. *Such a pretty broken doll.*

"Show me how weak you really are, slut. Show me what you are willing to do for another fix." I can feel the tic in my jaw pulsating as my breathing speeds up. I watch her grab the hem of the dress I provided her with, as she raises it up above her knees, then higher, until her pretty pink pussy is on display to my eyes. She doesn't stop until the dress is over her head and being thrown to the floor, as her chest rises and falls rapidly. *Fuck.*

"Give it to me, Diego, please," she whimpers. She's so needy and desperate, and it both makes my temperature rise and disgusts me in equal measure. Who has damaged her so badly to turn her into this creature before me?

"Get on your knees, whore."

Her eyes squeeze shut for a moment, as more tears silently make their way down her face. They call to me, begging me to show her kindness instead of cruelty, but I can't and won't. I keep picturing her offering herself to Raphael in my mind. My mind conjures the image of her willingly letting men fuck and use her for their depravity, all while she's high as a kite.

How many men have used my *Princesa?* How many of them have seen her blitzed out of her mind, and taken advantage of her weakness, her cravings? I will never let another man have her. I will never allow her to beg anyone else but me. *Mine.*

She falls to her knees, the sound of her flesh hitting the floor another nail in the coffin I will bury her in. Her eyes never leave mine as her whole body trembles before me, goosebumps sprouting across her pretty porcelain skin, even though the room is hot as hell.

I roll the bottle between my fingers, ensuring her jewel-tone eyes follow the movement as her lips part, and a needy mewling sound escapes her. "Look at how desperate you are, so pathetic." I pretend to drop the bottle to the ground, and she dives for it, her whole body hitting the floor hard in desperation.

I shake my head in annoyance at her and make a tsking sound, as she realizes that I have no intention of dropping the bottle and am just tormenting her. "Crawl to me, Issy. Crawl to me like the whore you apparently are. If you do everything I tell you, if you please me, my little slut, then I will give you a taste."

She hesitates briefly, anger and outrage crossing her features, and my breath stalls in my chest. *There she is, my girl.* My fighter is trapped in there, and she's ready to hand me my balls. As quickly as the expression appears, it disappears, and she gets on her hands and knees. Her body trembles as her full, round breasts sway below her, as she arches her back like a feline and crawls across the floor to me.

Fuck. She is perfection. Her skin calls to me to paint it red with the print of my hands. To leave all of my fingerprints across that porcelain surface, and to carve my name into her flesh so all who admire it, can see that she is mine. *My property. My whore. My doll to play with.* The desire to dig my fingers into her hair, and yank her around with it like a leash is almost overwhelming.

She stops crawling when she reaches the edge of my black combat boots and sits back on her bent legs, her chest rises and falls with her rapid breathing, and her eyes stare up at me with her dark lashes clumped together with diamond tears. She is so beautiful in her desperation, pure sinful temptation for a weaker man.

"Undo my pants, Issy, and pull out my cock. Open your fucking whore mouth and put out your tongue."

I brace myself into a wide stance as her fingers crawl up my pant leg and reach for my zipper and button without hesitation, opening both and then slipping inside and unleashing my hard, throbbing cock from the confines of my boxers. My crown is already slick with precum along its surface. She uses her thumb to brush across it, spreading more of my weeping pearls across the sensitive flesh, which has a shiver racing up my spine.

I bite the inside of my cheek to prevent the moan that wants to escape my lips. "Put me on your tongue, slut," I instruct her, moving my lower body slightly forward so that I can graze the tip of my cock across her pouty, pink lips. Her hand tightens around my girth as she strokes me once, then again, and places my cock on her waiting wet tongue.

I use the hand not holding on to the bottle to reach forward and grasp a fistful of her hair, forcing my hard cock further into her mouth until I hit the back of her throat, making her gasp and choke on my length. She splutters and tries to pull back, tears cascading down her face, but I tighten my grip further. I fuck hard and fast into the back of her throat with powerful thrusts, the sounds of her gagging and choking on my length egging me further on, to unleash more of my violence.

I want to hurt her. I want to destroy her like needing her is doing to me. She makes me feel weak in my desire for her. Hopeless because I cannot let her go, even though every fiber of my being knows I should walk away from her, and never look back.

"Look at what a cock whore you are, Issy. How pretty you look swallowing my dick. That's it, baby, take all of me down that pretty, delicate throat. Swallow me, all the way down until you choke, baby," I grunt, thrusting and fucking her face without mercy.

Her breathing is coming in harsh pants, and her body is both trying to pull away from my relentless treatment and move closer. I watch as she tightens her thighs, rubbing them together to try to give herself some friction on her needy clit. My whore is turned on by the violence I'm showing her. I shouldn't really be surprised; Issy enjoys being degraded and used. She enjoys being treated like a slut. *My slut.*

"Don't you dare cum, slut. You don't get anything out of this other than the fucking drugs you crave." *Thrust.* "That's what you desperately want, isn't it, Issy?" *Thrust.* "It's what you're willingly giving me your mouth and your body in exchange for, isn't it?" *Thrust.*

The words are getting harder and harder to utter, as electric tingles race up my spine with the coming orgasm. I shove my cock as far down her throat as I can go, until her airway is completely blocked and her nose is pressed against my pelvis, her wet tears and saliva coating my skin. She smacks my thighs and sinks her nails into my flesh, trying desperately to force me to release her just as my orgasm reaches its peak, and I cum in thick spurts down her throat.

Fuck, that feels amazing. Her throat is so tight as I cum inside of it. She gags and chokes on my length, and cum pours out of the sides of her lips and down her chin, making her look like a dirty, messy whore at my feet. "That's it, my dirty, drug whore; swallow all of it down, baby. That right there is your drug. *I'm* your fucking drug, Issy."

She tries to pull away from me again, and I release her, letting her skid backward as she swipes at the dribbles of my cum and spit on her cheeks and chin. Her blue eyes glow with an inner light as she stares back at me with watery lashes, the tears continuing to fall as she tries to catch her breath. Her chest is pink with a blush and wet with my cum. I watch as a drop makes its way between her full breasts, to continue its journey south toward my heaven.

Fuck, I'm still hard. Even face-fucking her like a savage mere moments ago has done nothing to cool my craving for her or, worse, my rage. Would she have let Raphael face-fuck her for a shot of morphine?

My hands tighten into fists, almost crushing the bottle in my grip. The answer is right there in front of me, in the form of a woman who would let me further use and debase her, even now. Her eyes are locked on my fist holding the glass bottle. Jesus fuck, how much of this shit have they been giving her to get her to this state?

Some part of me knows it's not right to use her addiction against her. To debase and humiliate her for something she is struggling to control. Something she was trying to move past before I threw her in a fucking hole, and let one of my men pump her full of painkillers, unknowingly bringing her back to this version of her before me.

Addiction is an illness, and my Issy is fucking sick, and I want to be her cure. To do that, I'm going to have to shatter her some more, in the hopes that when she hits rock bottom, she takes my hand to pull herself back up.

"You're just a broken little girl hiding under the Stratford name and all your money, aren't you, Issy? You're weak and pitiful, nothing like your sister or grandmother." I crouch down before her, her gaze holding mine even as small, pathetic sobs leave her lips.

I reach forward and grab her chin with my fingers, tightening until she flinches. "I won't allow you to be weak. I won't give you the satisfaction of escaping me, Issy. Not your body and certainly not your fucking mind. You belong to me now, and I can do what I want with you, and Issy? No one is going to stop me, not even you."

I return to my feet and take a few steps towards the door, her eyes following my every movement. "DIEGO!" Her voice comes out choked as she calls for me in a panic. God, I love the sound of my name on her lips, but not like this. I never want to see her like this again.

I lift the bottle of the drugs she was willing to do anything for, that she would have betrayed me for. This small, clear glass bottle signifies all of her weaknesses, the broken parts within her, the ones I want to put back together, even if they are jagged. With one last look at her beautiful, deceitful face, I throw the bottle against the wall and watch as it shatters, spilling all its contents on the floor and wall.

Her scream as she rushes towards it reminds me of an injured animal, one that knows it's about to be eaten by a predator.

"There will be no further drugs, Issy, you could be fucking dying, and I will make sure you are given nothing. You will never be this weak again, or I swear to you, I will end your fucking life, but not before I take your sister and grandmother from this earth."

I open the door and leave the room, slamming it behind me and locking it, to ensure she can't escape. A loud thud crashes against the door, followed by high-pitched screams. I drag my hands down my exhausted face; every part of me is tense.

The threats are piling up at my door, trying to find their way inside my haven, and the one person I have sacrificed everything for was willing to betray me for a little glass bottle.

Maybe my father is right, and I'm in over my head. The question is, do I send her back to her family and allow her to live out her days without me, or do I show her mercy and take her life here in the jungle, so she can never breathe another breath without me?

CHAPTER NINE

Issy

"You can't always get what you want, but if you try sometimes, you might find, you get what you need."

Mick Jagger

I pace back and forth, like a zombie from one of those shows my sister loves; *The Walking Dead*. My head spins as another bout of nausea assaults me, making me clutch at my abdomen, knowing it's only a matter of moments before I'm retching out what meager food I managed to consume an hour ago. The groaning sounds leaving my lips, and the rumbles in my stomach, certainly sound like they are coming from the undead.

It's been four days since Diego savagely face-fucked me in this room, and then destroyed my only hope for oblivion. Four days of withdrawal symptoms which have made me feel like death would have been a kinder mercy. A mercy that fucker is incapable of granting me. *I hate him, I fucking hate him, don't I?* Everything in my brain feels scrambled, and all my emotions are charged and on overdrive.

My whole body aches, my muscles spasm involuntarily, my nose won't stop running, tears escape my eyes unwarranted, *fuck*, even my hair hurts at this point. I'm struggling to keep even water down, and I can feel myself getting even weaker. Soon, I won't be able to rise from the bed at all.

Diego's promise that no further drugs would be given to me has come to fruition, and even the antibiotics have been stopped at the boss's command. Raphael still checks on me twice daily, but now it's Santiago and another man I don't know the name of, watching him interact with me. I guess they fear I may try to seduce him again. How sexy I must look, covered in my own vomit, hair a tangled mess, reeking of body odor and sweat. Every man's dream, apparently.

I haven't been allowed to leave the room of my four-walled prison to shower. My skin itches from the insect bites that are still healing and the cold, sticky sweat that clings to my skin. My greasy hair is piled on top of my head, using a torn piece of fabric from the bed linens I destroyed. The one and only dress Diego allowed me to keep is covered in stains, sweat, and filth, forming like a second layer to my skin. How it got on my body after I passed out still remains a mystery to me. One that I don't want to look too closely at, so it doesn't push me over the edge.

The room was cleaned of my destruction by Diego's men, while he held me against a wall with his forearm pressed against my neck, and a fist full of my hair in his grasp, so that I couldn't attempt an escape, not that I was in any shape to try, anyways. That was the last time I saw him in the flesh, though I have no doubt that he is keeping tabs on me. *His prisoner, his fucking prize. Psycho.*

Some prize I turned out to be. A pained chuckle escapes my lips at how angry he must be that he chose the wrong sister. He wanted a fucking queen for the empire that he was building. Instead of going with his original choice; my sister, Mia, he decided that he wanted me. Maybe it was because she would have never let him control, degrade her, and bring her to her knees like I would, and have.

No, my sister was more likely to stab him through the eye than cower at his feet. Poor, miserable Diego got a *dud*, a defective Stratford instead of a real Stratford. I almost feel sorry for him, but then I remember where I am, and that he threw me in a fucking hole and pumped me full of drugs, ending the months-long hard work of sobriety.

Heat rises up the back of my neck, and I surge towards the bucket Santiago has placed in the middle of the room. I drop down to my knees, emptying the contents of my stomach as dizziness overtakes me and my vision gets spotty.

Fuck, I need to lie down, just for a bit. *Rest, yeah, that's what will help.* I'll just lie down right here and have a nap, and then when I wake, I'll demand to see that devil.

He can't keep me confined to this room indefinitely, can he? My head makes contact with the wooden floor, and my eyes close automatically. My last thought before darkness takes me is an image of my sister's face. I wish I were more like her, because she would never have allowed this to happen to her.

I'm swimming in darkness, feeling like I'm trapped in deep molasses. It's so warm in here, so hard to form a clear thought. I must be trapped in a dream-slash nightmare made of my fucked up desires for that bastard, Diego. My dream lips release a whimper at how good I feel right now. There is no pain or turmoil, just bliss.

Why does it always have to be him, or the other one with his piercing blue eyes, invading my unguarded thoughts? For once, why can't it be some sexy figment of my imagination? Hell, I would take any of my morally gray book boyfriends at this point. Make him a dark, unhinged Fae prince, and you have checked all my boxes. Anyone but these two, who won't let me have some peace in this miserable world I'm confined to. *They both would have given you the world; one promised light and laughter, the other darkness and depravity, yet you chose neither, and that's on you, bitch.*

I could swear it's Diego's strong, muscular arms that are wrapped around me, his scent that is assailing my nose with its spicy, earthy musk. A small groan leaves my lips, and a soothing touch across my neck accompanies it, the sensation cooling, as if water is being poured slowly across my feverish skin. It can't be, because he doesn't have a gentle bone in his body. The demon devours small children for snacks. The thought has a chuckle leaving my dream state lips.

If this is a dream, I am not sure I ever want to wake up again. I feel light as air as my body is cradled, and more of that water sensation happens on my stomach and then across my hips, pussy, and thighs. *Fuck, it feels too good.* In my dream state, I arch and moan, spreading my legs wider so that the cooling sensation can cleanse me.

"*Descansa mi amor, déjame cuidar de ti.*" The words are whispered so low that I can barely hear them, or make them out. The tone is so soothing and gentle, that it must be a dream.

A soft touch across my pussy lips has a shiver racing down my limbs, and goosebumps break out across my skin. My eyes flutter but refuse to open, the darkness refusing to release me from its comforting grasp. The touch flickers over my clit softly, tenderly rubbing small circles on my throbbing nub as my nipples pucker in the cooled air, and more of that water sensation is poured over my pussy. I take it back; whoever this dream lover is, he's just fucking perfect, and I hope he doesn't stop what he's doing.

The stirrings of an orgasm are starting to wake inside of me, making my skin feel tight, and the sensation of small electrical pulsations race across my back, chest, and neck. Something wet slides across my lips, and I ache to open them, to drink in whatever is touching me, calling me to let it have its way inside of me.

The electricity continues to rise inside of my poor, abused, and malnourished body. My toes tingle, and my hands fist, as something warm and hard is inserted inside of my core, causing it to tighten and my abdomen to clench painfully. It's too much; whatever is inside of me, moving slowly in and out to a soft rhythm that I swear I can hear, feels like it's gradually breaking more of my soul away. I try to force myself to wake from this dream that I am trapped in, even though my body is warring with my mind, and wants to stay in this safe, pleasurable haven instead of the hell of my reality.

"*Eso es todo, mi amor. Toma lo que necesites de mí,*" the gentle, soothing voice whispers.

The speed of the rubbing on my clit increases, and so does the thrusting, until my body is betraying me and following the motion, arching my hips and spreading my legs wide, aching for the release that is just right there, waiting to take me away.

It can't be Diego, but maybe one of his men is in here with me. One of them is touching me, being merciful to me, and bringing me pleasure in this hell that I am trapped in. Guilt immediately rises within me, and I try to close my legs again to stop the sensation.

"Noooooo," the word leaves my lips in a mumble, as I try again to open my eyes. My hand reaches out and touches a hard, warm wall of flesh, and another moan leaves my lips.

No, I have to stop this. Whoever this is will die at Diego's hands. Their moment of mercy and kindness will have signed their death warrant. I can't have anyone else's death on my conscience, and I don't want to know that I am responsible for him hurting anyone else.

The sensation increases, and so do the tingles that race across my chest. My body tightens, and the orgasm takes me over, coursing through my limbs, making my back arch and my lips open in a hoarse scream. I shatter in the arms cradling me, as they continue to push me over the edge, with a gush pouring from my core.

"Tan completamente hermosa," the voice whispers, as it stops its ministrations inside me, and the cool water sensation is back now across my thighs and calves. Exhaustion overwhelms me, and the deep, murky darkness calls me back to its depths, and I go willingly.

My dream companion is the first man to offer me gentleness and kindness, without asking for anything back in return, besides my father and grandfather. How I wish this were real, that I was somewhere with someone who wanted me for me. Not for my name or my fortune. Not to use me as a prize or as a shield. Someone who wanted Isabella, and not the Stratford heir.

He does, he always wanted you. His desire for you was pure; he loved you, but you left him behind. You broke your promise and his soul. You destroy everything that is good, even him. An image of bright blue eyes try their best to break through the darkness, but I refuse to allow them through. I'm not strong enough to face those demons anymore; they will crush me under the weight of my regret.

No, that world is gone. That life ended long ago, with a girl who didn't know what she had until she lost it all. It's far too late now, and he can't save me even if he wanted to.

CHAPTER TEN

Diego

"I am obsessed with you, fascinated by you, infatuated with you. I hunger for your taste, your smell, the feel of your soul touching mine."

Jack Llawayllynn, Indulgence

"How is she today?" I question, as I continue to look over the latest manifest of goods my father is shipping from our home back to our contacts in Europe. A smirk quirks my lips as I read what the container reportedly has for the legitimate documentation. *Dildos.* Fucking hilarious that my father is hiding our guns in crates full of dildos of every shape and size.

It would be highly amusing to see a transport inspector's face when he opened one of our crates, to see nothing but a bunch of rainbow-colored dicks awaiting him. I wonder if I should divert a few of those toys here, so that Issy has something to play with?

Fuck, and now my cock is getting hard at thoughts of watching Issy sliding a big, hard dildo inside of herself and bringing herself pleasure, as she cums all over it. I wonder if she could take me and the dildo at the same time? It's the only way I'll ever share her with another fucking cock. That sexy, pink pussy belongs to me, and I'm not one to share my toys.

Unlike her sister, who has four fucking boyfriends, my cousin amongst them, to fill each of her holes and then some, my Issy will never get to experience having all her holes used at the same time unless it's with toys. It's not that I'm against fucking with others. I've had various threesomes and orgies before, with women and with other guys.

No, the problem is Issy. Just the thought of another man touching her creamy, porcelain skin, sliding inside of her tight heat, and listening to those breathy moans she makes when she's getting fucked hard and fast, makes my blood pressure rise, and makes me want to commit mass murder.

I give my head a little shake, and clue back in to the fact that Raphael has been speaking this whole time, while I was daydreaming about dildos and Issy's cunt. *Fuck, pay attention, asshole.* "Repeat that last bit," I demand with a frown.

Raphael's Adam's apple bounces in his throat as he shifts from one foot to the other, wary and giving me wide owl eyes. He's still nervous around me, worrying if I might have his head ripped off his body, and place it on a stake outside of the compound for what he did to Issy, for what I ordered him to do, that has led to days of her going through withdrawals.

She's been so sick and pitiful when I've checked up on her at night while she's sleeping. Every time I look at her fragility, I'm reminded that I had a hand in causing her the pain and torment she's experiencing. There's a part of me that wants to get down on my hands and knees and beg for her forgiveness, but that would be showing weakness, and knowing Issy, she would use that against me. My *little prize* is filled with venom in her veins, even if she hasn't quite figured it out yet.

He clears his throat, the tension radiating off of him. "Better today. She's managing to hold down more fluids and isn't as disoriented. She's... umm... requesting a bath, sir. I... I think it would make her feel better. She's... ahh... been cooped up in that room for over a week now. It would be... beneficial to her healing."

What the fuck is this asshole suggesting? Is he suggesting that I let him accompany Issy into a bathroom where he watches her bathe? I get up so quickly from my chair that it slams back into the wall with a huge thud. I move around the desk and wrap my fist around his throat, tightening my grip and lifting him off the floor.

"NOOOTTTT WIIITHHH... MEEEEE!" His words howl out of his lips as I continue to tighten my hold, and stare into his frightened eyes. I hope he sees his death right now, because he's about to go make the acquaintance of all his ancestors.

I release my hold, and he tumbles to the ground, grasping at his throat and coughing painfully, his face a bright shade of red. "Aaalonee... that's what... I... meant," he gasps.

Well fuck, I may have just overreacted a little. My eyes rise to the doorway of my den, and I see the shocked faces of two of my men, who were drawn to the room with the commotion. I stare them down with a cold, menacing glare until they both back away and go back to doing their jobs. *Cabrones.*

I slip my hands into my pockets, to help prevent them from wrapping back around Raphael's skinny neck. Ever since Issy tried to seduce him, I can't stand the fucker. I know it's not rational and that he's been loyal; the cunt ratted her out instead of taking advantage of her. But, still, *fuck,* I just want to smash his pretty boy face to pieces.

Unfortunately, though, I need this fucker; he's the only medic we have out here. I should really get my father to send me a replacement. The way things are going, I don't see Raphael surviving for long.

"Get out," I order through clenched teeth, as I watch him scramble backward to get away from me.

He stops at the doorway's threshold and looks like he wants to say something. His mouth opens and closes, but no words come out, and then he turns and races out of the room. Fucker might be more intelligent than I give him credit for. *Run, little lamb, run; the big nasty monster is coming for you.*

I drag my hands forcefully down my face. I'm so fucking tired. It feels like I haven't slept in weeks. I've spent the last few nights watching Issy sleep, ensuring nothing happens to her. Every single night, without fail, she has nightmares. What they're about, I have no idea, but I can only guess that I have a starring role in most of them.

What could have happened to her in her perfect, privileged life to make her this way? Who else is starring in those nightmares, and how do I protect her from them, especially if I am her villain? So many questions and so many unknowns with my girl. How many secrets is she hiding, and who is she calling out to in her dreams to save her?

I know it's not me that she reaches for, or calls out to, and that both saddens and enrages me. I want to be her everything, her salvation, and her destruction. The desire to ensure that every breath she takes, she does because I allow her to keep breathing, her heart to keep beating at a tempo that only sounds for me.

Maybe if I give her what she wants right now, she might be willing to answer a few of those questions for me. Even if she doesn't, giving her the bath she's requesting might be worth it. I'm not sure how thorough I was with my cloth bath a few nights ago, when she was completely out of it, covered in vomit and sweat, and I found her passed out on the floor.

Should I have done more than just cleaned her and put her back to bed when she was so vulnerable? Probably not, but do I regret fingering her sweet pussy and giving her an orgasm, *fuck no*. It was spiritual watching her come undone in my arms. Her little mewing cries are music to my ears. If I could spend every moment of every day watching Issy come at my touch, I would.

I fist my hair in aggravation, knowing that when she's awake, she detests me. That, if given the choice, she wouldn't allow me to touch her, or bring her the euphoria that I have in the past. Right now, she can't see past my kidnapping her and holding her as my prisoner. She doesn't see that everything I have done is because I can't let her go, that I've never felt for anyone what I feel for her.

It's a good thing I am not easily swayed by what she wants. If I were, I never would have kidnapped her. In fact, I never would have touched her that first night back at her sister's house, when I lured her out to the grounds and fucked her hard against a tree. All while she moaned like a slut, her pussy tightening around my cock like a vise, while she spouted words of denial, that she didn't want me.

It's an overwhelming feeling to know a five-foot-nothing, buck-twenty-wet Manhattan princess has you so messed up in the head, that you can't function properly without her. Isabella Stratford has turned my whole world upside down, and it will never be the same again.

One of my burner phones beeps on the top of my desk and captures my attention. I swipe at the screen, and a devilish grin crosses my face. *Carter Pemberton*, my bro from another ho.

> **Listen bitch, I get you want to play with her,**
> **but this has gone a bit too far.**
> **Stella is losing her shit**
> **& will kill you.**
> **Bring her back.**
> **Not a request, cunt.**

I throw the phone down, completely disregarding his message. I don't give a fuck what Stella thinks or wants, and as much as I like Carter, *but would never admit to it,* he isn't going to do shit to me. His threat is annoying, like a fly swatting at an elephant. If I have to squash the motherfucker if ever he comes for me, so be it.

I stroll out of the den, passing my armed men with stoic, menacing faces, and down the hallway toward my greatest desire, and also the largest provider of my stress. I don't bother to knock, as I unlock the door and enter the space. My sudden arrival has her spinning around from her position at the window, and the air becomes trapped in my lungs.

I take her in as she stands there and glares at me. *Fuck, she's stunning, an angel lit by the sunlight that shines through the open shutters.* My eyes narrow on the white sleeveless dress she's wearing. The one I had placed on her body when I washed her a few nights ago. The way the sunlight is framing her, the whole fucking dress is entirely sheer. Did my men see her like this? *I'm going to gouge out all of their eyes if they fucking did.*

Her pretty, pink pussy and rose-colored nipples are plain to see through the thin, lightweight fabric. Her dark hair is tied up with a ragged piece of cloth, but even from here, I can see it's dull and lifeless. Dark shadows stain the space below her eyes, and her face appears thinner and more gaunt than yesterday.

Dammit, I thought Raphael said she was doing better today? I watch as her chest rises and falls, and she swipes the back of her hand across her runny nose, and looks away from me to stare at a spot over my shoulder. I roll my eyes at her attempt to rebuke me. "Heard you want a bath?"

Nothing, only silence greets my words. I take a step forward, and her whole body flinches. Her lips are pressed tightly together, and I watch as her small hands tighten into fists at her sides. *Ah, the silent treatment.* Issy is throwing a tantrum like a fucking petulant child, and she thinks this will work on me.

If she wants to act like a spoiled brat, I will treat her like one. "Last chance to answer me, Issy. I don't really care if you sit in your filth forever. When I want to use your cunt, I'll fucking hose you down."

Her angry sapphire eyes meet mine, her nose flares with anger, and I brace myself for the attack that is probably coming my way. In the physical state she's in, it won't take long to exhaust her. I don't have long to wait before she races across the room, and tries to launch herself at me like a dark-haired banshee. She's a butterfly swatting at a lion, adorable but annoying.

"I hate you, *Diego Cabano*. I fucking hope you *die* out here in this jungle. That your men turn on you and bury you in a shallow grave," she screams in my face as I restrain her, and yank both her arms behind her back, holding them with one arm while my other hand slides up her heaving chest and grasps around her neck.

Her words sting, even though I know they are said from a place of anger and anxiety. Does she really wish I was dead? Would that bring satisfaction to her worthless life?

"I don't give a fuck if you hate me, baby. I don't need you to like me for what I want you for. The only thing I need is the use of your tight cunt, and your womb to bear my sons, Issy. I might take that smart, vicious mouth to shove my cock inside of and abuse, but trust me, your opinion, wants, and desires, mean very little to me."

My fingers tighten around her neck as her eyes widen and tears slide down her face. The anger that is strumming through my veins at her words overrides my good sense, and the knowledge that she's sick, and I squeeze until I am sure she's seeing stars and almost out of air.

I'm about to give her the prettiest of hand necklaces so she can wear it, knowing that she can never escape me. Just as she's about to pass out, I release my grip on her, and she tumbles to the floor, a pretty rag doll at my feet.

She splutters and gasps on the floor as I crouch down next to her, watching her try to reintroduce oxygen into her lungs. Watery blue eyes meet mine, filled with fear, as she tries to drag herself further away from me. The strap of her dress droops along her arm, and the tops of her creamy breasts are visible to my sight. The perfection of her creamy skin calls to me, and makes my mouth water with the desire to leave the imprint of my teeth on its surface.

I need to see all of her, all that flesh and sexy curves on display for me. I want to touch her, taste her, even fucking inhale her very soul. I scoop down and lift her into my arms, and she immediately finds the strength to fight my hold. She thrashes like a little bird caught in a snare, and it brings a chuckle to my lips.

"Release me, you piece of shit!" She demands, while slapping my chest and shoulders.

I swat at her ass hard and then hoist her higher into my arms. "Behave, or I will strip you naked, tie you to my dining room table, and let my men each have a turn inside your cunt."

Nothing could be further from the truth. I would kill any man who even looked at her for too long, never mind touched her, but she doesn't know that. She doesn't understand that she is more than a plaything to me; she is my long game. My future is wrapped up in a small, beautiful, annoying package named Isabella Stratford, even though she doesn't want to be.

She instantly stills in my arms as her frightened eyes look around frantically, as we leave the room that has been her prison for more than a week. From this moment on, she won't be returning to it. No, my *Princesa* will be sleeping in my bed, and waking to my cock in one of her holes daily.

I lower my head and allow my nose to graze the side of her head, inhaling her scent. Even unclean, her scent is an aphrodisiac to my senses. The feel of her weight in my arms helps to soothe some of the rage that cycles within me, demanding destruction and that I breed her, making her forever mine.

"You smell like shit, *Princesa*. I guess you're a long way from being a Manhattan socialite now, aren't you?" I chuckle to myself at the outrage on her face, as I carry her into my suite and use my foot to slam the door behind us.

CHAPTER ELEVEN

Issy

"For love is no part of the dream world. Love belongs to Desire, and Desire is always cruel."

Neil Gaiman, The Sandman, Vol. 2: The Doll's House

The door slamming has my blood pressure rising, and my attempts to get him to release me increasing. I don't want to be confined to a locked space with him. Not because I actually fear that he will hurt me; no, I'm a masochist, and I know I will *enjoy* every painful moment of what he does to me. I crave his brand of destruction, his insanity.

No, the real fear is that I have no willpower around him, and he knows it. He flashes those intense green eyes and that malicious, naughty smirk in my direction, and I fall to my knees to take his cock deep in my throat. I want to be his *good girl* and please him.

Pathetic. That is what I am. Who else would crave the villain who abducted them from their family, took them away from all that they have ever known, threw them into a life filled with perils and danger, and only remembers her when he needs to come?

Me, that's who. Right now, right in this very moment, I swear to myself that I will be stronger, that I will resist him and his devilish charms. I need to find my Stratford backbone, or I will always be Diego's prize. A victim to his whims and desires, with little or no choice in her future.

I struggle in his grasp, raking my jagged nails down his arms until he releases me, and I stumble onto a huge four-poster bed covered in netting, and bounce with the impact. The sensation of landing so hard is jarring, and makes me bite down on my tongue, my mouth filling with the taste of blood. A reminder that he would have me shed even more of my blood to satisfy his depraved needs. *Fucking demon.*

I watch from the corner of my eye as I slowly crawl to the other side of the bed, as he walks back to the door, locks it with a key from his pocket, and turns his sights back on me. His intense gaze penetrates me to my very core, causing a slight tremor to race through my body. *Fuck, how am I going to get that key?*

"You can stop with all your scheming to escape, Issy, you're going nowhere. Even if you somehow managed to get out of this room, which is doubtful, and past the guards in the house, you wouldn't make it five feet outside of the compound before my men were on you, never mind the beasts that inhibit this jungle."

He moves slowly, a sleek predator assessing his prey towards the opposite side of the room, his perceptive gaze never leaving its assessment of me. His words give me pause. Is it a scare tactic, or is he telling the truth?

No, he's lying, trying to scare me. He would say and do anything to keep me here and as his. There has to be a way out of here. A way back to freedom and all that I love. This can't be my fate, and I refuse to accept that it is. *Fight, Issy, fight!*

A deep, aggravated sigh leaves his lips, his shoulders hunching forward as he continues towards an open doorway. Seconds later, I hear the sound of rushing water filling the space. He walks back out of the room, and before I can even think to escape him, he's surging forward and grabbing me by the arm, yanking me back into his strong embrace and dragging me into what must be the bathroom. I try to kick my feet, landing shots to his shins and attempting to yank myself away from his demanding hold, but he doesn't relent. Instead, his fingers tighten until I am sure I will have bruises in the shape of his fingers tomorrow.

"Release me, you fucking demon!" I scream, trying to headbutt him.

"Stop acting like a fucking child, Issy." He gives me a shake that has my teeth rattling, and drags me through the doorway.

Once my vision stops spinning, I take in the space, which is shockingly beautiful; the floors are all made of rough, warm, neutral stones, and the walls are made of the same material but done in a beautiful mosaic pattern that has an indigenous feel, and represents the sun and the jungle, with detailed glass work imitating fauna. A large glass shower with pebbled floors and the same stone walls is off to one side of the room. A rainfall shower-head cascades water into the space, and looks inviting and cool.

Damn, if he weren't forcing me into this room, I would race to get under that water, but because he is, I have to fight my visceral need to get clean. A whimper leaves my lips at the thought that I will never get to use it.

The vanity isn't really even a vanity, but a beautiful piece of dark stone suspended against the wall with a sink carved into it, and a black faucet sprouting from the stone wall. In the middle of the room, a huge sunken copper tub that could easily fit three or four people sits, ready to soothe your sore muscles. The sun shines from the glass skylights in the ceiling, and the large open windows in the space. The humid jungle air gives off a fragrant smell, nature calling you forward to relax in this impressive space.

It's devastatingly beautiful, yet I have to act like it's not. I can't give him the satisfaction of seeing how much I want to use these amenities, how they call to the spoiled privileged girl inside of me. I wrap my arms around myself and refuse to look his way, or at anything, preferring to stare at my dirty, bare feet.

"Get undressed, Issy, and don't be a brat, or I will fucking rip that dress off you." He moves away from me towards a wood-paneled wall, which opens with a click of his hand. Inside of it, you can see row after row of neatly folded white, fluffy towels ready for use.

Because I am a brat, and a disobedient one at that, I ignore his command and inch towards the vanity, searching for anything that I might be able to use as a weapon against him. I get momentarily distracted by all the beautiful glass bottles on the counter, which look suspiciously like the bottles of the products I used back home. *What the fuck?*

"I told you not to be a brat." He releases a rough sigh of frustration and grasps onto the back of my dress, and before I can stop him, he yanks and tears the material straight down the middle, leaving my back and asscheeks on display to him.

Mortification fills me at his treatment, and I try desperately to hold on to the fabric, keeping it clutched to my body, but he pulls me towards his chest, my hot skin landing against his fabric-clad body with a bang. "Are you being shy now, my little slut? What happened to the woman who, just days ago, was willing to give herself to a complete fucking stranger, *hmm*, Issy?"

His words are sharp daggers piercing my skin and my heart. He's right, and knowing that he is brings me further shame. I was so desperate for a hit of the drugs that I didn't think through my actions. Actions that it seems, Diego will never forgive me for. *Why do we even care? He kidnapped us?*

The knowledge that he witnessed my weakness, that he was party to my humiliation and desperation, stops me from fighting his grip. My heart begs me to give in, and my mind stops its incessant call for escape. With just a few cruel words, he has once again laid waste to my defenses, bringing me low, like he intended. *You're a whore, a dirty whore.* The soiled fabric falls down my arms, exposing my chest to his waiting eyes.

He roughly grabs me by the back of the neck and marches me towards the shower, opening the door and shoving me inside, while I splutter at the warm water that instantly soaks me. I flail around, almost losing my balance and falling to my ass, before I use the stone wall to steady me. Diego doesn't laugh as I expected him to. Instead, he mumbles unintelligible words under his breath, closing the glass door and moving towards the bathtub without a further look in my direction.

With his back turned to me, I quickly drop the remaining pieces of the dirty dress and slip under the cascading water, rinsing the grime off of me and rushing through, washing my body the best I can with my back turned towards him.

My eyes connect with a stone ledge on the shower wall, and on the surface, I view bottle after bottle of the shampoos, conditioners, and body washes that I use. *What the fuck?* How did he get all of this here? How did he even know? It's not like he was ever in my room with me back at my sister's.

I quickly grab the bottle of fragrant shampoo and wash my hair, roughly cleaning my long tresses to remove all the grime. When I'm done rinsing it, I throw on a messy glob of conditioner, and reach for the body wash and a loofa hanging from a hook. I wash my body as quickly as possible, taking extra care not to reopen the insect bites that litter my skin. When I go to spread my legs to wash between them, a groan sounds in the air, and has me pausing and looking over my shoulder.

"Don't stop on my account, baby, I was enjoying the show," he smirks, his green eyes twinkling mischievously, and for a brief moment, I see the Diego I was first attracted to. The naughty, playful man who made my heart race, and the blood in my veins feel like hot lava spread within them. A ruthless psycho lived under that facade, as I have unfortunately had to discover the hard way.

I bare my teeth at him as a growl leaves my lips, and I turn back around, trying to ignore him, even though I can feel his heated gaze on my skin, and it causes my flesh to pebble.

"Where does the water come from, and how is it heated out here in the jungle?" I question, needing something to distract me from the fact that he's watching me clean myself. *Fucking pervert.*

"Solar panels are stationed all around the compound, and we have reservoirs to catch rainwater, which then goes through a purification process, so it can be used to bathe, drink, and cook with." His voice changes, and I can hear pride and excitement in his tone, which has me turning to look at him over my shoulder once again.

"It's a system I designed, one that I want to bring to Columbia, where I grew up, so that the poorer communities can have eco-friendly access to clean water, that they can use to survive and grow their own foods. I... I want to help the folks who have very little, and struggle daily even to get clean water."

He turns on the tap in the bathtub, and clean water pours into the tub. The sound of it hitting the copper tub creates a pretty melody, that has me relaxing further into the warm water cascading over my skin. I quickly rinse off the conditioner and body wash as he continues speaking, the loss of his gaze somehow cooling me, even though I would never admit it out loud.

"I have a few other projects that I think might help, like living roofs where the people can be given the resources to grow organic produce on their roofs, and ways to allocate proper internet to impoverished communities, so that the kids have better access to education."

He gets a wistful look in his eyes as if he can see these people, these communities that he speaks of. I listen to his words as he reflects with such passion about his projects, and the initiatives that he wants to produce, to help others who have less than him, and I realize that I know very little about Diego Cabano, and the type of man he really is.

Have I misjudged him based on the ruthless, corrupt, and power-hungry image he portrayed when I first met him? I mean, he was trying to force my sister into marriage with an alliance at the time. Is he that man, or this one who wants to help impoverished communities? Could the problematic truth lie somewhere below the complicated surface of both versions of the same man?

Remember that he kidnapped you! It doesn't matter if he intends to save the world, because he took your world away from you. The words hiss through my mind, but they don't have their usual impact.

I turn off the water and wrap one arm around my chest and another over my crotch, very aware that I am wet and naked, and he's fully clothed and staring at me with hunger on his face. He's eyeing me as if I am a little, tiny rabbit, and he is a hungry wolf ready to devour me.

"Towel, please," my voice sounds breathless to my ears, as my heart pounds in my chest. He turns away from me, not acknowledging my request, and shuts off the water in the giant tub, which is now more than two-thirds full.

"You won't need it, at least not yet." He trails his hand through his thick dark hair as my eyes become riveted to him. "Come here, Issy." He beckons me with his words, the tone seductive and filled with need as he firmly strokes himself over his pants, the prominent bulge clearly evident. Before I can think clearly, I take a step forward but stop myself from going any farther. *What the hell am I doing? I can't allow myself to become dicktimized.*

"Release me, Diego. Return me to my family before someone fucking gets hurt. You know that you can't keep me here forever as your prisoner," I demand of him, but I can immediately see that my words will not move him. A scowl races across his face as he takes the short steps to reach me, and pulls me roughly towards the tub, his fingers digging into my skin.

"Get in the fucking tub, Issy, or I swear to fuck, I'll drown you in it." He eyes me like the unhinged, temperamental asshole that he is, his expression relaying his thoughts clearly. He might actually enjoy drowning me. He wants me to fight him, so that he can hurt me. As much as I want to push boundaries with him and see how far he'll let me take them, I have no desire to swallow a bunch of water.

The wistful, calm Diego of moments ago disappears, and the broody asshole makes a reappearance. How could I have thought that there was something else to him? This is *Diego Cabano*, a man who won't take no for an answer, and would readily use violence and coercion to get what he wants. He's a killer, a deranged, possessive psychopath, and utterly without mercy or a conscience.

I step into the tub awkwardly and hesitantly, trying desperately not to lose my balance. Self-consciousness courses through me, knowing he's getting an up-close and personal look at all my parts, and it makes me immediately sit down, hoping that the water will help camouflage me.

I watch from below my lashes as he grabs the back of his shirt in one quick movement, and rips it over his head. The shirt falls to the ground, and his hands move to the button of his jeans, releasing it and pulling down the zipper, his long meaty cock becoming visible between the parted fabric. *Jesus, fuck.*

My mouth suddenly becomes parched, and I forget what I had even asked him for. My eyes center on the purple mushroom head, and the large veins that protrude along his length. My eyes follow what I know graces that amazing cock, a tattoo of a serpent that starts below his balls and wraps around his base, circling around his long length and ending with the serpent's mouth open just below the ridge of his crown. It's a stunning piece of art, beautiful in its complexity, shading, and colors. It looks so realistic that you would think he truly had a serpent sliding on his skin.

Fuck, I can already feel my core tightening, and the desire to run my tongue all along that tattoo is almost overwhelming. Diego has the most impressive cock I have ever seen, and the fucker knows it. He uses it as a weapon and as a drug. *Here I am, an addict, just waiting for his mercy. His own personal slut.*

He makes a motion to step into the tub with me, and my whole body recoils away from him, my knees bending and my arms wrapping around them as I make myself as small as possible. "What the hell do you think you're doing?" I question in a hoarse tone.

He stops midstep and stares down at me, the scar on his face pulling taut as his eyebrows rise towards his hairline. "I thought that was pretty evident, *Princesa*. I'm getting in the bath with you."

CHAPTER TWELVE

Diego

"Desire is the kind of thing that eats you and leaves you starving."

Nayyirah Waheed

I watch as her lips purse with obvious dissatisfaction, and a pink blush rises in her cheeks and makes its way down that delectable neck of hers, the one that is missing the imprint of my fingers as a warning to anyone who looks at her, signaling that she's all *mine*. The ache to wrap my fingers tightly around it is almost all-consuming, causing a quiet buzzing in my head with visceral need.

The water sloshes around the tub as she tries to make herself as small as possible on one side. Her beautiful porcelain skin is still marred with insect bites and bruises, and she looks thinner than she had been before I brought her to this jungle. The fear that her sexy curves will continue to diminish if I keep her a prisoner, is a hushed whisper in my mind, reminding me that I am the cause of all her misery at the moment.

Bringing her here was a mistake. She won't survive, my mind seethes.

"The fuck you are! Get away from me, you psycho," she cries. Her body trembles with fear and rage that makes itself visible on her delicate, doll-like face. I can see into the facade that she wears like a second skin, the one that urges her to be strong but knows that she's not, at least not yet.

She is so perfect, so small, so very fragile. Mine.

I deserve her anger and her hateful words, but they still piss me the fuck off and make me want to force her to her privileged knees, so that I can shove my cock to the back of her throat and make her swallow her venom, and her truths.

My hand snaps forward as I step fully into the tub and tangles into her wet hair, yanking her forward until she is forced to her knees with a scream, as more water sloshes over the side of the tub. "You have a vicious mouth, *little one*. One that I think needs occupying since you seem to think you can make demands around here. In case you didn't notice, *Princesa*, you are my fucking prisoner, not my guest."

She tries to pull back from my merciless grasp, but I don't release her, and a pained cry leaves those pouty lips of hers instead, as dark strands of her hair are ripped out with the movement. *Fuck.* The sound shouldn't excite me, but it does, and it causes my cock to swell further with the desire to hear more of those cries leave her. *Fuck yes, baby. Cry for me.*

"Stop trying to fight me, Issy. You will never win against me, and you will never escape me. *You are mine.* The sooner you accept your fate, the easier things around here will be for you."

Even though I utter the words, the reality is that I never want her to stop fighting me, challenging me, and keeping me on my toes. I need the constant push and pull from her, which reminds us that we are alive. Our relationship may be volatile and plagued with issues, but it's ours.

Her dark blue eyes flash with malice and rage, a fire within them that I am willing to fan if it strengthens her, and gives me what I want. A queen to stand by my side, proud and strong. One who is ready and willing to face my enemies with me, and bring future generations of Cabanos into the world. Little dark-haired replicas of her who will run rampant, destroying the world around them.

I wonder what would happen if I let her know that I had her IUD removed, when I first drugged and kidnapped her from her sister's house. That all the times that I have taken her cunt and filled her up with my seed since then, she has been unprotected, and could be carrying my child. My cock hardens further at the thought of Issy's belly swelling with my baby inside of it. Excitement rises within me to ensure that if she's not pregnant yet, I make her so immediately.

If that makes you hard, just wait till the bitch realizes you branded her lower back with your name. Then she really will lose her weak mind, that little asshole in my head snarks.

A smirk crosses my lips at the knowledge that she hasn't seen the tattoo I had placed on her lower back that first day we arrived here, when she was out cold from the drugs we gave her. She has no idea that right above her ass, my name is printed like a tramp stamp, a brand of my ownership over her. I'm going to guess she's not going to be too happy with me when she finds out.

Her eyes leave mine and are immediately drawn to my dick standing proud, long and hard between us. I know she has a fascination with my snake tattoo that circles around my length. How many times had she traced it with both her fingers and her tongue when we were at her sister's? She's looking at it now, though, like it truly is a serpent come to life, one ready to strike at her.

"He won't bite, baby, at least not much." I drag her forward by her hair until the tip of my cock brushes against her lips, coating them in my essence. "Open up, slut. Show me how much you enjoy taking me to the back of your throat."

She gasps as I yank on her hair, forcing her lips to open with a pained cry. She inhales sharply before I can get more than just my tip inside the warm heat of her mouth, as she stares up at me with tears racing down her face, and an emotion I have never seen on her features before. It has me hesitating in my forward motion, an uncomfortable buzzing rising in my mind.

"Kill me," she mumbles against my hardness, the rumble of her words vibrating up my length, causing shivers to race across my flesh. My chest tightens painfully with, not only her careless words, but the sound of her losing any hope she had behind them.

I pull back from her lips and stare down at her. At the sadness and devastation across her features. *My beautiful broken doll.* She's giving up instead of fighting back, and a part of me wants to grant her request for her weakness, but I never will give in to it. I can't; it would be as if I took my own life. I know that I can no longer see a future for myself that she is not a part of.

My queen, my love, my everything.

"If you won't release me, kill me. I don't want to spend my life as your prisoner, as... your whore."

Her words have me releasing my hold on her thick tresses, and taking a step back and then another inside the tub, until I can't move away from her without stepping out from its interior. My heart thunders in my chest, the sounds of my own blood whoosh in my ears, and my hands fist at my sides with the need to wrap around her neck once more, but this time not release her until all of her breath is spent.

I understand why she's asking me for death, asking me to grant her a mercy that I would never entertain. How could I kill the one person who is my everything? How could I continue breathing without her? How does she not realize what she means to me? How fucking dare she even utter those words?

Issy has always been filled with a deep sadness that I failed to comprehend, an emptiness even when in a room filled with people. Is she hoping that with death, that emptiness she feels will disappear, and that she'll finally find the freedom that she seems to be searching for? She won't, because it will follow her even into the next life, just like I will.

The only time I have ever seen a glimmer of something else is when she was in my arms, and I was fucking the very breath out of her, taking her to the heights of depravity that she craves, the ones she refuses to admit she needs. Then, she was filled with life, emotions, and desires. Even in her submission to me, there was fight, there was a war that stirred between us. In those moments, she was alive, filled with passion and destruction. That is the Issy I crave to bring to life. That is who I want to spend the rest of my days with, whether they be long or short, and to stand by my side.

She has always worn a mask around everyone else, even her sister and grand-mother. Is it because she believes that she is less than they are? Anger rages inside of me at the thought. Nothing could be further from the truth. She is unique, delicate, brilliant, and perfection walking this earth, even if she is a little shattered from within. I long to know the source of her trauma, who damaged her and made her this way, so that I can bury that person in an unmarked grave.

The problem with Issy is that no matter how many times someone tells her that she's beautiful and intelligent, she always seems unable to believe it, as if her mind can only see and comprehend her inadequacies. The weight of the Stratford mantle must truly be crushing.

That is why I need to make her a Cabano so that she can shed her skin, like a snake, and be reborn into what she is meant to be. There is a spirit inside my girl that is broken, and it's my fucking job to mend it. To push her to fight for herself, even if that fight is against me. Hell, I'll enjoy watching her self-destruct, so that I can be present and cheering her on for her rebirth.

"You want to die?" I take a step forward and then another, and watch her tremble. I hunch down in the tub until we are at eye level. "Death comes with pain and at a price, Issy. Are you sure that's what you truly want?" I quirk an eyebrow, my eyes looking deeply into hers, green clashing with vibrant blue in a never ending war.

"Death would be preferable to being your whore for eternity," she replies with a defiant lift to her chin.

"Be careful what you wish for, *Princesa*; you might realize too late that you made a mistake." I stand back up and yank her hair roughly, lining up my cock against her lips. "You want to die, baby? Let me take your very breath away."

"Diego-" She tries to speak, but the rest of her words are choked off, as I slam into her mouth and hit the back of her throat. I don't give her a second to adjust to my size, beginning a relentless, punishing rhythm that makes her choke, and gag on my hard cock each time I push a little farther down her throat. I will fuck the weakness right out of her, or both of us will perish with me trying.

Her fingers rake down my thighs as she attempts to pry herself off of me, the sting causing my cock to throb inside of her tight throat. Saliva drips down the sides of her mouth, and her nails dig into my flesh. The water sloshes all around the tub with her frantic attempts to get me to release her, but I don't give a shit. She wants to fucking die, I'll make her regret ever uttering those words to me. I'll make her fear death more than she fears life.

"That's it, baby, go ahead and choke to death on my cock," I grunt as her teeth graze my length. My fist in her hair pulls her off of me, and I quickly dunk her under the water. Her surprised scream chokes her as water pours down her throat. She struggles, all of her limbs trying desperately to fight my unrelenting grasp. I hold her down tightly until the fight starts to leave her, and then I yank her back out and shove my weeping cock down her throat. She will find no mercy at my hands, if she desires death more than she desires a life with me.

Her lips tremble as she gasps for a breath around my length. I pull back slightly, allowing her to suck in some oxygen before I slam back inside her warm, wet mouth. My muscles tighten, and a zing races up my back with electricity. I need to hold off a little longer, even though I am desperate to cum right now down her tight throat. She feels so good, so fucking right, as if she was made for only me, and my need to consume and own her.

Isabella Stratford needs to be taught a lesson, one that I hope she doesn't learn effectively, so that I can repeat these moments over and over again, with my cock shoved inside of all her holes. I plan to fill her with my cum daily, maybe even hourly, if I can keep up.

Her fight suddenly stops, and she stares up at me through her thick, wet lashes. Her blue eyes are filled with such profound sadness, my broken, beautiful doll. Her lips tighten around my thick length, her hands sliding up the front of my thighs and her soft, delicate fingers reaching for my balls.

I brace myself, guessing that she's about to make me scream by fisting or punching them. I wouldn't put it past her, because that's precisely what I would do to regain some of my power if I were in her position. It doesn't stop my brutal forward thrusts, or her gagging sounds every single time I hit the back of her throat. At the savage pace I'm going, she's going to be sore and unable to swallow, when I am done with her. *Too fucking bad, princess.*

To my surprise, her fingers grace my delicate testicles as she rolls them around gently, lifting them and caressing them. The added sensation has my body tensing, overriding my desire to hold back and not release in her mouth. The look in her eyes alters; the sadness and anger are still present, but now it's intertwined deeply with desire as her breathing picks up, her mouth sucking me deep as she twirls her tongue along my length, becoming a willing participant rather than a forced one, or at least that's what I try to convince myself of.

Goddamn, this is heaven right here. She is my saint and my sinner, my salvation and damnation, all in one. The one woman I would die for, but also set the world on fire for. How could she possibly think I would ever let her go? How could she possibly think to ask me for death?

I cum in long spurts down her throat, and a moan vibrates through her and along the crown of my cock. *Fuck.* My eyes threaten to roll into the back of my head, but I force them to stare down at her beautiful face. She's even more stunning like this, surrendering in submission. Enjoying the depravity that I bring to both of us.

She doesn't realize that there's strength in her submitting to me. That from her knees, she actually holds power over me. The day that she does figure that out, I know that I'll become her slave instead of her master. That knowledge should bring fear with it, but instead, it brings anticipation. I can't wait to witness her coming into her power, and bringing the world to its knees at her feet.

My eyes trail down the length of her body, her knees spread wide in the water, and one of her hands disappearing below its warm depth. The movement of the water tells me that she's bringing herself pleasure even in this moment of punishment. *My naughty, little doll.*

I pull back from her lips, and her mouth makes a sloppy, popping sound that has my balls tightening. My cock is still rock hard, despite cumming just moments ago. It's as if it knows that once is never enough with her; his greedy desire to be inside of her is relentless.

"Are you touching yourself, my slut?" I question as her hand drops away from my flesh, leaving coolness and the feeling of loss in its wake.

No words greet my question as her breathing picks up and becomes choppy, little moans leaving her throat, signaling that she's close to her own release. As much as I want to watch her come undone before my eyes, I also want - no, I fucking *need* to teach her that I own her. That if she wants to orgasm, it will be solely with my permission.

"If you cum without my permission, I will drag you out of this bathroom, tie you to a fucking post in the yard, and let every man in this compound take a turn filling that pretty, pink pussy. I'll blindfold you, Issy, so that you don't know who is inside of you, and using you like the whore you are."

My words are harsh but have the effect intended, and her trembling hand rises out of the water with a frightened cry. She tries to move away from me, but at the cold look I give her, she stills as more tears slide down her face.

So beautiful. I wonder what frightens her more, the threat of men fucking her without her being able to see who it is, while she's forcibly tied against her will, or the fact that I would let that happen to her? Little does she know that I would rip their heads off their necks if they even tried to touch her.

"You want to cum, my broken doll? Then beg me. Beg me on your knees like a whore, with those pretty, pouty lips to allow you to reach your bliss."

CHAPTER THIRTEEN

Issy

"Somewhere between love and hate lies confusion, misunderstanding, and desperate hope."

Shannon L. Alder

"You want to cum, my broken doll? Then beg me. Beg me on your knees like a whore, with those pretty, pouty lips to allow you to reach your bliss." His words bring nothing but rage in their wake. Who does this asshole think he is? Beg him to cum? I'm more likely to try to castrate him right here in this tub.

Sure you are, you're not your sister. The best you can do is cry. Why not give in and beg? After all, you do it so prettily, my mind calls me out for my nonexistent threat. Even my subconscious knows that I am nothing but pathetic and weak, even when I want to stand up for myself.

"Motherfucker, you don't talk to my sister like that, she's a Stratford, not one of your little whores, Dominic." My mouth hangs open as my sister comes flying out of nowhere, and throws a punch at my ex-boyfriend without even hesitating.

Dominic outweighs her by over a hundred pounds and is built like a brick house, but does that stop her? Not even for a second. The little savage follows the punch with a headbutt that has him stumbling backward, and falling into his laughing buddies, his ass hitting the hard asphalt with a thump.

"Fucking cunt," he seethes, as his friends scramble away from him, leaving him to deal with my sister's fury alone.

"Cunt? You wish you could have a cunt like me, instead of those tiny fucking raisins you call balls. If I ever catch you with my sister's name on your lips again, I'll rip out your fucking tongue and shove it up your ass." She lifts her heeled foot and slams it down on his cock, until he screams bloody murder.

Her furious gaze lands on me, and I want the ground to open up and swallow me whole. "Issy, what have I fucking told you about anyone disrespecting you?" A tear slides out of the corner of my eye as I try to pull myself together. She's so strong and capable, I desperately want to be just like her.

Her gaze softens, and she pulls me into her embrace, squeezing me tightly in her arms. "I love you, Issy, but I will not always be here to fight your battles, baby sister. You have to learn to fight back. You're a Stratford, Issy, and no one gets to ever fucking hurt you."

No! This fucking time I am going to resist. I refuse to keep allowing him to push me around and use me any way he wants. I'm not a delicate porcelain doll like he thinks I am, one that he can play with and then discard, when he gets bored. I can't keep letting him win. I lose a little more of myself to him every time he does. Soon there will be nothing left of Isabella Stratford, the wayward Manhattan princess who was set to inherit a kingdom.

All I will be is Diego Cabano's whore, his prisoner for life in the shackles of my own weakness. I can't let that happen to me. I know he won't grant me my demise, and to be at his mercy forever might be a punishment more gruesome than a vicious death. A stillness enters my mind as I process that thought, and defiance rises within me.

I slip my hand down into the water as his eyes narrow on the movement, and he watches my hand disappear under the warm depth as I caress my clit. With my eyes centered on his, anger sparking deep in their depths, I slip a finger inside of my needy pussy and then another, widening my knees so that he can see that I am defying him. My other hand trails up my stomach and grasps onto one of my full breasts and squeezes. A moan releases from my lips, his gaze pulling away from my fingers sliding inside of me to my mouth.

Gotcha, fucker, do you see me defying you? Your threats mean nothing to someone who wants to die. I don't belong to you. I don't belong to anyone but myself.

There's a tic jumping in his cheek, the rough skin of his scar pulled tight across his face, and his green eyes blaze with a fire filled with both anger and hunger. His cock is still standing erect against his stomach, looking like a delectable piece of marble that makes my mouth water.

The truth that I will never utter out loud is that I enjoy it when he uses me, when he's rough and takes what he wants from me. Does that make me a slut? *Maybe*, but that is the least of my sins.

I release another moan, using my fingers to pull on my nipple roughly as the fingers inside my core speed up, in a rush to bring me to the pinnacle of euphoria. One that he wants me to beg him to receive. *Fuck him, and his need to control me.* I honestly believe his threats are empty, that he is too territorial and possessive to allow his men to use me. He stole me from my family for himself, not to share me with others.

In fact, I'm counting on it as I barrel towards my orgasm, my chest tightening as shivers cascade across my skin, and my core tightens down on my digits. *Fuck*, I'm going to cum, and there is nothing he can do to stop it from rolling over me.

"Fuck, fuck, oh my God," I moan.

"Don't, Issy. I swear to you I will fucking punish you if you cum."

My eyes threaten to roll in the back of my head as the electricity races across my skin, causing the hair on my arms to stand on end, and my breath to leave in little moaned pants. I use my thumb to add pressure to my clit, slipping a third finger into my pussy as the orgasm peaks, and throws me right over the precipice as he watches on.

"Fuck, fuck, fuck," I pant, as my whole body tightens and my head falls backward, my eyes closing as heat encompasses me. The sensations of the warm water lapping against my skin, and his eyes watching me come undone, have aftershocks hitting me, one after the other.

"Jesus, fuck," he groans.

When I can finally catch my breath, I release my hold on my nipple and pull my fingers from inside of my core, raising my head to meet his eyes with defiance. The look on his face is not what I expected. Instead of being angry, or even filled with desire, he looks amused.

There's a stupid fucking grin gracing his full lips, his eyes sparkle with enjoyment, and his hands are braced on either side of his hips, bringing my eyes down to that pronounced 'V' that he has that makes me stupid when I look at it.

A deep chuckle leaves his lips, stretching them wide as he steps out of the tub and grabs a towel from the towel warmer next to it, wrapping it tightly around his trim waist but leaving his sexy, chiseled chest on display. His body is a work of muscled art, littered with various scars, tattoos, and a scattering of dark hair that trails down to his impressive cock, which, *thank fuck*, is now covered.

I'm instantly filled with rage that he's laughing at me, as if I'm some pathetic joke to him, but I'm also wary of his unpredictable behavior. He reaches down to his discarded pants and pulls the key out of his pocket. The very one he used to lock the bedroom door, tucking it into the towel around his waist, my hopes of escaping him evaporating instantly.

We can fight him, get it from him, my mind tries to reason, but I can barely swallow the lump that has formed in my throat at his calm demeanor.

"Oh, Issy, you really are adorable. You remind me of a puppy: cute, mischievous, harmless, and easily brought to heel. Are you feeling satisfied with your act of defiance, *hmm*... my pretty doll?" He questions as he moves determinedly back in the direction of the tub, holding another towel in his hands, his actions causing me to shift to the farthest section away from him. My body is starting to panic, while my mind is screaming that we are in grave danger. *Fuck, fuck, fuck.*

Fear and doubts slither across my mind in rapid succession. Is he going to hurt me? Did I just fuck up? Did I overestimate how possessive he is about me? *Fuck, what have I done?*

"Get out of the tub, Issy." He motions towards the fluffy white towel that he holds in his hands, but it might as well be a rattlesnake waiting to strike out at me. I want nothing to do with that towel, or the look that graces his features.

I grapple over the side of the tub and try to move as far away from him as possible. My wet feet slide across the stone floor in my haste to put much-needed distance between us, and I slam into the wall, the air getting knocked out of me. My hands rise to ward him off, as if that action alone would really be able to keep him from doing what he wants with me.

"Stay away from me, asshole!" I screech and try to move around him, my eyes wide and frightened. I can feel the water sliding down my skin from my wet hair; a cold chill is making itself present, or maybe that is the feeling of death approaching me.

I try to move to the right in an attempt to make it towards the door, but he blocks my access, forcing me to go in the other direction towards the shower area. "Don't make this harder and more painful than it has to be, Issy. You chose to be a defiant, fucking child when I explained to you the consequences of your actions. You wanted to play, baby, so here is the fee."

"Leave me alone, you fucking psycho! I'll fucking kill you if you touch me."

Another chuckle leaves his lips, this time making his body shake with mirth. I can't believe this asshole is laughing at my threats. *Of course, he's laughing at you, because he knows they are empty. You are nothing but a weak, scared little girl playing at being a badass, trying to replicate your sister, except you're not her, and you will never be good enough or strong enough to be her.*

"Issy, you're a pretty moth, and I'm a fucking lion. The lion doesn't worry about the threats the pretty moth issues. You're too small to hurt me, baby, and we both know that you aren't going to kill me." He strikes quickly, reaching forward and wrapping a hand around my throat, pulling me forcefully until I crash against his strong, wet body. My naked, wet limbs pressing flush against his heated flesh, and feeling every single thick ridge pressed against my chilled skin.

I scream and thrash in his hold, but his fist tightens, squeezing, as his eyes glare down into mine. I no longer see amusement in their olive-green depths.

Now, I see the anger, frustration, and desire to hurt me. *Fuck, he's going to hurt me, and not in a way that I will enjoy.* My one moment of defiance will have brought me nothing but regrets and pain.

His other hand trails up my back and yanks on my hair, pulling my head to the side and exposing my neck to him. "Do you want to beg for my forgiveness now, baby? Are you regretting your actions, Issy? Was that orgasm worth your impending punishment?" His warm breath skates over my skin and causes goosebumps to rise along my arms, and the hairs at the back of my neck to stand on end.

I couldn't get a word out even if I wanted to, with how tight he's squeezing my throat. My chest tightens with the lack of oxygen, and pretty white dots dance in front of my vision. Maybe I'll get lucky, and he will kill me in his fit of rage. Wouldn't that be fantastic? I would die having orgasmed, and having given him a giant *'fuck you'* at the same time.

His eyes darken as they stare into mine, their intensity adding to my already frightened state. "Oh no, *Princesa*, you aren't going to die. At least not at this moment. First, you're going to pay for defying me, for giving yourself pleasure, when I told you to beg me for that release," he leans closer and utters, as if he can read the thoughts scrambling in my mind. He releases his hold enough that air siphons into my poor, abused throat, and I start to choke.

He shifts me to the right and stops, using my neck and his grip on my hair to bend my body forward. "Pick up the towel and wrap it around yourself, or I'll make you walk out of here naked, so my men can feast their sights on your sexy body."

Fear courses through my body, and I don't hesitate, reaching forward and grabbing for the discarded towel on the floor, and wrapping it tightly around my body, covering my nakedness from his sight. *Would he really allow his men to stare at me naked?* My lips tremble as tears fall down my face and coat my lips, continuing south to meet his tight grip around my neck.

Once the towel is snug below my arms and wrapped around my body, hiding all of my delicate parts, Diego pushes me in the direction of the bathroom doorway, using his brutal grip on my hair. My whole body trembles in his hold, as I come to the realization that he is going to punish me the way he said he was. That I miscalculated in thinking that he cared for me, that he wanted me only for himself. For all I know, he stole me, not for himself, but to blackmail my grandmother. I was just an easy, gullible fool who believed that he wanted me for more than my money, and the power that comes with the Stratford name.

I'm a fucking moron. He's about to allow a bunch of men to use me like the whore he named me. My legs tremble, and I stumble as we cross the bedroom floor, and head towards the doorway leading to the rest of the compound. "Die... go," I try to beg, but his fingers retighten in a brutal grip that doesn't allow any more words to escape.

"No, Issy, the time for begging is now over. Reach back and take the key from me. Open the door," he demands, his voice clipped and cold.

I refuse to raise my hands to the doorknob, trying desperately to pry his grip from around my neck, but it's no use as he shoves me flat against the door using his upper body, his bare chest melding with my back and wet hair, to restrain me further. "Open the door, Issy. Nothing and no one will save you. You need to learn that you are at my mercy, and every time you disobey me, there will be a punishment."

He shoves my face into the wooden door as his grip on my hair releases, and he forces my hand to insert the key and turn the doorknob.

"Pleeeeaaassseee," I hiss, but it makes no difference as the door is pried open. He forces me out of the bedroom and into the hallway, my feet barely making a purchase with the ground, and his hold on my hair and neck the only thing keeping me standing.

Rugged men's faces flash past me as we continue moving forward, and fear like I have never felt before fills my body, like a tidal wave threatening to suffocate me. I'm long past the point of panic, as we continue moving toward the doors that must lead out to the courtyard. I can hear muffled steps behind us, men joining in to watch the spectacle that he is making of me.

"Ve a buscar una cuerda, ahora," Diego roars, and I watch a man run past us to obey his command. *Fuck, what did that mean? Did he just tell him to kill me?* I hope that's what he said rather than telling them to fucking rape me.

I'm going to die! He's going to kill me, but before he does, I will live through every woman's nightmare come to life. Why did I defy him? Why, in this moment, did I decide to stand my ground? *I am so stupid, so utterly stupid.*

We approach a large, tall, rooted tree with rough bark that sits in the middle of the compound. More men seem to appear out of nowhere to watch the commotion, as I continue to struggle against Diego's hold. The man who ran off returns with a long length of rough-looking rope in his hands, his dark eyes appraising me like a hyena's, salivating, and ready to eat me for dinner.

Male murmurs can be heard all around the space, as more footfalls approach us. My heart is trying to climb out of my throat, and my body is drenched with sweat as it trembles. This is it, the moment where what little sanity I had left leaves me. He's going to let these men rape me, to teach me a lesson about obedience.

"Plllleeeassse," I beg with what little air I have.

Diego pushes me up against the tree, my towel-wrapped chest pressed firmly against the rough, thick bark, the humidity in the air and the dense smell of vegetation all around us. My body loses the ability to remain standing. All of my energy is suddenly gone with the knowledge of my impending doom, and my legs give out below me.

"Tie her arms around the tree, and find me something to blindfold her with," Diego barks the order with venom, with no evidence of affection left. I played my poker hand at this game, tried to bluff and channel my inner Stratford, and look where it has gotten me. Tied to a fucking tree, a prisoner of a cartel boss, and about to be assaulted for disobeying a ridiculous order.

If only my grandmother were here, she would murder all these men. She would ensure that not a single one of them was left breathing when she was done, that their complete bloodlines were eradicated from the face of the earth, for thinking they had dominion over a Stratford.

Picture Stella and her rage, and imagine the violence she would unleash. You can survive this if you tuck yourself away in your mind, and keep yourself safe until you are ready for revenge.

My hands are stretched and tied at the wrists around the tree, yanking me forward and up on the tips of my toes. They dig into the dirt and skid across the coarse tree bark. Diego's warm, heavy breath pants behind me, sliding across my neck and cheek, and causing a shiver of both desire and disgust to spear through me.

How can any of this be turning me on? He's about to use me, share me with his men like I don't matter at all to him, and am only a hole to shove his cock into. Hungry, dark gazes meet my eyes from the men watching me be strung up as an offering. A lamb brought to the slaughter for ravenous beasts. Most of them don't even try to disguise their interest, adjusting themselves as my towel shifts and slides.

"Aparta tus malditos ojos. Si alguno de ustedes la mira, les arrancaré la cabeza y los alimentaré a las bestias de la selva."

Diego's commanding, brusque voice is so loud behind me that it causes me to press further into the tree, my trembling body threatening to shut down entirely, with fear now saturating every one of my pores. He releases his hold on my neck and hair, and the only thing left holding me in place is the thick rope digging into my skin, keeping me a prisoner, as a piece of dense fabric is wrapped around my eyes and tied to the back of my head, yanking on my hair in the process.

"No, please! I'm sorry. I'm so sorry, please!"

"Remember you asked for this, *Princesa*. You wanted to be used like a whore." His words slither across my ear, and a wet sensation slides across my chin. Did he just fucking lick me? "Your tears and fear taste like heaven, *little one.*"

Chapter Fourteen

Issy

"Loving you was a sacrifice, you know. I gave you the power to destroy me, and that's exactly what you did."

Unknown

My heart beats savagely in my chest, threatening to rip itself through my sternum in an attempt to escape what is about to happen. His words compete against the loud sound of my blood whooshing in my ears, and my lungs struggle to absorb any of the warm, dense, oppressive air.

"Are you sorry now, little doll? Do you want to beg me for forgiveness?" His words slide across the skin of my neck, sweltering and repulsive. I try to pull my head away from him, even as the rope digs further into the skin of my wrists, and my fingers start to feel cold and numb. *I am truly a prisoner now.*

How could he do this to me? Was it all a lie? Did he never feel anything for me?

All the feelings that I have held inside of me for weeks, the desire for him, the need to be with him, even the thoughts of leaving my grandmother behind when everything was done with my sister, and starting a life with Diego against my grandmother's wishes now seems trivial, immature, and those of a naive idiot who didn't know she was being played.

This was all a game, and I was an idiot who took the bait, the spoiled princess falling for the villain in her guarded ivory tower, who would rip her heart out without the slightest hint of regret. Shame fills every molecule inside of me at how stupid I have unquestionably been.

How could I have been so blind to the reality facing me? He never truly wanted me. All those whispered words in the dark of night, while we hid our relationship from my family and friends, were nothing but the false actions of a manipulative man.

What relationship? My mind snarks, *you were a dirty lie told in the dead of night, a slut who got to her knees for false promises.*

Some irrational part of me rises to the surface, demanding that I not bend, that I not become this pitiful, weak creature he believes me to be. He's going to abuse me regardless, so why give him the pleasure of proving him right? Why cement the fact that I am unequivocally weak?

I bite down hard on the inside of my cheek, trying to silence the fear-induced whimpers from leaving my lips. The taste of rich copper gives me something to focus on, rather than my impending doom. I will not beg, not for his mercy, and not for my life. I am a Stratford and a woman, and both those entities demand respect. He will pay for what he is doing to me one way or the other, because my soul will not allow this to go unanswered.

The image of a pair of crystal blue eyes tries to enter my mind, offering with it a moment of respite against what is happening here to me, but I force it away. I cannot hide inside thoughts of him when I am in trouble. He is not my savior, the white knight coming to save the princess. I burnt that bridge long ago, and I must learn to stand on my own two feet, even if it means I tremble and fall. *There is no going back to the past, and after this, there will be no looking to the future either. Death and retribution will be what I crave.*

A warm, rough hand slides up the outside of my thigh underneath the edge of the towel, and has my breath hitching. I no longer try to move my head away from him, instead pressing my forehead as hard as I can against the coarse texture of the tree. The pain it causes helps me to distance myself from the here and now.

Focus on the feeling of the bark, Issy. Ignore what is happening. You will survive. You must survive.

His rough fingers reach the apex of my thighs, and brush against the swollen flesh of my pussy lips, causing my breath to stutter in my chest, and the mantra I am repeating in my head about surviving to stall momentarily.

"Such a pretty pussy you have, baby. How I enjoy filling it. My men are going to enjoy filling it, too. Maybe I'll let them take your ass too. Would you enjoy that, my whore?" His words slide against my skin with a hint of malice in their tone. A shudder runs through my frame, even as I implore my body not to betray me.

"Beg me, Issy." His teeth meet the delicate skin where my neck and collarbone meet, as he bites down, and a pained cry escapes me. The sting is harsh, but I know it could be so much worse. I know what violence he is truly capable of. He's a ruthless killer, a cold machine when he needs to end others' lives.

Yet he never used it against me until he stole me from my family, and brought me to this ill-forsaken place. There has always been pleasure between us, even when there was pain. Even when I questioned my sanity for wanting him. He introduced me to my greatest desires, unleashing them, and opening the door to my need for pain mixed with pleasure, to be degraded and used. I should have known with those introductions, he was chaining me to him.

I believed I was special to him, that I was the woman he wanted, more than he coveted my sister, our empire, or to live without me. Back in Casbury, he treated me as if I was a piece of fragile glass, giving me pleasure while ensuring I became addicted to him as he bided his time, all the while knowing that he was going to shatter me.

His hand trails down my back, as my breath puffs out in the cold air surrounding us. Every noise has us on alert that we could be discovered by one of my grandmother's guards, or by my sister. I'm not sure which would be worse, but my guess is that Mia might actually try to kill him.

Would they tear him away from me? Would they remove him from the compound, from my life, if they knew their precious Isabella was sleeping with the son of the leader of one of the most dangerous cartels in the world? I can't imagine that my proud and dignified grandmother would not order his death for thinking to touch me. After all, it makes me soiled goods. The Stratford heir tarnished beneath the filth of the Cabano name.

What she doesn't understand, and probably never will, is that I crave the danger. I want Diego Cabano to soil and use me up, until I become something other than what I am. I want to be his in all the ways that matter, and I am willing to sacrifice everything I am to make that happen.

Does that make me naive or perhaps insane? Probably, but I have never felt this intensity with anyone else, not even with the man who haunts my dreams, and fills me with regrets.

Light blond hair, blue eyes, and a gentle smile fill my mind. No, don't think about him now, Issy, don't allow your mind to return to the past. Diego is your future, and there is no going back. I shake my head, trying desperately to stay in the moment and clear my thoughts.

This insanity between Diego and I is a burning inferno that neither of us is willing to put out. We are consumed by each other, in a way that I have never been with anything or anyone else. In a short period of time, he has taken over all of my thoughts and desires. He has become a drug that I can't, and don't wish to, breathe without.

"Your skin is velvet, my pretty, broken doll." His warm breath skates across my shivering flesh, and my core tightens with the obvious need in his tone.

"Why do you call me that?" I whisper.

"Because it's what you are, beautifully broken and precious to me, and what you are is mine, Issy. You are mine."

I push back against his tall, firm frame, his long hard cock slipping between my asscheeks, and making a whimper leave my lips as he nudges my back hole. I'm so wet already that it's dripping down my thighs. The need to have him fill and stretch me is almost painful. I should be embarrassed with my wanton reaction to him, but he makes me feel beautiful and desired. My forehead presses against the metal wall, its coolness a balm to my overheated flesh.

"*What a good girl you are, my slut. Look at how you crave my cock inside of you. You want me to fill you up, baby? Does this sweet pussy need a good fucking, or shall I take this tight ass tonight?*" His dirty words are whispered in my ear, and cause my whole body to tremble against him.

My legs threaten to give out and prevent me from standing, as he presses me further into the wall of the gardener's shed. His arm cradles around my middle while his hand grips my hip in a tight clasp, forcing me to keep standing.

"*You are mine, Issy, this cunt is mine, and only I will ever fill it. Do you hear me, baby?*" The crown of his cock nudges my back hole again, and has my core tightening in anticipation. Fuck. I need him to take me, to use me, and leave me filled with his cum.

His hand wraps around my neck and tightens firmly, preventing my next breath from entering my lungs. "*Tell me that you want me, Princesa. Tell me that you belong to me.*"

The crown of his cock pushes forward through the tight ring of muscle, and an instant sharp pain assaults me. He hasn't prepared me enough to take him in that hole. My body tries to fight the intrusion, my asscheeks tightening even as my vision starts to spot as he constricts his hold further. He pulls back and lines up with my pussy, not even giving me a moment to adjust from one hole to the other, before he slams inside of my wet core with a feral growl.

"*So fucking wet, always ready to be used,*" he grunts as he starts a forceful rhythm inside of my pussy, the sound of flesh hitting flesh loud in our quiet, hidden spot. He releases his grip enough for me to drag much-needed air into my lungs. His hand rises and grabs a fistful of my hair, using the grip to drag my neck back, so he can see my face clearly as I pant like an animal out of breath.

"*Tell me, Issy, or I swear to you, I will fucking tear you in half and fill all your holes with my cum, before I send you back to your Abuela.*"

His rough words, and the menacing look across his features, don't have me doubting that he would, in fact, send me back to my grandmother, tarnished, and dripping from all my holes. If there is one thing Diego enjoys above all, it's watching his cum drip out of me, while I squirm as I'm forced to interact *with others. He gets a perverse satisfaction in knowing he has dirtied me up, the Manhattan princess in waiting.*

"Yoooouuurrrs," the word escapes my lips with a ragged moan, and my core tightens around his thick girth, as he hits the spot inside of me that has my eyes wanting to roll to the back of my head. I can feel the electric current racing across my skin, the orgasm ready to burst inside of me, promising to take me to heaven in mere seconds. Just as it's cresting and my chest is trying to force more oxygen into my lungs, he pulls out of me, leaving me empty and spasming.

"NOOOOOOOOO!" I scream, fighting against his hold.

A harsh chuckle leaves his lips before he bites down on my shoulder, his teeth breaking the surface of my soft skin with a sting. "FUCK!" I scream with the pain, before he pushes his stiff cock between my asscheeks once more. Before I can even utter another word or plead for him to be gentle with me, he's pushing inside of my back hole. Burning and pain assault me instantly, and my whole body locks up tight.

"You will always be mine, Isabella Stratford. My slut, my whore, and one day I might even make you my wife." His words are an aphrodisiac to my heart. I want all that he's promising. I want to be his in every way.

The memory fades as I bite down harder on the inside of my cheek, refusing to utter the words that may, or may not, stop all of this from going any further, the Stratford stubbornness demanding I hold firm against Diego. The darkness of the blindfold is my friend at this moment, because at least I don't have to witness his depraved satisfaction. The glee in those green eyes when he sees the dread, hurt, and disbelief in mine.

A finger slips between my pussy lips, rubbing against my clit and causing a jolt to race through my body, forcing me to balance precariously on the edge of my toes. The finger rubs tight circles in rapid succession, and I can feel my body falling into the trap, as wetness starts to slip from inside of my core, coating my pussy lips and the sides of my thighs. All of the adrenaline racing through my body spikes further, bringing with it a sense of being on a rollercoaster ride, racing to the very top with the anticipation of the rapid plunge into madness that is about to engulf me.

"Give in to me, *Princesa*, you know you want to." I can hear the smirk in his voice, even if I can't see it.

"Noooooo," the pained word leaves my lips on a moan. A moan that I can't seem to swallow, even as my body defies me and follows the movement of the fingers caressing me, my thighs spreading wider against my wishes.

"That's it, baby, use your words. Tell me what you want. We both know that you don't want me to stop. You enjoy being used, being taken roughly like the rich, spoiled whore that you are." Wetness greets the side of my neck, and I am sure the fucker has licked me.

"Look at how you're dripping, baby. Is it because they're watching, or is it because you're waiting for each of them to take their turn inside this perfect, rich cunt?"

He doesn't wait for a reply, and I feel the towel lifting from behind and the humid air against my exposed asscheeks. One of his feet pushes against my own, forcing my stance to widen further as his other hand slips behind my back. The movement causes me to feel his bare, rigid cock pressed against the seam of my ass before it slips between my cheeks.

"Should I take your ass, baby, and leave your dripping cunt for my men? Should I let them fill you with cum, until you're dripping like a dirty faucet, Issy?"

Another moan escapes my lips at the mere image of my pussy dripping with cum, of Diego stretching my ass with his large, hard cock and filling all of my holes. A sense of self-disgust tries to rise within me, but it's overridden by all the emotions and sensations circling within me.

The head of his cock meets my back hole, pressing against the ring of muscle and causing a pained cry to leave my lips. It burns; he's too large, and I'm not prepared to take him. He knows he's going to hurt me and tear me apart, but I don't think that will dissuade him. I'm just a whore for him to use now. No, I'm even less than a whore; at least a whore gets paid for what she does, but I'm just here at his mercy. *Prisoner*, my mind supplies the world that slices me emotionally from the inside out.

He slides the head of his dick from my back hole across my soaked slit, a groan leaving his lips. He bumps my clit, again and again, forcing me to rock back and forth on my toes, my own body betraying me as it angles to try to force him inside of me.

"So needy already, baby," he groans. "If you won't beg me, Issy, then you will have to learn your lesson the hard way."

He pulls away from me, and a pained sound of disappointment leaves my lips. *I'm so weak and useless.* I press my head further into the tree's bark, wishing that I could meld right into its aged surface and cease to exist.

The towel must still be lifted above my ass, because I can feel the humid air against my exposed skin. Shame fills me, knowing his men are watching all of this, staring at my bare ass and perhaps even getting themselves ready to fuck me. That I am nothing but a vessel with holes to be used for their pleasure. *Fight back! Don't blindly go into this fate. Remember who you are and who you come from!*

"What's it going to be, *Princesa*? Will you beg or become the jungle whore?"

He's going to hurt us... they are going to hurt us. We will never survive this fate.

I bite down on my bottom lip, refusing to utter any words that would have him believe that he has won, despite my mind and heart warring within me. One demands I hold firm, while the other begs that I save us from an action that can never be undone, one that will crush our very soul.

Does Diego not realize, with what he is about to allow to happen to assert his control and dominance over me, that he will lose me forever? He won't have to kill me after this; I will find the strength to end my own life.

"Who's up first? Who wants a taste of my rich, Manhattan slut?" His taunting words ring out over the courtyard, and I can hear steps shifting on the ground somewhere behind me. I tighten my eyes shut behind the blindfold, even as tears soak the fabric and pour down my face.

"Si alguno de vosotros le pone un dedo encima, os mataré. Ella es mía. Ella necesita aprender la lección, pero ninguno de ustedes es el maestro. Sigue el juego o muere dolorosamente."

His words are uttered in a demanding, sharp command that echoes over the space, and my chest rises and falls with an impending panic attack. This is it, the moment I realize how little I truly mean to him. Did he tell them to use and hurt me? To make it as horrible as possible, so that I learn my place? *Oh, how the mighty Stratford princess has fallen. Not even my grandmother will want me back after this.*

She took Mia back after what happened to her. Yes, but I am not Mia; I am worthless, damaged goods.

I feel another presence next to me, a hot breath blown against my face, the scent of tobacco and onions making me gag. "You are so pretty, *chica*," the words are spoken with a rough voice that I don't recognize. My hair is moved away from my face, and the lump in my throat threatens to suffocate me. Blackness calls to me in my panic, promising respite and oblivion from the horror about to be done to me. *I can't breathe, I can't fucking breathe, I'm going to die tied to this tree.* My heart will explode from inside of my chest, finally killing me once and for all.

Terror slithers across my body as a hard cock is notched at my opening. There is no going back now, and I will never be the same again. A guttural grunt assaults my ears before the cock is forced inside of my pussy. My core tightens against the large invading feeling, and at that exact moment, a hand slips between my body and the tree, squeezing my breast roughly and forcing a cry from my lips. The cock inside of me fucks me with hard thrusts, forcing my body to press against the tree bark, even as I'm compelled to widen my stance. They hit the end of me repeatedly, starting a rising tide within me.

No, no, no. Please no! I beg my body as it tries to fight the sensations within me, but it's almost impossible. The feeling of electricity is starting to spread across my limbs. My ears pick up the subtle groans and shifting of the other men around us, even as this stranger fucks my pussy like an animal, and sharp cries leave my lips. Just as I'm starting to reach the pinnacle of a release I don't want to crest, he pulls out and leaves me empty and spasming in his wake.

A scream leaves my lips, and male chuckles sound all around us. Warm fingers cradle my face before tightening their grip, and forcing my chin to the right.

"Did you enjoy him inside of your cunt, baby?" Diego pants viciously into my ear, and a shiver slides down my back.

"I will kill you!" I scream, trying to pull away from his grasp.

"Not before I break you, Issy. Not before you realize I own every part of you, and can do whatever I want with you." His touch gentles, almost becoming soothing as he strokes my face, pushing my hair away from my clammy neck.

"Next," he barks the command, and someone else moves to my side. I can tell it's a different male by the stench of their sweat in my nostrils. Repulsion fills me at the exact same time my core tightens, knowing yet another man is about to use me.

The head of a cock is slipped inside of my cunt and then pulled out again, sliding in and out over and over again with shallow thrusts, never deep enough to hit me where my body craves. Never deep enough to truly fill me. Large, rough hands tighten on my hips, squeezing my flesh painfully. My lower body angles backward, trying to force the penetration to become deeper, even as loathing fills me with the knowledge that I want this, that in some depraved way, I am enjoying being used.

A deep, rough moan fills my ears just as whoever is inside of me pulls rapidly away, and I feel wetness hit my feet. A chuckle rents the air. "Looks like he preferred to cum on the tree than fill your whore pussy, Issy."

His words are my undoing, and whatever strength I had left to fight him, to continue my defiance, leaves me. "Pleaaase, Diiieeegggo," I sob, the shame of my demise filling me.

"Have you learned your lesson, *Princesa*? Who do you belong to?" I can hear the note of satisfaction in his deep voice, and I hate it. I hate him.

He knows that he has won and broken me, but what he doesn't realize is that there will be no repairing the damage he has inflicted. No part of my mind and soul can survive, not only what he's done but knowing that, on some level, I enjoyed it. *Dirty, weak whore.*

"You," my voice sounds broken and defeated to my own ears. The sound of the man shuffling away from me gives me a moment to try to inhale a ragged breath, one that becomes immediately trapped in my lungs, as another hard cock slides inside of my pussy without warning, taking me hard and rough. Pushing me savagely into the tree bark and forcing my skin to rub against its surface. My breasts are crushed below me, but the friction from the soft towel and the rough bark pressed against them has that electricity soaring within me, immediately igniting.

"*Vuelve al maldito trabajo*," Diego yells, and more tears pour down my face. Even my breaking for him, admitting defeat, won't have him calling off this punishment. He's determined to shatter me, and so he shall until there is nothing left of my mind, body, and soul but dust.

The man uses me selfishly, without mercy, his actions filled with contempt, as if this is all I am suitable for. A doll made to be his plaything and nothing more. A whore to use any way that he deems appropriate, even if that means he shares me with his fellow soldiers.

Fingers brush against my clit, sliding between my pussy lips even as his cock keeps up a punishing rhythm. A thumb rubs circles over and over on my hard nub, causing all the hairs on my body to stand on end. A rich scent invades my senses, trying to get me to process that I recognize it, but my head is in a dark place right now, and my thought processes are all overwhelmed.

"That's it, beautiful doll, shatter for me. Show me how much you enjoy me fucking you like a whore, while my men watch."

Relief fills me to hear his voice and know that it's him inside of me, that he hasn't let yet another man use me. Diego bites down on my shoulder, his teeth stinging along my flesh. "Come for me, baby."

His words are my undoing, and my orgasm spills over me, causing heat to flush my body as every one of my limbs tightens against the tree bark. My body absorbs each of his harsh, powerful strokes, my cheek pressed against the bark of the tree as his forearm presses against the back of my neck, giving me not even an inch of control over my own body.

I cum all over his cock, squirting and soaking him, and my shaking thighs. My release drips down my legs as he grunts one last time, and fills me with his cum. He stills deep inside of me, breathing harshly next to my face.

I swallow, his heavy breath mixing with my ragged own. "Please... Diego. Please... please don't hurt me anymore. I... I'm... yours."

My words are my signal of defeat, my white flag flying high and present against my enemy. An enemy who has not only won, but also shown me how weak and inadequate I am at the game. Every part of me is exhausted and drained. There is nothing left to fight with, nothing left to give.

He's not only an enemy, but is a psychopath, willing to use anything at his disposal to force me to realize what and who I truly am. How is he not aware of how psychotic his actions are, and how he's hurting me, not only physically, but emotionally? *He doesn't care; you are a prize, nothing more.*

My body is tense against his, the tremble of pain racing through my limbs even as I continue to shake below him. He leans forward, and my breath becomes even more distraught, waiting for how he will hurt me next. Confusion cycles through me when his lips land tenderly, and almost reverently, against my shoulder.

"Eres mi todo, princesa."

The emotional tone in his voice has me releasing all of my weight, and sagging in the restraints and against him. I have no idea what he's just uttered, but the tone alone assures me that, for now, he is done punishing me.

At least, that is what I pray for, but with Diego Cabano, mercy may be a pipe dream.

CHAPTER FIFTEEN

Diego

"I want her to melt into me, like butter on toast. I want to absorb her and walk around for the rest of my days with her encased in my skin."

Sara Gruen, Water for Elephants

H er body sags against me, entirely depleted of everything. She finally submitted to me thoroughly, and it was beautiful. Beautiful in a way that I only dreamed was possible. In a way that I will forever cherish in my soul, because it confirms the truth. I know in my heart that she was meant for me. *She is mine.* Her words echo in my mind on repeat, and I almost regret my actions for a moment. Regret that I had to go to these lengths to force her hand.

"Please... Diego. Please don't hurt me anymore. I... I'm... yours." Her voice sounds shattered, as if a part of her has come utterly undone. A sense of foreboding enters my mind, and causes a chill to race down my spine.

I've no doubt in my mind that those words will play on repeat in my nightmares for years to come. How could she honestly believe that I would allow anyone to hurt her? That I would permit any man to lay a finger on her, never mind insert their cocks inside of her, while I stood and watched? My *Princesa* still doesn't seem to understand what she means to me.

This game I just played with her was dangerous. I can see it by the hungry expressions on my men's faces, as they move silently away from us and back to their duties. Would any of them attempt to touch her, now that they have seen how beautiful she looks and sounds as she comes undone? How many more men's lives will I have to end before this is all said and done?

She's worth it. I meant what I just whispered to her. She is my everything, she's just too stubborn to see it.

One day, I hope that Issy realizes that the only man who was inside of her was me. The whole time, it was me touching her, bringing her pleasure. Although my men stood by with their backs turned away from her, and participated in my vicious game of deception as I commanded them to, she was never truly in any danger of them being inside her. My cum is what slides between her legs, and it was my load that landed on her feet.

I reach around and untie her arms from the tree trunk, and her knees instantly give in, causing her to slump. I grab her petite body and pick her up, cradling her in my arms bridal style as her head snuggles into my chest. I don't bother to look in my mens' direction, giving all of my attention to the small, fragile creature who attempted to defy a demon in my arms.

We should tell her it was us the whole time, my mind hisses. I know that I should, that what I have done to her will leave scars on her soul, and on mine, but I needed her to break for me. I need her to finally surrender, and know that she is irrevocably mine. If I tell her now that it was, in fact, me, she could revert back, and she could fight me again. I can't have that. I can't have put us both through all that for nothing.

I carry her back into the compound, never stopping until we reach the safety of my bedroom, using the heel of my foot to slam the door behind us, and lay her across my white sheets. She's out of it, completely groggy and sluggish, as I maneuver her on the mattress, removing the soiled towel and releasing the wet makeshift blindfold from around her eyes.

She looks so petite against the large bed, her dark hair matted and spread around her in thick, damp waves. Her pale skin now looks a shade darker than my sheets. My perfect doll, so beautiful that, even in her current ragged state, she is still the most beautiful woman I have ever seen.

Her face is red, blotchy, and streaked with dirt from all her tears, and the turmoil I put her through. She has red abrasion marks across her porcelain skin, where it rubbed against the tree. Blooming bruises are already sprouting on her slim hips from my ruthless hold while I fucked her, and my teeth are imprinted along her neck and collarbone. She looks devastatingly stunning, covered in my marks. Each one a reminder of her defiance against me, a defiance that I was proud of.

Issy is mistaken, thinking that I only want to break her to make her compliant and reliant on me. That couldn't be further from the truth. My desire is to break her of her weakness and lack of self-confidence. I want Issy to fight me. I want her to believe in herself, and see herself as the powerful creature that I know dwells underneath the facade of a broken doll.

Her thick, dark lashes flutter, and her stunning sapphire eyes stare up at me. There is still fear present in their depths, and it causes a pain deep in my chest. I don't want her to be afraid of me. I want to be her safe haven, not the monster in her nightmares. *Good fucking luck with that now, asshole.*

"Rest, baby, it's over now," I lean forward and gently kiss her forehead, and her breath leaves her lips in a sigh as her eyes close again.

I get up and head into the washroom to get a cloth to clean her. As I'm running the small, white hand towel under the running water, I look at myself in the mirror, and the man I see staring back at me surprises me.

I still see the ruthless killer that I was made to be. The cartel boss who would end anyone who gets in my way. The image reflected back also shows me a man littered with scars, both externally and internally. More importantly, and surprising, is the man who can't deny what he feels for the woman lying in the other room.

In the past, turning my emotions off has helped me survive this cold and dangerous world that we live in, the one where any weakness can and will be used against you. The world determined to exterminate my very bloodline. The cartel life has no mercy or forgiveness. *Ruthless. Cold. Deadly.* Those are the words that we live by.

The deep scars on my body are a road map to my success, and tell a story of the unforgiving life I have lived. One that I know deep down, my *Princesa* won't survive, at least not in her current state. My mother didn't, and she was stronger in spirit than Issy is. She was born into this world, and was used to teach my father a powerful lesson, one that I am doomed to repeat if I can't keep my Issy safe.

Dangerous is what I have been raised to be so that I can survive, and now a pretty broken doll is trying to wear down all the strong and impenetrable walls that I have taken years to put into place. The thought that I should return her to her grandmother once again runs through my mind. *She's not safe with me.*

Wouldn't it be better to watch her from a distance, thriving, instead of watching her wither away or possibly die here with me? Is my need and desire for her more important than her survival?

I walk back into the bedroom to see her still lying in the same position I left her in. My eyes trail over her face, down her delicate neck, and over the rest of her body, my cock instantly stirring despite having just cum numerous times. *Fuck, I want her again.* I want to keep filling her until she's bursting with my cum in all of her holes.

I make my way over to the bed and run the soft, wet cloth against her legs, wiping away the debris from the jungle floor, and the tree I forced her against. She has a gash on her shin from where she must have banged it against the tree. I lean forward and run my tongue over the tiny, red beads of blood on the surface, enjoying the explosion of her rich taste on my tongue. She moans and spreads her legs further, giving me a front-row seat to her pink, swollen pussy, which is still leaking some of my cum.

I run my tongue up the inside of her knee, spreading her warm thighs further, wiping any debris away with the cloth, as I follow behind with my lips and tongue. Cherishing every single drop of moisture on her skin, mixed with her own taste. I drop the cloth on the bed as my tongue reaches the apex of her thighs, and use both hands to spread her glistening pussy lips.

The combination of my cum and hers is still on the surface, and peeking from her swollen entrance. I run my tongue along one pink lip, and then the other, moaning deep in my throat as I get hints of her taste combined with mine. *Salty and sweet, fucking delicious.*

My tongue strokes against her hard, little clit, and a moan leaves her lips, as her head thrashes against the sheets. I use my forearms to keep her legs open wide and let my tongue feast against her swollen, slick flesh. Sucking and licking as her moans become hoarse cries, and I slip my tongue into her entrance, fucking her as deeply as I can with it.

"Dieegggoo, oh my God!" Her calling my name soothes a part of my abrasive soul, the one that had always been pitch black before I laid eyes on her.

I keep tongue fucking her, letting my fingers rub through her slit and helping to coax another orgasm out of her, with my thumb strumming against her sensitive clit and flesh. "That's it, *Princesa*, ride it out, baby. Soak my face; I want to taste you gushing in my mouth."

"Too much!" Her cry makes the tip of my cock weep pearls of cum. I need to have her swallow me as I consume her. I maneuver my body, forcing it to suspend above her on my forearms and toes, until my cock is against her lips, pressing between their warm depth, and my face is snug against her delicious pussy.

My tip slips between her lips, and her tongue lashes at it with a moan. I keep licking her clit and slip two fingers inside of her soaked cunt, fucking her slowly and as deeply as I can go, while my cock starts a slow thrusting rhythm inside of the warm heat of her mouth. The sounds of her slurping and gagging on me push me closer to the edge, and I thrust deeper into her throat, forcing her to take more of me down her tight column.

Her whole body tightens as I grab onto either side of her thighs, spreading her legs wide so I can lick down her pretty cunt and down to her crack, taking pleasure in her stunted moans, as an electric current runs up my spine, warning me I'm close to spilling inside of her mouth.

I slide my tongue inside of her back hole as I slip another of my fingers within her swollen pussy, and I pick up speed inside of her cunt. Her core tightens on my digits, strangling them in a tight hold at the same time her back hole compresses on my tongue, as a gush of warm fluid soaks my face. I love that Issy squirts. I know that it embarrassed her when we first started fucking, but it's so incredibly hot.

I lick her through her orgasm as my own tightens my balls and races down my length, forcing my legs to wobble a bit and threatening my body to collapse and suffocate her. I pull back from her sweet cunt and lift my body off hers, my dick pulling out of her mouth with a wet plopping sound. A dribble of my cum drips down her lips and covers her chin. I move up her sexy body, my hand grabbing for her chin and holding her firmly, while my tongue slides out and licks up all the mess she left behind. My salty taste, combined with the rich taste of her release on my tongue, causes a deep growl to escape me.

Fuck, she tastes delicious all on her own, but the combination of the two of us is something I will never get sick of, and is quickly becoming my favorite flavor. My cock bobs against my tense stomach, refusing to relinquish its hardness. Who the fuck needs Viagra when there is an Isabella Stratford living and breathing? She's a hundred percent more potent than any drug would be for my dick.

I pull back and realize with a chuckle that she's passed out again. The deep purple stripes underneath her eyes worry me. Maybe I pushed too fucking hard. She's still recovering from being sick and going through withdrawal. *I'm a fucking psychopath.*

Issy has this sweet innocent look when she's passed out. One that calls to the monster who lives inside of me, the one with no self-restraint and respect for anyone else. She beckons sweetly to him to come closer, to rip her apart, hurt her, and it takes all my strength not to allow him free. Not to allow him to further damage the precious woman lying in front of me.

Guilt fills me as I walk back to the bathroom to get another clean cloth, determined to finish cleaning her and to let her rest. When I'm done wiping her down, and her body rests peacefully on the bed, deep in a dreamless slumber, I allow myself to lie beside her, cradling her in my arms, with my nose buried in her dark hair.

The beast and the beauty, a demon lying with an angel, those thoughts make a smile cross my face. I reach for her small hand, intertwining our fingers and pulling them to my lips.

"*Te haré mía y no querrás dejarme nunca más. Tu corazón me pertenece, Isabella Stratford.*"

Chapter Sixteen

Issy

"That's the thing about trust. It's like broken glass. You can put it back together, but the cracks are always visible--like scars that never fully heal."

Hope Collier, Haven

I wake up alone, even though I was sure that Diego was in this bed with me and had me wrapped tightly in his arms, which makes little to no sense to my muddled brain. Why would he want to hold me after what he had allowed to happen? Why show me gentleness and affection after terrorizing me? Is it just another way for him to manipulate me, to hurt me? What is his end game?

Various aches and pains make themselves known, as I stretch under the white sheet that covers my naked body. My core feels swollen and sore, all of my muscles tense, flashes of images reminding me of why, putting me instantly on edge as I try desperately to avoid thinking about last night. The heat is already swirling around the room, and the bright light streaming through the curtains tells me it's probably late morning, if not later. I suppose it doesn't really matter what time it is; where does a prisoner need to go? It's not like I have any appointments to keep.

An urgent pain in my full bladder demands that I get up and make it to the washroom. I sit up, my head spinning a bit as I try to maneuver my exhausted body off of the plush, wide mattress with a groan. When my feet finally make it to the cool floor, I stumble and have to grasp onto one of the bed's four posters to keep standing.

Jesus, I feel like I've been on a week-long bender. My whole body shakes, and I take one trembling step, and then another, in the direction of the open doorway leading to the bathroom. Once I enter the spa-like space, I rush for the toilet. My whole body protests the movement of lowering myself to a sitting position. My pussy burns as I try to pee, causing a pained gasp to leave my lips, and tears to slide down my face. *Fuck, it hurts so bad. I'm going to punch him the nuts the next time I see him and that one-eyed snake of his.*

Shame once again fills me with the knowledge of how many men were inside of me, that the soreness that I'm feeling is from being so thoroughly used. My hands clench in my lap as I force myself to deal with the memories that assault me. Reliving every second of what happened to me, what Diego allowed to happen to me. All of the pain, the struggling, and even my pleading for him to stop, and finally giving him what he desired most; my broken soul laid bare at his deviant and destructive feet.

Rage like I've never felt before races through my body, threatening to drown me in its hot, fiery depths as it demands that I stop my self-pity and self-deprecation. Yes, I pushed him and acted like a spoiled brat, but there was nothing that I did that deserved that type of punishment.

Was it a punishment? My mind questions with doubts. Did I not enjoy at least some parts of what happened? Am I going to sit here in denial that I relished being used, degraded, and treated like a plaything? That I didn't get off on the depravity of what happened. Am I gaslighting myself?

All of my emotions become tangled in a sticky web: rage, lust, pain, and shame, all mixed together, the worst of them forcing me to realize that I was a damn fool. The truth is, it doesn't matter if I enjoyed it or not. What matters is that Diego was willing to go to those lengths to break me down and control me. *That's not love.* None of what happened here yesterday was genuine affection, just the actions of a madman who wanted to flex his power, and show me how utterly powerless I am in my own fate.

Tears prickle at my swollen eyes, and I swipe at them angrily. *No more tears, Issy, be strong for once in your life. Straighten your spine and refuse to allow anyone else to beat you down. Be a fucking Stratford for once in your pathetic life.*

The truth is that all of my ill-fated decisions have led me to where I am now. Not a single turn in my road of life could have prevented me from my fate. I was always meant to fall in love with a monster. Even when I once had a prince who I discarded. I was always destined to be a pitiful queen with a serpent for a lover. Nothing could have stopped it, not my grandmother, not my sister, and certainly not my common fucking sense, if I even ever had any.

It's why I have always hated making decisions for myself. All my life, I have avoided them. Call it weakness, inability, hell, call it a lack of faith in myself and my capabilities, if you will. All I know is, every single decision I have ever been forced to make has ended in destruction.

There are no exceptions, no what-ifs. Every one of them has created a road map of small, jagged fissures that have continued to grow, and further splinter. Every single one of them has led me here to where I am now, a prisoner of an unhinged psychopath with obsessive tendencies and control issues.

I finish my business and look longingly at the stone shower, as repulsion fills me at the state of my own body. I can see the various markings of fingers along my thighs and hips, already turning an ugly shade of eggplant on my pale skin. My body yearns to be clean from the filth of the experience I was forced to endure.

I turn on the water and slip into the stall, letting the cold water propel over me and pelt my skin with tiny shards of ice. Maybe if I stay under here long enough, I can freeze what is left of my emotions. I can freeze my heart to a solid piece of ice, so that way, no one can ever hurt me again.

The truth is, if I had a blade, I'd cut the miserable, useless organ out of my chest so that I never had to feel anything ever again. If I was lucky, I would die in the process, and this life would finally come to an end. *Wow, look at the self-pity queen, just wallowing in her shit rather than trying to overcome it. Get over yourself, spoiled brat.*

I scrub at my skin roughly, raking my broken nails down the surface, wanting to shed it from my body, so that I don't have a constant reminder of who and what I am. My eyes spy a few bottles on the stone ledge, and my fingers tremble as I lift the bottle of shampoo, with the knowledge that Diego must have had these brought here for me.

So what? He afforded his prisoner some comforts from home, but it means nothing. Get it together, Issy. He's a fucking monster.

I wash quickly, refusing to acknowledge any more of the products that I see. Whatever his reasoning for bringing them here makes no difference now. He wanted a prisoner, and that's what he will get.

I shuffle out of the shower and saunter to where I remember seeing the towels are kept, the warm air making my skin dry almost instantly. My eye catches on a white, soft-looking dress neatly folded on the stone sink counter, a stunning violet orchid placed on top of it. My fingers trail over the soft, delicate petals, lifting it gently to my nose and inhaling its rich scent. The reflection in the mirror catches my attention, and I stare at the broken, naked girl on its surface.

My hair is a thick mass of dark, wet tendrils down my back and over my shoulders. Red and purple angry bruises and welts cover portions of my skin, as do healing insect bites. My ribs look pronounced on my petite frame, showing me clearly how much weight I have lost since being kidnapped. The finger marks along my neck are pronounced, like some fucked up necklace the size of Diego's hands.

I lean forward and trail my finger along the imprint of his teeth on my shoulder and neck. The fucking savage looks like he mauled me. My chest clenches with the sobs that threaten to rise and the tears that fill my eyes. I'm a mess; I look like I've been through a traumatic event. I look like my sister did, when she was finally brought home after being taken by a lunatic. The difference is Mia found the strength to fight back against her monster, and I'm here shaking like a leaf.

I crush the soft petals of the orchid in my hand, crumbling it and allowing it to fall from my fingers and hit the ground. That flower represents me: *pretty, delicate, soft, and weak.* All the things that allow a monster like Diego Cabano to use me in any way he desires. I straighten my shoulders and look back in the mirror, and the reflection that greets me is a shimmering vision of my grandmother when she was younger. Stella Stratford would never allow anyone to hurt her. She would never allow her fate to be dictated by anyone. I am her granddaughter, her spitting image, some say. I need to start acting like it.

I throw the dress on over my nakedness and prepare myself to be a captive, but one with a plan. If Diego Cabano won't release me, I will try to escape, and if that doesn't work, I'll make him kill me. Either way, my days in this jungle are now numbered.

I walk out of the bathroom and head for the door of the bedroom, turning the knob. I'm surprised to find it unlocked. Cautiously, I slip from the room and immediately meet the dark eyes of a guard stationed across the hall. Embarrassment and fear slide up my back, causing my face to feel hot. Is he one of the men who fucked me yesterday?

I almost step back into the room in horror, but I force myself to stand firm, to take another step away from the door, and meet and hold his dark glare. I will not be weak. I am a fucking Stratford, and I will not cower before this man or any other. "*Señorita*, the *jefe* says for you to be escorted to the dining room for a meal. Please follow me."

He doesn't wait to see if I will follow him, walking away with a quick stride down the hallway to the right. For a moment, I hesitate, looking in the other direction that I know leads to the exterior of the building, rather than further within the compound. Could I make a run for it? How far would I get before one of his men captured me?

Not far. Play the game, Issy, and bide your time.

I follow the man down the hallway that opens into a large living room/dining room combination. The walls are all made of rich wood and stone, with large windows allowing the bright sunshine inside, and an angled glass ceiling, that enables you to look up into the canopy of jungle trees that surround the compound. It's stunning, a work of architectural art that seems to blend with nature rather than try to subdue it.

If I wasn't a forced captive, I might actually enjoy the space, all the abundance of nature, and the experience I could have of living in the jungle, but I am. I wasn't given a choice; I was stolen by a thief who didn't care about my fundamental right to choose for myself.

A small elderly woman, with pure white hair pulled back into a bun, stands with a welcoming smile next to a large, round wooden table laden with food. Her sleeveless dress is bright with an ethnic embroidered print; the rich reds, blues, oranges, and yellows of her clothing cause a smile to tug at the corner of my mouth, and her rich caramel skin to look like it's glowing.

"Hola, linda muñeca." She greets me, her arms reaching out and embracing me in a warm hug. I try to hold firm and rigid in the embrace, but her welcoming scent of citrus and honey, and how she tugs and squeezes me, have me melting against her.

"Hello," my voice comes out small and husky, as I meet her lively, dark eyes.

"I..." She points at her chest as she pulls away from me. "Alisa, you call me." Her attempt at English is endearing, and her warm brown eyes make me feel safe in a place filled with perils. She pulls me by the hand and leads me to a chair at the table. "Eat, *muñeca. Demasiado flaca.* Skinny."

I stare at the banquet on the table before me. So many different varieties of fruits, some meats, and rice are just waiting to be served. My mouth waters at the same time my stomach rumbles.

"Eat, *niña bonita,*" she hums as she starts piling food on my plate, and ignores my attempts to stop her. I wish I could understand all of her words, as her presence is soothing and makes me feel safe like my grandmother does, but without the lingering judgment that Stella always has.

Once she's satisfied that I have a mountain of food to consume, she wanders off to one of the room entries, and I immediately feel bereft without her presence. My eyes wander around the room, and I take in the beautiful pieces of art that adorn the walls, and the crisp linen fabrics on the sofas. Everything here is bright with saturated colors. The yellows, reds, and blues calling out to you, but at the same time, not trying to outdo the presence of the jungle surrounding us, but instead, somehow seeming to compliment it.

My eyes slide over the mens' large frames guarding each exit point, and the ones I can see beyond the windows, standing guard along the veranda that must run the length of this side of the compound. Each wears similar camouflage attire, and has weapons strapped to their impressive frames. My body begins to tremble, and my hands feel slick. *Did all these men watch me last night? Who amongst them took their pleasure inside of my body?*

My appetite disappears instantly, and nausea turns in my stomach just as Alisa walks back into the room, carrying a black comb and bottle in her hands. Her eyes connect to mine, and whatever she sees in their depths has her cradling my chin in her aged hand. "It's okay, niña. No hurt." Her dark eyes turn towards the men who are doing their best to avoid meeting my gaze.

"Afuera! Todos ustedes! Ella no puede comer si la miras como animales."

Whatever she yells at them has them shifting uncomfortably in their stances, and staring at each other. Alisa stands with her wrinkled hands on her hips and stares them down, as if she were about to fight a jungle cat, and I watch as grown men shuffle with wary looks on their faces, and leave the room. *Holy fuck! How did she do that?*

Alisa comes around and pats my arm. "Eat!" She orders, and a grin slips across my lips as I put a piece of fruit inside my mouth. She hums a tune as she comes around behind me, her hands pulling my hair from my back and laying it across the back of the chair, before she pours whatever is in the bottle on my strands, and combs it through my long matted tresses with her hands. The smell of jasmine and orange blossoms fills the air.

She gets to work, untangling the mess that is my hair, gently combing through my long, dark waves while I do my best not to disappoint her, and get some much-needed delicious food down. Heavy footsteps echo off the stone floors and make their way closer to us. I restrain myself from turning to see who it is, and try to swallow the forkful of rice that now tastes like ash.

"Hola, mamá. Cómo estás en este buen día." The voice is deep but familiar to me. Santiago appears in my sightline, reaching across the table to grab a piece of meat from one of the trays. *Mamá?* I know that word means mother. Alisa is his mother?

"Los espíritus de nuestros antepasados han visto que vivo un día más," Alisa responds, never stopping her soothing ministrations of my hair.

"Good day, *señorita.* I see you have met Alisa, my mother. She is one of the fiercest and meanest cats in this jungle," he laughs.

Alisa must have an idea of what he's saying about her because in the next instant, the comb whacks him on the back of the neck, and she goes right back to combing through my hair. A chuckle escapes me at their antics.

"She does seem fierce, and also lovely." I watch as his eyes soften, and stare into mine with compassion. He rubs his large palm across the back of his neck and fidgets as he takes a seat.

"How are you feeling today, Isabella?" He inquires cautiously, his eyes assessing my condition quickly, and whatever he sees must bring him some relief because his features relax.

"Still a prisoner," I scoff while pushing the plate away, my appetite truly gone now.

"Ehhh, yes, but also a no. The *jefe* has sent me to tell you that you have free rein of the house and gardens. No more locked doors for you, *chica.* He... emmm," Santiago rakes his thick fingers through his salt and pepper hair, his face showing a measure of regret. "He said to remind you who you belong to."

His words cause a deep sense of resentment to lodge in my chest. How fucking dare he? Now that he has abused me, broken me, and made me beg, now I have free rein in his fucking jungle kingdom? *Well, fuck him.*

"Where is Diego now?" I question, with my head cocked to the side and a raised eyebrow.

Santiago wipes at a bead of sweat on the side of his face. Whatever he must see on my face has him wary. Does he know that I want to strangle his boss? Perhaps the way that I am holding my fork, as if I might thrust it into his eyes, is an indication of how I feel right now.

I turn in my seat and reach for Alisa's hands, cradling them gently in one of mine and bringing the back of her hand to my lips. "Thank you, Alisa. *Gracias.*" I attempt the word, not knowing if I am pronouncing it correctly, but based on the smile that breaks across her lined face, I must not be too far off.

I move out of my seat and towards the middle of the room, stopping and looking over my shoulder and giving Santiago cold eyes. "Are you going to take me to the devil, or shall I go searching for him myself?"

Santiago stands wearily, a frightening smirk crossing his lips as he moves towards me. "Be careful what you wish for, girl. The devil is always listening and ready to take your soul."

I would laugh, except this particular devil has already taken my soul, and destroyed parts of me that I didn't even think were left to be devastated. I have nothing left to lose except my life, and right now, that no longer means much to me, especially if I can deprive him of having me.

CHAPTER SEVENTEEN

Diego

"The world was collapsing, and the only thing that really mattered to me was that she was alive."

Rick Riordan, The Last Olympian

I stare down at the man on his knees at my feet, his head sagging low on his neck, blood pouring from a gash on the side of his head, and trickling into his already swollen-shut eye. His nose oozes more blood, no doubt shattered from one of my fists, and the pained groan escaping his damaged lips is music to my fucking ears. *More, cause more damage,* the monster inside of me rages.

One of his arms hangs limply at his side, from where I dislocated his shoulder and snapped his forearm, along with all of the fingers on his left hand. His heavy breathing, due in part to the stab wound in his other shoulder, is getting on my nerves. He's still refusing to give me the information that I need, even though he knows there is no way that he's escaping this compound with his life.

My arm flies out and meets the side of his battered face, forcing it to slam to the side. More blood splatters across my stone floors, and I'm pretty sure that's a tooth that just fell out. "Tell me which family sent you," I demand.

Impertinent silence greets my demand and has me stalking around him with my blade. How I long to fucking gut this piece of shit, from his miserable throat to his groin, and watch all of his guts spill across my floor. That way, I can strangle his worthless neck with them.

Someone bravely and stupidly sent him here to die on a mission to murder me. A mission that, *thank fuck*, we were able to intercept before he killed more than one of my men. The thought that he could have actually gotten to me, or worse, to Issy, makes my blood boil, and my vision only sees *red*. The only thing that can calm me now is to see all of his blood spilled, and send his severed fucking head back to who sent him.

"You will die here, make no mistake about that, *coño sucio*. The only question is how long it will take before you get to meet your maker, and how many pieces of you will be missing by then."

I slide forward and cut through the cartilage of this ear, as his screams rent the air around us. My men stand against the walls, watching and waiting for their own turns to rip pieces off this asshole who thought he could slip in under our defenses, and try to attack us. No, not just attack us, but murder me.

"You... cannot... escape your fate... forever... *serpent*. They... are coming," his words hiss out in a pained groan.

I grasp onto his other ear, ready and willing to give it the same treatment, but noise at the entrance to the den has my eyes tearing away from the man before me, and meeting a pair of terrified sapphire eyes, her loud gasp the only sound in the room. I watch as she takes in the scene before her. Blood splattered on the floor and walls, splashes of crimson along my carpets, desk, and priceless art. My cream linen shirt sticks to my chest, with rivulets of blood sliding down my neck and forearms. It's a gruesome scene, especially for a pampered princess to walk into.

The man's head tilts to the side, and a sinister chuckle leaves his busted lips. "She will... die too, but not before they make you watch... her scream for mercy."

I slam my clenched fist into the back of his head, making him slump forward, and his face hit the stone floor with a thud. My eyes remain on the vision before me as she trembles, her arms wrapping tightly around herself, as if she could ward off the evil in the room.

"Did you require something, *Princesa*?" I inquire nonchalantly, my voice even, as if I didn't have a man beaten almost to death and bleeding on my floor. *She has to get used to the sight if she will be your queen.*

Her mouth opens and closes, blue eyes so wide that I almost don't see any of the white. *Come on, Issy, show me what you're made of. Show me you can handle this life at my side.*

I know it's utterly unreasonable of me to want her to walk into a room filled with blood, and a half-dead man, and be able to get past what she sees. This is not the world that she was raised in, despite her grandmother being a bloodthirsty bitch. It is, unfortunately, the world she will have to become accustomed to, as my wife, and the mother of my children.

She seems to come to some of her senses, her head slightly shaking as if waking from a fog, and I watch with my breath held as she takes a step forward and another, her glare never wavering from mine, and her head held high. Her arms unlace from around her waist and instead become clenched hands at her side. *That's it, baby, show me the vicious feline asleep within you.*

"What is going on here, Diego? Who is this man?" Her upper lip curls with disgust as she appraises my appearance. *That's it, my broken doll, show me that fire you hide deep inside of yourself.*

"This doesn't concern you, Issy. If you don't require anything, get the fuck out," I growl through clenched teeth.

"Doesn't concern me?" She splutters with rage, a pink flush starting at her delectable neck, still marked with my fingerprints and rising to her cheeks. "I'm a goddamn *prisoner* here! Everything concerns me! Did this man come to save me? Is that why you are torturing him?"

She moves further into the room, her shrill voice bouncing off the stone walls, and her fear long forgotten. Her bare toes make contact with the blood splatter on the floor, and a momentary expression of disgust and horror crosses her features, but she doesn't step back. *She. Doesn't. Step. Back.*

"You are mistaken, my pretty doll. No one has come to save you. No one *will* come to save you, and do you know why that is, Issy?" I take a few steps forward towards her, my bloody fingers grabbing onto her chin and squeezing.

She doesn't answer, but I feel the slight tremble in her body, and the lump she swallows in her throat. I lean forward until my lips are pressed close to her ear. "They will never find you, Issy. You have disappeared from this earth unless I choose to change that."

Her hands wrap around my wrist, trying to pry my hold away as her nails dig into my flesh. Before I can say another word, a loud, gruff noise sounds from the man behind me. "You stole the Stratford princess?" His laughter gets louder before he chokes on the blood in his mouth. "You're as much of a dead man as I am, *puto*."

I watch the impact of his words on Issy's face; her eyes widen, and a haggard breath leaves her lips. I drop my grip and move away from her. This fucking guy is really getting on my last nerve, and my patience is at an end. If he isn't going to give me any answers, then his time is up, and he has a one-way ticket to meet the devil.

I move forward and grab a fistful of his hair, wrenching his head back, lifting him off the ground slightly, and then slamming him back down with a hard shove. The impact makes him fall to his ass. "Who sent you? This is your last chance to tell me before I cut you apart, piece by fucking piece." I motion to my men, and two of them move forward, one with a machete in his hands.

"Fuuucck you," he slurs, his body slumped in on itself. Anticipation for more bloodshed, and glee at the prospect of more violence fills me, and has adrenaline racing through my limbs.

"Take him to the yard, tie him to the tree, and start carving body parts off of him until he squeals like the pig he is. Make sure Raphael keeps him alive. We don't want him to die quickly."

"You will die, Diego Cabano! The devil is waiting for your black soul!" The man shouts.

My men nod, and each of them grabs onto one of the fucker's arms and drags him limply out of the open doorway that leads to the courtyard. My glare returns to Issy, who is looking paler by the second, my bloody fingerprints on her chin a harsh contrast against her porcelain skin. Her chest rises and falls rapidly, as she struggles to get enough air into her lungs.

"The rest of you get the fuck out," I shout with malice and aggravation. "I'm not in the mood for one of your hysterical tantrums, Issy," I warn her.

"*Tantrums?*" The word leaves her lips with fury, and in the next moment, she's launching herself at me, sliding across the streaks of blood on the floor and slapping me with her arms, hands, and knees, everywhere she can land a blow as she attempts to hurt me.

"You psychotic fucking *asshole!* I'll show you a fucking tantrum! You kidnapped me from my home and treat me like a fucking *whore!*" Her screams are so loud that they threaten to burst my eardrums. One of her hands manages to land a hit to my nose, which has tears stinging in my eyes. *FUCK THAT HURT!*

I try to restrain her, but it's like holding on to grains of sand. She keeps squirming and hitting me with everything she has, and I can't get a good grip on her without physically hurting her. After last night, I swore I would try not to do that anymore, but she's making it almost impossible with her banshee behavior.

"ISSY, FUCKING STOP! Stop before I hurt you!" I demand as I manage to restrain one of her wrists behind her back, but the little bitch headbutts me in my chin for my effort.

"HURT ME! ALL YOU DO IS HURT ME!" Her ragged scream fills the air and has my heart thumping painfully in my chest.

I grab a fistful of her hair at the back of her head and yank, causing tears to slide down her pretty face, and her movements to halt momentarily. FUCK, I don't want to hurt her anymore. "Issy, please, baby, calm down."

Tears continue to slide down her face, a river of diamonds making their way to her chin before disappearing. She goes limp in my restraining grip, falling to her knees before me in the pools of blood, and I release my hold. I drag both my hands down my face in an attempt to keep them from reaching for her, from wrapping around that slim column of her neck.

Fuck, yes, I much prefer her on her knees than trying to claw my eyes out. Her luscious, submissive mouth calls to me, begging me to plunder it and take what I want from her. To pull my hardening cock out and slam into the back of her throat, stopping her from breathing until I allow it. *MINE.* The thought slides across the possessive, animalistic part of my brain that wants to claim his mate.

The problem is that once I start, I can never seem to stop with Issy. One moment is never enough, and my body craves her like the very drugs that she was addicted to. She is my drug and my weakness, and my fear is that others are starting to realize that, too.

My show of force yesterday, to get her to realize her predicament, didn't seem to curb her need to scream and act like a little spoiled shit. This threat that happened on the same fucking night might be a coincidence, or maybe one of my men sent a message that I was weak. Do I have a traitor in my midst? How did this fucker get so close before one of my men spotted him?

"Diego, you have to let me go. If you ever cared for me, let me return to my family before it's too late."

CHAPTER EIGHTEEN

Issy

"She knew she shouldn't feel that way about a monster, but right then, she wanted nothing more than a monster of her very own."

Holly Black, The Coldest Girl in Coldtown

"Diego, you have to let me go. If you ever cared for me, let me return to my family before it's too late." Tears continue to slide down my face with my words. Words that feel like rough pieces of sandpaper scraping against the inside of my throat, threatening to choke me of my very breath, and leaving me bloody in their wake.

Why did I even bother to speak them? Just staring up at his stoic face, covered in another man's blood, I know that he will never let me go. It's not a matter of if he cared for me; he's unhinged, and there is no way that he could care about anyone. Everyone in his world is a tool to get what he wants, and I am no different.

His stunning green eyes narrow on mine, as if they can see right into my mind and know of my plans to leave him, one way or another. He will try to stop me, no matter which route I decide to take. He leans forward, his hot breath on my skin, and he drags his nose along the side of my neck, breathing me in, scenting me like animals do to each other. It's both a terrifying and exhilarating sensation, and my core tightens with need.

"No, Issy. The answer will always be no, and if you try to leave me, I will make what I did to that man, and you yesterday, seem like a walk in the fucking park or a Sunday dinner. Don't ever utter those words to me again."

Fear and rage combine inside of me, tightening my muscles as they wash over me. One urges me to try to run away from the madman in front of me, while the other dares me to fight him and let him end our lives. I have nothing left to lose either way, because I'm already dead inside.

I do neither, keeping my face as neutral as possible while drinking in his features. The face of a man I honestly believed at one point would be my future. One I could have loved, and spent the rest of my life with, if only things hadn't turned out the way that they have.

That's the crushing thing about fate; it never quite works out the way you planned, and sometimes it leads you down a dark, winding path to your own destruction.

He drags me up to my feet and out the door that leads to the courtyard, the very one that his men dragged the bleeding man through, and the minute we step outside, I see the tree. The one that just the night before bore witness to, and aided in, my own punishment.

"No, fuck, no." Panic starts deep within me.

I try to drag my feet and pull away from his relentless hold, but it's useless; his grip is too tight, and he's determined to get me there. What Diego wants, he seems to always get, regardless of the wishes of others.

"Release me, Diego." My voice sounds full of terror to my own ears, and my heart rate has skyrocketed in my chest.

The bleeding man has been hoisted up and strapped to the tree, his arms stretched across two branches as his back presses against the thick, gnarled tree trunk. It almost looks like a horrid crucifixion, one that has the scream that wants to escape my lips, trapping in my throat and choking me of all my air.

The sounds of his whimpers are loud in the otherwise quiet space. Men stand around watching, waiting for what will happen next, for the orders from their boss, a psychopath, who will dictate the punishment that needs to be met by this stranger who tried to kill him. *Kill or be killed;* that is the law of the jungle.

The predator consumes the prey in order to survive, and so Diego Cabano must do the same, to prove he is the strongest predator within these jungle walls.

A thrill of excitement mixes with the trepidation and fear inside of me, until it becomes all mixed up in a ball of overwhelming emotions, and brings with it nausea that threatens to have me purging the meager amounts of food that I consumed earlier.

Diego releases me when we are only a few feet away from the restrained man, and one of his men steps forward and passes him the machete, the sunlight glinting off the metallic, menacing blade. Saliva pools in my mouth as my head spins. *He can't do this. He can't be this barbaric, can he?*

"Who sent you?" Diego's voice is calm and steady, unlike my own racing heart, which is threatening to burst out of my chest, and run as fast away from this situation as possible.

The man whimpers in obvious pain but refuses to utter any words. I want to speak out and urge him just to give Diego the name, and save himself from the pain and torment that is about to happen to him, by his refusal to speak, but instead, I bite down on my bottom lip to restrain my own whimpers.

The blade arcs in the air as Diego swings forward, catching the man on his upper thighs and embedding the blade deeply into his flesh. The scream that leaves his lips is hoarse, and sounds more animalistic than human. Diego drags the machete away, and a gush of red taints the roots and bark of the tree below the man. There is so much red already, and we are nowhere near done. I feel the sour taste of bile rising up the back of my throat, but I force it back down.

"Who sent you to kill me?" Diego moves to the right of the man, his bright green eyes shining with a depraved light from within. The monster he keeps confined shines through their depths, and surfaces to play with its food.

He's terrifying and yet somehow beautiful like this, filled with rage and bloodlust. A general ready to enact battle, and protect himself and his men from their enemies. My stomach clenches as my hands become clammy. I realize I'm actually less horrified by him, and that I am incredibly attracted to him in his current form. The part of me that craves submission wants to prostrate at his feet.

"Fuuuck you..." The pained words barely leave the man's lips before Diego raises the machete again, this time slicing through part of the man's bare foot. The cut isn't clean, parts of flesh and muscle still lingering in its wake, as he yanks the blade back.

The smell of copper and iron overwhelms me, as does the stench of urine. The man has lost control of his body functions, even as he refuses to give Diego a name, refuses to save himself any more pain. I gag, no longer able to stop the burning bile from racing up my throat, and turn to the side, bracing my hands on my knees and emptying the contents of my stomach. The sounds of my retching are so loud, and it seems as if time stands still in this bloody garden.

"Come here, Issy." Diego beckons to me with his hand covered in the blood of his enemy. I use the back of my hand to swipe at my mouth and think about running, even as my legs tremble. He must see the look on my face, and be able to read my thoughts, because his head nods slowly, and a look of pure menace crosses his features.

"If you attempt to run, I will hunt you down, and you will take his place. Is that what you want, my broken doll? Hmm, do you want to be strapped to the tree again, or would you rather stand at my side?"

There is no real choice that he is offering me, and he knows it. I know that if I take the man's place, death would not come for me, only punishment. I step forward, my bare feet sinking into the tainted red dirt. A breeze passes over my skin, and the call of a bird overhead steals my attention away from the horrors I'm presented with, but only momentarily. All this beauty, and he chooses to taint it with death.

"Take the blade, Issy." He doesn't give me a choice, reaching forward for my hand and wrapping my fingers around the thick, solid wood handle tightly. My hands are slick with sweat, and the cooling blood just makes it worse. The minute he releases his grip, the blade almost slips from my grasp, and I have to use my other hand to help me continue to hold it.

Diego moves behind me, pressing his broad, muscled chest into my back until I can feel every inch of him firmly against every inch of me. Heat radiates off his form, and into my overheated flesh, as perspiration slides down my body. I'm trying desperately not to lose my mind, not to allow my body to cave in on itself, and have a massive panic attack. My blood rushes through my veins, the sound loud in my ears.

His breath lingers on my neck and blows against my hair. My body trembles in the over-warm embrace. His fingers wrap around my left wrist, and my right forearm, as he pushes me forward. One step and then another until we are closer to the man. *NO*, my mind screams, and I try to push against his hold. My feet sink into the ground, determined not to move another inch. I want to grow roots deep into the earth like the old tree, to stop him from forcing me forward.

"He would have raped you if he got his hands on you last night," his voice slithers across my skin. "He would have taken you back to his men and let them all rape you. Over and over, they would have taken their turns on you, Issy. You would have been a prisoner used to teach me a lesson, before they murdered you, and sent me and your grandmother your body parts."

He takes a deep breath, and his lips touch my temple in a soft caress. "That is, if they didn't make you bear their spawn first, or sell you to the highest bidder. They would have gotten a pretty penny for you, *Princesa*."

I shut my eyes, the images that he is painting causing further nausea and fear to churn in my gut. He's right, and I know it. This man would have hurt me, used me to teach the Cabanos a lesson, regardless of if I was an innocent pawn in this game between cartels.

The problem is that Diego has also done everything he spoke about to me. He, too, has abused me and shared me with his men. He, too, has taken me from my loved ones and held me hostage, and although I know my fate could have been even worse than it is now. I am nothing but a prized piece to be stolen, and used by anyone who is willing to take the risk.

The hypocrisy of his words are lost on him, but not on me. I recognize him for the manipulator and monster that he is. He would do anything to get what he wanted, and that has anger brimming through my limbs. When will he ever stop trying to use me to further his agenda? *Never, not while you have breath left in your body.*

His lips meet the shell of my ear, and his tongue licks around the delicate skin, causing shivers to race up and down my body. "You know I speak the truth, Issy." His teeth sink into my ear lobe, forcing a whimper to leave my lips. "They can't have you, my slut, you are mine. I will be the only person to fill your pretty pussy, and make this belly swell."

My lungs expand and contract at a rapid, terrifying rate that has my head spinning, and my vision threatening to blur. How, even now, can his words have me teetering off a cliff, willing myself to dive head-first into his depravity?

I can feel the pulsing in my core and wetness slipping out of me. It should fill me with disgust. Disgust at my own depravity and weakness where Diego is concerned, but it doesn't. Instead, it's as if lightning hits my body and fills me with bright, hot energy that courses through my veins. Rage, an all-consuming rage, envelops me and promises me sweet vengeance against the world that keeps playing with me like a toy.

Diego raises my arm and forces it to swing, until the end of the blade meets the side of the man's abdomen, and blood arcs and sprays my hands and arms with the impact. "Again, Issy! Show them all that you are not weak, that you will not lay down and die. That you are my queen waiting to take her fucking throne."

A buzzing penetrates my skull, drowning out the sounds of the man's pitiful cries, his barely-there voice no longer a concern of mine. When I stare at his mangled and bloody body, I no longer see him, nor do I hear Diego's voice urging me on. Instead, I see the man who abused my sister, and all the men who have used me in the past to get what they want, and would continue to use me. I see everyone who has made me feel weak and helpless, made me feel small, less than, and worthless.

I see my grandmother with her sad, disappointed eyes staring at me and my sister, who always feels the need to protect me. I see the coffins of my mother and father, who left me in this world as an orphan, alone and unloved. The images of every person who has ever hurt me race before my eyes.

My arms swing without my mind giving them direction, and the blade lands in the middle of the man's chest, slicing through fabric and skin until all I see is red. I swing again, this time landing a blow to the man's arm and severing it from its confined hold. The impact sends a jarring pain back up my forearms, but instead of causing me to drop the blade, it makes me tighten my grip further.

A sort of madness takes over me, and I swing again and again until my body is spent of energy, and my arms can no longer lift the blade. A wet sensation covers me, sliding down my face and neck, causing the fabric of the dress I wear to be plastered to my skin, and covering every inch of me. I use one of my hands to swipe away at my face, and it comes away drenched in blood.

I should be horrified at my actions, should be screaming at what I have done, what he has urged me to do, but something inside of me has cracked open, and instead of fear, for once in my life, I feel euphoria. I feel alive, and filled with something that I can't name, something that calls to me and urges me to not stop.

That thought brings me back to the reality of the moment, and I stare at the red mass in front of me, more bloody red meat than man. He's dead; his head hangs low, and his body is still. At some point, he must have died from all of his injuries, but the bloodlust I was under didn't stop me from continuing to slice him open.

I. Did. That. I killed him. It was me who took his life.

"Such a *good girl*, you are perfect, baby. Fucking perfect." Diego's voice penetrates the fog surrounding me as he pries the blade from my hand, and I hear it clank down to the ground.

The horror of what I've done tries to hit me, but instead of succumbing to it and falling on the floor in the fetal position, I push away from Diego and walk back toward the house. My limbs feel wobbly, and that buzzing sound is back, louder than before. My chest feels tight, as if it's constricting all the air inside of my lungs and trying to suffocate me.

I enter the den the same way I was forced to leave it, only this time, I am no longer Issy, but some creature that has taken a life. I am a murderer, regardless of if that man was sent to kill Diego or me, regardless of if he would have done unspeakable things to me, if he was able to get his hands on me. The proof of my villainous actions covers me, sliding along my skin, and sings to the madness that wants to take me in its grasp.

I killed someone. I, Isabella Stratford, am a *murderer*.

My eyes lift and meet my reflection in a mirror outside of the den, but the woman staring back at me doesn't look like me. She resembles a demon from hell, covered in blood. *Lilith* in her finest hour. Is that who I am? Is that who I was always meant to be? Perhaps my weak facade was just that, a facade hiding a monster just as sinister as that of Diego Cabano.

Perhaps that was why I was instantly attracted to him. *I am just like him.*

I stare at the reflection, and the corners of my lips rise unbidden back at me. The sight is so startling that I take a step back and then another, until my back comes up against a firm, warm surface, and I pry my eyes away from the creature in the mirror and meet two green orbs that stare back at me with nothing but insanity, pride, and lust.

In that very moment, I realize I'm unequivocally a monster just like he is, and I'm not even the slightest remorseful about it. Diego Cabano wanted to break, rebuild, and force me to be stronger. He may have just succeeded, but what I bet he didn't count on, was that I would turn into a monster that would rival his own.

CHAPTER NINETEEN

Diego

"When you spend so long trapped in darkness, Lucien, you find that the darkness begins to stare back."

Sarah J. Maas (A Court of Mist and Fury (A Court of Thorns and Roses, #2))

I stare at her reflection in the mirror, covered in my enemy's blood. The corner of her lips rises in a sinful smirk that has my balls tightening in my pants, and my cock rock hard instantly. She looks like a dream, a sinful, dark dream with an avenging angel sent down from heaven to wreak havoc on mankind. *Fuck, she doesn't even look real.*

My mind should be telling me to turn and run; self-preservation should be kicking in right the fuck now. I should be terrified at the look on her face, which promises nothing but dark deeds, and signifies that she has finally cracked, and splintered all her restraint and control. I've never been great at keeping myself out of harm's way, and fuck knows, I won't be starting now.

Issy has never looked more insane, beautiful, and sexy than she does at this moment. Her sapphire eyes shine through the red haze she's covered in, and in their depths, I see the same insatiable madness that lives inside of me. The one that has corrupted everything that was once pure within me and turned it dark, and now is doing the same to her.

I should be worried that I have broken her, that she has finally snapped and is tarnished beyond repair, but instead, all I feel is desire racing through my bloodstream. The desire to chase her and run her to the ground like a beast, force her to take my cock, and hear her scream my name is paramount. It's a live wire of electricity running through my veins, looking for an outlet. *Mine.*

My chest presses firmly into her small back, and a shiver races through her limbs, the slickness of her skin and the beating of her heart thunderous against my own. It's not enough. Being this close to her is not enough, and even if I crawled inside of her, it would never be enough.

I slide my hand forward and grip around her throat, the feeling of her pulse below my fingers a sensation that further increases the blood flow to my already painfully hard cock. *Thud, thud, thud,* what beautiful fucking music it makes. The sound of her finally alive. *My Issy, my whore, my whole world, mine.*

I release my grip, even though my desire is to tighten my fingers further, and feel her breath stall inside of her chest. I need more of her. I need everything she has, everything she will ever be, to be mine, *only mine.* I grab her arms and push her away from me, that feeling mounting inside of me until it threatens to tear me apart. My hands clench tightly into fists to prevent me from hoisting her over my shoulder, and taking her somewhere dark and confining, where I can keep her entirely at my mercy, chained to a fucking wall, and I can unleash all of my dark, depraved fantasies on her sinful body.

Her beautiful eyes, alight with bloodlust, life, and unleashed madness, continue to hold my stare in the reflection, and her pink tongue slips out and swipes at her bottom lip. The lip that is still covered in my enemy's blood. That snaps the last vestige of strength and restraint that I have left. "RUN, ISSY!"

She doesn't hesitate even for a moment, turning on her bare feet and sprinting away from me, as my chest heaves with the effort not to chase her. I am more wolf than man at the moment, and my prey is getting away. The sound of her feet slapping across the stone floors as she leaves me behind is a ragged tempo beating in my heart.

Chase, run her down, make her fucking cry, punish her; the thoughts swirl inside my head, with the sound from the '*Purge*' movie as their soundtrack. A feral growl leaves my lips, and I slam my fist into my wall, trying to control the raging emotions that are careening through me. I need to garner some control before I hurt her. *My prize, my queen, my dark angel.*

I see Santiago out of the corner of my eye, cautiously trying to approach me as if he knows that I am just moments away from snapping, and becoming more beast than man. I bare my teeth to him in a warning. In his eyes, I witness a morbid curiosity, but also fear. He doesn't know what to make of Issy's actions, of her violence, or my reaction to her. He doesn't understand that I have just shattered and rebuilt her, in an image that will rule by my side. *My dark queen, and I will be her serpent, filling her with venom and ensuring she never leaves my side.*

"Do not interfere, no matter what sounds you hear," are my parting words before I give chase to my broken doll. I tear through the main rooms, searching her out. Her bloody footsteps leave an easy trail to follow, that is, until it leads back outdoors, and I lose her in some of the thick fauna.

Fuck, yes! My *Princesa* wants to play, and I'm amped up and ready to chase her through the fucking jungle.

I move slowly through the thick bushes and fauna around us, the scent of earth, vegetation, and humid jungle air helping to clear my senses. The call of birds and wildlife above me makes it harder to determine where my beautiful prey has headed. The heat is already rising all around me, and sweat starts to bead on my hairline, further irritating me. The need to catch her and sink my teeth into her soft flesh is paramount. I want to ravish her, leave my marks all over her delectable body, covering her in my scent, and fill her with my cum until it drips out of her, so I can claim her as my own.

Isabella Stratford is more than a woman to me, and she is more than a prize to be stolen from her family and forced to my side. No, Isabella Stratford is an *obsession,* one that I never wish to be cured of. She is my heart, soul, and future, wrapped in a small, damaged package.

Up ahead, I hear branches stirring and dart in that direction, but emptiness greets me when I part the thick, green leaves. *Fuck, where is she?* As much as I love the chase and want to run her down, my cock is weeping and hard in the confinement of my pants, the desire to bury it inside of her making it difficult to concentrate on the chase. My body fills with unhinged primal desire, and the need to dominate.

"Where are you, *Princesa?*" I call out with humor, knowing full well she is not stupid enough to bother to answer me.

I keep moving forward, straining my ears to hear any sound that will help me determine where she is, and focusing my eyes to search for any hint of her. This jungle is wild and untamed past the limits of the compound. I'm not the only predator that she has to fear. That knowledge has another shot of adrenaline racing through my tense limbs. I need to find her and keep her safe from everything but me.

I push forward, and up ahead, something red flutters from a branch. I reach out and pull it from the broken limb, holding it in my fingers up to my face, only to realize it's a piece of her bloody dress. *Jackpot.* She came this way and can't be far now. Issy has no fundamental survival instincts or experience. She has never had to fight for her life. I'm counting on that making her sloppy and careless, and helping me to track my delicious prey.

Just as I'm turning around to pursue her further into the jungle foliage, something whacks me on the back of my head so hard that it has me falling forward to my knees, and seeing double. Before I can even shake off the double vision, something jumps on my back, limbs wrapping around my neck and pushing me further into the ground. My ears fill with the sounds of vicious snarls, even as a pair of strong, blood-streaked legs wrap around my waist from the back, and try to hold me down, squeezing me like a boa constrictor and taking what little breath I'm siphoning in.

What. The. Fuck.

A hand digs deeply and painfully into my hair, yanking on the strands, and pushes my face into the dirt. I try to use my strength to lift both of us back up, but the little psycho headbutts me hard on the back of my head, before sinking her teeth into the nape of my neck.

FUCK! The pain of her bite adds another level to this already out-of-control situation, and pushes me to a state of almost complete madness. *Primal mad-*

ness, where all I want is to fuck her hard until she's no longer breathing. *Control; try to get some control before you obliterate her. We don't want to hurt her.*

"You're going to pay for that, Issy. Every fucking mark you leave on me, I will make sure to double on your body," I grunt the words with a mouthful of dirt, my restraint hanging on by a tiny, insignificant thread.

"Promises, promises," she hisses in my ear and snaps her teeth, biting down on the cartilage of my ear like a rabid animal. *FUCK, she's really enjoying herself now!*

I get my knees out from under me and lift myself back up to my feet, struggling with the banshee who has wrapped herself around me, and is trying to maim me. Her ankles cross tightly around my waist even as her forearm digs into my throat, causing me to choke on the little air I have. Her teeth latch onto the side of my neck and bite down hard, eliciting a scream from my lips that sounds like an animal dying, and has all the birds in the nearby trees taking to the air for safety. I try to yank on her body, but like a feral monkey on my back, she refuses to relinquish her hold.

"Let... go... and I won't... fuck you... into a... coma."

I have zero intentions of complying with my own words, regardless of whether she releases me or not. She'll be lucky if she's still fucking breathing when I'm done with her.

Instead of listening to my fucking words and releasing me from her tight hold, the little unhinged psycho slams one of her fists into the side of my head, forcing me to stumble while trying to hold the both of us upright. *Fucking cunt, she's going to pay for that.*

"Stop telling me what to do, you kidnapping psychopath!" She screams, her breath hot on the side of my face.

I stumble back another step, almost tripping over the thick roots of a tree, and slam her into the trunk, the impact jarring both of us, and groans echo in the humid air. Her constraining hold releases as the air is knocked out of her. I turn my larger, heaving frame until I can get an arm up between our bodies, and I can grasp one of her soft breasts tightly. I squeeze hard until a murderous scream flees her lips. *There she is, my sexy little slut.*

Pressure builds within me, rising uncontrollably until I fear for both of our safety and sanity. The need to hurt her, to force her down to her knees, so that she can stare up at me with those large, midnight sky eyes overriding all my senses. I want her to worship at my altar, to prostrate herself before me, and reassure me that I am her God.

"Fuck, stop, Diego!" Tears slide down her blood-streaked face, as her nails dig into the back of my hand, trying desperately to release my hold.

I lean my shoulder into her chest, pushing her further into the tree and holding her up with my much larger body. Her feet don't even touch the ground as she dangles, suspended by my body and my will. "*Never.* I will never stop, Issy. You can fight me and try to run, *but, baby*, I will never let you go."

Chapter Twenty

Issy

"I would like to be the air that inhabits you for a moment only. I would like to be that unnoticed and that necessary."

Margaret Atwood

My breath catches in my throat as he continues to tighten his hold on my poor, abused breast. *Fucking savage!* My tearful eyes meet his, and I see nothing but madness in their deep, olive-toned depths, with gold specks shining in the filtered sunlight.

This is the true him, the monster that lurks leashed inside a cage that he tries to contain. The one he knows will destroy the world around him, if he doesn't control it with an iron restraint. The monster I can't tear my eyes away from, even though warning bells are ringing inside of my head. *Run. Run as fast as you can from the danger,* my mind warns, yet I stay rooted to the same spot.

My monster, my savage, my heart's fucking desire.

As much as it terrifies me that my actions have unleashed him, and that he's going to hurt me, because there is no doubt in my mind that he will now, it also brings with it an intense feeling of exhilaration. I want to chastise myself for pushing him beyond the point of no return, but the condescending, fearful bitch who lives inside of me is currently hiding. *Hiding from the sadistic monster before us.*

My throat constricts painfully with the scream that I'm trying desperately to swallow. I don't want to give him any more of my weakness, even though he has me cornered. I refuse to allow him any further free reign over me. I want to show him that I can, and will, take him on. That the weak, broken doll he loves to use as a whore, will fight him every, single, fucking chance she gets. *I will, won't I?*

My eyes trail over his rugged, angry features. His lips are pulled back in a bloodthirsty scowl, baring his perfect, straight, white teeth, even as it pulls on the flesh of his scar that some would say is an imperfection, a deformity to a stunning canvas.

To me, it just enhances his handsome face and shows me and the world his strength. That nothing and no one can ever take Diego Cabano down. He's looked death in the face countless times, and refused to cower or break. Not even the *Grim Reaper* can take his soul, if he even has one.

My heart thuds painfully in my chest, and the sound of my blood whooshing in my ears is so loud that all of the sounds of the jungle just seem to disappear. My lips part with snarky words at the ready, but I swallow them down like a lead balloon.

He means every single word he just said. He has no intention of ever letting me go, and no amount of pleading or violence will change that. No amount of bloodshed will stop him from keeping me as his prisoner, latched to his side for all of eternity. It should repulse me, the knowledge that he truly believes that he owns me, that I'm his. It should make me fight harder to get away from him. To run into the wild jungle, and take my chances with the beasts that inhabit it, and the elements, but instead, my pussy floods, and my core tightens painfully with desire.

Desire for a man who enjoys using and hurting me in sadistic ways, who will control all of my wants and needs. One who is determined to bring me to my knees with his particular and sinister brand of insanity, until I'm just as unbalanced as he is and utterly consumed and addicted to him.

His other hand trails up my stomach, then my sternum, until it reaches the base of my throat, where his fingers still. Moans breathlessly leave my lips, and the blood inside my veins races through my limbs, causing everything to tingle in its wake. Fight or flight is still engaged, and the rational part of my mind, the part that is not currently succumbing to lust, urges me to fight and flee.

On the other hand, danger calls to me like a sweet siren, urging me to take all he offers. She encourages me to let him have his way with me. Promising that the pain and ecstasy that he'll deliver will be worth everything that I've endured, even losing my mind for good.

Diego's eyes are laser-focused on mine, refusing to release me from their hold, as if he can read the thoughts going through my mind. He leans forward, his scent invading all of my senses, and trails the tip of his tongue along the edge of my jaw, the sensation causing goosebumps to rise on my blood-streaked skin.

"You're wet, aren't you, baby?" *Lick.* "You know that every inch of you is mine, don't you?" *Lick.* "You want to be my savage little whore, on your knees, willing and waiting to take my cock any time I want to fill you, don't you, Issy?" *Lick.*

I want to dispute his words, to argue that I belong to myself and that I'm not his whore, but I know that if I open my mouth, only more moans will escape me. My nipples pucker as the flat of his palm rubs against my sensitive tips under his brutal ministrations. *Fuck, fuck, fuck.* I need to stop this. I need to fight him off somehow, even though my body recoils at the mere suggestion.

"Open your mouth, Issy," his voice has gone husky with his demand as he treats me to a sinister smirk, one that has a shiver racing down my spine. When I don't comply quickly enough with his request, his fingers tighten painfully around my throat, constricting my airflow and causing a ragged gasp to leave my lips. "Open. Your. Fucking. Mouth."

His head leans forward, his lips pressing against my bottom lip as his teeth sink into the pillowy, soft flesh that still tastes like his enemy's blood. He bites down and pulls until my mouth is forced to open and widen for him, and a tear makes its way down the side of my face, the saltiness hitting both of our lips simultaneously. *Fuck.*

"Fuck, your tears taste delicious," he groans.

He gathers spit in his mouth, and before I can pull back or try to close my mouth again, he spits deep inside my mouth until his taste is mixed with mine at the back of my throat. "Swallow, *Princesa*." Satisfaction shines in his depraved eyes when I do, a growl vibrating from his throat.

Holy shit.

His fingers dig painfully into my throat, so much so that I know I will have a new hand necklace to accompany the one that he had already left, as he eyes me questioningly. I don't know why that thought has me strung tight, with heat flooding across all the planes of my skin as desire courses through me.

He releases his hold on my breast, and his hand makes its way to my face, caressing my cheek reverently, gently even, before slapping it. The sound is instantly swallowed by the jungle surrounding us. There are no birds, no wildlife, and not even the sound of the wind blowing through the thick canopy of trees. There is only *us*.

"So beautiful. So delicate and broken." I open my mouth to cry out, and he takes that opportunity to spit inside once again. It's crude, disrespectful, and repulsive, but it's also one of the hottest fucking things he has ever done to me.

His grip on my neck forces me down to my knees at his feet. The feeling of the rough dirt and the jungle floor digging into my bare flesh, as the ruined dress sticks to my body, is just another element that causes further longing to race through my bloodstream on overdrive.

Dirty fucking slut, the words slither through my mind, and rather than avoid them, I embrace them.

So what if I enjoy his brand of degradation, depravity, and insanity? That I savor his willingness to use me. That deep inside of me, inside those parts that I hide from the light, I want him to control my very breathing, and make me his puppet. Does that make me a whore? Does it make me his broken doll, as he claims?

At this point, I no longer care. Let me be whatever he wants me to be, just don't let this feeling, this need inside of me disappear. It fills the hollow, dark, and tundra-like parts deep within me. It gives me a purpose where there wasn't one, even if that purpose is just to be his plaything.

"Pull your dress off slowly. Show me what belongs to me."

His eyes darken with lust, the pupils blown and swallowing all the pretty green as his breathing picks up. His chest rises and falls and I'm mesmerized by its actions, by the fact that it's me having this reaction on him. His hands release their grip on my flesh, and instantly, my body craves them back. I feel bereft without the heat of his touch.

I slowly pull the hem of the dress up my thighs, taking the time to run the soiled fabric and my fingertips along my heated flesh, then higher towards my aching core, exposing my naked pussy to him with a mischievous quirk of my lips.

An anguished groan leaves his lips when he gets his first glimpse of my swollen flesh, which I can feel is glistening, waiting for his touch. The wetness coats my pussy lips and the sides of my thighs, warm and slick. He licks his lips, hunger evident on his face, and it gives me a spike of energy, makes me crave to push him further, to have him completely lose control.

I continue to move the bloody fabric past the planes of my stomach and over my ribs, teasing him with each inch that is revealed to his waiting eyes. His nostrils flare, a bull waiting to charge, and I can see his impatience and need flowing through his body's tightness. His shoulders flex, and his strong throat swallows, forcing his Adam's apple to bob. I want to bite it. I want to suck on it and leave my own marks.

I clench my thighs tightly, trying desperately to produce some friction for my needy clit, which throbs, waiting for attention. He catches the movement, and one side of his mouth rises in a knowing smirk as he raises one dark brow. *Fucker*. Of course, he knows how much I want him. Yet I'm not alone in my needs, and the huge twitching bulge in his pants tells me he's just as ready to ravish me as I am him.

I stroke my fingers just below the round globes of my breasts, teasing my flesh as I slowly raise the fabric further until my areolas are exposed to the warm air, and I hear his sharp intake of breath. Not wanting to miss even a moment of his reaction to my body, I rip the fabric over my head and discard it to the side. My breasts feel swollen and achy, needing to be touched. Both my nipples are stiff peaks, waiting for his fingers and his mouth.

"Pull on your nipples and roll them between your fingers. Show me how you like to touch yourself."

His voice is pure sin, growly, and incredibly hot. I can hear the tight leash he has on his control, allowing no room for negotiations, just demands, and I want to smash it. To see him wholly shattered, just like he does to me. I hanker for his actions to turn unpredictable, and to have him decimate and devour me whole.

I grab both of my nipples, pulling on the tips, rolling them between my thumbs and pointer fingers before squeezing them tightly, the bite of pain making further wetness flood my pussy. *Fuck, I want his mouth on me.* I want him to suck and bite down on my nipples, and make me scream like only he can.

"Spread your legs wider, baby, and show me that sweet, soaked cunt. Trail one of your fingers down between your slit and have a taste of yourself." I oblige and begin spreading my thighs wide, opening myself up to my touch but also so he can see me. I need him to watch and to crave me, just like I desire him. *Insatiably, demandingly, and overwhelmingly.*

I trail one of my fingers down my abdomen, across my hips, and let it skate over my throbbing clit. The sensation of the caress pulls a gasped cry from my lips as I use my middle finger to rub circles around my nub, making my legs tremble with how wide open I am. I'm so close already, and it won't take much to get me to orgasm. The race through the house and into the woods already had me primed; the rest has just been prolonging the rush.

I slip my finger down between my pussy lips until I reach my entrance, rimming it over and over, but not slipping it inside, delaying the gratification and increasing the torture. His hand makes its way to the top of my head, his fingers digging into my strands and pulling on my dark tresses, until pain lances across my scalp.

"Slip your fingers inside of your tight hole, fuck yourself slowly for me, and let me see how you stretch yourself. I want to see how many your pussy can take until it's full. Show me how your cunt swallows them, my slut."

My eyelids flutter as heat surges up the back of my neck, and I slip the first finger deep inside of me, a second one following with a moan. I slowly fuck myself with small, even thrusts that have tiny shockwaves soaring through my core.

"More, baby, stretch that pretty pussy for me," his words sound almost hummed to my ears. *Fuck, he's enjoying this.*

I slip a third finger inside of my needy core as it clenches down, and a gasp is pulled from my lips. Fuck, it's already tight as I bear down and pick up speed with my thrusts, riding my hand, bringing myself close to the pinnacle of the mountain I want to throw myself off of.

"You can take another, Issy. Fill that cunt up for me, and let me see your gap stretch. Show me what a slut you are."

I try to regain some of my composure, even though my body is soaring out of control with lust and the need to cum. I slip the fourth finger inside of me, the stretch almost too much to bear, and a mewling sound releases from my mouth. Diego's hold on my hair gentles briefly, before he's once again yanking on my strands. *Fuck, fuck, fuck! I need to cum. I need it more than I need air right now.*

"That's it, baby, fuck your fingers, ride them like you do my cock, nice and deep, my dirty whore."

The pull of his command has me speeding up and losing complete control. I can feel and hear the wetness of my pussy as it soaks my fingers, and slides down my palm all the way to my wrist. Fuck, I am so wet and so close, so very close to exploding. I use my thumb to stroke over my clit, causing electricity to race through my limbs, and then to tense painfully as the orgasm starts to race through me. *Yes, fuck yes!*

Just as I am about to let go and reach my peak, his fingers tighten around my wrist, yanking it away and pulling my digits from inside of me forcefully. Denying me the chance to cum as I release a scream.

"NOOOOOOOO!!!"

"Yes! I never gave you permission to cum, my little whore. So needy, so desperate to explode on your own fingers." His voice is laced with authority, as if he and he alone has agency over my body and when I cum.

"Please... please," I beg with desperation, like the slut that I am, the needy ache growing inside of me.

My eyes rise to his, and I take notice of his clenched jaw and his rapid breathing, as his tongue dips out of his mouth. "Slip them inside again, fuck yourself with them, but don't cum. If you do, Issy, I will punish you."

I clench my molars to stop the objections and swear words that want to leave my mouth. The desire to tell him to go fuck himself is rising within me, and so is the need to be a disobedient little brat, and fuck myself all the way to completion. I don't fear his punishments anymore, even though I probably should.

He must see the defiance on my face because he bends down, his face coming to eye level with mine. "If you disobey me, I will tie you to a fucking tree, and whip both your ass and pussy with my belt, before I fuck this pretty cunt over and over again, but never let you cum. Don't test me, *Princesa.*"

I go to slip my fingers back inside of myself, but his grip on my wrist doesn't release. Instead, he forces my hand up to my lips, my wet fingers sliding over my mouth and chin, making a fucking mess of me and covering me in my own arousal. "Tongue out, lick your fingers clean."

I don't even hesitate; my tongue slips out, and I lick across my fingers like a fucking cat, consuming some yummy cream. My flavor hits my tastebuds, sweet and musky at the same time, eliciting a moan from my lips as I continue to clean each digit off.

"Fuck, Issy," a rumbled growl leaves his lips, "look at how fucking sexy you are." His lips slide forward, his mouth a mere inch or two away from my own, when his tongue slides out and licks my lips, then my chin, cleaning me off as he swallows my taste down. "So fucking good, baby, you have the best-tasting pussy ever made."

I slip my fingers back inside of myself, my eyes never leaving his as I race to reignite the spark that had me almost cumming. I try to reach that spot deep inside of myself that has my eyes crossing, while strumming my swollen clit, and my eyes almost roll to the back of my head. *Jesus, fuck.* The electricity races once again through my body and up my spine, making my mouth go dry.

"That's it, my slut, look at how well you're filling that sweet pussy." His words are almost my undoing, almost push me over the edge, and at the last second,

I yank my fingers away, but it's too late; a gush pours out of me as my core contracts, and a primal scream leaves my lips. I couldn't stop the orgasm from cresting, and now my body has fallen off the mountain, head first. My body shakes and shivers with the aftershocks of one of the best orgasms I have ever given myself.

"Oh, Issy, you naughty little whore," he says with a lamenting sigh, even though I know he enjoyed watching me cum. His breath is labored as he struggles to keep himself in control.

"Now, I have to punish you, baby, but that's what you wanted all along, isn't it? You get off on my brand of depravity. You enjoy it when I use your cunt for my own needs."

I don't bother to reply, because we both know he's speaking the truth. My whole body is spent, warm lethargy setting in, and the desire to move, never mind speak, is escaping me. A frightening smirk lifts his lips, and I know that I am in big fucking trouble as he releases my hair and starts to remove his clothing, pulling his belt from around his waist and folding it in one of his hands. I watch as golden skin is exposed one delectable inch at a time until all of his muscles and scars are on display for my viewing pleasure.

Fuck, this is going to hurt.

CHAPTER TWENTY-ONE

Diego

"To burn with desire and keep quiet about it is the greatest punishment we can bring on ourselves."

Federico Garcia Lorca, Blood Wedding and Yerma

The naughty little minx defied me, despite knowing that I would, in fact, punish her. It looks like my broken doll enjoys being a fucking brat, and getting a rise out of me. Watching her cum all over her fingers, after forcing her to delay her gratification, and then watching her lick her cream off of those same fingers, almost did me in. I almost caved and unleashed my cock, and shoved it down her pretty, tight throat.

My cock is so painfully hard right now, with pearls of precum dripping down the sides of my length. I use the hand not grasping my belt, to stroke myself from root to tip as Issy watches. Her eyes are intense on the motion as she bites down on her lip. She looks so innocent, a porcelain doll with those massive blue eyes, and pouty red lips. All that pretty skin just waiting for my fingers and mouth to leave their brands.

The taste of her pussy is still flooding my senses, but it's not enough to have cleaned it off her mouth and chin. I want it directly from the source. The desire to bury my face in her cunt and have her ride it, is all my mind can think of, well, that and fucking her throat. I need her over me, under me, and spread wide so that I can fuck and use all her holes.

I raise the black leather belt clenched in my fist, and watch as fear washes over her features. She has seen what I'm capable of. She knows that I'm a murderer, unforgiving, and a monster. Does she fear for her own life at the moment? I slap the belt down on my own large, muscled thigh to test the sting. The sound of the leather hitting flesh is loud in the air around us. Her whole body flinches as she tries to move away from me, but a vicious grin splits my mouth. *She won't be getting away from me now.*

"I wouldn't attempt to run, baby, or it will make it so much worse. You decided to act like a brat after I explained the consequences, and it's time to pay up."

"Diego... please." I release my cock and grab onto her face, spreading my precum into her skin and squeezing her chin, until she swallows the remainder of her words.

"*Shhh*, Issy, the time for words is over."

My cock bobs up and down against my stomach, leaving precum in its wake as my balls feel heavy and achy with the need to cum down her pretty throat. Before this day is done, I will fill all of Issy's holes with my cum, making her drip, so that she knows who she truly belongs to.

My hand with the belt strikes out, catching her on the top of her asscheeks, and the cry that leaves her lips has a tremble racing down my spine.

"DIEGO! FUCK!"

Fuck, that sound is beautiful, I desperately need to hear it again. I lift the belt again and strike her with it. This time, she's prepared and tenses, as she tries to swallow the sound. *No, I can't have that. I own all her screams, and my ears desperately want to hear them.*

My control is starting to frazzle, and the need to hear her screams, to be inside of her, is becoming visceral. Yet the knowledge that I don't want to damage her, at least not permanently, sounds like an alarm inside my brain. *Calm down, calm the fuck down, you'll hurt her, calm down.*

My eyes trail over the area around us, looking for a way to not only restrain her, but so that I can continue her punishment without killing her in the process. I spot a large flat rock jutting out from an area of soft leaves that will make do for what I have in mind.

My hand on her face squeezes her skin once again, forcing her lips to pucker, and a red blush to race along her cheeks and neck. "Get down on your hands and knees, baby."

Her eyes go wide with my words, and she tries to pull away from my grasp. I don't wait for her to comply, grabbing the length of the belt and wrapping it around her neck like a leash. She struggles and tries to yank it off, panic filling all of her limbs, but I thread it through the buckle and pull her off her knees, until she's forced to brace with her hands or smash her pretty face.

"Diiieeegggooo," she wheezes.

"Crawl, *Princesa*. If you want to act like a little disobedient bitch, I'll treat you like one. Crawl to me, baby, and I might take mercy on you and let you cum again, before I'm done filling all your holes."

Her sapphire eyes meet mine, and they're filled with murderous fury. She's forced to crawl forward as I pull on the belt and lead her towards the rock. "Such a *good girl*," I praise her, even as she looks ready to rip my fucking eyes out. *Fuck, I love it when she's angry.*

Once we reach the rock, I tug on the belt and force her back to her knees. Her chest is heaving with labored breaths, the leather biting into her neck, and sweat beads at her hairline as her matted dark tresses slide across her porcelain flesh. *What a beautiful, broken doll she is.*

"Move forward and bend over that flat rock, place your hands behind your back, and spread your legs wide for me, baby." I wait with bated breath to see if she will comply with my order, or if I will have to punish her for disobeying me.

She hesitates, her mouth opening and closing as if she wants to object to my command, but the look I give her must have her realizing that I won't waver, and neither am I feeling merciful. She will receive her punishment, but if she fights me, and I fucking hope that she does, she'll receive double.

She stumbles awkwardly over the rock, looking hesitant and unsure as she places her upper body against its flat, gritty surface. She turns her head so that she can watch me over her shoulder, as I loosen and remove the belt from around her throat. Her breath hitches, as I trail my fingers down the length of the smooth column and stop at her pulse, caressing the point with my thumb before removing it.

"Hands, Issy, now," I demand, and she uses jerky motions as she moves both her arms behind her arching back, where I use the leather to bind them together tightly.

Once I have her confined, I press my palm into the flat of her back, letting it skim over her warm flesh until I reach the top of her ass. My hand strokes the red marks, already swelling from the belt, and she flinches.

I think I hear her mumble the word '*asshole*' under her breath which has a giant smile sliding across my face. My fingers continue their exploration, sliding down her right asscheek, rubbing and caressing until I squeeze the perfect round globe tight, and then release it.

Fucking delicious... I just want to take a bite out of her. I repeat the motion with her other cheek, even as her lower body sways on her knees, pressing firmly against the side of the rock surface. *So responsive, my doll.*

My hand rises and falls with a slap against her right cheek, quickly following with a slap to the left, before I caress the sting away. "You've been naughty, *Princesa*. I think it's time you learned how to behave, don't you?"

My hand rises and falls with four more slaps, two for each of her asscheeks, until they are both bright red, and she's crying out and panting harshly against the rock. My cock throbs, and I know I need to get some relief if I'm to continue with her punishment, otherwise, I will be cumming like a schoolboy in front of her, and we can't have that.

I move around to the other side of the rock, stepping through leaves until her mouth is lined up with my cock. "Open your mouth, and relax your throat."

I thread my fingers through her hair, using it to raise her head until her neck is arched, and she's ready to receive my dick. She does as requested, a crystal tear sliding down from her right eye, and trailing southbound on her cheek to disappear off of her jaw. Her tears won't move me to stop her punishment, rather, they help to excite me. *She's so pretty when she cries.*

I slip the crown of my cock between her warm lips, and her tongue immediately lashes at it the way she knows I enjoy. I pause for a moment, allowing her to lick, suck, and clean the precum off my mushroom tip, before pushing further into the warm heat of her mouth.

Fuck, yes, so good. I keep going, not rushing, but also not allowing her the time to acclimate to my size. Warm saliva coats my cock, and slips from the corner of her lips as she starts to choke. I hit the back of her throat, pushing my way in until she gags, the sound pure seductive music to my ears.

I pull back, allowing her a chance to get a quick breath in, before I start a punishing rhythm of thrusting into the back of her throat, while I hold her head immobile by my grip on her hair. She's mine to use now, and I can't wait to get to her two other holes.

"That's it, baby, swallow me down. Choke on my cock, be a *good girl.*" My hips jerk back and forth, each time forcing my cock back down the snug confinement of her throat, as a growl leaves my mouth. "You're doing so well, Issy."

A shudder races through me as her tight throat constricts around my cock, causing fireworks to race up my spine and explode along the length of my body. She hollows her cheeks, using her tongue to suck and caress my length, as I fuck her face and use her for my perverse gratification.

"God, yes, baby, your mouth is perfection. Your throat feels so tight around my cock. What a *good girl* you are swallowing me whole."

I push forward until her nose is pressed against my pelvis, and I know she can't get any air in. Her body tries to lift off the rock, to fight my hold on her hair, but I shove her back down, forcing her to take all of me as my orgasm races across my length, and I start to cum down her throat. She gags and chokes, the sounds ragged and vicious as I continue to pour into her, until her body starts to sag with the need for air.

I pull back until only my tip is still inside of her pouty, red lips, and strings of saliva and cum decorate her mouth and slip down her chin. *What a messy girl she is. So perfect, so mine.* "Breathe, baby, don't waste a drop. Swallow and show me your mouth."

She pants hard, trying with desperation to catch her breath even as more tears slide down her face, mixing with the snot, cum, and saliva. She opens her trembling lips and pushes out her tongue, showing me her empty mouth. "*Good girl, my perfect slut,*" I praise her, as I release my harsh hold on her hair and stroke her face.

I move away from her, my cock still rock hard as I make my way back around her body. The tips of my fingers slide across her slick skin, as rays of sunlight beam down on her, making her pale skin seem to glow. *Beautiful, she looks otherworldly in this light.*

I slide my fingers between her reddened asscheeks as she clenches them and moans, and it has a chuckle leaving my lips. My fingers find her puckered hole, and I stroke them across it before reaching her tight hole. She's fucking drenched, my naughty girl.

I slip my pointer finger inside of her shallowly, not allowing her to get off but coating it, before withdrawing it and sliding it through her swollen folds, until I reach her needy clit. I run the tip of my finger in a circular motion, stroking her nub until her lower body pulses and moves against the rock's side. I don't even know if she realizes the mewling sounds that she's making with pleasure.

I slip my middle and ring finger inside of her cunt, thrusting as deep as they can go while continuing my ministrations of her clit. I feel her pussy clench down on my digits, signaling that she's not far from cumming again, but I have no intention of allowing that to happen.

No, my girl will get her full punishment, while I get off on filling her up until she's bursting at the seams. I pull my fingers from inside of her, and the sound that leaves her mouth is filled with anguish, frustration, and anger. My lips break into a huge grin at her expense. *Too bad, baby, you should have listened.*

I grab onto my cock, stroking it from root to tip, coating it in her wetness before slipping it between her drenched folds until I nudge her clit, rubbing it back through her soaked folds until my tip is at the entrance of her tight hole. "Beg me, *Princesa*. Beg me to let you come undone."

"Fuck you," she hisses the words, defiance in every syllable. It's too bad I didn't have a ball gag shipped with the rest of the items I had brought to the jungle. I have a feeling I will need one of those, and a few paddles to deal with Issy and her bratty ways in the long term.

I slam forward, pushing her body roughly into the rock and bottoming out in one go, and I'm hitting the end of her. I'm not a small man, and I know my cock is stretching her, filling her up until there is no more room inside of her. Her protesting cries do nothing except spur me on to thrust inside of her, taking her roughly, until the sounds of skin slapping skin are all around us.

Her body squeezes my cock like a tight vise, trying to hold on to me. I start a brutal rhythm, thrusting inside of her over and over, as the sounds of her weeping, mixed with pleasure, reach my ears. My grip on her hips is punishing, as I use her body's momentum to slam her back into me with every forward thrust.

"Too much, too much... please," she gasps as she starts to fall apart at the seams, and has me giving her everything I have, until I start to feel her pussy spasm against my cock. I quickly withdraw from inside of her tight heat before she can come, an outraged scream accompanying my departure. "MOTHER-FUCKER!"

"Watch your mouth, my slut, or I will take away your ability to speak."

My cock throbs with the need to come again, coated in her slickness, as I once again move around the rock and in front of her face.

"Lick. Lick yourself off of me, Issy." I slide my cock across her cheek, chin, and lips, coating her face in her own juices. I grab onto the base of my dick and slap her mouth over and over, with amusement, as her eyes rage at me from behind dark lashes.

Her tongue slides out and curls around my crown, as a moan escapes her lips when her taste hits her. She greedily sucks, licks, and slurps my cock, licking all of herself off my aching length, and all the while, her body sways against the rock, seeking friction to abate the need inside of her. She's desperate to cum, and I can see it in every tense line of her body, in the dark pools of midnight blue in her eyes.

I pull out from her mouth with a plop, move around her once more, and without giving her even a moment to adjust, I slide back inside of her waiting cunt and start a punishing race toward my own completion. My fingers spread her asscheeks apart, giving me the perfect view of her puckered hole, and I gather spit in my mouth and let it fall over it. I use my finger to push the spit inside of her clenching, puckered anus, using slow, methodical circles until the digit slips inside, followed by another one. I scissor my fingers inside her back hole, stretching her, as hunger looms inside of me.

"Diego... please... please," she moans.

Fuck, I need inside of her here. I need to mark every part of her, so she finally understands that she belongs to me.

She starts tightening even as my name becomes a mantra on her lips. "Diego, fuck, fuck, fuck, Diego." The sound of her fervent prayers has my eyes wanting to roll to the back of my head, and sends bolts of pleasure down my spine.

"That's it, baby, cry for me. Let the jungle hear who you belong to, who your master is." Surge after surge of pleasure is racing through my body, a spiraling vortex of sensations, every nerve ending alive with sparks of electricity. I'm going to cum and fill her tight pussy until she's overflowing, but before I do, I need a taste of her ass.

I pull out, my heart hammering in my chest as beads of sweat slide down my body, and the rush of adrenaline has me trying to catch my breath. "Fuccccck-kkk, noooo, please, please, Diego," she dissolves into tears, and begs so prettily that it almost has me giving in, and letting her have her release. Her forehead meets the flatness of the rock as her whole body trembles against me. Jesus, that was fucking close; I could feel my orgasm about to slam into me like a tidal wave, and my cum about to shoot out of my tip.

"Are you mine, Issy? Tell me who you belong to, baby." I push the head of my cock between the seam of her asscheeks, as I use my harsh grip to spread them wide. My cock nudges her back hole, even as she tries to angle her body away from me, pushing against the rock and no doubt hurting herself. That's the thing about my Issy, though; she enjoys a little pain with her pleasure, so I have no doubt it's helping to arouse her further.

My tip pushes through the narrow ring of muscle even as she screams like an injured animal. "Oh, fuck, fuck, fuck. You're so tight, baby, that's it, keep gripping my cock, strangle me. Be a *good slut* and give me more."

I push forward, breaching her hole and bottoming out inside of her. I try to give her the briefest of moments to adjust to my intrusion, but it's short-lived as my balls tighten painfully, and the shiver of electricity warns me I'm so close to cumming again. *Breathe, motherfucker,* I remind myself, the tightness of her ass making me forget my own need for oxygen.

Her body thrashes underneath me as I fuck her ass in long strokes, my fingers digging into her hip and asscheek so roughly, that I know she'll have bruises all over her tomorrow. *Fuck, I can't wait to see them decorate her skin.*

I can't hold on any longer; the need to explode inside of her is overwhelming my senses. My body strains, trying to get as close to her as possible, to pull her to me so every part of me touches a part of her. I slide my hand underneath her body, using it to cradle her away from the rock so I can deepen my angle, as my chest presses against her back. My face meets her neck and I inhale her delicious scent, my teeth biting down on the soft spot where her neck and shoulder meet.

"FUCK, baby! So fucking good. You're perfect, my perfect slut." The orgasm explodes over me as she clenches down hard on my dick, milking me of my cum and even trying to steal my damn soul. Her body continues to attempt to thrash in my hold, as ribbons of my cum paint the inside of her clenching ass. *Fuck, so warm, so tight.*

My body slumps against hers even as her small body trembles against mine. Her clenching ass squeezes me over and over again, causing some aftershocks to race up my length. *Fuck, she will be the death of me.*

My thighs are coated in her wetness as they press firmly against her, and with a groan, I lift my heavy body off of her petite frame, my cock objecting to being parted from one of its favorite places, even though it's now spent. A grin splits across my face as I take in the perfect imprint of my teeth on the base of her neck.

She is indubitably going to lose her fucking mind, and try to maim me, when she gets a look at all the marks I have left on her body. *It will still be worth it.* I pull out of her tight ass with a groan, and a whimper escapes her lips. My cum slides out of her puckered hole, and I use my fingers to push it back inside.

Fuck, I should have filled her pussy with my cum, to make sure if she's not already pregnant with my baby, she soon will me. Her body is still wired tight and filled with tension, letting me know she didn't cum but is close. I slide my cum coated fingers inside of her pussy and fuck her hard and fast, rubbing against the spot inside of her that I know makes her see stars. "*Good girl,* baby. Cum for me."

Her pussy immediately clenches down, and within seconds, her body is spasming and cumming. Her pussy floods, and her release gushes around my fingers, her internal muscles holding them hostage. "FUCK, FUCK, DIEGO!" She calls out, and it's music to my ears.

CHAPTER TWENTY-TWO

Diego

"Love is giving someone the power to destroy you... but trusting them not to."

Paulo Coelho

I pull my fingers away from her needy cunt, slipping them inside my mouth and licking off her taste. *So fucking delicious. She always tastes like the finest nectar, and it's even better when I can taste the combination of me and her together.* She's an addiction I can't do without. Her whole body slumps against the rock, completely zapped of energy now that I have allowed her to reach her orgasm.

This right here is paradise; being with her, in her, around her, and consuming her, is what I dream of when I close my eyes. It's better than winning the lottery or being at the top of the food chain. If I could stay alone with her forever, I would, and wouldn't even miss the rest of humanity.

I pull away from her, taking my heavy weight entirely off of her, and pushing her hair back from her sweaty face to see her lips are parted, her eyes are closed, and she's passed out. A chuckle leaves my lips before I can stop it; I blissed her the fuck out. That orgasm must have torn right through her.

My eyes trail every line of her face, neck, and body, that is still streaked with my enemy's blood. My own marks on her skin add to the mess that she is. Fuck, she's a beautiful disaster, one meant to destroy everything I know, and bring me to my knees. She is mine; she was made for me, and I will never let her go. How could I? It would mean the death of me. I can no longer live without her.

A nagging begins at the back of my mind that she is probably exhausted. Her time here has been anything but restful, between being in the hole for days and then going through days of painful withdrawal. Not to mention the trauma of helping me kill a man. I should have been gentler with her. *Fuck, why am I such a fucking monster?*

My hands shake as I loosen and remove the belt, releasing her strained arms, and rubbing her wrists and forearms to get the blood flowing again. A small moan slips from her lips, but her eyes remain shut and her body unmoving; she's utterly spent. I slowly and carefully turn her body over in my arms, cradling her abused flesh from rubbing further against the rock.

Fuck, her upper thighs and lower stomach are scraped, from rubbing against the edge of the rock, tiny red dots of blood appear on their surface, and the rock below her is streaked with red. I fucking hurt her, again. Even though I know she enjoys the pain, a lump of self-loathing rises inside of me, at the way my depravity takes over when she is near. I can never seem to control myself when it comes to Issy, going from one extreme to the other, like fucking kidnapping her and hiding her in the damn Amazon jungle.

Jesus, what the fuck is happening to me? Who is this man that I am morphing into? I lean forward, allowing my lips to caress her soft skin and leave kisses along its surface, in an attempt to make it up to her.

I rise with her in my arms, cradling the diminutive bundle of perfection close to my chest. My nose rubs against the top of her head, inhaling her rich scent. Fuck, how can one small, fragile creature have become so important to me? How could this woman who comes from a completely different world, a world I loathe, become my everything?

Do I love her, or is this merely an infatuation, an obsession that knows no limits? I look at her beautiful face at rest, tracing all the small details, like the seven freckles on her nose, the small mole on the side of her right eye, and the dark, thick lashes that skim her high cheekbones. How one of her eyebrows has a small scar just at the very end of it, and how her upper lip is shaped like a perfect cupid's bow.

She is perfection, and everything about her speaks to me and calls to the deepest part of me. Her name is written across my very jaded and weary soul. The one who has seen everything he has ever loved destroyed and taken from him. I can't let that happen to her. I can't lose her too. *You may be the very thing that destroys her.*

I know the truth, even as my heart hammers painfully against my chest. This is not just about infatuation or obsession. No, it goes past that. This dark-haired beauty, with all her issues, complexities, and even her snobbish privilege, has stolen my heart. I'm in love with Isabella Stratford, and have been from that first moment my eyes met hers back in Casbury, and she took my breath away.

Fate, opportunity, and circumstances brought us together, but my strong will and love for her will keep us from being parted. She thinks she wants to escape back to the world she came from. Wants to run from what we have because it scares her.

The truth is, she was never truly herself in that world. She was a shadow of what she could be. The dark, crushing weight of the Stratford title held her down, and made her believe she was not worthy of the name. Not equal to her sister or grandmother, just because she's not a bloodthirsty bitch, like they are.

Nothing could be further from the truth. There has always been a dormant strength inside of Issy, one that called to me and begged me to help coax it out of her. To save her from herself and the feelings of inadequacies that haunt her. That is why I'm so determined to break her from the shackles she has surrounded herself with. Fracture the constraints she puts on herself, and the weakness that bleeds the life out of her. I want her to be strong, for me and for her. I want her to never doubt that she is a powerful entity. Her actions back at the compound, when she helped destroy one of my enemies who sought to end my life, prove it.

My eyes scan the jungle around us, trying to determine how far we made it from the compound. I should be on high alert out here. This was reckless chasing her into the thick jungle while men seek to end my life. I should take her back immediately and place her under lock and key, but hesitation fills me. I want to enjoy basking in her beauty and softness a little longer. I don't want our connection to immediately fade, with the reminder that she is my prisoner, and bringing her back to the compound will only ensure that.

As I scan our surroundings, I recognize a part of the scenery up ahead through the thick trees from when we first arrived, and I explored with my men to determine our defenses. I'm pretty sure that way leads to a pool of fresh water, and a small waterfall. We haven't made it that far from the compound after all.

Excitement rises within me at the thought of showing her that little slice of paradise, and I begin moving in that direction. As leaves and branches brush against me, I'm reminded that we are both naked, and I didn't bring any fucking weapons out here with me when I chased her.

It's just one more example of how she turns my head upside down. It's careless of me, and could have deadly consequences. I'm not only being hunted by other cartels who want to end the Cabano's bloodline and power. I'm also being sought out by her psycho grandmother, and the mercenaries she hired to end my life. Enemies in every direction surround me now. If that wasn't enough, there are always the beasts who call this jungle home that would enjoy making a meal out of me and my *Princesa*.

Does any of that dissuade me and force my feet in the other direction as common fucking sense demands? Do I head back to the compound where my men are armed to the teeth and can protect us? No, I fucking don't, because I want to show the woman I love, a waterfall. *God fucking save us from my stupidity.*

As we make it another few feet through the thick fauna, with me cradling an unconscious Issy tight against my chest, protecting her from the branches digging into my flesh, the trees finally give way, and the beautiful crystal water pool opens up before my eyes. The canopy of trees is a little thicker here, with only filtered sunlight making it through and illuminating the waterfall, the crystal blue-green pool of the water, and the fragrant flowers all around us.

The first time I saw it, I knew this place was special. It has an otherworldly feel, as if you're cocooned from the rest of the world, and nothing can touch you here.

Thick green vines hang down from different trees, giving it a curtained effect. The small waterfall has clean, fresh water cascading down its various ledges, and filling the pool below it. The smell of earth, mixed with the fragrance of fresh water and vegetation, fills my senses. The sounds are magical, with the water rushing against the stones, birds calling from overhead, and the sounds of nature going about its business, unaffected by the two humans invading its space.

I move closer to the pool of water, my skin itching with sweat from the harsh heat and humidity, and my strenuous workout on Issy's body. It craves the cool, refreshing reprieve from the liquid before me. I walk right into the pool, still cradling a sleeping Issy in my arms, and I keep going until the water rises past my waist, and is lapping at our skin. A moan leaves her lips as her eyelashes flutter with the contact, and a satisfied sound escapes her mouth.

Her eyes finally open, and I am treated to her stunning blue irises, as they fill with confusion and panic. Her body tenses in my hold as one of her arms reaches up and snakes around my neck, and the other rises to cradle my face. I lean my head down and brush my lips across hers in a barely there kiss. "Welcome back, *Princesa*."

"Where... where are we, Diego?" Her head moves around as much as my hard chest will allow, as she tries to take in the sights around us. I watch her eyes grow large on her face as she takes in the thick trees and the waterfall. A hint of excitement and color rises on her face. "It's so beautiful!" She exclaims with a gasp.

"Yes, it is, but... I have seen more beautiful things in my life," I reply while never taking my eyes off of her, and a pink blush races across her cheeks and down her neck.

I keep moving further into the deep pool until the water has covered both of us, and reaches our chests, cooling down our overheated bodies and giving our muscles a much-needed refresher. Still, I don't release her, relishing the feeling of having her body in my arms, holding her tight to my heart, a place she has invaded and all but taken charge of.

"I found it a few weeks back, when I was scouting and assessing for danger with the men. I knew that you would love it here. It's hidden and peaceful, and it looks like a spot right out of one of those fantasy romance novels that you like to read."

Her eyes widen, and the blush on her face grows more profound, as a chuckle leaves my lips. She didn't realize that I knew about her naughty reading habits. My beautiful girl loves to read spicy romance novels, but hers usually involve elves and fae doing naughty things to each other. I can't wait to see her face when she realizes that I stocked the den shelves with all her favorites, and a bunch of the ones that were on her Kindle TBR.

I left nothing to chance when I drugged and stole her away from her family. I want Issy to have everything she needs here in our secluded hideaway, for as long as it takes to get her to accept that she belongs to me. That, and to get Stella Stratford to pull her bounty from my head. Maybe a great-grandbaby will have her seeing reason. If not, perhaps I will have to kill the matriarch of the Stratford clan. One way or the other, Issy will never leave my side.

I made sure that all of Issy's various products were packed up and sent here, including the books she likes to read, and comfortable, lightweight clothing for her to wear. I even had her favorite snacks sent by the crateful, so she didn't have to do without her precious almond chocolates, and the disgusting red berries candy she loves to eat by the handful.

No, nothing was left behind when I decided to go down this route with the guys from Casbury, who were all too eager to steal her nonsensical sister away, and needed my help to pull it off. Did I take advantage of the situation to steal my own Stratford princess? *You bet your ass I did*. I knew it would be my only opportunity to do it, especially after she told me we were over, at her grandmother's behest.

Fuck Stella Stratford and the high horse she rode in on; Issy and I will never be over, not while there is still breath inside of my body. She can try to separate us, but she will lose every single fucking time. I will not be parted from my

Princesa by some demanding, Manhattan power-hungry queen, who can't see that we are meant to be together. I also won't allow her to use Issy to further her family's empire. I am fully aware of the bullshit she tried to do to Issy's sister, Mia. Forcing her to agree to a marriage of her choosing, in order to save one of her lovers.

Fuck that shit. I'll kill Stella Stratford with my own hands, if she tries to pull that with Issy.

My legs push off in the water, and I move us underneath the waterfall's spray, eliciting a charming melodic laugh from Issy, as the cool water lands on our skin. She reaches out and runs her hand through the spray, turning her face up and enjoying the feeling of the water as it cascades over her, and soaks her long, dark hair.

She reminds me of a water nymph from one of her stories, naked and basking in the water and sunshine. Yeah, I might have indulged in reading one or two, or maybe five, of her books. I wanted to see what she was interested in, what turned her on, and what made her tick.

I'm a grown-ass cartel man, a badass killer, and some of the shit in those pages had *me* blushing. It's what helped me to determine that my Issy has a praise fetish, and enjoys being called a *'good girl'*. The minute I started calling her that, I realized there was no turning back, because every single time I used those words, her pussy flooded with moisture.

I bite down on my bottom lip to stop a groan from exiting my mouth; my cock is already getting hard at just the thought of her tight pussy flooding again, even though it can't be more than twenty minutes since the last time I was inside of her. Fuck, I was never this insatiable before Issy came into my life. Yeah, I fucked a lot of women before laying eyes on Isabella Stratford, sometimes a few at a time, but since her beautiful sapphire eyes met mine months ago, no one else can even compare. No other women interest me, and my desire is only for the same fae-like creature in my arms.

I can feel the crown of my cock prodding into her backside, and by the widening of her eyes, I know she can feel it too. My eyes watch as she sucks her bottom lip inside of her mouth, and she shifts in my hold. Instead of pulling away from my cock, though, she squirms until the crack of her ass is right over the crown.

She's got to be sore with how rough I took her, so I shouldn't even be considering fucking her again so soon. Just as the thought crosses my mind, her hand snakes into the water and strokes my cock, tightening it in her small fist. "Fuck, Issy, you need to stop before I fuck you here in the water. I know you have to be sore."

The tip of my mushroom head slides between her soft cheeks, and those sexy mewing sounds she makes leave her throat. My restraint is barely hanging on by a thread when she leans her face forward, and presses her lush lips to mine. "Fuck my pussy, Diego. I need to have you fill me up until there is no beginning and no end to us. I'm yours. I belong to you."

Her words, spoken in that sexy as fuck whispered voice, snap what was left of my good intentions, and I switch my hold on her body, forcing her legs to wrap around my waist and her breasts to press against my chest, as I take her mouth in a blistering kiss and push my cock inside of her tight hole. We both groan into each other's mouths as our lips fuse with an all-consuming hunger.

I move her up and down on my hard length with my hands braced on her ass. Her pussy squeezes my cock for dear life as she circles her hips, and increases the pace so that her clit is rubbing against my pelvis, and giving her the friction her clit needs to chase her own release. This time, I have no intention of preventing her from seeking her oblivion. Instead, I want to fall into heaven with her.

My strokes deepen, my thrusts going harder inside of her until I am hitting the end of her over and over. She breaks the kiss, a long, ragged moan escaping her lips. Her head dips back and arches her neck, allowing me to scrape my teeth along the slim column currently decorated with the imprint of my hand.

"Fuck, Diego... you... feel... sooooo... good," she moans.

Fuuucckk, that hand necklace looks so pretty on her. I reach up, bracing her with just one arm while she tightens further on my throbbing length, and I wrap my fingers around her neck, slowly squeezing. Her pussy clamps down on my dick like it's trying to suffocate it, and I can feel the tremor running through my body, as my balls tighten with the need to fill her pretty cunt with my warm, thick cum. I need to hold off, because I want her to accompany me this time.

The thoughts of filling her with all my creamy, thick cum, and putting a baby version of us inside of her, have my legs threatening to give out on me. Fuck, I need to get her pregnant, need to see her belly swell with my child.

"Baby, rub your clit for me. I want you to cum when I tell you. Can you do that for me? Can you be my *good girl*? My *perfect slut,* and cum when I do?"

"Yes, *God*, yes, Diego." Her hand slips between our bodies, and I back away a bit, angling my body and giving her room to work with, which also increases the angle I'm pounding into her sexy pussy at. Fuck, I won't be able to hold off much longer. Her pussy is milking my cock, demanding that I release inside of her.

Her fingers start to move in jerky quick movements, circling her clit, and her cunt tightens painfully on my dick, making me falter in my next upstroke. *Jesus fucking Christ, this woman is literally going to bring me to my knees.*

"Baby, I need you to get there. I need you to cum with me." Her pussy spasms again at my words, and her breathing becomes ragged, as I keep bouncing her up and down on my cock. My feet dig into the watery ground as I try to keep us both upright, and the orgasm starts to tingle up my spine. "Cum, Issy! Cum for me now, baby!"

A scream tears from her lips, causing the birds around us to take flight, as I slam one final time inside of her as hard as I can and hold her to me, my cock twitching and emptying inside of her, and filling her to the brink with my cum. My vision threatens to go out on me, and my legs shake with the effort to keep standing.

Fuck, that was amazing and devasting all at once. To hear her tell me that she's mine, that she belongs to me, while asking me to fuck her. I feel like the fucking king of the world right now, one who is trying desperately not to drown us both, as I try to regain my breathing.

I slide her off my semi-hard cock as I move us closer to shallow water, where I'm sure she will be able to stand without going under. She slides down my body and leans against me, still trying to get her breathing under control. Her beautiful, thick hair floats in the water all around us, my sexy water nymph, and I can't stop the feeling of happiness that crests over me.

I grab her jaw with both my hands and cradle it softly, staring into her gorgeous eyes. My lips touch hers in small feather-light kisses over and over, unable to get enough of her. "I love you, Isabella Stratford. You are mine, and you will always be mine."

Her eyes fill with tears that slide down her face as her lips tremble. She wraps her arms tightly around me, burying her face into my chest with an anguished sob. She doesn't say it back. No words leave her lips affirming that she feels the same for me, and my heart feels like it plummets to my feet.

She doesn't say it back. Fuck, does she not feel the same way?

CHAPTER TWENTY-THREE

Issy

"In time, the hurt began to fade, and it was easier to just let it go. At least, I thought it was. But in every boy I met in the next few years, I found myself looking for you."

Nicholas Sparks, The Notebook

It's been two weeks since that fateful day when I took a machete to a man. No, not a man, an enemy, and I helped end his life here in the tropical courtyard that I'm sitting in, soaking up the sunshine next to a chatty Alisa, who, for some inexplicable reason, has me peeling potatoes. *I*, Isabella Stratford, who had never held a potato before today, never mind used a potato peeler.

The very same courtyard where Diego Cabano had me strapped to a tree, and later let his men use me for their depraved pleasure, to teach me a lesson, to make me understand how powerless I truly am in the world of the cartels, weapons dealers, and monsters.

Two weeks since the man who kidnapped me from my family, and held me prisoner in a hole, made the sweetest love to me underneath a jungle waterfall. Then he shocked the hell out of me by confessing that he loved me, and I said nothing back. Not one single word escaped my lips as he poured his heart out to me, while I stared into his deep, soulful green eyes.

I know I hurt and angered him with my silence; I could feel it change the air around us the minute I didn't say it back to him. I keep going over that moment in my mind. Why didn't I say it back? Why didn't my lips part and let spew the words that I knew were right there? The ones that he looked desperate to hear.

How about because he's a psycho who drugged and kidnapped you from your family, dragged you out to the jungle, and has done nothing but continuously try to break your will since you have been here? My mind snarks.

I have feelings for Diego, strong feelings, all-consuming feelings, feelings that terrify me down to my very core, despite all that he has done to me. Ones that I have only ever had for one other living person in my life, and I destroyed that man, and myself, with my weakness and selfish ways. I detonated us into such tiny fragments that there was no way to ever put us back together again. We became dust in the wind, gone as if we had never been.

A year ago.

"Where are you going, Isabella? Why are you always running away from me, huh? Am I not good enough for the rich heiress? Am I not worthy of being with a Stratford princess? Are you fucking embarrassed to be with me?" His blue eyes shine with misery as his strong jaw clenches. I can see it in every tense line of his body, how he wants to reach out and grab me, hold me against his wide chest, and never let me go.

A part of me wants that, too, but I know it will never work. He can't fill the empty parts inside me. What is broken within me is no longer repairable, and I won't drag him into my world. A world that would chew him up and spit him out, with no regard for the decent man that he is. The honorable man who it would corrupt, until he was just a passing memory.

My grandmother has warned me of the consequences of bringing him into our world. He would have to change everything about himself and adapt to survive, and therein lies the problem. I don't want him to change who he is, the person I love, respect, and admire. I don't want him to have to feel inferior just to stand by my side, and he always will as long as he is with me.

My world is toxic and destructive, and he is a ray of bright, warm light.

He comes from humble beginnings, and I come from a line of wealthy tyrants who built an empire with an iron grip, and will not settle for less than the best for the next generation, ensuring our name never dies, and our legacy lives on forever.

I am a Stratford born to a world of privilege, and he is but a simple man from a small town with no ambitions to rule the world. We could never work, and that knowledge breaks what is left of my heart.

"It's over. Don't make it harder than it has to be. We don't belong together, and we never have, and you know that. Nothing you say now will change that. Nothing can change the roads we both must travel, and your path is not in the same direction as mine, Kai. Let me fucking go, I... I don't love you anymore."

"You are a liar, Isabella. You lie to yourself, and you lie to me."

He moves forward, and his hand rises as he grasps my chin, the sensation of his touch against my skin searing right into the deepest part of my soul, as his eyes blaze into mine, with so much devastation and emotion in their ocean-blue depths. My words have wounded him, my denial of my feelings for him, ravaging him from the inside out.

That is what I do, what I am a master at. It's the one talent that talentless Isabella Stratford has. I ruin everything around me. My self, my family, my grandmother's hopes, and now even the man who I know genuinely loves me for me, not my name, power, or wealth.

I am the villain in our fairytale story. The roles are reversed, and he's Cinderella. Except there is no fairy fucking godmother, no ball, and no carriage, and at the stroke of midnight, I will turn into a monster instead of a damn pumpkin.

My chest tightens until it's pounding and constricting so painfully that I'm struggling to breathe. A tear cascades down my face, even though I'm trying my best to hold them back. I bite down on the inside of my cheek to prevent the sobs from leaving my lips, as I wrench myself away from his hold.

"Don't do this, Isabella. Don't run from me. I know you're fucking lying."

Show no weakness, Isabella, remember you are a Stratford. Don't let them see you cry, my grandmother's voice echoes in my head. I use her words to strengthen my resolve and my spine. I have to do this. I have to walk away from him. He doesn't realize I'm doing this for him, so he won't one day look at me with disgust and hate in those gorgeous eyes.

No, you just won't be able to look at yourself in the mirror ever again, after demolishing his heart.

Fuck, I'm hurting him. I know that I am, but it will be so much worse if he tries to stay with me. Then he will truly see what I'm made of, all the worst, malignant, and insufferable parts that live and breed inside of me. The dark, smoldering ash that tries to suffocate me daily, pouring from my mind and filling all of my crevices with its grit. I'm worthless inside, irrevocably broken, so how can I love him, when I don't even know how to love myself?

"I don't want a life with you, Kai. You were just a way to pass the time, a handsome distraction, nothing more." One more dagger slams into my heart, slicing me open from the inside and assuring me that I will bleed to death from my self-inflicted injuries, once this is done.

He inhales sharply, his blue eyes a storm of chaos. "You are a liar, Isabella, and I feel nothing but pity for you. You are so broken inside that you can't even see what is happening around you. You are losing yourself, piece by fucking piece, to your own self-sabotage, and soon, there will be nothing left of the woman I love with all my heart."

His words are nails, hammering deep into my flesh with their truth. I can see that he's still holding onto a kernel of hope that I won't end us, or walk away from the best thing that has ever happened to me. I can't let him continue to hold on, to let him believe that there will ever be a chance for us, because there won't be. Our love has to end, even if it rips my soul apart. I know with my next words, I will demolish everything that we were, ensuring that I end us forever.

I don't want to utter them; they burn like acid in my throat, but I remember the way Stella looked at him, as if she was dissecting him piece by piece. Searching for his weakness, and the best ways to hurt him, so that he would leave me. The way everyone in my world has looked at him, as if he was fresh meat for their vicious claws. They will destroy him until nothing is left of the man I love.

"I slept with my dealer... I let him fuck me raw, while I was high as a kite on snow. He filled me up with his cum until it dripped out of me, and recorded it while he did it. Still think I love you? Still want to be with me, Kai?"

He staggers back a step and then another, his face paling, even as he tries to discern if I'm telling him the truth. His mouth opens and closes, but no words leave his clenched lips. I watch as his throat bobs with the effort to keep breathing, to swallow down the venom of my words, and his body trembles, struggling with the effort to keep standing, with the crushing truth that I have dealt him. The worst part is that it isn't even a lie. I committed those crimes. I succumbed in a moment of weakness to my demons, and in the process, set my world on fire, guaranteeing that I would lose him forever.

He swipes his trembling hands down his face, his body tense with suppressed violence. Does he want to reach out and hurt me, like I have done to him? Would he even be capable of violence towards me? My sweet, compassionate Kai, who has never hurt a fly in his life. The man destined to try to heal the world, and who mistakenly fell in love with a tarnished, self-destructing woman like me.

My heart screams that I love him, that we can't lose him. That he is our future, but my mind knows the truth. We were never meant to be; only a monster can love another monster, and Kai is as far from being one as possible.

"One of these days, someone is going to find you dead somewhere of an overdose, Isabella. It will no longer be my problem, though. You're fucking right, we're done. I never want to see your whore face again."

He turns and walks out the hotel room door, his head held high as he slams it in his wake so hard that it rattles the walls. The sound is horrifically loud in my ears, and it replays over and over until it's all I can hear, aside from the sound of the last shards of my heart breaking.

He's gone, it's over. Now I can crawl into a hole, like the reptile I am, and die. Alone, always alone, that is my fate.

I burnt our love and our life to the ground, and left it smoldering in a fiery wreck, while I walked away with the scars on my heart and soul, and never looked back. Maybe that's why the words refused to leave my lips, because, with them, I could doom us too, just like I did in my past.

Diego is not Kai. They are not even remotely similar, other than the fact that they both loved you.

Perhaps the words that Diego craved to hear refused to leave me due to everything that has happened since we arrived in this isolated jungle, most of it traumatic and heartbreaking. How can the man tell me he loves me, when he took me away from all that I know? Stole me like a thief from my family. How could he claim to love me, when he was willing to share me with his men? That is not love; that is possession, *no fuck*, with Diego, it might actually be an obsession. He wants me, but only on his terms.

He wants me to be who and what he wants, carving out all my weaknesses, as if I were made of clay that he could mold. Then he could shape me into a version that he approves of. A version who can withstand this deadly life that he lives, whether I consent to it or not.

That happened in my past, too, with Kai. He, too, tried to mold me into being what he perceived was the version of me he could love. Someone who was good, honest, and caring, and could deal with her demons. It seems that I will never be enough for anyone. There is always something about my personality that needs changing, something that causes the other person to want to alter who and what I am. *Why can I never be enough?*

The image of large, bright blue eyes enters my mind again, followed by a crooked, mischievous smile. The sound of his carefree and cheerful laughter skates across the darkest recesses of my mind, and brings with it a longing for a past I cannot change. *He's gone, and I was not what he deserved. I could not be the person he wanted me to be. I am never what anyone truly wants or needs. I am nothing.*

History has a way of repeating itself, if the lessons fate tries to teach you are not learned. I have yet to learn my lesson, it seems. I keep losing myself to others, trying to reinvent the sad girl who lives deep inside of me, instead of trying to heal her. The truth is, I have no idea who I am anymore. Nothing feels like it belongs to me, not the sadness, weakness, or desperation to survive. *Do I even want to survive?*

Am I the wealthy, spoiled Manhattan heiress, or the drug addict willing to give herself away for just a hit? Could I be a cartel boss's wife, or how about a simple doctor's wife? Who is Isabella Stratford, and how do I find her? *She doesn't exist; she never did. She's an apparition walking amongst the living, unable to move forward, and stuck in the past.*

I release a deep, miserable sigh at the thoughts circling endlessly in my mind. It's like someone came in and scooped out all my insides with a rusty spoon, and left me empty, lost, and poisoned. Who am I now that I can't be the person I once was? Am I even truly alive if I don't know who I am anymore, or have a purpose? Was I ever alive to begin with? Have I ever had a purpose? *All I've done is cause pain and bring headaches to my loved ones. I'm a problem, a mistake they are always stuck trying to solve.*

There are so many questions, and no answers that I can see forthcoming. I give myself a shake, trying to pull myself out of the melancholy that threatens to drown me. It doesn't matter anyway; I know I will never leave this jungle unless Diego allows it, which seems highly unlikely. The last two weeks have been a rollercoaster of emotions, bringing with them highs and lows.

He's held me tight every single night in his arms, moving me into his room and sharing his space, as if we were a couple. He fucks me every chance he gets, filling me with his cum as if he's insatiable, and *thank fuck* he can't get me pregnant. On more than one occasion, the staff has caught us in compromising situations, and I have been too embarrassed to meet their eyes for days afterward.

Then there are all the surprises he has orchestrated, like all my favorite books in the den, the products I used back home, movie nights under the stars, and picnics at the waterfall. He even had the candy I craved like a fiend shipped by the boxload. He left nothing to chance, ensuring I would have everything I needed here, as if there was no probability of me ever returning to my old life. That thought terrifies me, that I may never see my grandmother or sister again. *He wouldn't do that; he loves you.*

Diego whispers words to me in Spanish with such gentleness when he doesn't think I can hear them, and I've managed to pick up a word or two and translate them, with Santiago's bemused help. It seems my lover does know how to be gentle, poetic, and sweet, but it's a shame he only seems to show me that side of himself when he thinks I'm asleep. Then there are the words he hasn't repeated since the first time at the waterfall. I'm not even sure I want to hear them; all I know is that not hearing them hurts me too.

"Chica, me estás escuchando?" Alisa taps me on the thigh with her potato peeler, and I snap out of my thoughts. I have no idea what she just asked me, so I just smile brightly and nod my head. A hearty laugh leaves one of Diego's men who are watching us. There is always someone watching and waiting for danger to arise, or maybe that is to keep a princess from escaping her captivity.

"She asked if you were listening to her, *señorita*, which obviously you weren't." Another chuckle leaves his lips at what seems like my expense. *Asshole.*

My eyes narrow and slide over him, taking him in from his large feet encased in black combat boots to the camouflage-printed cargo pants, and the tight, sleeveless gray tank top that exposes his large, tattooed, muscled arms. My eyes keep moving upwards until they meet a large grinning mouth, with what I can only describe as a seventies pornstash, a bulbous nose, warm chocolate brown eyes, and a head with dark, closely cropped hair.

I side-eye Alisa, who keeps on peeling potatoes as if she's getting ready to feed a small army, which I guess she is. I have no idea how many men are here in the compound, guarding us from who knows what dangers, but I know that Alisa and I are the only women. That knowledge made me uneasy, but when I expressed my concern to Diego, he said I had nothing to worry about, that his men were loyal, and they knew that I belonged to him.

"Sigue pelando las patatas mientras empiezo con la carne." Alisa puts her peeler down and wipes her wrinkled hands on the apron at her waist, before she wanders off in the direction of the kitchen, and I'm left curious at her words.

"What did she say?" I question as I keep attempting to master the peeler, but my poor potato looks like he went through a massacre.

"She... um... she said for you to keep peeling, but no offense, *señorita*, I don't think you should. There will be no potatoes left for dinner if you do." His mustache twitches on his face as he tries to swallow his laughter.

My own lips quirk as I look at the mess around me. I should probably stop, at this point, we would likely starve if I was the one required to feed us. I put the peeler down in the large stainless steel bowl Alisa placed on my lap when she told me to start peeling.

"Perhaps you are right." I start to rise from my chair, the bowl cradled in my arms, intending to go back inside, out of the heat and sunlight, and maybe find a good piece of fae smut to read, when the man sits down in Alisa's vacated chair. He leans in towards me, the smell of his sweat and tobacco filling my nostrils.

Apprehension immediately fills me, and I move farther into the chair, putting as much distance between us as possible. Usually, Diego's men don't speak to me unless absolutely necessary, with the exception of Santiago. Raphael, the coward, even turns around when he sees me in a room, and avoids me as if I had the bubonic plague.

"I'm Paulo, and you are Isabella, no?" He questions, his dark eyes roaming over my face, down my braided hair, and stopping at my breasts that are covered by one of Alisa's colorful indigenous dresses. The heat from his perusal has my skin becoming clammy, and the sensation of insects crawling along it in repulsion. He hasn't made any aggressive moves towards me, but that's what I sense from him.

I nod my head but don't understand what is happening here. Is this man trying to befriend me, or does he have another purpose for getting so close to me? He must know that Diego is uber possessive of me; it's not like fucker attempts to hide his tendencies. Why would this man risk his wrath?

My intuition is telling me to run, to get away from him, that he doesn't mean me well. I try to rise from the chair once again, prepared to keep walking away, even if he continues to speak to me. I would rather be rude than end up punished by Diego, if he misinterprets this man's friendly attempt at conversation.

Just as I try to get to my feet, his large hand slides across the arms of the chairs, and he presses his palm against my abdomen, holding me in the seat. I almost release my hold on the bowl with my meager potatoes, with how stunned I am at his actions.

"What's the rush, señorita?" All the friendliness leaves his features, as if he took off a mask that he was wearing. "We are just having a friendly conversation. There is no harm in being friendly; one can always use friends."

My hand moves to remove his from touching me, but he leans across the chair, his tobacco-scented breath sliding over the skin of my arm and collarbone, as he presses further into my flesh. "I think you need a friend, Isabella Stratford, especially if you ever want to see your *abuela* again."

At the mention of the word '*grandmother*,' my breath stalls inside my throat, choking me until I can't breathe. What does this man know of my grandmother? Instead of leaning away from him, or making a further attempt to dislodge his hold, and get up out of the chair, I lean closer.

"What do you know about my grandmother?" Alarm bells are ringing inside my head, as my heartbeat accelerates inside my chest.

"I know she hasn't stopped looking for you, *niña bonita*. In fact, she seems determined to tear apart the world to find you." His words are said with a deadpan expression, as if it's every day that you tell someone that their relative is still searching for them, after they have been kidnapped.

"I could help you. I could get a message to your *abuela*, give her the right direction to look in... for a price."

A snort leaves my lips at his words. "Diego would kill you, you know that, don't you? Painfully, he would murder you painfully, and then bathe in your blood."

"He doesn't have to know. I can make sure that he never finds out, and that you manage to get away from him. That's what you want, isn't it, *Princess*?" The way he says the word '*princess*' gives me the creeps, and causes goosebumps to rise along my arms, even with the high heat.

Is this some kind of *test* from Diego, to see if I will attempt to escape? I wouldn't put it past the *fucker* to be testing me with one of his men. He's such an *unhinged bastard*, and he sees me as a prized possession, one he refuses to lose.

"I don't trust you. I don't know what you are attempting to do, but leave me alone. I don't want to be punished by Diego." I push away his hand, and rise from the chair with my back straight and head held high.

"Your grandmother is offering a hundred million dollars for your safe return, Isabella. Eventually, others will find you, and when they do, there will be bloodshed. He will die either at their hands or at your grandmother's. It's only a matter of time."

I keep walking, and I don't look back, refusing to acknowledge his words even though my insides are burning like hot lava, and nausea is threatening to suffocate me. I pick up my pace and rush into one of the guest bathrooms, dropping the bowl on the ground in my haste to make it to the toilet before I vomit up all my breakfast.

One hundred million dollars for my safe return. God help us all; my grandmother will have started a war. No, that's incorrect. She technically didn't start it, Diego did by kidnapping me, but by the sounds of it, my grandmother aims to finish it and take Diego's life in the process.

Kidnapping me will be his death sentence. The thought has me collapsing to the cool tiled floor with hoarse sobs. *I don't want him to die.*

CHAPTER TWENTY-FOUR
Diego

"Parts of me wanted to ask you to stay. To keep fighting for me. To fight for us. But a certain ideology impeded me from doing so. The idea that when someone loves you enough, they will stay on their own, without you asking them to."

Mirtha Michelle Castro, Letters, To The Men I Have Loved

"Enter," I call out to the knock on the den's wooden door, and watch as a wary Santiago enters the room, his beaten, sweat-soaked hat in his rough hands. His dark eyes meet mine, and I can immediately tell something is wrong. This man has been with my family since I was a small boy, and while not related to us by blood, he is more family to me and my father than some who carry the same genes as we do.

"*Jefe... I... lo lamento,* I don't mean to disturb you." He rubs at the back of his head, clearly uncomfortable with having to speak to me. "We have had reports of mercenaries two hundred miles southeast of our position, actively searching for us in the jungle."

Fuck, that's close, too fucking close. Stay calm; your men look to you for leadership. If you show them you're weak and frightened, they'll be too. We need to stay the course, stay hidden, and above all, I need to keep Issy. No one is going to fucking take her from me.

"They've been in the dense jungle before and haven't found us." Even as I say the words, I know I'm wrong since that man we hacked to death with the machete managed to find us. He never divulged who had sent him before Issy put him out of his misery. My money was on one of the other cartels, but there's a real chance he could be one of the men Stella hired to find her. The relentless bitch put a target on my back... well, maybe I did that myself by stealing her precious heir.

"We are getting reports of them approaching the local villages, seeking out someone to guide them through the jungle. It's only a matter of time before someone takes them up on their bribes, Diego."

Years ago, when we first built this compound as a safe haven for my father and me, we worked with the ingenious tribes and villages within the jungle, to ensure we were left alone but informed of anyone seeking to harm us.

The agreement between them and us has held for years, with us providing them with food, needed equipment, and weapons to protect themselves, and in return, they provided intel. Not once has this compound been mentioned to an outsider. I know because I have paid moles inside each of the villages. Call me overly cautious, but I would rather be that than have a knife stabbed in my back.

"Do we know if they have been sent by one of the other cartels, or is it the Stratford witch?"

The possibility that someone in the villages could sell us out is a real problem. I don't have an army here, just enough men to keep us safe and push back any enemy that comes for us, but Stella will keep sending men our way. As long as she can buy soldiers, we will be in danger.

"My money is on the *Reyna de Hielo*. She will never stop looking for her, Diego. That woman is more dangerous than any of the other cartels. Your father is worried, and I am, too. You taking this woman could mean death to us all. Are you ready to die, us along with you, just to have her?"

His tone is accusatory, as if I am playing some sick game. Doesn't he realize that I share the same fears, and worry that taking Issy will cost all of my men their lives? Stella won't stop, and she will take Issy from me at her earliest opportunity.

She's MINE! Anger soars through my veins, and the desire to slam my fist into his mouth, and make him bleed, almost overrides my good sense. I need to calm the fuck down and get control of myself, or my emotions will lead me down a dark path.

He might be right. You are playing a deadly game with an opponent who will not back down, my mind whispers the reminder, as if that fucking thought doesn't circle inside my head on repeat.

I rub both my palms down my face with exhaustion. I haven't been sleeping, laying awake night after night, next to Issy while she dreams away. I hold her in my arms securely, knowing that at any moment, she could, in fact, be taken from me. I feel like a noose is rapidly tightening around my throat.

I should hire a mercenary of my own, and have Stella Stratford murdered, so that she leaves us all in peace. I would be doing the world a favor by ridding it of that pestilence. The only reason I haven't, is because I know Issy will never forgive me if I do. She loves her grandmother dearly.

We have been out here in the jungle for almost three months now. Three months that I have had what is mine solely to myself, but I feel a time bomb ticking away in my brain. *Tick, tick, tick,* it threatens me with the loss of the woman that is mine. They are coming to take her away from me; I can feel it deep in my soul. Will I be able to keep her safe and still with me, or will I lose her and my life in the process?

"Double the patrols. The men are to stop drinking and stay alert. Send feelers out into the villages to see if anyone has been disloyal. If they have, make sure to send them to see their maker, and leave a reminder to the villagers of the consequences of breaking my trust."

I can tell by the expression that Santiago tries to mask that is not what he wants to hear, but I also know he will do his duty to my family, and carry out his orders. He is a general in our cartel, and the men look to him as much as they do to my father, and me, for their directions. He is loyal to the Cabano line, and if there is one man in this fucking jungle I don't have to worry about slitting my throat, it's him. He would never betray me.

"Diego... *mi mamá*, she mentioned the *señorita* hasn't been herself the last two days. She seems agitated and restless. She is not eating again, and what little she does manage to eat is not staying down. You should have Raphael look at her again."

What the fuck is he talking about? I haven't noticed a change in Issy in the last couple of days other than her looking a little pale, and I just put that off due to the high heat and humidity we are experiencing. Could she be sick again? Could she still be dealing with more withdrawal symptoms? It's been two months since she last had any narcotics. Would she still be experiencing side effects from me forcing her to go cold turkey?

Whatever is going on with her, when I'm with her, she doesn't seem restless or agitated, quite the opposite. She seems to cling to me now, seeking me out on her own and wanting to spend time with me. She returns my affection openly, without me having to force her. *Shit,* we've had sex across all of this damn compound, much to my cock's happiness and her embarrassment.

Having Issy to myself, holding her and touching her these last couple of weeks, has only cemented my feelings for her further. I'm not only whole-heartedly infatuated with the woman, but I also find myself craving her every minute of the day. Maybe I am the addict now, and my addiction is to a five-foot-two, dark-haired, blue-eyed princess who keeps my cock perpetually hard.

Doubt and worry start creeping up my back, and I clench my hands on my neck to avoid yanking on my hair, the hair my *Princesa* loves to run her delicate fingers through. She's sick again, not eating, and I didn't notice. How can I claim to love her, if I don't see these things?

Fuck, I know I have a lot on my plate, with all of the deals for weapons going through across the world, to strengthen our reach further within the underworld. The other cartels are trying to do their best to undermine us, and murder my family one by one.

It also hasn't helped that we are being hunted through the jungle by paid mercenaries. Every day, I worry that today will be my last on this planet, and what will happen to Issy if I am gone. None of this has been a walk in the park. Add to all of this shit my father's constant demands that I return to him, and help him grow our empire, and I'm lucky I can even still see straight with the stress that plagues me.

For fuck's sake, I stole her from her family though. The reason we are in this fucking jungle is because I am hiding her, otherwise, I would be at my father's side right now. How am I missing what is happening with the woman I have risked it all for?

"Get Raphael to check her, but have your mother present in the room. I don't want him left alone with her."

"I don't think you have to worry about Raphael, *jefe*. He's terrified of her, and I'm pretty sure he believes you are the *diablo* incarnate, but it's not a bad idea to have *mi mamá* also with her. She could use the support of another female... she is all alone here."

His words are daggers to my heart, even if he doesn't intend them that way. I know Issy misses her family, especially the company of her sister, Mia. I wish it hadn't had to go down the way it did. I would have preferred that I hadn't been forced to take her away from her whole world, and that we could have built our relationship on a solid foundation, instead of this dangerous house of cards. The one that could come crumbling down at any moment right on top of us. I just couldn't risk losing her, and I knew she would cave to Stella's demands to stay away from me.

I'm pulled from my self-pitying thoughts as Santiago shifts away, and heads towards the door. Fuck, I am so distracted that I didn't even realize he was still standing there, never mind in the damn room. I drag my hand through my hair, trying to pull my focus back to the here and now before I get myself killed.

"Santiago," I call out, and he stops, looking over his shoulder at me. "Thank you for your loyalty. You know you and your mother are family to my father and me."

Now there's a thought that I do want to indulge in. I've been filling Issy's pussy with cum every chance I get, in order to knock her up. She, of course, doesn't know that, and would probably shank my ass if she ever found out that's what I am doing to further tie her to me. If I have my way, she will never leave my side, not even on our deathbeds.

I had our bathroom stocked with all the needed necessities for a woman's menstruation, but she hasn't used anything yet. I know, because I'm a psycho who checks. I'm not surprised, though. I had done some research on IUDs, and I know they can often cause women to stop menstruating. It can also take months after their removal for a woman's cycle to return to normal, and for her to be able to get pregnant. It's been three months. I hope that we are close now. I hope that one of these days, my fucking sperm will take root, and my baby will grow in her womb.

The image of a little, dark-haired girl running through these rooms, and racing towards me with open arms and a wide, toothless grin, is so realistic that it has my heart thumping painfully in my chest. I want that; I want a child with Issy, no fuck, I want a whole soccer team of children with Issy. I just need a chance to win her over completely. I know that she loves me even though she refuses to say the words. Her actions give her away, especially when she doesn't think I am paying attention.

I catch her staring at me when she doesn't think I am looking, and her need to constantly touch me when we are in the same room. The way she gets a shy look of pleasure on her beautiful face when I compliment her, and I know she's been actively trying to learn Spanish. I've caught her repeating words back to herself. These all point in the direction of her growing feelings for me.

The question, however, is not about what I want; it's about whether she would stay if given the option of her own free will. I know deep down I can't keep her a prisoner forever. That's not the life I want for us. Maybe if I hold her close and show her how much I care, she will decide to stay. She'll choose me.

I rise from my desk, the need to see her hitting me like a stampede of elephants. Perhaps, if she hears the words again, it will be enough. Enough to make her want to say them finally back to me. One way or another, I must ensure she is mine for the rest of our lives. I can't let her go; I can no longer live without her.

She will always be mine.

Chapter Twenty-Five

Issy

> "I had trusted him. I had even trusted him after he betrayed me. I was too open for my own good. I still gave that man my heart even after he destroyed it."

Jacqueline Simon Gunn, Let Love Rule

God, this fucking heat is ridiculous. I lift the heavy braid off the back of my neck and let the air hit the spot. It's so disgustingly hot that it's making me physically sick. I'm sitting here in the courtyard out of the sun, drinking a glass of some fruit concoction that Alisa made for me and insisted I drink all of it. I can see the worry in her eyes. I haven't been keeping food down the last few days, and my stomach is perpetually queasy.

The problem is I think I know what's wrong with me. My stress and anxiety levels have gone through the roof since Paulo approached me. I feel his dark eyes on me whenever I leave mine and Diego's bedroom. A part of me wants to run to tell Diego what he said, and the other part chastises me to keep my mouth shut. I don't want to be stuck in this jungle forever. I miss the city's noise and lights, my family, and fucking air conditioning. So I've done nothing but debate my choices, and the consequences, in my head.

Trying to decide between hoping that my grandmother finds me, and that she never does, is causing an internal war within me. Paulo's words haunt me day and night. I now even dream of my grandmother's hired men finding us in the jungle, and executing Diego before my eyes, which is playing havoc on my nerves. If I know my grandmother, she has given her men a *'shoot to kill'* order, and they won't hesitate to follow it.

Last night, I woke with my heart in my throat, and a scream trapped on my lips. Diego wrapped his large arms around me, squeezing me tightly against his beating heart, before fucking me into a coma. It did the trick, and I was able to sleep for the rest of the night, but the minute my eyes opened this morning, the anxiety set right back in.

I look across the courtyard and spy Paulo creepily watching me, while pretending to be interested in his conversation with another of Diego's men. His eyes seek me out no matter where I try to hide, making me feel cornered and trapped. I need to do something about him, but I just don't know what. Fuck, if only I could ask my sister, she would know what to do, but of course that's impossible.

I've thought about approaching Santiago for help. He's been decent with me, and his mother has been kind, but I know that his loyalty is to Diego, and he will run to tell him, the minute the words leave my lips.

I place the half-empty cup on the small bamboo table, knowing full well that Alisa will wag her bony finger at me for not finishing the drink, and start walking toward the little vegetable and herb garden that is set up. It really is a marvel, all of the self-containment and off-the-grid amenities that Diego has created here. If only he could use his powers for good, instead of trafficking weapons that kill people. It could be worse, I suppose, he could be in the drug market or human trafficking.

A chill goes down my spine at the thought of Diego dealing in human trafficking, particularly trafficking women. I inhale a deep breath through my nose and release it through my mouth, the queasiness rising once again, and threatening to have me on my knees in the bushes.

I don't know how I know, but a feeling deep inside of me reassures me that he wouldn't do that. He and his father don't partake in those types of ventures.

Diego Cabano is brutal, violent, and a psychopath, but he does have honor, and there is none in selling women for nefarious reasons.

I remember both of their reactions when my sister was taken and abused by a madman. He would have helped her boyfriends set the world on fire to find her, and ripped that man apart with his own two hands.

I wander over to a plant with some small, red, fleshy fruit. Alisa picks them daily and puts them in our breakfast food. The smell is sweet, but the fruit itself is sour and tangy. The little elderly dictator stands with her hands on her hips, until I at least consume a few pieces of the fruit every day. Diego just laughs as she mutters under her breath, and gives him a stink eye. I actually don't think she fears him at all. I've watched her whack him with a large wooden spoon before, and she once threw a slipper at his head, to my astonishment. Which Santiago referred to as the flying *'chancla'* with a laugh.

I'm so distracted that I don't realize that someone has managed to come up behind me, until I feel the heat coming off their body, and the scent of sweat and tobacco reaches my nostrils, making me instantly gag. *Paulo.*

I whirl around with my fists clenched, ready to do some damage to his face if he tries anything. The expression on his face, as it meets my gaze, can only be described as sinister. He doesn't step back, giving me the needed space to make my way around him. Instead, he shifts his body forward, crowding mine into the bush. "What the fuck do you think you are doing?" I question, but I can hear the tremble in my voice.

"Such an unladylike mouth on a wealthy *Princesa*. Makes a man wonder what other parts of you are filthy, *hmmm?*" He leans forward and sniffs my hair like a damn psychopath, and I shove both my hands into his chest, trying to force him to move away from me.

An unhinged chuckle leaves his lips at my attempt to move him. "Poor little spoiled girl, out here all alone, a prisoner of a murderer and a tyrant." One of his knees slips between my legs and forces me to be unbalanced, the branches behind me starting to dig into my skin.

"Get away from me!" I pant, the combination of his smell, the heat, and my fear making my body break into a cold sweat, and my head spin. I can feel acidy bile rising at the back of my throat, just waiting to escape me.

Don't back down, don't show fear, hold your ground.

"Have you thought about what I told you, Isabella? You're running out of time. Every day, your *abuela* gets closer and closer. Very soon she will find you, and then you will have to watch your lover die." His hot breath blows across my cheek as his hand rises, and he trails his fingers down my shoulder, his touch leaving revulsion in its wake.

"Why are you doing this? You're one of his men, so shouldn't you be loyal to him?" I pull my body as far back as I can into the bush, preferring to allow the branches to impale my skin, than let him touch me.

He reaches out again, this time grasping onto my long, thick braid and forcing me forward and into his body, until his sweat-slick skin touches mine everywhere my pretty dress doesn't cover me. He wraps my hair around his fist and yanks my head forward, his lips close to mine, and a cry of pain leaves my own. *No, fuck no!*

"I'm loyal to myself first, Isabella, and I want to stay breathing and get the fuck out of this jungle, and you, *hermosa*, are my meal ticket to never work another day in my life. You're going to come with me, and together, we will reach your grandmother's men, and then she will reward me for saving her princess."

An evil smirk crosses his face, and it terrifies me. "But first, I think I will get a little taste to see what makes you so special to him."

His lips slam onto mine, forcing a gasp to escape that he takes full advantage of, and slips his slimy tobacco-tasting tongue into my mouth. His other hand wraps around my neck, pulling me into his body and forcing all the air out of my lungs, as he holds me tightly, while he plunders the inside of my mouth, and I try in desperation to push against him, to force him backward and away from me.

NO! I don't want this. I don't want this fucking psycho to touch me, never mind to kiss me. *Oh my God, I'm going to vomit. I'm going to pass out from the lack of air.*

I need to get him to release his hold on my neck and hair, before I run out of air and pass out, leaving me at his mercy. I struggle, trying to put all my anger and energy into removing his hold. My teeth bite down on his tongue, as I try in desperation to pry his fingers from my neck. The taste of blood, mixed with his vile breath, is almost too much for me to handle.

One moment, he's touching me, forcing me to endure his violent hold, and the next, he's ripped away from me, with a loud growl sounding through the trees, and he's flying backward through the air. Paulo releases a harsh cry as he lands haphazardly on the ground, and before he can even move more than an inch, a large body is on him, slamming a fist into his face, and knees into his stomach and chest.

"MINE!" The word is roared loudly, and vibrates against the earth and vegetation.

The sound of skin slamming into skin, and bones crunching, is so loud and disgusting that it has me falling to my knees. The bile I desperately tried to hold back forces me to purge the contents of my stomach, and my head spins rapidly, disorienting me. *Get up, you weakling! Get up, he's going to kill him.*

"I'll fucking kill you!" *Crunch.* "She belongs to me!" *Crunch.* "Mine!" *Crunch.*

I try to rise back to my feet, but I'm unsteady and my head swims, causing me to see not one Diego pummeling Paulo, but two. I fall back to my knees and crawl in their direction, even as the sound of a fist hitting raw meat has me struggling to breathe. "Diego... stop... stop!"

Paulo tries to struggle against Diego's ruthless blows, but I watch with horror as his movement slows, and his limbs become jerky and then fall to the ground, as he must lose consciousness. Diego doesn't acknowledge my words. He keeps hitting him, and making feral animal noises, even though Paulo makes no attempt to fight back. The only word I can make out is '*mine*' as he slams his fist over and over into Paulo's face.

I finally reach them, and I try to grasp onto Diego's shoulder, to pull him off of Paulo before he kills him. The sight before me is right out of one of those terrifying horror movies, with so much blood, and Paulo's face all mangled and unrecognizable from the impact of Diego's fists. A sob manages to exit my lips, and is instantly swallowed by the sound of flesh striking flesh. Why I'm trying to save the fucking asshole who just assaulted me, I'm not sure. All I know is I don't want another death on my conscience.

"Diego..." I try again to pull at his black shirt.

His hand strikes back at an odd angle and grasps onto my neck, tightening its grip, and I instantly can't breathe. "I'll deal with you after I kill this miserable traitor, slut." He puts all his force into throwing me back, and I land on my elbows and ass. Tears slide down my face at the impact, and the burn of my flesh scraping against the hard earth, but also at his cruel words.

Run, Issy, run now. He's lost his fucking mind!

He grabs onto both sides of Paulo's head in his large hands, and snaps his head to the side, the sound loud, depraved, and ominous. *Holy shit, he just snapped his neck.* He releases his hold on Paulo, and he falls like a dead weight beneath him, his head hitting the earth with a sickening thud.

His green eyes are alight with an inner fire, filled with insanity, as he gets to his feet and moves towards me, a beast tracking his prey. I crawl like a crab to get away from him, panic invading every part of me. Fear like I have never felt sears through my very soul. He's going to hurt me. My Diego is gone, and has been replaced by this feral monster before me. "Pleeaaasee, Diego."

He quirks one of his dark brows. "Please? Please what, Issy?" His voice is rough and filled with rage. "Did you think he could help you escape? Were you trying to score drugs from him? Is that why you have been ill, or are you just that much of a whore that my cock alone can't satisfy you?"

"He... he attacked me." Tears continue to slide down my face as I keep crawling backward, until I'm pressed up against the trunk of a tree with nowhere else to go. "It's not what you think!"

"Sure he did, Issy. He's only been loyal to my family for years, and never been violent with another woman, to my knowledge, but out of the fucking blue, he attacked you."

The disbelief and disgust on his face decimates what little pieces of my heart he had mended with his affection over the last couple of weeks. He doesn't believe me. He doesn't believe that I wasn't trying to score drugs off that piece of shit lying dead mere feet from us. Fuck, if he wasn't already dead, I would kill him myself for ruining what peace we had managed to attain.

"You need... to believe me... please. I... I only want you." My words stumble out of my mouth in ragged sobs. How could he do this? How could he believe that I would do something like that?

He reaches out and grabs a fistful of my hair on the top of my head, yanking until I feel strands being ripped right out of my skull. "I don't believe you. It's your M.O., Issy. You offer yourself up to men to get what you want. You had me convinced there for a bit, that you actually care about me, but you don't, do you, my broken doll?"

"I... do." I tremble at the ferocity in his eyes. He's lost all control of himself. He's going to hurt me, to do something that we will never be able to come back from. "Please!"

"You're a whore, Issy, and it's time I started to treat you like one." He yanks me forward until my body is forced to comply with his hold, and I am back on my hands and knees. "You still don't understand that you belong to me, that you are mine, and I own you and can do whatever I want with you, that you live in a cage because I allow you to continue breathing, but we can fix that, *sweetheart*. I can train you like a fucking dog to heel and come at my command."

He drags me over to Paulo's bleeding body, his face resembling bloody ground beef. "No! No, Diego!" I beg while trying to stop my body from being dragged forward, even as I tremble uncontrollably, my limbs scraping along the ground.

"Yes, Issy!" He stops when I am right next to a dead Paulo whose dark, empty eyes stare into nothing. Diego yanks the hem of my dress from behind, pulling it over my ass until it pools on my lower back. "Remove your underwear, *Princesa!*" His voice is tight with emotion as he slips behind my body and gets to his knees.

"Don't do this... please, Diego, please!"

"Save your tears, Issy. They don't fucking work on me, because I know now what you are." The sound of material ripping rents the air, the tug against my hip stings as the side of my panties snaps and tears, the material sliding down my legs and pooling at my knees.

"Diego... please, I beg you, listen to me," I sob uncontrollably.

His hand snakes in front of my face. "Spit, slut. It's the only lube you'll get, and the only mercy I will show you."

Horror fills me as I absorb his words, and he doesn't bother to wait until I comply with his command, forcing two fingers into my mouth and almost making me vomit again. Saliva slides down the side of my face and mixes with the tears, and he rubs the flat of his palm against it. "So pretty when you cry, baby. I'm going to enjoy fucking you with your own tears."

"Diego, please, not like this! I... I love you!" The words escape my lips in a panicked rush, but it's too late. He slams three of his wet fingers inside of my core, making my back bow with the intrusion, and a scream squawks from my lips. His fingers begin a punishing rhythm inside of me, opening me up and stretching me.

Pain and pleasure start to rise inside of me, even as I try to fight against the sensations. My body impulsively bucks my hips into the feeling of fullness in my pussy, trying to chase away the horror, and replace it with carnality.

"Look at how your cunt is squeezing my fingers, Issy. You're strangling them even as your pussy weeps, baby." His grasp on my hair loosens, and I hear the sound of a zipper being released.

"Diego... please, not... like this." My words escape me in a whimper, and my core clenches as he rubs that soft spot inside of me that makes me lose my mind.

I try to force my eyes to look away from a dead Paulo before me. The scent of iron and blood is all that I inhale, and I can taste it from Diego's fingers being inside my mouth. The fingers he's now fucking me hard with, covered in this dead man's blood, along with my tears and spit.

"Reach forward, Issy, and rub your hands in his blood. Get them nice and wet, baby, so that you can lube up my hard cock. I'm going to fuck you with the blood of the man who tried to take what is mine."

Jesus fucking Christ, he's completely lost his mind. Tears pour from my eyes and blind me to the sight before me. He nudges the crown of his cock at my entrance, rubbing it through my slit, even as his fingers keep up their unwavering pace, and the hand still grabbing my hair forces my face to look across Paulo's dead body.

"You can either use his blood for lube, or I'll make you lick up the fucking mess with that traitorous mouth of yours. The choice is yours, *Princesa*, but either way, I'm going to paint one of your holes red."

Sobs wrack my body as I reach forward, bracing myself on just one hand and my knees, as I trail my fingers through the blood on Paulo's neck and upper chest, coating them in nothing but red until they are dripping, the feeling of his still warm blood forcing me to gag.

"Reach back and stroke me, baby, get my hard cock nice and wet," he growls. "That's a *good girl*, what a *good whore* you are."

I reach back and coat his throbbing cock with Paulo's blood, even as I clench my eyes tightly to stop myself from seeing the dead man in front of me. His fingers continue to move within me, stroking me in the spot that makes my eyes want to roll into the back of my skull, despite the ghastly situation I find myself trapped in.

Searing heat and electricity dashes up between my thighs, making my core spasm and my legs tremble, and I bite down on my lip to stop the aroused cries from leaving my mouth. *What the fuck is the matter with me? How can I be getting off on this? This is sick!* I can feel myself dripping and slickening my thighs, the orgasm starting to rise within me as he mercilessly finger fucks my pussy.

He suddenly stops and pulls his digits from inside of me, and a groan of objection leaves my lips. "What a dirty little slut you are, getting off on being fucked next to my dead enemy." He slams his cock inside of me, bottoming out in one painful go, and stretching me until I think he might break me open.

"FUCK! Diego, please!" I scream.

"You will take all of me, again and again. I'm going to pour my cum inside of you, mixed with Paulo's blood, until you drip with it. Until you cry out for your release, beg me to cum, and admit that you're a whore, and tried to betray me."

His body bends over mine, pushing my limbs further into the dirt, and closer to the bleeding mass of dead flesh before me. His warm breath slides across my cheek before he licks a line from the corner of my eye to my jaw. "That's what you want, isn't it, Issy? You want to be my whore, and you want me to come until you're sated from being used, don't you, baby?"

The way he's pounding into my body, making it rock forward and hitting the end of me continuously, has me seeing stars and my mouth hanging open, as I desperately try to drag much-needed oxygen inside of my seizing lungs. Prickles of heat rise within me, and I'm unable to stop them from climbing the mountain; the promise of darkness is too addictive, even though I should try not to submit to my arousal. It's sick, unhinged, and depraved, what we are doing. He's literally fucking me with the blood of the man who forced himself on me.

"Cum for me, baby. I can feel you clamping down on my cock, strangling him. You feel so fucking good," he pants. "So fucking wet and tight, as you try to suck my soul right into this perfect traitorous pussy."

His hand releases from my hair, and makes its way down my face and around my neck, his fingers tightening but not impeding my air, at least not yet. His other hand pulls brutally on my hip, forcing me to take all that he has to give. "Tell me who you belong to, *Princesa*. Tell me who owns you."

I'm enthralled by his words, my body clenching down as he keeps pushing me higher and higher. I look down between my swaying breasts in the gap of the bodice of my dress, and I can see where we're connected. His cock pushes into me in deep, hard strokes. My pussy lips and his cock are tinged bright red, so much fucking red. Fuck, I can't hold on. I need to explode, even though I know I shouldn't, that this is wrong.

"Say the words, Issy, or I will leave you fucking empty and cum on your face."

The words leave me in a deafening scream. "YOU! I... belong to you!"

"That's a *good girl*," he utters, before pushing my face down into the bloody mess of Paulo's chest, picking up speed and force, and fucking me so hard that it hurts. I can't breathe as his hold on my neck keeps me pressed up against Paulo's hard chest.

Fuck, I'm going die, it's the last coherent thought I process as my body tightens painfully, and the waves of energy float over me, making me clench down on his thick cock as heat explodes through my body. The release is so intense that all I can hear is the blood rushing in my ears, and my skin tingles everywhere. As I struggle to get any air inside of my lungs, it forces my eyes to close and roll to the back of my head.

"FUCK, FUCK, FUCK!" I scream into Paulo's dead chest, my words muffled by the fabric and blood.

He thrusts twice more and cums with a roar inside of me, joining me in our unhinged oblivion. My eyes snap open, and all I can see is the tinge of red as my body comes back to itself, and, with it, an awareness that my face and upper body are covered in Paulo's cooling blood. My mind and body threaten to revolt as panic sets back in, and I feel myself being pulled apart at the seams.

An unsettling coldness blankets my mind and body, forcing my limbs to feel numb and weighed down. A blackness that crawls up from the earth, wrapping itself around me, piece by fucking piece, and like a snake filled with venom, tightens, strangling what is left of me, one weak section at a time, until it promises that nothing will be left in its wake.

My body crawls forward until he releases me from his hold, and I feel his cock slip from inside of me, and the sensation of his cum oozing out of me. Nausea threatens me once again as my head spins, and I take huge lungfuls of air to stop myself from hyperventilating. I'm covered in death; he's made me a willing accomplice to this insanity, and I hate that I enjoyed it, that I reveled in it, and that was the most powerful orgasm I've ever had at the expense of another living creature.

What does that say about me? Does it certify that I'm just as psychotic as Diego is? Maybe I'm worse because he at least had his reasons, demented as they are, but I didn't have a reason for enjoying what he was doing to me. I could have, and should have, continued to fight. That's what any normal, unbroken woman would have done, except I have never been normal. This just fucking proves how very abnormal I am.

"Issy... fuck," his tone is low and cautious.

I stare over my shoulder at him, even as his deep, panting breaths are the only sound besides mine in the jungle. It's as if nothing else even dares to inhale, or make a noise, at this moment. The world is utterly still, holding its breath for what is to come.

A trick of my vision makes him look like he's entirely made of swirls of black and red. As if the darkness and savage bloodlust within him are pouring out for me to see. This is who he is, who he has always been. He will continue to be this way despite my love, despite my willingness to give him all of myself, and eventually, he will destroy what is left of me, corrupting me into this person I don't want to be.

I don't want to be a killer or relish in brutality, but if Diego has his way, that's what I'll become. The other side of him, the strong and ruthless woman he wants at his side. The fucking *queen of serpents*, because that is what he is, after all, a venomous snake willing to kill without mercy and consume his prey, and I will be his mirror image.

Despite my feelings for him, and my heart seizing inside my chest with the realization that I'll never be enough for him and I can't stay with him, I can't let him have me because I'll be destructively empty if he does. He will continue to hurt me whether he realizes it or not. I have to save what is left of me and escape him.

Crushing defeat races through my veins, and my heart begs me to stay, while my mind and my self-preservation urge me to run, to get away from the monster who has taken a portion of my heart and soul, and will eventually take my life.

He must see some semblance of my thoughts across my features. His blazing gaze trails across my skin, leaving metaphorical blisters in its wake. "I won't apologize for taking what is mine, Issy! You are fucking mine! You're still not understanding it. No other man will ever have you, and no one will ever get to fill your pussy but me."

"Except those you decide to share me or punish me with, right, you fucking bastard?" The words calmly leave my lips, despite the inner turmoil within me trying to seep out of all my pores.

"No one will touch you. No one *has* touched you, Issy. You are my slut only."
He reaches down and tucks his red-tinged cock back inside of his pants, and the
corner of my lip lifts in disgust, both at his actions, and the reminder of what
he just did to me.

"I'll never forgive you for what you just did, not even if we're in this fucking
jungle for the rest of our miserable lives. What you did to me wasn't love, Diego,
it was hate. You don't know how to love, and you're just as fucking broken as I
am."

"I don't need your forgiveness, Issy. I will continue to do what is best for us.
As for loving you, you have no fucking idea what I've sacrificed to have you.
The enemies I've made that could destroy my family, my whole fucking world,
because I couldn't give you up."

His words should sound romantic to my ears. Isn't that what every woman
wants and dreams of? Isn't that what all those naughty, dark romances claim we
want? A man who will give up everything, sacrifice his whole life, and set the
world on fire to have you.

Yet, they sound hollow to my ears, refusing to ignite that part of me that
would have me once again kneeling at his feet, and bring with them only sorrow
and misery. I never asked him to give up anything to be with me, in fact, I told
him we were over, and look where it led me.

We are death walking hand in hand, *Hades* and *Persephone* doomed to be
together for all eternity. His darkness slowly but surely infecting my light, until
I too, will be consumed by it. He will continue to hold me prisoner, and use any
method at his disposal to keep me trapped in his world.

CHAPTER TWENTY-SIX

Diego

"Someone I loved once gave me a box full of darkness. It took me years
to understand that this, too, was a gift."

Mary Oliver

A rustle in the trees around us has me on high alert, my body immediately
preparing to fight off anyone who tries to harm us. No one will fucking take her
from me. I will murder every fucking person breathing on this earth if I have to,
in order to keep her. *You'll destroy her, and nothing you love will be left standing.*

There's an alarm bell blaring inside my skull, my mind warning me that I've
crossed a line that there is no turning back from. Insanity has gotten its talons
deeply embedded inside of me now. I just killed one of my own men for daring
to touch her, so how much farther would I go? Would I kill all of them for her?
The truth pours in like a hurricane, disrupting and tearing everything I know
about myself apart, until only rubble and shambles remain.

I would end the world for her, set it all up in a fucking blaze, until we were the
only two people left. There is no limit to what I will do, no person that I won't
end, if they try to take her from me. The knowledge has me rising to my feet,
prepared to take on whoever is coming for us. May God have mercy on their
soul, because I won't.

I spy Issy as she takes an unsteady step forward, and I release a growl in warning that has her freezing in her spot. Her face and body are covered in red tinges of blood. The front of her dress is wholly plastered to her skin, and outlines every curve in the blood of a man who wanted what is mine. She stands there trembling like a leaf, shock across all of her beautiful features, and terror in her sapphire gaze, as she stares down at Paulo's corpse.

I feel no shame or remorse for taking his fucking life, regardless of if he had been with me for years, a loyal soldier to my family. He saw an opportunity to deface that loyalty, and seek out a taste of what belonged to only me, and for that, the penalty was death. I hope he's enjoying his entrance into hell, and his meeting with the devil. The monster lurking within me is beaming with pride at defending our mate. *Did you, though, or did you punish her along with him?*

I feel positive that my mind has finally succumbed to madness. A part of me irrevocably cracked when I saw Paulo touching Issy. When his hands were caressing skin that belonged to me, and his mouth was on lips that are mine, inhaling her air. The air I allow her to breathe.

A large, burly shape bursts through the thick fauna, followed by a few more, and they come to a grinding halt, the sounds of their heavy breaths grating on my already frazzled nerves. "I heard screaming! What has happened? Are we under attack?" Santiago's panicked voice makes its way to my ears. It has me standing tall, a demonic warlord about to show them the darkness which resides within me, so that they understand that they should fear me. Everyone should fucking fear me, now that I have finally released my hold on the restraints that had me a prisoner.

"*Santa mierda*, Diego... what have you done?" Santiago's voice, filled with disbelief at the sight before him, breaks me from the spell that has me trapped in this fucked up insanity.

I haven't heard him this panicked since the day one of the other cartels took my mother, as a way to punish us for reaching too high in the world of the underground. They sent her back in pieces to us, and none of us were ever the same.

The image of my mother with her large olive-toned green eyes wide open, staring sightlessly, and her mouth shaped in a scream, while the rest of her body was in pieces found in crates, enters my mind. Someone took her away from me, the only woman I had ever loved, and they destroyed her. I won't allow that to happen a second time. No one is taking Issy.

My head slowly turns in his direction, the menacing look on my face forcing Santiago and the men with him to take a step back. I know what they're seeing before them with disbelief. I'm covered in Paulo's blood, the mask of rage is still on my face, and I can feel my eyes blazing with an inner fury, that has me sending out a message to all who are present that I'm long past the point of rationality. I bare my teeth at them, like a rabid wolf in warning to stay away from my mate.

"Mine, she is fucking mine, and I'll destroy anyone who touches her, or thinks to fucking take her from me."

"*Jesucristo!*" One of the other men utters and takes another step back from us, putting more distance between the monster that lurks at the ready within me, and himself. *Smart fucker*, even though the beast begs to be released and give chase, calling for more blood to be spilled. One of the other men performs the sign of the cross, as if I were the devil standing before him, and moves as far away from me as he can, without turning his back on me.

"Paulo is... is he dead, Diego?" Santiago's Adam's apple bobs, and he tenses his frame, staring at the unhinged menace before him and trying not to show a hint of weakness, so as not to provoke me further.

I'm a monster who literally just snapped a man's neck like it was nothing, and fucked Issy into the ground with that man's blood as lube, and got fucking off on it, not to mention made her cum like a slut. My cock is still even now in a semi-hard state, just with the fresh memory of the sounds that escaped her, and how tightly she clenched around me.

Fuck, if anything, I dare any of these fools to make a move towards her, so that I can take their lives too, and bathe her in their blood. This time I'll fuck all of her holes, and paint her from the top of her pretty head to her dainty little feet in nothing but red. She would look absolutely stunning, with only her sapphire blue eyes peeking out through all that crimson.

A whimper behind me has me snapping out of my depraved thoughts, and coming back to the here and now. "The fucker has gone to meet the devil, and if you try to make a move towards her, you will be joining him."

A cascade of emotions crosses Santiago's face, everything from fear to worry and disgust, before he nods his head at my words. *"Déjanos, ahora!"* He orders my men in a calm but forceful tone, giving them no option to argue, and out of the corner of my eye, I see them slinking away back into the vegetation.

His eyes never waver from holding my own, refusing to slide to Issy as if he knows how close I am to the edge, and how I could perceive that as a threat. "Is she hurt, Diego? She is covered in blood and trembling, *jefe*. She looks like she is mere moments from collapsing."

His words have me tearing my gaze away from him, and the other three of my men disappearing from my sight, and staring at Issy. I take in her bloody state, but look closer and finally notice how pale she is. How her lips are pinched in pain and practically white, and her eyes are so large that they look ready to pop from her very skull. She's swaying on her feet, attempting to keep herself standing, but about to lose the fight.

"Issy," I move towards her, but before I can get my hand around her bicep, she collapses to the jungle floor in a dead faint, her eyes rolling to the back of her head as a wheeze of air escapes her lips. The thud her body makes with the impact destroys whatever was left of my hold on reality, and I dive to the ground, pulling her into my arms and cradling her into my body.

"Issy, fuck, baby. Please, baby, speak to me."

My heart thunders in my chest, and my monster roars with fear as my breathing becomes restricted. I press my ear against her chest, begging the sound of her heart to calm my own. *Thump, thump, thump*, it beats strongly against my ear, and has the boulder of fear passing down my throat, until I can take a deep breath. *Jesus, fuck.*

"Jefe, please... we must get her back to the compound. We are not safe here out in the open, exposed like this. She is not safe here." His words register through my mind, and I also hear what he refuses to say out loud: *she's not safe with me, either.*

I want to refuse him, to take her further into the jungle and hide her away from all those who would seek to part us, but as I stare down at her, worry fills me. She looks so fragile and frail. He had said she was unwell, that's why I came looking for her in the first place, and found her with Paulo. Now I have just put her through more emotional and physical hell. What the fuck was I thinking?

You weren't thinking. You let the monster control you, and he took full advantage to leave death in his wake. You could have killed her in the process. The whispered words penetrate my brain, and I cradle Issy to my chest, rise, and start moving toward the compound, Santiago putting space between the two of us in case I were to attack him.

"Diego, what about Paulo?" Santiago inquires.

I don't even hesitate in my steps, because for all of Paulo's previous loyalty, he betrayed me in the end. "Throw him further into the jungle for the beasts to consume. He was a fucking traitor."

From here on forward, anyone who even looks at Issy too long will meet the same fate, regardless of who they are. I hope the word of what happened here spreads amongst my men, so that they realize that even looking at her is a death wish, one that I will gladly grant.

Isabella Stratford is about to become the most prized and feared creature in the jungle, and I'm her gatekeeper; all who seek her should be prepared to perish at my hands.

CHAPTER TWENTY-SEVEN

Issy

> "A great fire burns within me, but no one stops to warm themselves at it, and passers-by only see a wisp of smoke."

Vincent Van Gogh

A knock on the door startles me from wallowing in my dark, depressing, and self-deprecating thoughts. I've been sitting here watching the torrential rain pour down, like thick sheets of opaque glass, for what feels like hours with my arms wrapped securely around my legs. As if I just made myself smaller, maybe I could escape or disappear from this place, from this very stifling and oppressive life.

The images of what happened with Paulo have been constantly repeating in my mind, so I can now tell you a second-by-second account of what happened that afternoon, mere days ago. I keep circling back to the fact that, if I had just told Diego about that first conversation with Paulo, none of what followed would have transpired. Although that isn't entirely true. I know with certainty that it wouldn't have saved Paulo. The minute he approached me, he was destined to die. He was willing to betray Diego, for the pot of gold my grandmother is dangling out to anyone who can find me.

I want to be angry with Paulo and my grandmother, because both caused what happened in their own way, but I also have to take responsibility for my actions. While painful and harsh, the truth is that some part of me wanted to escape, and leave this jungle and Diego behind. That's why I didn't go to Diego, and tell him about the escape that Paulo was offering me.

The weakness ingrained deep within my bones constantly tells me to run, be a coward, and come back to the protective embrace of my Stratford family. That my grandmother and sister will keep me safe from any more harm. Safe even from myself, and this new realization of who I am deep inside, and what I'm capable of. *Murderer.*

The darkness, depravity, and need for pain, call to me in a sweet lullaby sung in Diego's voice, and I want to go to him and lay myself at his feet, and ask him for more. Ask him to take me to my very limits, and then throw me over the sharp, dangerous pinnacle until I'm reborn. Reborn as the woman at his side, the wife he wants, and the queen who rules his empire without regrets or limitations.

What does it say about me that I'm sitting here thinking about how he almost beat a man to death, then snapped that man's neck and proceeded to fuck me using his blood, but I not only enjoyed it, I came harder than I have ever in my whole life. Not only that, but I know that if I reached below my flimsy cotton dress and into my panties right now, I'd find myself soaked just from the memory.

Yup, I'm a fucking psychotic bitch. I guess it makes perfect sense why I'm so incredibly attracted to Diego, despite him not being my typical type. I'm just like him, just as damaged, filled with anger, and now apparently bloodlust. Like calls to like, and here we both are, together in the fucking jungle, unable, it seems, to part from each other, even though that would be best for both of us in the long run. *He will never give you up. You're his prize.*

"Enter," I release a sigh, unwrapping my arms from around my legs and turning towards the door. I already know it can be only one of three people. It's either Santiago with his dark, worried eyes, his mother, Alisa, with her motherly acceptance and constant hovering, or Raphael coming to check that I haven't somehow slit my own throat, but who is still terrified to touch me in any way.

I haven't seen Diego since he killed Paulo. He no longer sleeps in his bed or eats meals with me. In fact, if I didn't occasionally hear him bark orders from somewhere within the compound, I'd think he had abandoned me. *Maybe he finally realizes you're not worth all these headaches.*

Santiago steps into the room, his dark eyes meeting mine, and in their depths, I see a profound sadness that wasn't there before Paulo was murdered. His hands clench his hat tightly, as if he needs it to keep himself from wrapping those strong hands around my neck, and ending my hold on his boss.

I know that Santiago has never approved of me being brought here. He believes that I've procured nothing but trouble for the Cabanos. I'm Helen of Troy, a cursed destroyer of a kingdom, because a prince dared to fall in love with me. Will the Cabanos crumble under the strain of my grandmother's larger army, intent on getting me back? *History practically guarantees it.*

I watch him warily, refusing to be the one to speak first. I have no idea what to say. I haven't had a moment to discuss what happened with him, or anyone. Do I apologize for getting one of his men killed? Do I try to explain what happened, what Paulo was attempting to do? Would it even matter at this point? I doubt he would believe me. No one ever believes me, always choosing to think the worst of me, but I guess I haven't given them much of an opportunity to think otherwise. *It's because you're weak and pitiful, unwanted.*

"Ummm... how are you feeling, *señorita*? *Mi madre* says you are still not eating? Do you need me to get Raphael?" I can see the concern wrapped up with the doubt in his features; maybe he believes I'm faking it to get attention. Perhaps Santiago thinks I'm a spoiled princess who wants everyone's sympathy, and to have them at my beck and call, when the reality is that I just want to disappear into a hole. Ironic, isn't it?

A chuckle leaves my lips at that thought. I never, in a million years, would have believed that I'd crave to be back in a hole in the ground, but here we fucking are. This is what my life has become. It seems like the safest solution for ninety-nine percent of my problems at the moment. If I'm genuinely fucking lucky, I'd die down there this time. I wonder if I can convince Santiago to push me back into that hole?

Santiago gives me a quizzical look. I'm sure I look utterly insane, chuckling to myself and disregarding his well-meaning concern. See, that's part of the problem; he's not a horrible person, even though he's helped his boss keep me trapped in this jungle for months.

"Where is Diego?" At my words, the concern bleeds instantly from his face, and is replaced by a mask with no emotions. Ah, there it is, the limit to Santiago's compassion and concern.

"He is dealing with business, which is none of your concern. If and when he chooses to see you, he will." His tone's coldness has me wrapping my arms around my waist. At my action, his face seems to soften, as if he realizes how harsh he's being with me, and a bunch of words in Spanish leave his lips in a rapid tangent, most of which I'm certain are nothing but swear words.

He steps further into the room and closes the door firmly behind him, which instantly has me on alert. Since Paulo's death, no one has been in a room alone with me with a closed door except Alisa. As if the mere thought of being alone with me could mean their death. *It probably does. Have you met Diego fucking Cabano?*

"Listen to me, *chica*, you need to leave this place, to get away from him." He comes closer until he's a mere two feet from me, and I notice all the deep grooves on his face and the dark shadows under his eyes; he's not sleeping any more than I am.

"I have known that man since he was three years old. He's like a son to me, Isabella. I've seen him at his worst, but I've never seen him like this, not even when the cartels took his mother and sent her back in pieces, or when they captured, tortured, and scarred him for life." A haunted look crosses his face at the memories that he speaks of.

"He's sick, *chica*. You make him sick." He drags his hand down his face in agitation, even as his other fist clenches tighter to his hat.

"Loving you is destroying him from the inside out. Your love is nothing but a curse, and you are hurting him. *This* is hurting him," he motions around at the compound walls. "Because he is like a son to me, I will not allow you to continue to do this to him. Loving you is toxic and destructive. I will kill you before I allow you to take him to hell with you."

"I... I love him, Santiago... I don't want to hurt him." Tears cascade down my face as sobs choke me. Fears races through me, not for my own life, but for Diego's. What if Santiago is right, and I'm destroying Diego? What if loving me ends up costing him his life? *It will, you already know that. Your grandmother will murder him, that is, if his men don't turn on him first.*

"I'm giving you one chance to live, Isabella, only one. I will help you escape, but you must not return to your family. You can never go back, or he will find you again." He drops to his knees, his hat slipping from his fingers as he grasps my hand tightly.

"Promise me, Isabella, that you will not return to your *abuela*. If you ever loved him, ever had any feelings for him, you will disappear and make sure he can never find you."

Shock gallops through my body, bringing with it a sandstorm of emotions. I want to immediately rebuke his words and deny his request, but almost instantly, it is followed by a meager trickle of acceptance. What my heart wants to refuse, my mind knows as nothing but the truth. He's right; together, Diego and I are toxic and destructive. We will end up destroying each other, along with the world around us, and take everyone we love down with us. I can't allow that to happen, not to the people I love, nor to him.

"Where... where would I go?" Uncertainty seeps from all of my pores. What he's suggesting seems so radical; how can I just hide and live without my family? What he is demanding of me is akin to a death sentence. I'd be all alone in the world. Surely there has to be another way. My grandmother can keep me out of Diego's clutches, can't she?

The truth hits me like a battering ram, taking my breath with it and causing my chest to constrict painfully. He'll never stop trying to get me back. Diego has already started a war with Stella Stratford, one that he had no way of ever winning, yet he was willing to risk it all to take me. How far would he go to get me back? How many will die in the process, and will he lose his life in the effort? *It is the only way he will ever stop trying.*

"I will make sure you get out of this jungle, but where you end up after that is not my concern, nor do I want to have those details. You, Isabella Stratford, are a *plague* on everything you touch, and to have you gone will be a blessing."

I'm overwhelmed by his crushing words, and my body begins to shake as the tears blind me. This man hates me; I can feel it radiating off him in waves, and blistering at my skin. Would he rather murder me if he could? One look into his dark eyes tells me he's giving me mercy against his better judgment, that his first choice would be to provide me with death.

Can I even trust that he will get me out of this jungle? Who is to say that he won't try to kill me as I make my escape from the compound, and then blame it on me? Should I try to reach Diego, and tell him what Santiago is trying to do? *NO! Don't be stupid and weak!* My mind screams.

This is my one chance to do what is right: save Diego from himself and me. The words that Santiago spewed echo through my mind: *toxic, plague, destructive, curse,* I am all of those things and more. I know that I can never be the woman Diego needs at his side, and right now, I need to save myself. I need to finally be fucking strong, and protect myself without counting on someone else to do it for me. From this moment on, I will be completely alone.

"How... when?" The words become tangled on my tongue, as thoughts race through my mind.

"Your grandmother's mercenaries are mere miles away from the compound, and will find us by nightfall. They will help create a diversion, and occupy Diego and the men. I will help you slip out of the western part of the compound and into the jungle, where a cousin of mine will lead you through the jungle, until you have reached safe passage. They will have a new identity waiting for you, Isabella."

His hand tightens painfully on mine, crushing my bones and causing the blood to stop circulating to my fingers. "You must let Isabella Stratford die in this jungle, *chica*. When you step out of the jungle, you will be someone new, and that woman is no longer a Stratford, do you understand?"

Sadness threatens to overwhelm me with his words, and the meaning behind them. Isabella Stratford, the woman I have struggled to be all my life, will die here, and in her place, someone new will be reborn, perhaps even someone I can finally be proud of.

"I understand." With my words, I seal my fate and agree to end my life as I know it forever. I just hope that I make it out of this jungle, yet at the same time, I can already feel the longing to stay with Diego. Will my heart be able to survive losing another man that I love?

It survived before, didn't it? You are still alive and will continue to live, with or without a heart; that has always been your fate.

Chapter Twenty-Eight
Santiago

"It is easier to forgive an enemy than to forgive a friend."

William Blake

I pace back and forth in my quarters, running my rough and scarred hands through my thinning hair. The knowledge of what I have done, weighing me down, as if dark tar was plastered on my body. I have lied and conspired against the man I have always been loyal to, and considered a son.

Am I doing the right thing by removing this woman from his grasp? Yes, no, I no longer know what the right thing is. All I know is that I am watching him self-destruct, because of his love for her. A love that will ultimately lead to his very death. Stella Stratford will have him murdered for abducting her granddaughter, and if she doesn't, then his own men will become traitors and turn on him.

I've been listening to the grumblings, and the whispers, for months since we brought Isabella to the jungle, but now dangerous words are being uttered by angry voices. The men not only fear Diego, but they believe that he's entranced by a witch, who has stolen and corrupted his very soul. After what occurred with Paulo, the men are terrified that they might be next to die for merely looking at Isabella, and are ready to abandon him, or cut him down, to protect themselves. I can't let that happen. I can't let them turn on Diego.

That is why I secretly reached out to Diego's father, Manuel. I explained to him what has been happening here, and together we came to this agreement to save Diego, not only from himself, but from destroying what is left of the Cabano empire, just to have this woman who does not deserve him.

I know I'm being harsh with my thoughts on Isabella; she is not an evil person. At least, deep inside my heart, I don't honestly believe that. She is just not the woman who is meant for him. She is too weak, selfish, and stubborn to survive in our world. That weakness will get Diego killed, especially if she were ever to fall into the hands of the other cartels like his mother did.

The memory of Julia Cabano slides into my mind. Her smile lit up the night sky, and her dark eyes were always filled with mischief, much like her son's were when he was a child. I miss hearing the twinkling of her laugh, that always reminded me of bells at Sunday mass back home in Columbia. The truth I will carry to my grave is that I was in love with Diego's mother for years. She became my sole reason for staying with the Cabano family; originally, my loyalty was only to her. *My Julia, mi corazón.*

She is the one who begged me, with her sweet lips and words, to protect her son, as if he were my own. It is that promise I made with my own blood to her that has kept me at Diego's side, as he grew from a child into a ruthless man. Despite the many obstacles and hardships that have been thrown in his way, including losing his mother so brutally, and being abducted and kept prisoner for months, at the hands of a rival cartel, he has flourished. He has become a man I am proud to follow and support, in any way I can, except in this.

This woman has been a curse from the moment he laid eyes on her back in Casbury. I urged Manuel to intervene then, but the greedy bastard that he is, he wanted a Stratford heiress. To him, it didn't matter which sister Diego chose, as long as he ended up with one of them.

Personally, I believe he would have been better off with the other one, Mia. Yes, she is mostly insane, reckless, and more than likely to plunge a blade into your skull, just for looking at her the wrong way, which always caused fear to rush down my spine anytime I was in her presence. She's also the type of woman Diego needed at his side, one he could grow his empire with. A ruthless queen, fearless, loyal, and unwilling to bend or break, instead of a weak woman destined to only bring hardship in her wake.

Yet there was no convincing him once he laid eyes on Isabella Stratford. I watched as she consumed him from that first moment. She became everything to him within such a short time that I worried for his very sanity, and I was right to. Look at what has befallen us, enemies in every direction, and us hiding in this damn jungle just waiting to die.

I hear the sound of my door sliding open quietly, and soft footsteps making their way across the stone floor, and I turn around to greet my elderly mother. I can't believe I let fucking Manuel talk me into bringing her into the jungle, to care and cook for us. I must have truly lost my mind to be willing to risk her safety.

At least, after this, I will be able to get her far away from here and the Cabano family. My shoulders sag, with the sad knowledge that I may never see my mother alive again, after what is about to transpire. I need to remove her from Diego and Manuel's reach, and send her off to live with relatives they don't know about. I can't allow her to be harmed when, and if, Diego realizes what I have done to help Isabella escape.

"Hijo, estás bien? Está todo listo?" Her soft, weary voice makes my heart ache. I love my mother dearly, and I wish I didn't have to be parted from her. She's my only true family, but I need to save her from the boy I think of as my son.

"Sí Madre, we are ready. It will be just a few short hours before that witch's army arrives at the compound gates, and then I will have Salvio ready to take you in the opposite direction of Isabella."

"Estás seguro de esto? Qué pasa si estás equivocado?" She lays her wrinkled and age-spotted hand against my face, her small, frail body not even reaching my chin.

"She will be his death. I have no doubt about that." Although it hurts my heart to know that what I am doing will only cause Diego pain and anger, I honestly believe in the long run, I am doing what is best for him, by removing this woman from his grasp. In due time, he will be able to heal, and find someone more worthy to rule at his side. Isabella Stratford was never meant to be his.

"*La niña está embarazada, Santiago. Le quitarás el hijo a Diego. Cuando descubra lo que has hecho, no te perdonará y te matará.*" A crystal tear slides down her lined face as she reaches up and kisses my cheek, before moving away from me and leaving the room.

The silence is almost deafening in her absence. Her words dig into my heart and soul. Fuck, she's absolutely right. If Diego ever finds out that I had a hand in taking Isabella away from him, especially with the knowledge that she's carrying his child, he will murder me.

Only one person other than my mother would know that Isabella Stratford is leaving this jungle pregnant: Raphael. I have to make sure he doesn't make it out alive during the attack on the compound. He must die.

What about Isabella? She will be out there alone in the world somewhere with Diego's child. Perhaps I should rethink what I am about to do; it is unforgivable to take a man's child away from him. Doubts whisper in my mind, reminding me of my faults and how this can go terribly wrong in so many ways.

No, I need to stand firm; in this case, it is the best that can be done, the only thing that can be done. That child will tie Diego forever to that woman, and with it, she will ruin him until there is nothing left. I have to protect him from her, and from himself. My hands are tied, and my priorities lie in the promise I made to Julia to protect him, even if that means protecting him from himself.

In a few short hours, Isabella will be gone from our lives forever, and we will be able to get back to business, as if she was just a minor blip in our history. Manuel assures me he has already lined up a marriage alliance with one of the other cartels to strengthen us. Diego will still have children to rule, and carry the line forward, *ones he will be aware of. All will be well in the end, I hope.*

CHAPTER TWENTY-NINE

Issy

"I'll always want him. Until every sun goes dark in every sky, until I am nothing more than long-forgotten cosmic dust, I will want him. And even then, I suspect my particles will long for his."

Ann Aguirre, Doubleblind

The vibration of various sounds accosts my ears, and increases my heart rate. It sounds like we are under attack. I can hear the loud and terrifying echoes of gunfire, explosions, and the screams of what must be injured men. The walls shake in my bedroom, making it seem like they are about to fall in on me.

Terror races through me with the understanding that my grandmother's hired men have finally reached the compound, and are attacking us. Fear for Diego, and his safety, has my lungs seizing. I want to race out there and go to his side, tell him I love him, but my limbs quiver and refuse to move toward the door.

Santiago's words repeat on a malicious cycle in my head, until I fear they will never end. That man hates me, but he loves Diego, and although I wanted to deny the verity of his words, the truth is they are accurate. I'm poisonous and destructive, and mine and Diego's love is toxic, if you can even call what we have love. I need to get away from him, for my own safety as well as his.

The door slams open, and an apprehensive Santiago rushes inside. "Isabella, come with me now. We must go, *chica!*"

For a moment, I don't move as panic sets in, and I want to run in the other direction, to get away from him, but at Santiago's stern expression, I know that he will drag me out of here kicking and screaming. One way or the other, he plans to remove me from Diego's life by force. Whether I'll still be breathing by the night's end is a mystery.

He grabs onto my bicep and drags me forward, my mind reeling on whether I should fight his hold or not. *Get it together, bitch. Stay strong; this is our one chance to get out of here.* I pull back on Santiago's hold until he releases me, and I glare at him, daring him to try that shit again.

"You either come willingly, or I will put a bullet in your head, Isabella. You choose whether you want this to be your last night on earth."

His words mimic my thoughts and bring a chill to my spine. "I will go, but please tell me he's safe."

"He will be safer when you are no longer here, *chica*. Come now, we have only a small window of time to get you out of the compound unnoticed."

I follow him like a lost puppy, through winding hallways into a section of the compound I have never entered, until we reach a room in the farthest western point. Santiago moves forward, rips open a window with no bars on its frame, and then turns back to face me. "This way. This is the furthest part of the compound. We must climb out of this window and move silently through the trees. I will climb out first and help you. Don't try to run, Isabella. I was not bluffing. I will kill you."

I watch as he heaves himself out of the window, and then reaches back to help me. I climb out the window on trembling legs that threaten to buckle under my weight. His arms instantly surround me and yank me forward, until we both stand precariously on a small pile of wooden pallets. We jump off the four-foot height, and Santiago urges me towards a thick area of trees. "There keep going, head towards the trees."

I follow his instructions, the material of my lightweight dress snagging on the thick branches as we move through the trees. Up ahead, I see a small firelight, and Santiago urges me in that direction. The sounds of gunfire erupting all around us, and screams in the distance, help to block out the noise of my panting and my racing heart. When we come closer, I notice a man dressed all in black, with two dark backpacks resting at his feet, and a machete gripped in his hand. The menacing look on his face doesn't exactly give me warm and tingly feelings, and once again, I wonder if I just walked myself to my own death.

"Isabella, this is my *primo*, Francisco. He will lead you through the jungle, and to one of the trading villages just over eighty miles away. There, I have a man who will have your new identification ready, and will help you get out of the country. Remember your promise to me, Isabella."

He grabs onto both my arms and shakes me until my teeth rattle. "You must let Isabella Stratford die in this jungle, and never contact your family again. I am giving you a chance at a new life. Don't make me regret it."

"How... how do I know... you're not trying to... kill me. That you don't plan... to kill me or have me killed in the... jungle?" I question with terror. I meet his dark gaze, and I witness fear, and what I also believe is hope. He wants me gone, as he honestly thinks I will be the end of Diego, which terrifies him and motivates him to help me escape.

"You can't know that, and I won't promise you that you won't die out in that jungle trying to escape, but it won't be by my hands or my orders. Your fate is in yours and God's hands now, *chica*. I hope for your sake he hasn't forsaken you."

He turns away from me and clasps his arms with Francisco in a burly man hug, slapping his back. "May God keep you safe on your journey. Get as far away from here as you can. Do not stop until you can no longer hear the sounds of gunfire, and even then, keep going, *primo*."

"*Dios te bendiga a ti también, primo. Te veré cuando te vea, mantente a salvo.*" Francisco releases him and grabs one of the bags, throwing it over his shoulders and slipping his arms through it, before handing me the other one.

"Let us go, *reina de las serpientes*. Time is a-wasting, and death breathes down our necks."

I throw the heavy pack around my shoulders, its weight both cumbersome and reassuring. They wouldn't bother with supplies if they planned to kill me in the jungle, would they?

Francisco steps forward towards the thicker fauna, and I fall into step with him. I turn to look back over my shoulder, and see nothing but Santiago's retreating back. Fuck, am I actually doing this, running away from the man I love? Leaving him to face my grandmother's army, and possible death, while I escape. I either don't love him enough, or love him too much, but which is the most accurate description of my feelings for Diego? The truth is I don't know anymore; my mind and heart are all tangled up.

What other choice is there? Diego will die trying to keep me. He will never let me go, and will end up killing me with his obsession, and irrational need to control me and make me stronger. Santiago has given me a chance to leave this frail and useless woman behind here in this jungle, and be reborn as something stronger. A person with no past, and no defined future, all I have to do is keep going and not look back, and let my heart irrevocably break.

Tears slide down my face as I put one foot in front of the other, and keep up with Francisco's steady pace, moving us stealthily through the jungle, and farther away from the place that has been both my home, and my prison, for months. The sound of heavy gunfire, and a larger explosion, has Francisco darting back and pulling me low into a thick grouping of bushes. He raises his fingers to his mouth, urging me to be quiet.

Two men are up ahead, not more than forty feet from us, both dressed in dark blue army attire. They each hold a rifle strapped across their chests, and I can hear the faint sounds of their conversation being spoken in English. "Chances she's still alive might be slim. I hope for that fucker Diego Cabano's sake, she is. Stella Stratford has no mercy."

"He's going to wish for death if he's still alive, when she gets her hands on him. Either way, it makes no difference to me. We get paid regardless."

Francisco grabs my wrist and points in the direction he wants me to go, urging me to stay as low to the ground as possible. I crouch down and keep moving forward, but I've taken about ten or more steps when I realize he's not with me. I search over my shoulder for him, and observe as he stealthily sneaks up on one of the men as he relieves himself against a tree. The metallic shine from a blade in the moonlight, as it slams below the man's chin and he collapses forward against the tree, is the only sign of his death.

Francisco pulls the blade out and moves towards the other man, who has no idea that his companion is now dead. With an almost unbelievable speed, Francisco darts silently from the foliage and throws himself on the man's back, wrapping his arms around his neck and taking him to the ground. The soldier tries his best to roll on the jungle floor, and turn the tables on Francisco, but he holds on tightly, and before I can even make a sound, he slits the man's throat from one ear to the other, and blood bursts from the wound, dark red in the moonlight. *Jesus fucking Christ.*

I tightly shut my eyes and bite down on the inside of my cheeks, to keep the whimpers that want to escape me silent. Nausea threatens to have me purging my stomach, but I force myself upright and continue moving in the direction Francisco had indicated, as he quickly makes his way towards me.

"Keep going, girl, we have a lot of ground to cover, and more than one predator in this jungle with us," he hisses as he moves past me to retake the lead, and dread slithers down my limbs.

We continue forward for what feels like hours, my legs and feet aching with all the miles we have put between us and the compound. Every once in a while, I watch as Francisco pulls out a digital compass and stares at it, to ensure we're still going in the right direction. I want to beg him to stop and allow us to rest a moment, but nothing comes out every time I open my mouth to speak.

Keep going, Issy, don't be weak. Freedom is this way; you can do it.

The night sky starts to lighten as night gives way to daybreak, and I inhale a deep breath of warm, earthy jungle air. "We will stop up ahead and rest, but we cannot stay long. We have to put many miles between us and Diego."

He marches towards the trunk of a large tree, surrounded by thick bushes, and removes his pack, pulling a metal canteen from it and taking a deep gulp of water. "Don't drink too much. You will get cramps, and I don't know if we will find fresh water again before nightfall returns."

I replicate his motions, dropping the pack at my feet, pulling the canteen out, and taking a drink. The cool water feels refreshing, and I'm tempted to keep drinking, but I feel his eyes centered on me, and I stop, using the back of my hand to wipe my mouth, and place the canteen back inside of my pack. "How much further until we reach the village?"

"Sixty or more miles. We have much walking to do, and we must cross the river before then. The heat will slow us down, but we have no choice. We must keep moving, or they will find us."

"Why are you helping me escape?" I question with apprehension as I sit down at the tree's base.

He groans as he sits down next to me, leaving a distance between us, and rubs the back of his sweaty neck with his large hand. "My *Tia* Alisa, said you are not a bad person. You are a trapped, gentle little bird, ready and waiting to be eaten by the serpent. She asked me to help you, to ensure you could get away. She helped raise me when my parents died, and I would do anything for her." He shrugs as if leading me through the jungle, while we're possibly being pursued by Diego, and my grandmother's men, is no big deal.

"Do you think they are still alive, and have been able to fight off my grandmother's men?"

A chuckle escapes his lips, and a grin breaks across his face, making him look younger and less harsh. "Santiago is a cat with nine lives, and Diego is the devil; no one can take them down. Worry about you, *reina de las serpientes*. You're much easier to kill."

"What does that mean, *reina de las serpientes*? Why do you call me that?" I butcher the words saying them, and another amused chuckle leaves his lips.

"Means you are the queen of serpents: snakes, *chica*. I call you that because you seem to be a snake charmer. At least, that is what I witnessed with Diego, and my *Tia* confirmed. You were able to tame him for a while until his venomous nature reemerged."

I process his words, and a smirk lifts the corner of my lips. I was able to tame him? In what world was I ever able to get Diego to do anything he didn't want to do?

"Issy, what the fuck!" Diego yells as I launch another vase towards his head.

"You son of bitch, you need to help those four fuckers find my sister, Diego. You need to use your men to scour all of the fucking state to help them locate who has taken her." I can't breathe. I feel like I'm being suffocated by the weight of the loss of my sister. Thoughts race through my mind on who could have taken her, and whether she's still alive. She has to be alive, because she's one of the strongest people I know.

"Jesus, Issy, fucking breathe, baby!" Diego demands as he wraps his large arms around me, and tries to comfort me, but there's none to be had while my sister is out there somewhere.

"Promise me you will help find her. Promise me you will kill whoever has done this to her." I grab tightly to his face, and his olive green eyes meet mine. Worry and anger swirl together in their depths, combined with something else that I can't name.

He raises his hand and cradles the back of my neck gently, before brushing his lips across mine in a tender kiss. "I promise you, Issy. I'll end them. I'll help to find her, but not because you are begging me, but because you are mine, Princesa. Anyone who hurts you in any way will pay with their lives."

I snap out of the memory and realize that I did have some power over Diego, at least before I told him that it was over between us, and that I didn't want him in my life anymore. That was the catalyst for the change in our dynamic. That was when his heart became a cold fortress that I no longer held the key to. It was then that he must have come up with this deranged plan to steal me from my grandmother, putting in motion events that would change both our worlds forever.

"Sleep, Isabella. Soon enough, we must keep moving, or the devil and his hell hounds will find us."

I close my eyes, exhaustion settling on my limbs like a weighted blanket. I'm filled with regrets for the life I've lived, the love that I have wasted with my immaturity and selfishness. All the different people I've hurt along the way; my grandmother and sister, my friends, or at least what few I had, and I turned my back on Kai, and now Diego. Where does the suffering that I've caused end?

You have a chance at a new life, a new beginning, and you can be a better person. You can heal yourself, this weakness inside of you, and live a life worth living. Shed yourself of this self-loathing, and become who you were always meant to be. There is strength buried under the weakness. Otherwise, you wouldn't be trekking through the jungle to save yourself but, more importantly, to save Diego from you.

I love him, the thought crosses my mind as sleep envelops me, but before the darkness swallows me, a pair of bright blue eyes sear my mind, reminding me he's not the only one I've ever loved and hurt.

Chapter Thirty

Diego

"Being deeply loved by someone gives you strength, while loving someone deeply gives you courage."

Lao Tzu

One moment, I'm sitting down to dinner alone in my den, as far away as I can get from the woman who makes my heart ache, and drives me insane simultaneously, and in the next second, parts of the glass ceiling are falling down around me, with an explosion from outside of the compound.

My skin stings as some of the smaller pieces of glass become embedded in my arms, and the back of my neck, which are exposed by my black t-shirt, and my ears ring loudly, forcing me to raise my hands to cover them. I race to my feet and stumble to the window, only to see the darkening sky lit. *Holy fuck, they are setting everything on fire!*

It looks like a war has broken out in my courtyard, with my men running in every direction, carrying weapons and firing back at the intruders. Who the fuck has found us? Could it be one of the other cartels, or is this Stella Stratford and the mercenaries she has waved a pot of gold at?

Another massive bang sounds from further within the compound, and has me running out of the den and toward my bedroom, where I know Issy was sleeping. *Fuck, I have to get to her now, I have to protect her at all costs.* I push debris out of my way, bile racing up my throat with the fear that threatens to choke me, as I try to maneuver down the hallway, and past my men rushing past me.

"Who the fuck is attacking us?" I yell, but the sounds of gunfire drown out my voice.

I grab one of my men by their shirt and pull him towards me. He's covered in blood and debris, and his eyes are prominent in his head. "Who's attacking us? Where is Santiago?"

"*Jefe*, mercenaries, they have surrounded the compound and are firing rockets at us, and shooting anyone who is outdoors. They have killed most of the men who were on patrol."

Mercenaries means they're Stella's men, fuck, why are they throwing rockets at us? Do they want to risk killing Issy along with us? There is no way that Stella authorized that. She would never risk injuring her granddaughter. That means some of them have gone rogue, and are willing to kill all of us. FUCK!

I push the man away and race down the hallway, reaching the door to my bedroom at the exact moment another bomb goes off. I hear the windows shatter, and the walls let out massive creaks. I force myself past the door; a scream logged in my throat as I take in the destruction before me. The bed is on fire, the ceiling has caved in where it leads to the washroom, and glass is everywhere.

Panic fills me as I search for Issy, flipping broken items out of my way and trying to find her underneath them. *Please be alive, please be safe.* I keep the mantra going in my mind, refusing to allow the possibility that she may be hurt or dead to register. I run into the bathroom, where further destruction greets my eyes, but other than the chaos, I don't spy my *Princesa*.

"ISSY! ISSY, WHERE ARE YOU?" I scream until my voice becomes hoarse, as I once again search the bedroom. The sounds of panicked men greet my ears, as the gunfire gets closer to the compound. Fuck, they will be upon us shortly. I have to organize my men and push them back, or we will be overrun.

With no signs of Issy in the room, I dash back into the hallway, yanking on whatever man crosses my path, and trying to get as many of them to follow me as possible. I frantically search all the faces around me, but still don't lay eyes on

Santiago or Issy. My only hope is that he was able to get to her first, and has her hidden and protected.

"How many are out there? Do we have a number? How many of our men are still standing from guard duty?" I roar my questions at my men, some of whom are already showing signs of battle.

"*Jefe,* at least ten or more are dead out there. They managed to get the drop on us silently coming in from the jungle and, without warning, launching rockets at the compound," Miguel replies.

"Has anyone had eyes on Santiago or the women?" I question with a lump in my throat threatening to stop my airway, and my hands clenched into tight fists as each of the men assembled shake their heads. Fuck! Where are they? Are they safe? Could they have already been captured?

Just as the thought crosses my mind, Santiago strides across the main room towards us, blood sliding down the side of his head, and an angry grimace on his features.

"*Jefe,* they are almost past the perimeter. We have to launch a counterattack! You have to activate the defense measures now!" He shouts above the loud sounds coming in from all the destroyed windows.

"Where are the women, Santiago?"

"*Mi madre* is safe. I was with her when the bombs started to go off. I have not seen Isabella since lunch." His large eyes meet mine, and I witness nothing but fear in their depths. Fuck, where is she? Where would she have hidden? She has to be so scared right now.

"Issy was not in my room, I checked. She must have hidden somewhere else in the compound when we were attacked. Take two men and search room by room, Santiago. I want her fucking found and brought to me now." I turn my attention to the rest of my men, and force myself to focus on what needs to be done right now, even though all I want to do is go search for my girl myself.

"The rest of you take up arms and positions like we have practiced. We must repel them, or we will all die before sunrise." With my parting words, I run towards the hidden security room within the compound's depths. Once I reach the door, I use my thumb to unlock it and seal myself within.

My eyes find the cameras hidden all over the compound and in the jungle, seeking out how many mercenaries are now at my door, ready to capture or murder me. *God fucking dammit*, we are overrun. There has to be at least forty or fifty men out there loaded down with weapons. Fucking Stella has sent a small army to do her bidding.

I search one camera after another, to see if I can get a glimpse of where Issy might be hiding, but all the cameras on the furthest western side of the compound have been disabled, probably from the rockets the bastards are launching at us. With no signs of Issy anywhere, I begin enabling all of the defense measures that we have hidden.

I activate the hidden electric wires around the perimeter, and release the gates on the guard dogs' pens. The emergency bulletproof shutters slam into place on all the window openings in the compound, and I can see that three of my men have now made it to the roof-mounted machine guns, and are returning fire against the intruders. A few others have made it into the tree-lined sniper's nests, and are picking the mercenaries off one by one.

Even with us attempting to defend ourselves, there are still so many blue uniformed fuckers on the screen. My eye catches movement in one of the lower screens, and I see Santiago moving from room to room, searching for Issy with two of my men. They are turning over debris and searching every section for her. *Fuck, I hope he finds her.*

I'm out of time, though. I can't stay hidden in this room, or join in the search for her, no matter how much I want to. I have to help my men fight off the intruders, or it won't matter if we find her, because they will take her away from me and return her to Stella's arms, probably before shooting me down like a rabid dog.

I can't let that happen. I can't have done all of this only to lose her in the end. *You knew that was always a possibility*, my mind seethes. Yes, I did, but I refuse to believe that my story with Issy ends here. That all the sacrifices I have made for her were for nothing. I can't let her go, not even now, when I know turning her over could save most of my men.

I know deep down it's selfish of me to allow all of their possible deaths, so that I can keep my beautiful prize. *Fuck,* it was selfish and insane of me to kidnap her, and drag her to the jungle in the first place, hoping I could have more than a slim amount of time with her before her grandmother found her. Time to correct her belief that we don't belong together, that she's not fucking mine, and I'm not hers, despite what her cunt of a grandmother says.

Now I'm out of time, and I only hope that at the end of this, she will want to stay with me of her own free will, but after everything that has happened, and the way I treated her with Paulo, I know she is going to run from me the first chance she gets. A cold film of sweat and dread coats all my limbs, with the almost certainty that she won't even look back when she does. *She's already left you, idiot, you just don't want to believe it.*

I broke and rebuilt her into something stronger, or at least that's what I hope I did. The image of her covered in blood, and hacking at my enemy, enters my mind and forces my breath to leave my lips in a whoosh. She was so beautiful and powerful in that moment, owning all the rage that had festered inside of her over the years. My queen, my little broken doll, put back together. Will she use her newfound strength to leave me?

Are you really so deluded that you don't already know the answer? The monster inside of me snarks, as a wave of despair tries to overwhelm me, and bring me to my knees. I can't fucking lose her. My world only makes sense when she is in it.

She says she loves me, but that was when I was traumatizing her. When I gave her the opportunity to say it before at the waterfall, or anytime we lay together in my bed in the weeks after that moment, she never did. Not once did she utter the words that my heart craved to hear. Not once did she reassure me that she would stay with me of her own free will.

If these fuckers get their hands on her, they will tear her away from me. I can't and will not allow that to happen. Nothing, and no one, is taking my *Princesa* from my grasp. I will fight for her to my very last breath.

I grab a few of the guns and knives off the wall, and strap them to my body, preparing to wage war on those who thought they could come in here, and take what is mine. They will all die, and I will feed their bones as an offering to the jungle beasts, and then I will have Stella Stratford's head for thinking she could take me on.

CHAPTER THIRTY-ONE

Issy

"The most terrible poverty is loneliness, and the feeling of being unloved."

Mother Teresa

"Isabella, come here, love, come taste this!" The sound of his excited voice lures me around the corner, and into the small kitchen of the cramped apartment. The rich smells of tomatoes and garlic reach my nose, and have my stomach growling loudly in demand of nourishment. When was the last time I ate anything?

I enter the small room that can barely fit his large frame, and watch him move about easily and gracefully. He stirs a pot on the diminutive stove, the muscles in his back and arms rippling with the movement, pulling his light blue button-up shirt tight across his form. Some of his blond hair covers one of his bright blue eyes that I love, and even from the side, I can tell he's smirking.

He's so handsome to look at; he should be on the cover of a magazine somewhere, instead of doing his residency at a tiny not-for-profit public hospital, one that barely pays him enough to live in this run-down apartment that feels like a stifling shoebox.

Whenever I mention it, or even the possibility of getting him a better-paying position, at a private hospital where my family are donors, and have wings named after us, he scoffs and brushes me off. He wants to help those who cannot help themselves. *Wealth and power are nothing to him, and he seems utterly immune to their temptations. I've never met anyone like him. I'm not even sure that anyone else exists like him, and because of that, I live in perpetual fear that he'll realize all the rot that lives inside of me.*

I'm a weak fraud, one who cannot go more than a day without living under the influence of the drugs that constantly flow within my veins. Right now, my hands are trembling, and my body aches with a need for more, as I come down from my high.

I try to avoid him when I'm like this, but the problem is that I've become more and more dependent on the oblivion that they provide, and yet, despite the need to be high, I also crave him just as much. Even when I try to stay away from him, I find myself in his gravitational pull, returning to where I know I should not linger. I can't stay away from him, because he has become a soul-deep addiction, just like the cocaine I can't live without.

I stumble as I make my way over to him, my limbs loose and uncoordinated, and he reaches out to grab my elbow and steady me. "Are you alright?" He questions as he stares deeply into my eyes, and I see when he notices I'm not. Why did I think I could hide it from him? I'm so stupid, so fucking stupid.

"Fuck, Isabella! We talked about this! You promised me that you wouldn't take any more of that shit," he roars, dropping the wooden spoon on the counter and splashing tomato sauce everywhere.

I can't hold his gaze as shame and guilt fill me, and threaten to smother me. Why the fuck did I come here? I knew this would be his reaction, that he would be angry and disappointed in me. Like everyone else in my life, he is no exception to feeling let down by Isabella Stratford, the Manhattan princess who has everything you could ever dream of at her fingertips, but craves oblivion more than life. More than him.

Weak, useless, discarded, empty. Those are the words I use to describe myself, which I'm sure everyone who has to deal with me would agree on. So, why did I come here? Why did I come to the one person I'm certain without a doubt loves me, only to hurt him?

Does he love you for you, or for the version he has in his head that he thinks he can save? Is that what I am? A project, a weak lamb to be rescued from the hungry jaws of a wolf? Does he believe he can save me from myself?

He grabs onto both of my biceps and shakes me with his tight grip, forcing my head to spin and my breath to become trapped in my throat. Fuck, the nausea that was already threatening to rise begins to do just that, and I know I'm mere moments away from spilling the meager contents of my stomach.

What, the fucking booze you drank earlier? You're such a lost cause, Issy. You would have been better off taking a little more and never waking again, my mind snarks, and despite not wanting to agree, I know it speaks the truth.

"*Kaaaiiii... I'm going... to vomit.*" *I try to get the words out between clenched teeth. He instantly removes his fingers from my skin, as if touching me now disgusts him, and takes a step back to put room between us. The expression of pure disappointment on his face makes my chest clench tightly, adding to the sensation of light-headedness and self-loathing.*

"*Why, Isabella? Why this constant need to self-destruct? What was it this time? What could only drugs have solved?*"

He's not wrong; I do indulge in nothing but self-destructive endeavors, and it's a testament to how well he has gotten to know me, that he can predict that something happened to push me back towards the snow that I snorted hours before.

An argument with my grandmother, over my sister being allowed to return to Casbury to seek revenge on those who wronged her, was the catalyst for this particular drug binge. My precious, strong-willed sister, who can never do anything wrong in my grandmother's eyes, is leaving me here alone at the mercy of my grandmother, and her whims, without a thought of how that would impact me. When I adamantly suggested that I go with Mia to Casbury to stay by her side, my request was immediately denied.

My grandmother's reasoning? I would only be in the way of Mia completing her tasks, and Mia had enough to worry over. That a period of distance would be good for both of us, so I could learn to stand on my own two feet, and fight my own battles.

If you read between the lines, all you see is, "You're not worth it. You'll only get in the way. You're useless." My response to that was to shove as much coke up my nose, and vodka down my throat, as possible. That was two days ago, and I'm only coming off that binge now.

My first coherent thought was that I needed to see Kai, to be wrapped in his arms, and know some semblance of love from someone. Yet here I am once again, being nothing but a disappointment. Even the man who claims to love me, can't stand all the broken, weak parts of me.

Will there ever be someone who loves me for me? You don't even love yourself, so how can you believe someone else can love you?

I turn away from him, not wanting to continue seeing the judgment on his face, and the hurt in his eyes. "Nothing, I don't need a reason."

"Isabella, please. You can't keep doing this to yourself. This is not the right way to handle your problems. You can't just keep running and evading them. Let me help you get clean, and into a program." His hand reaches out and tries to pull me back towards him, but I step out of his reach.

I'm so sick of him telling me this is not how to handle my problems. What does he know of my problems? He has his purpose, a loving family to support him, parents who dote on him, and a brother who adores him and would never think to leave him behind. I have nothing and no one, no parents, no purpose, no life of my own. Half the time when I am with my only remaining family, they don't acknowledge that I am there, unless I have created a scandal they must fix. Even my sister, who I thought would never betray me, is willing to leave me behind.

"I don't want your fucking help, Kai. There is nothing wrong with how I handle my problems. We can't all be perfect and golden like you are." I take a step towards the door of the apartment, ready to make my escape from his judgment, and sermon on how drugs are harmful to me. Like, no shit, asshole, that's why I do them in the first place.

"Let me call your sister and grandmother, and between the four of us, we can figure out how to help you, Isabella." I whirl around and bare my teeth at him with a growl, and his eyes widen dramatically.

"You will do no such fucking thing. I didn't ask you to put on your savior cape, Kai. I don't want your help or anyone's help. I don't want to be saved. If you can't accept that this is who I am, we shouldn't be together." I pry the apartment door open, and step out into the dingy hallway that reeks of sweat, a mixture of different foods, and garbage.

If only Stella Stratford could see how her granddaughter likes to slum it, she would be horrified. Oh well, it would just add to my long list of sins committed. That list grows daily, as she likes to remind me.

"Isabella, please don't leave. We can talk about this. Come back in and let me feed you at least."

I don't bother to turn around, though, because I have no intention of being manipulated by him or anyone else. As much as I think I love him, I don't want to change for him. I don't want to be saved by anyone. All I crave is destruction and chaos, because at least then, I don't hear the voices in my head reminding me that I'm nothing.

Chapter Thirty-Two

Issy

"In the depth of winter, I finally learned that within me, there lay an invincible summer."

Albert Camus

I wake from my dream with a start, the sounds and smells so vivid that I can almost taste the garlic and tomato sauce, and my stomach rumbles with hunger. My eyes search the area around me. Night has started to creep forward, and with it, the jungle looks ominous.

I had to beg Francisco to stop for a few hours as my legs felt like jello, and the blisters on my feet were aching, and making every step feel excruciating. He took pity on me once we had come close to the river he mentioned. I bathed and cleaned my blisters, and tucked myself at the base of a tree for a few hours of rest, and now, as I look around, I don't see him anywhere.

I scramble to my feet and try to restrain the need to shout for him. It's not safe. He repeatedly reminded me to be silent as we traveled through the jungle, so as not to garner unwanted attention from the humans, and beasts, that may be hunting us.

Has something happened to him while I slept? Has he abandoned me? Left me to die in this jungle alone, without any idea of the direction I have to travel, in order to reach safe passage. Was that Santiago's plan all along?

The quiet sound of a twig snapping has me pushing back into the fauna around me, and sliding my hand down to the ground to grasp the small blade he gave me hours ago to protect myself. Just as I hoist it, ready to slam it into whoever or whatever is before me, an arm snaps out and grabs my wrist.

"Easy there, no need to stab me, girl." Francisco's amused voice greets my ears, and the breath I was holding leaves me in a wheeze. I have never been so happy to hear anyone's voice. I was positive he had abandoned me.

"So... rry. Sorry, I thought... I..." I don't finish my sentence now, feeling foolish for having thought that he would have abandoned me, and that Santiago betrayed me with his promise to get me out of this jungle.

His dark eyes meet mine, and I see a look of understanding cross his face. "I won't abandon you, Isabella. I promised my *Tia* to see you safe, and I don't break my promises."

"Thank you," I whisper, and he releases his grip.

"Come, I found some berries and nuts. We need to eat quickly and get across the river before the light completely disappears. It won't be safe to be in the water after dark, and I fear we are still too close to the compound."

I sit down on the tree trunk, and he hands me a piece of fabric with berries and nuts wrapped in its center. I'm so hungry that I don't even hesitate to start eating, the delicious tart and sweet combination of the berries exploding on my tongue. "How far are we from the village?"

He pulls out the digital compass and shows it to me. "We need to keep heading in that direction," he points to the far right. "Once we cross the river, we are still just under fifty miles away from the village. The terrain will get harder now, as denser jungle is on that side. It will slow us down, but we have to keep pushing."

"How long do you think it will take us?" I question as I eat more of the sweet berries that he has provided.

"A day, maybe two at the most, if we don't stop for long." I immediately get what he's saying without speaking the words. I have to find the strength to keep moving, and keep up with his pace, or we are doomed. I'm the reason we haven't made it farther.

My mind wants to call up all my weaknesses, but I shove them away. There is no time for self-pity, and I will not allow anything to derail the opportunity to escape. I promised myself that I'd leave Isabella Stratford in this jungle to die, and that is what I intend to do.

My thoughts travel back to the compound and Diego, and my chest tightens with worry for him. Is he safe? Were they able to fend off the attack from my grandmother's men? Has he been captured? So many thoughts circle inside my mind, until nausea starts to rise again in my stomach. I stop eating, wrap what is left of the berries back up, and place them in my pack.

"He doesn't need your worries, *chica*, he will survive. Even the devil doesn't want to go toe to toe with him. Focus on leaving this jungle and the freedom that awaits you." Francisco lifts his pack out of the thick bushes and places it back on his back, motioning for me to do the same, as he makes his way back down to the river.

"We need to cross here; this is the shallowest part of the river. I hope you can keep your balance, *chica*, and swim, otherwise, the currents will drag you further downstream." *Fuck, I hope so too.*

We make our way into the river, the cold water rising quickly past my knees until I'm chest-deep inside of it, and my teeth begin to chatter. *Fuck, it's so cold and moving so quickly.* I step forward on the sandy bottom, slide across a rock or some smooth debris, and almost lose my balance. Francisco reaches back and steadies me, until I find my footing again. *Keep going, Issy. We are almost on the other side.*

It feels like it takes forever to make it through the river and across to the other side, fighting the currents the whole way. My entire body is frigid once we reach the muddy riverbank, my hair is plastered to my back, and my breath leaves me in heaving pants. We did it, though; we made it. We are that much closer to getting out of this jungle.

"What... what will happen... to you once we get to the... village?" I question as my teeth chatter, and I wring the water out of my hair and dress, which now clings to every inch of me. Thank fuck I wasn't wearing white; at least the dark green isn't see-through.

"I will return to Columbia, and my *Tia* Alisa. Santiago has made arrangements to hide her from Diego and Manuel." He says it so nonchalantly, as if he wasn't implying that Manuel and Diego would harm a sweet old lady, in order to punish Santiago for helping me escape.

"You think they would harm Alisa?" I ask with worry.

"You are a multimillion-dollar prize to the Cabanos. A way to further their reach with your name and your womb." He nods toward my stomach. "They would kill anyone who helped you escape from their grip."

Jesus fucking Christ, I hope he's not right. I know that Diego is ruthless, but even he has to have a conscience and empathy, and understand that Alisa was not part of this. That she doesn't deserve to be harmed just because I got away. *He might be dead, and you are worrying about nothing,* the thought appears in my head, but I slam a door shut in my mind, and refuse to engage with the self-destruction that is beckoning me.

We travel for hours through the thick jungle. The sounds of insects and wildlife are all around us. More than once, I see eyes glowing from deep within the jungle, watching us. When I motion to Francisco, he tells me in a hushed whisper to keep moving, but he grips his machete tighter and picks up the pace, until we are almost at a jog.

Just as we are about to leave a thick treed area, something huge and black lunges from one of the trees at us, and lands on Francisco's back with a snarl. He tries to fight it off, but the jungle cat is too large and growls, biting into the side of his abdomen, and taking him to the jungle floor with a wretched scream.

A cry leaves my lips as I race for the machete that Francisco dropped, and raise it above my head, slamming it down on the giant predator's back. The jaguar momentarily releases Francisco, looking back over its enormous, sleek, muscled back at me before snarling, all its sharp, bloody teeth on display. *Oh my God, I am going to die!*

"HIT IT AGAIN, ISABELLA! AGAIN! NOW!" Francisco shouts frantically, as he tries to fight off the cat and get it to release its claws, which are digging deep into his shoulders.

I raise the machete, my hands slipping on the handle, and force it back down on the large cat, getting one of his hind legs and then raising it again to hit his lower back, the blade slicing his fur, and exposing the tissue and bone. The cat makes a few more snarling sounds, but they are softer and muffled before he stops moving on top of Francisco, and he can finally push it off and to the side.

Francisco tries to scramble back to his knees, but he buckles almost instantly back down to the ground with a pained groan, as he clenches one of his hands on his side. There is so much blood covering him, both his and the jaguar's, that it's hard to tell how badly he's hurt.

"Francisco! Oh my God!" I drop the machete with a clang on the ground and rush to his side, bracing him and pulling him farther away from the cat. He groans with my grasp on his body, and his legs give in under him, taking us both down to the ground.

"You... make sure it's dead, now!" He pants, and I scurry back to my feet and grab the machete again as I approach the animal. Its whole body is still, its massive mouth open with its fangs exposed. Its luminous yellow-green eyes stare back at me without moving, and I finally release my pent-up breath.

"Dead. It's... dead." I rush back to Francisco's side as he lifts the side of his shredded shirt, and I can see a part of the wound. The big cat has managed to bite deep, ripping through the skin and leaving horrific damage in its wake. Muscles and bones are visible through all of the carnage and blood. I gag at the sight, and have to swallow the bile that rises up the back of my throat.

Fuck, I need to stop the bleeding, or he's going to die. I crawl to his discarded backpack, and rifle through until I find a long-sleeved shirt, racing back to him, and wrapping it tightly around his chest. I tie it as tight as I can, while he releases a guttural scream. My hands are covered in so much blood that they drip and shake. "It's going to be okay, we will get you help."

Panic seizes me as tears cascade down my face. Do jaguars hunt alone? Was that even a jaguar? Should I be worried that it has a pack that will be coming to hunt and kill us? My eyes search through the trees surrounding us, looking for any sign of more predators. What am I going to do if there are more?

"Isabella, you need to take... the compass and keep moving. I'm not... going to be able to make it like this. You... need to reach the village and... send help back," Francisco pants the words, each breath sounding more strained.

"No! No, I can't leave you here. I don't know how to navigate through the jungle." How could he even suggest that? There is no way that I could make it through the jungle alone. I would die trying. *You'll die here if you don't, especially when other predators smell the blood.*

"Go... to the river. Wash the blood off, or it will call... to other animals. Hurry, girl!"

I rush back into the river and throw myself under the water, submerging every part of me. I grab fistfuls of sand and scrub frantically at my skin and dress to get all the blood off. Once I'm clean, I race back to Francisco and grab one of the canteens, raising it to give him some water.

He takes a deep swallow, pain laced across his features. "Listen to me, *chica*, you are my only hope of survival. You need to take the compass and listen to my directions. Get to the village and send someone back." I grab the compass and hold it in my trembling fingers before him.

"The course is set on the compass; you just need to follow it. You see this?" He points to a part of the compass. "It must always be pointing in the same direction to ensure you are getting closer to the village. Don't deviate, just stay the course, and you will make it, but you have to go now. Take the machete with you, girl."

"What about you? How will you defend yourself? What if more predators come?"

"Open the pack, hurry, Isabella. Two guns... are inside; take one, leave... me with the other. You must go now." I stumble back to my feet, grab the other gun, throw it into the pocket of my bag, and heft my backpack, throwing it over my shoulders while I hold tightly to the compass in one hand, and the machete in the other. "Go now, Isabella."

I take a step forward, followed by another, leaving Francisco injured and behind me. Tears continue to slide down my face, but adrenaline and strength fill my limbs with determination to get to the village, and send help back for him.

I look over my shoulder but no longer see any hint of him, the jungle swallowing him from sight.

Keep going, Issy, we have to get to that village if he has any hope of surviving.

I keep moving for what feels like hours, and the night sky fully darkens and then starts to lighten again, as I force myself forward, deeper into the jungle, and check the compass for direction while keeping my eyes and ears open for predators near me. My body is fighting exhaustion, but still, I keep pushing, remembering that Francisco is counting on me to get help.

I fall down and pick myself up again, forcing one foot in front of the other. I'm drowning in nausea, nothing but acid seems to be in my stomach, and dizziness assails me. I fall once again as my head spins with the already rising heat, and empty my stomach into the bush, but nothing comes out. Pain radiates through my abdomen as cramps have me clutching my arms around my middle. I'm going to die out here in this wretched jungle, and I won't have saved anyone.

Get up, you fucking weakling, keep moving! We have to keep going, or we die.

I crawl forward, my legs refusing to carry me until my knees are bloody. I grab onto the low branches of a bush, pull myself up, and then use the trunks of the trees, stumbling from one to the other to keep going. *I will survive. I will be strong. I'm not dying in this jungle.*

The sun starts to set on the day, and I know I won't make it more than a few steps now. I need to rest for an hour, and drink some water, or I'm going to pass out from dehydration. I take the canteen from my bag and swallow deeply, despite my stomach's protests. I look around, spy some thick, leafy bushes, and stumble in that direction.

The stomach cramps are getting worse and making me want to double over. I lower myself to the ground, placing my pack next to me so I can lay my head on its surface. I hold the machete tight in my hand as I assemble myself in the fetal position, raising my knees to my chest. I'm asleep within moments, the darkness calling to me instantly and taking me away.

CHAPTER THIRTY-THREE

Diego

"I will be with her again, or I will die. There aren't any other options."

Julie Kagawa, The Iron Knight

It's been hours since the attack started, and we were able to repel Stella's hired men back into the jungle. I'm not deluding myself into thinking they have retreated very far and won't attack again. I know they will; they are just biding their time, recouping their losses, and treating their wounded, the same as we are, and then they will strike again. The bounty on my head guarantees it.

The compound is in shambles around me, many of my men are injured, and we still can't find Issy, and now Alisa is also missing. I worry that they have been taken by one of Stella's mercenaries. Either that or my *Princesa* has finally managed to escape me. The thought alone makes me want to race out into the jungle and search for her, to bring her back with a leash around her fucking throat, and lock her in a room so she can never leave me again.

However, I can't leave my men to hold off these assholes alone. I have to stand by their sides as they have mine during this stupid, idiotic plan of mine to take the Stratford heiress, and keep her for myself. "Diego, we have managed to get your father on the satellite phone," Santiago's weary voice calls out to me, as I stare through one of the open doorways into the jungle, daring one of Stella's hired fuckers to try to shoot me.

I bring the phone to my ear, but before I can even speak a word, my father is already yelling at me. "How many of our men have died, Diego, for this one woman? *Hijo*, I need you to see reason, release her, and return to me. This has gone too far, and Stella will see you dead."

So he doesn't know yet that we can't find Issy. I stare at Santiago and see the understanding in his face. He didn't want to be the one to tell my father that many of his men have died, and I lost Isabella Stratford in the process. My father, Manuel, was already unsure of this plan, and now it looks like I have failed him and, at the same time, failed myself.

How can she fucking be gone? There is no way Issy made it out of this compound without help. Someone got her out. Someone from within helped her escape. That seems more likely than one of Stella's men breaching our interior without us realizing it, and getting her out. The question is, who has betrayed me? Who took my prize away and now has a death sentence on their head?

"BOY, ARE YOU LISTENING TO ME!" My father shouts and brings my attention back to the matter at hand. The sound of his angry, disappointed voice causes further aggravation along my already frazzled nerves.

"Yeah, I'm listening. We have lost twelve men in the raid, six more are injured gravely, and three have minor injuries. We managed to push them back for now, but I need reinforcements, *papá*."

"*Reinforcements*? Have you lost your *goddamn* mind? You want me to send more men to die so you can keep that spoiled girl? No, Diego, I can't send more men to their deaths because you won't see reason. That *chica* is dangerous!"

"Issy's fucking gone. She escaped somehow during the raid. The men are to protect those of us trapped in this fucking compound under fire, or do you want to see them capture your only son again?" I let him feel the wrath of my words, and the harsh reminder that this won't be the first time an enemy has captured me.

No, I spent weeks being tortured, and chained to a wall, only a mere two years ago. I was barely out of my teens when I was taken by one of the other cartels, as a way to keep my father in line. I reach up and trace a finger along the scar on my face, a constant reminder of that time. That period of captivity changed me, making me colder and more ruthless. It also taught me that I can survive anything this world throws at me, anything that is, except losing Issy. *She's gone, and you will never get her back now.*

"The *chica* is gone?" A deep, annoyed sigh vibrates through the phone. "*Hijo,* I know you don't see it now, but it's for the best. She is not the one for you. She would only bring your death. You should have picked the other one; she was strong, and would have ruled at your side."

I pinch the bridge of my nose and press my lips firmly together, to prevent myself from telling my father to go '*fuck himself*'. It's not his fault he doesn't understand my feelings for Issy. He can't see past the weak shell that she shows the world. She can be, and is, as strong as her sister, but she just doesn't know it yet. I've seen glimpses of her internal power and strength over the last few months. Every time she fought back against me, she showed me her resilience.

She wouldn't have escaped if she wasn't strong, and left me here to die at the mercy of her grandmother's men.

My father doesn't understand that sometimes, your greatest strength comes from knowing your greatest weaknesses. No one can use them against you, if you don't allow them to. My Issy had to learn that for herself, and while I pushed her in that direction, she did the work herself and has come out fiercer even after everything I put her through. *That's how she found the fortitude to leave me behind.*

"It doesn't matter. I plan to get her back, and no one will take her from me again, not even you, *papá.* She is mine and will always be mine, and neither you nor Stella will change that. Send the men, or be prepared to dig a hole to bury your only son in." I don't wait to argue with him any further, disconnecting the call and slamming the phone down forcefully on the table next to me.

"Prepare the men who are still able to fight. We're not going to be sitting fucking ducks here waiting for our death. We will attack these assholes under the deep cover of night, and we have the advantage because we know this jungle."

A concerned look crosses Santiago's face, and it almost looks like he intends to argue with me before he nods. "*Si, Jefe*, right away."

"One more thing, Santiago. Someone helped her escape from me. That person is a traitor, and I will have their head, and the heads of every member of their family. No one betrays me and keeps breathing." He visibly gulps at my words and then turns without another word, leaving me alone with my thoughts and rage.

Once I have these fuckers pinned down or dead, I will be going after my *Princesa*, and when I get my hands on her, she is going to regret ever even thinking about leaving me behind. I know I'll thoroughly enjoy punishing her, for every moment of worry and anger she has caused me with her escape.

If she's not knocked up yet with my baby, I am going to make sure I tie her to a fucking bed and breed her until she is. She will never escape me again, and with her by my side and giving birth to the next generation, we will rule the world. Stratford and Cabanos united for all eternity.

An image of Issy on her knees, covered in Paulo's blood, enters my mind, her mouth pleading for mercy as she finally uttered the words that I craved so desperately to hear. Words used to attempt to placate me. Does she even truly love me? Did I do this all for nothing after all? Will she never find it in her heart to be mine?

I could offer her the world, bleeding at her feet, yet she chose to leave me the moment I had my back turned. She ran away from me as if I was a villain, and not the man who loved her beyond reason. She's my obsession, the reason my heart started beating again after all these years of lying dormant. I can't and won't go back to the way it was before her. I won't ever release her from our relationship, regardless of if it is toxic and all-consuming. Isabella Stratford was born to be mine; the fates brought us together, and no one, living or dead, will separate us.

It's time to send Stella Stratford a message, written in blood, that she can't stop me from having her granddaughter. No one can.

Chapter Thirty-Four

Issy

"Confront the dark parts of yourself, and work to banish them with illumination and forgiveness. Your willingness to wrestle with your demons will cause your angels to sing."

August Wilson

"Princesa, wake up now, my love. It's time to go; you have to keep moving," Diego's voice calls to me deep within the darkness, and a moan sounds in response. *"Come now, my beautiful broken doll, you're stronger than you think, and you will survive."*

I try to pry my tired eyes open, struggling with a groan. Every part of my body aches, and my legs feel numb, from the way I have them bent and pressed against my chest. I crack an eye open to see nothing but the canopy of thick trees and greenery above me. For a moment, I'm disoriented, thinking that Diego is here with me, and I'm back at the compound, but then my memory intrudes, and flashes of an injured Francisco have me dashing to my feet, as my breath catches in my chest.

How long was I asleep? FUCK! How could I have slept so long while Francisco was counting on me to get help? I drag my hands down my face as my stomach clenches with a painful cramp, which forces me to lean against a tree trunk. I breathe in through my nose as I try not to scream. I can't stay here, and I need to keep moving. There are more predators in this jungle, and I'm exposed. I bend down and lift my pack, almost falling back to the ground with its weight.

Get it together, weakling. You will die in this fucking jungle if you don't keep moving. Francisco is counting on you to get help. Diego will find you and drag you back, if you don't get to that village! Do you want to be a prisoner for the rest of your life?

The words spur me on to move forward, even as my head spins with light-headedness. I have to keep going. I know that I can do this, survive this jungle and escape. I can't let Diego take me back, and live a life where I constantly worry about what he will do next.

I pull out the compass, look at the direction that it's pointing at, and groan with frustration. I've already gotten off the path I needed to follow. Fuck! Okay, I need to adjust my course and keep moving forward, and sooner or later, I have to hit that village, right?

I'm going to save myself, and get the hell out of this jungle, and then I will run as far and as fast as I can from Diego Cabano. *You love him*, my mind reminds me. Love is not enough. It doesn't matter if I love him; our love is corrupted, and will have the both of us continuously hurting each other, and others around us, because of it. I can't live a life knowing that I'm continuously hurting him and myself.

I look at the compass again and charge into the thick jungle, my ears at the ready in case another animal attempts to attack me. I will survive. I have no other choice.

I've been walking for hours, yet still, there is no sign of the damn village, and I'm starting to doubt that I'll ever reach it. I'm losing hope that I won't die out here in this jungle, alone and eaten by beasts. Memories keep accosting me as I trek through the wilderness.

"Give me your hand, Princesa." The smirk on his face is endearing. I want to deny his request but end up giving him my hand, and he pulls me off the sofa

and drags me outdoors. The cool North Carolina night air meets my skin, and has goosebumps erupting all over my arms.

"Diego, it's cold. What are we doing out here?"

"So impatient. Come with me and find out." He drags me off the back porch and further down the yard towards the pool area. My mouth hangs open at the vision before me. The pool is completely lit up with candles on every available surface. There are even some floating on the water. One of the outdoor daybed's frames has been draped with soft white fabric, and inside, a mountain of pillows await, and a soft faux fur blanket is draped on its end.

"What is all this?" He keeps pulling me toward the daybed, with a silly grin on his face that causes his scar to stretch tight across his cheek, and his eyes to sparkle brightly in the moonlight, making him look younger and carefree.

"Netflix and chill, but outdoors?" He laughs.

I can feel my face getting hot at the naughty way he's wagging his dark eyebrows at me. I look back over my shoulder towards the house, but don't see any lights on in the rooms besides the one I just vacated. I worry what my sister and her friends will think, if they spy me out here with Diego making out, or worse, what if one of my grandmother's guards sees us and reports back to her?

"Diego, someone could see us." I grind to a stop, feeling self-conscious.

"Are you embarrassed by me, Issy? Who are you hiding me from, hmm, your sister, grandmother, or yourself?" He pulls me forward, and his finger tilts my chin until I have no choice but to stare into those stunning olive-green eyes. A look of disappointment crosses his face, and I instantly feel horrid for putting in there.

"Of course not. I... I just don't want to create any problems, and you're not exactly well-liked by my sister, especially after trying to blackmail her into marrying you."

"That's in the past, Issy. I never really wanted her, and you know it. She was just a means to an end." He leans forward and skates his lips along the edge of my jaw, "You, however, are a different story. I want you. In fact, I want to do very naughty things to you, baby. The kind of things that make that pretty pussy of yours weep, and those perfect cheeks go pink."

Heat floods my system, and I can feel my panties getting damp with his words. Diego has the filthiest mouth I've ever encountered, which never ceases to turn me on. He knows it, too, the bastard.

"Come lay under the stars, Issy, and let me lick that sweet cunt of yours, until you scream my name to the heavens."

Jesus fucking Christ, this guy will be the death of me. I'm a puddle at his feet whenever he says things like that to me. I'm pulled forward, and before I can protest further, he throws me over his shoulder in a fireman's hold. "Jesus, you're a fucking caveman! Put me down!" I demand and get a swat to my ass for my efforts.

"Hush now, baby, let me have this." He keeps moving towards the daybed and then drops me on its surface, and I bounce before landing on my back with my legs spread.

"Fuck, yes. Let me help you get rid of those clothes that are hiding my perfect pussy." My core clenches tightly at his words, and my clit throbs.

"It's not yours, psycho. It's mine, and I never said you could look at it, never mind lick it." My words sound all husky to my ears, and I know he knows that I'm turned on, and there is no way I will deny him. Since we started hooking up in the shadows here in my sister's house, I have never once been able to deny him access to my body, and for that, he makes sure that I come hard and frequently.

He braces himself on his forearms and toes above me, blanketing me with his smell and the heat from his body. Fuck, he always smells so good, earthy, spicy, and sweet. It's a combination that I can never seem to resist, and has become my favorite scent.

"Baby, everything about you is mine. From the pretty, privileged top of your head," he leans in and kisses my head. "To these pretty eyes," he kisses each of my eyelids. "To these delicious, pouty lips," he graces his lips along mine, and a whimper escapes me. "Right down to these sexy as fuck tits." One of his hands cradles the globe of my breast before he strums his thumb across the hardened peak covered by fabric.

My body is heating up, and I no longer feel the cold. His hand leaves my breast and slides down my abdomen until it reaches the waistband of my sweats, and he slips his fingers underneath to brush the very top of my pussy. "This pussy is mine,

Issy. It belongs to me. It weeps for me, baby, and do you know why?" He asks with a raised eyebrow as he bites down on his full lower lip.

"Why?" The word leaves my mouth with a shudder, as his fingers caress my pussy lips over the soaked fabric of my panties.

"Because you are my good girl, and my slut. Your pretty cunt knows who owns it, and who makes it cum, doesn't it, baby?" He slides my panties to the side, and his forefinger rubs against my throbbing clit, as my hips rise and chase the feeling of his fingers on my hot flesh.

"Fuck, Diego," I moan.

"You want to cum nice and hard, don't you, baby? You want my fingers inside of you, stroking you while you clench around them. You want me to stretch this tight, pink hole so my cock can fill you up, don't you, my slut?"

Fuck yes, I want that. I want all of him inside me, filling me up until there is no room left. Until he and I are one body with two beating hearts, and our souls combine in rapture.

His head moves forward until his lips are at the junction between my neck and shoulder, his warm breath causing a shiver to race down my spine. His tongue slides against my hot flesh and licks me before his teeth bite down, and a gasp leaves my lips. "Tell me that you want me, baby. Tell me whose sweet pussy this is."

His fingers slip between the folds of my wet pussy lips as he strokes me, then one meets my tight hole and plunges inside, forcing my body to bow below him as he bites down on my neck simultaneously. "FUCK!" The word is screamed so loud that I'm instantly worried that someone in the house will hear me, or it will send one of my grandmother's guards running in our direction.

"Diego, fuck! We have to stop, or someone is going to find us. The guards are going to report back to Stella." Even though I'm begging him to halt, I widen my legs further to give him better access to slip another finger inside of my core, and he doesn't disappoint me, filling me until my breath hitches in my throat.

His lips move down my neck towards my chest, and he mumbles against my skin, "you worry too much, Princesa. No one is coming in this direction even if you scream. I made sure of it."

He pulls up my shirt until my bra is visible and squeezes my breast, pulling the soft fabric cups down until I'm exposed to the night air and his mouth. His hot mouth seals over one of my hardened peaks, and has me biting down on my lower lip to stifle the cry that tries to escape.

"What... Jesus... did you do?" I can't think coherently, as he sucks and lashes my nipple with his tongue.

He pulls back, his lips shiny and wet, and a wicked grin graces his face. His dark lashes frame gorgeous eyes that twinkle in the candlelight. "Might have slipped something into their dinner so they could go nighty night a little earlier. Nothing that will harm them, just make them take a nap so I can eat my girl in peace."

He lowers his body to my side, increasing the speed his fingers are working me at, as his mouth returns to sucking my breast. Heat spirals in my belly and pulsates throughout my limbs. My toes curl, and my fingers find their way into his hair, holding him tightly to my feverish skin. 'My girl', that's what he called me, claiming me as his. The words bring me so much pleasure that they push me right over the edge, and force an orgasm to race up my spine. "Oh my God, oh my God, don't stop, please don't stop."

I snap out of the daydream and stumble down an incline, falling to my hands and knees and smacking my chin on the hard ground, until I taste copper in my mouth. *Fuck*, I groan as I try to get back up, as a sharp pain radiates through my forearm, and my bare knees throb. I sit down and take inventory of my new injuries. Blood dribbles down my chin from biting my tongue, there's a gash in my knee filling with blood, and my wrist is red and painful when I try to rotate it. *Fucking great, on a roll, Issy!*

All the emotions, the stress of the last forty-eight hours, and my injuries, overwhelm me at that moment, and huge sobs wrack my body. I drag my hands down my face, swiping angrily at the tears in frustration at my mental breakdown. Okay, we'll just cry it out for a moment, get it all out of our system, and then we're going to pick ourselves up and put on our badass girl panties, and get to that fucking village, and nothing is going to stop us, my mind rants.

Resolve fills me not to let this deter me. I'm going to get to that village. I will get the fuck out of this jungle, and save Francisco in the process. I'm leaving that weak bitch behind here, and when I emerge, I'll be someone new, someone who doesn't break down and takes no shit from anyone. I'll be in control of my destiny.

Despite the pain in my leg, I get to my feet, the backpack's weight trying to drag me back down. *No, keep fucking moving! Let's go!* I urge myself, pulling the compass back out, reassessing my location, and moving toward where the village is supposed to be. Hunger pains fill me, and my mouth is as dry as the Sahara desert. I pull out the water canteen, only to realize it's almost empty, and I haven't seen any signs of fresh water for a while. It's okay, it will be okay, water will appear, but I have to keep going. I unwrap the few remaining berries and consume them, their tart taste helping to soothe my aching stomach, and offset the gnawing hunger.

The next few hours fly by, as I continue to follow the compass's directions with no signs of water. The high heat and humidity cause my ripped and stained dress to stick to my flesh, and the backpack's weight to slow me down. My vision blurs with the pounding headache that is trying to shatter my skull. Nausea once again becomes my unwelcome companion, and my swollen wrist throbs painfully, until even holding the machete in that hand becomes unbearable.

I suddenly notice how quiet the jungle has become around me. The sound of birds overhead, and insects, have almost entirely disappeared, as if the jungle was holding its breath. *Predator.* The word makes its way through my mind and has my heart rate increasing. I slowly maneuver myself into the thicker vegetation and crouch down, just as the sound of loud footsteps and male voices perk my ears.

I try to make myself as small as possible, hiding behind some thick leaves, as I peek out and spy two large men heading toward where I was standing moments ago. They are both dressed in t-shirts and shorts, not military uniforms, and that makes some of my anxiety release. *Are you stupid? They are men! Men traveling through the jungle, and you are a woman alone. Get the fucking gun!*

I reach into the side pocket and pull out the pistol that Francisco urged me to take, removing the safety and holding it in a tight grip, camouflaged at my side. The men look like locals and are not speaking English, but I don't think it's Spanish either, which makes me believe they are not part of Diego's men. They are lost in boisterous conversation, and have almost passed my hiding spot when suddenly something wraps around my neck, and yanks me backward and off my feet. I panic and flail in their hold, trying to loosen the arm around my neck, while keeping my grip on the gun.

All the noise has gotten the attention of the other two, who I can hear making their way back through the fauna. *"O que é isso?"* One of the large males speaks as he gets closer. I manage to sink my teeth into the forearm of the man holding me, and he releases me with a shout. I scramble to my knees and point the gun at the one directly in front of me, and he immediately backs up, his hands in the air. *"Ei, agora, não atire."*

"Stay there, or I'll blow a fucking hole in your head," I shout. I back away slowly from the three of them, keeping the one who tried to strangle me in my peripheral vision.

"Ela é louca?" The one being held at gunpoint says to his companion. Fuck, I wish I understood what they were saying. "You, move towards your companions now." I motion with the gun towards the other two, hoping that at least one of them understands English, and my commands.

"Little girl, you are going to get yourself killed with that thing," the one who tried to strangle me responds, as he moves in the direction of his companions with a smirk.

"You speak English? Why did you attack me?" I question with fury at him calling me a *'little girl'*. Fuck him, I may be small, but I'll still put a bullet between his eyes. I have never been so happy that my grandmother Stella insisted that my sister and I learn to shoot guns for our own protection.

"Americana," the tallest of the three says, and I know at least what the word means.

"Why were you hiding?" His dark eyes trail over my body, taking in my ragged appearance. "You're hurt, you need medical attention."

"Answer my question. Why did you sneak up and attack me?" My arm throbs painfully, and I grit my teeth, refusing to waver and give them another chance to assault me. I take in all three; all are large and in their early twenties with dark ethnic features. I don't see any weapons visible, but that doesn't mean they don't have them on them. I won't allow myself to be stupid and let my guard down, because that would be a sure way to get myself killed.

The one who spoke English leers at me intimidatingly, and refuses to answer. To prove my point that I will fucking shoot them, I point the gun just over his left shoulder and pull the trigger making all three of them jump. "If I have to ask again, the next one won't miss."

A huge smile breaks across the psycho's face in pleasure. "I like you already, little girl. Why don't you put the gun down, and we can have a chat."

"Why don't you go to fucking hell, and answer the question before I shoot you?" I let a vicious smile cross my lips.

"Eu acho que acabei de encontrar minha alma gêmea." He chuckles to his companions, and at my look of fury, he turns back to me and translates, "I said to my friends that I think I just found my soulmate in the jungle of all places."

"Keep evading my questions, and you won't leave this jungle." I tilt my head and grin.

He clutches his chest dramatically in response. "So beautiful and deadly. How lucky I am to have found you." I roll my eyes at him, and his smile gets even wider, showing me bright white teeth against his tanned skin. "To answer your question, *beleza*, we are looking for something, a lost jewel. One of our elders sent us to search for it, so it can be brought to him safely."

His eyes appraise me once again, and their intensity causes my skin to break out in goosebumps. "You wouldn't know anything about a jewel in the jungle, would you, beautiful?"

"Where is your village? How far is it from where we are now?" Hope rises within me that the village is not far, and I'll be able to reach it. Will I have to injure or kill these three, before I can get to it? I don't know, but one thing is for certain: I won't allow anyone to stop me.

"What will you give us if we tell you?" His gaze narrows on my chest as he licks his lips suggestively.

I will literally pull the trigger and end these motherfuckers' lives, if they think they're going to rape or use me for their depraved pleasure. *Shit*, I'll blow my brains out before I let that happen. The days of me rolling over and allowing *anyone* to use me are done. That girl died in this jungle, and this bitch has no intention of playing along. "Your lives. I won't murder the three of you fuckers, and leave you as an offering to the jungle."

"Ela diz que não vai nos matar e nos deixar na selva se a levarmos até a aldeia." The three of them release hearty laughs at my expense. This fucker is not taking me seriously, and my patience is at an end. I have to get to that village to send help back to Francisco, and get out of here before Diego or my grandmother's men capture me. *"Ela é a joia que procurávamos."*

"Speak English, and the next words out of your mouth better be answering my questions, or you better say a prayer to whatever God you believe in." I'm done fucking around and fire at his friend's feet. All three of them jump in the air, and the humor disappears from their faces.

"Are you the princess? The one we seek? Where is your guide?"

"My questions first." I watch as one of them tries to distance himself from the other two, hoping I don't notice. I fire again, the bullet whizzing past his shoulder blade, and halting him in his tracks.

"Foda-se, okay," Mr. Humor raises his hands and motions to his friend to come back over. "The village is less than five miles that way," he points in the direction over the ridge. "Our village elder sent us; a woman was to be led by a guide through the jungle to our village, where we were to ensure she left the country. You are Isabella?"

I don't answer his question. Instead, I motion forward with the gun. "Take me to your elder and don't try anything further, or I will send you to hell." A cocky smile breaks over his face before he motions to his two friends to start walking. "A woman like you is hard to find, *preciosa*. Maybe we will keep you."

Fat fucking chance of that, asshole. One way or another, I'm making it out of this jungle. I hold the gun tight in one hand, lean down, and grab the machete with the other. It looks like I am a Stratford, after all.

CHAPTER THIRTY-FIVE

Issy

"Your absence has gone through me like thread through a needle. Everything I do is stitched with its color."

W.S. Merwin

Four months later.

I turn my face up towards the sunshine, the rays warming my skin, the smell of clean, fresh spring air rejuvenating all my senses as I sit here on the beach, looking at the crystal-clear waters of the Pacific Ocean. If someone had told me a year ago this is where I would be, I would have laughed in their faces, before I broke down and cried.

Yet here I am in a small coastal town, *free*. Free from the worries of my old life, and all the chains that confined me, and kept me a prisoner for so long. Free, not only of the man I loved, but also of the name and dynasty I was born into. Do I miss my old life and my family? *Like one misses a severed limb, forever feeling the ghost of the loss.*

Despite that loss, I know that this is where I belong. I know that if I contacted my sister or grandmother, another war would escalate, and I just can't allow that to happen. Despite the amount of pain I'm causing them, by letting them believe that I'm dead, I can't bring myself to go back to those chains. Is it selfish that I am out here living a new life while my grandmother and sister mourn my death?

Yes, but that is who I am, who I have always been, and despite many things changing and finding my way, that remains a part of me, one I'm no longer critical of. The truth is that Isabella Stratford died in that jungle, attempting to escape her lover's grasp and her family's demands. She never made it to that village; she died just like her guide, Francisco, did, consumed by the jungle, an offering to the old gods.

The woman who made it to that jungle village, with three men at gunpoint, is not the same person. That woman met the village elder and was treated for her wounds, and dehydration. She took a blade and sliced open her skin, removing the damaged tracking device her lover had installed in her own arm, as the men stood around and watched her with astonishment.

She forcefully demanded a new identity at gunpoint, and safe passage to a private airport, where she was taken in the dark of night, never to be seen again. Santiago followed through on his promise to get me to the village, and out of the country with a new identity and the means to start a new life. I will forever be grateful for the opportunity to become who I should have always been.

The weak woman who was once broken, traumatized, and a victim of her own failings, I'd like to think, is now gone, replaced with someone who finally has a reason for living. Someone who will never allow another person to own her.

It hasn't been easy, but once I made it out of the Brazilian jungle and back stateside, I had to decide where to go and how to survive without my family, my trust fund, and all my vices. Although Santiago gave me the means to start a new life, it wasn't one I was used to. A smirk crosses my lips at the memory of looking at the envelope with currency, and the note he sent with it.

Isabella,
If you are reading this, you have survived by God's grace. Take that as an indi-
cation never to look back. Start a new life far from the one you left in the jungle.

There is only pain behind you and a clean slate in front of you. Use this gift I have given you wisely. Remember your promise, or death will await you.

Santiago.

The currency didn't last more than the first month, while I lived in the shadows in perpetual fear of someone recognizing me, or realizing I was alive. By the second month, I came to the shocking realization that Santiago wasn't the only one who gave me a parting gift.

By then, the death of the heiress, Isabella Stratford, at the hands of her captor and lover, Diego Cabano, a ruthless cartel boss, was everywhere. It was on all the news channels and across social media, forcing me to use the meager funds I had left to ensure I could disguise my features.

My hand reaches up and touches my short, pixie platinum blonde haircut, my long, dark locks gone. The brown contact lenses that I wear hide my recognizable sapphire blue eyes. My prim and proper grandmother would have a heart attack if she saw my nose ring, or the tattoos that cover one of my arms. I have even managed to change my accent, hiding my recognizable New York twang. No one passing me by in the street would ever think I could be Isabella.

I now spend my days working at a small coffee shop as a barista, and my nights alone with the memories of those I left behind. I share a two-bedroom apartment with a roommate who doesn't ask any questions about my past, probably because she, too, is running from hers. It's a far cry from the riches of Billionaire's Row at Central Park West, and I wouldn't change it for all the money in the Stratford coffers.

I chose to come to this small town, where nothing ever changes, and people are happy with their quiet, mundane lives—a town filled with working-class families, little league baseball, and Friday nights spent at the local football stadium. I remember hearing the fond memories of someone I loved speak of its existence, and how it helped to shape him into who he was. I hope that it can have the same impact on me, and who I desperately want to be.

Diego and my grandmother are still at war. Somehow, he managed to escape that jungle, even after my grandmother sent an army to capture him, and bring me back. Diego retaliated by blowing up a few of her buildings, and sinking her yacht; thank fuck she wasn't on it at the time. Right now, he's sitting number one on the world's most-wanted list. My grandmother placed a billion-dollar bounty on his head, dead or alive.

Am I sad to know that my death didn't bring with it any sense of peace for either of them? *Yes.* Grief does funny things to people, and I don't believe for a second that either one of them has gotten past the anger yet of losing me. I haven't gotten past the anger of losing myself, even though I know with certainty that this was the only way I could live my life on my terms.

"Annabell? Girl, we have to do something about that tramp stamp." I look over at my companion and see the look of disgust on her face. I don't blame her; I wasn't overly thrilled when I finally caught a glimpse of it in a mirror four months ago. I can't believe that *asshole* branded me with his name, like property. Yet, despite the rage at knowing he did that without my permission, I have yet to remove it.

Some irrational part of me believes it is still a link back to him. A piece of him left on my body as a reminder of the love we once shared, regardless of if it was toxic. It certainly wasn't the only thing that he forgot to mention.

Three months ago.

"Miss Delburne, ma'am? We have your test results. The reason you have been feeling so tired and unwell isn't due to infection as we thought." The young female doctor at the community clinic gives me a look of deep sympathy, and has my hackles instantly rising.

"I know you said that you had an IUD and couldn't be pregnant, but we found no evidence of the IUD present when we did the ultrasound. Your bloodwork also confirmed my suspicions. You're pregnant, Annabell, just under five months along. You had lost so much weight that it wasn't noticeable."

I sit there, shocked to my core, not understanding what she is telling me. How can the IUD be missing? They don't just fall out. She has to be wrong; her tests have to be incorrect. I can't be pregnant. Then it hit me: the reality of the life I was living. That fucking bastard would have done anything to keep me with him. Even stooping so low as to remove my method of birth control, and impregnate me.

No wonder he couldn't keep his hands off of me. It was his plan all along to make sure that I would never leave him. He knew I wouldn't be capable of leaving my child behind, and I'm sure he never planned on letting me take it with me if I left him.

"You have choices, Annabell."

"No, I really don't." The mere thought of this baby inside of me, a piece of Diego and I together, forever intertwined, has me laying my hands on my mostly flat stomach. Joy replaces anger, and the need to nurture and keep it safe fills me. Mine. This child is mine. It is a blessing for a future I never planned on, but somehow, deep inside, I always wanted.

My grandfather Jaxon's words from long ago enter my mind and, with them, cement my decision. "Fate has a funny way of giving you what you need most without you even knowing it, my beautiful little doll. Trust that what happens in life is meant to be; fate makes no mistakes when it casts its weave. It's up to you to pull on the correct thread."

The thread was there for me to pull all along, just waiting until I was strong enough to bear the next part of my journey, and now I am. I will be this baby's mother, protector, and cheerleader.

I can never let Diego know that this baby exists. He would use it against me as a way to tie me to him forever. I'm sure he never counted on me getting away from him. A love forced, is a love scorned. He will never understand that, and I have no intention of going back to teach him.

Love will fill this baby's life; I will make sure of it. It will be the two of us against the world, and I'll give it everything I lacked when I was growing up. It will always know it is wanted, needed, and valued, and I'll destroy anyone who tries to hurt it. It may never get to know that it is a Stratford, but that won't stop me from instilling our Stratford strength into it.

I'm pulled back from the memory of the first day of my new life. The day I knew I had to not only survive for me, but for my baby. "I can't see it, so it doesn't bother me, Rachel." I smile and take a sip of my water as I turn away from my roommate, and stare back at the ocean.

So much has already happened since that day when I discovered that I was going to be a mom. Now, I'm once again facing a crossroads, and I'm unsure of the road to take. I wanted to do this alone, to hide away from the world and have this beautiful life with my baby, but life has once again thrown me a curveball. I have to do whatever I can to save my child, and for that, I need *him*.

Memories and dreams plague me in this peaceful town. Signs of him are everywhere, even though I never visited here with him. All of his stories have left his ghost everywhere I look.

I can no longer ignore what my heart is begging for; the need to reach out to him, and hope he doesn't betray me. Although I don't need a savior anymore, I still need him. *He wouldn't, he loved me.*

Yes, loved, as in past tense, as in no more. I live with the guilt daily that I caused that to happen. Do I even have the right to drag him into this mess? *Do I have another choice?* I can't keep going like this; this baby is my everything, and without his help, it may not survive to live a full life.

"I'll be right back, just taking a walk to stretch my legs." I smile down at Rachel as she gets the look of an overprotective mother hen. I know she's worried about me and the baby. If I'm being honest, I am too.

I grab my burner phone, walk down the beach, and dial a number I never thought I would again. My heart races in my chest, and I almost disconnect the call on the first ring.

"Hello?" The rough voice on the phone has my insides tightening, and sweat slickening my hands. What if I'm doing the wrong thing? What if this puts him in danger? What if my grandmother finds me through him?

Worst of all, what if he tells me to go to hell and hangs up the phone? What will I do then? How will I help my baby? *Survive, we will survive, with or without him.* My hand rests against my rounded stomach, the curve now present and impossible to hide on my small frame. I have no choice but to survive and keep going; it's no longer just about me anymore.

"Kai, please don't hang up."

"Isabella?" The name is said with disbelief. "What the fuck! Where are you? I thought you were dead. The news has been reporting your death for weeks. They say you were kidnapped and taken for ransom against your grandmother."

"KAI! I don't have much time. I can't explain now, but you can't tell anyone that I am alive. I am being hunted, Kai, and they will recapture and take me back." I brace myself against the beach wall, my legs threatening to buckle at just the thought of what Diego Cabano would do, if he found me now. The violence and ruthlessness that he is capable of terrifies me.

"Isabella, holy shit. Are you safe, baby?"

His voice soothes me immediately, and his use of the word 'baby' reassures me that I have done the right thing, and pulled on the right thread. "Do you remember where you told me the seagulls like to play in the sand, and waves feel like magic at twilight?"

"Seagulls, waves? Isabella, just tell me where you are so I can come to you to keep you safe, please, baby."

"Come find me in the waves, Kai, and keep me a secret, or it will mean my death."

I disconnect the call, pull the SIM out, and snap it, throwing both it and the phone into the nearest garbage can, and then continuing down the beach, waiting for my prince charming to arrive, while hoping the beast doesn't find me first.

"But he did not understand the price. Mortals never do.
They only see the prize, their heart's desire, their dream...
But the price of getting what you want,
is getting what you once wanted."

Neil Gaiman, The Sandman, Vol. 3: Dream Country

That is the end for now.

Get more of Issy, Diego, Kai, and the rest of the Casbury clan in **_Venomous King_**, the conclusion to this story. Preorder it **here!**

If you want to learn more about the original Casbury crew and Issy's sister, Mia. You can find her in **_Reign of the Queen_**. Get it **here!**

If you are intrigued about the original Stratford _"Ice Queen"_ you can meet Stella Stratford in **_Rise of a Kingdom_**. Get it **here!**

Acknowledgements

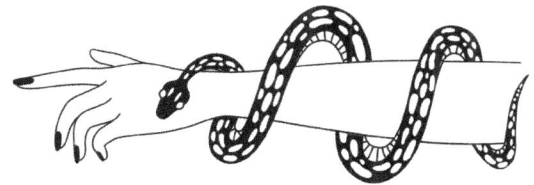

To the readers - If you have made it this far, I hope you still have your sanity intact, and I'm sorry for the scars I leave behind, but thank you from the bottom of my heart and soul for reading my books. Know that without you, there are no books! Thanks for giving this Canadian indie author a chance!

My ride or die - You have once again had to put up with my perpetually hangry, frustrated, and anxiety-ridden self. You are my favorite superhero and naughtiest villain all rolled into one. *I love you forever.*

To my daughter- I still love you, even though you think I am unhinged, depraved, and filled with darkness and can be mean to my characters. Thank you for being the first person to always read my books and to call me back from the dark to the light. I love you, *little momma*.

To my handsome son - Thank you once again for ignoring me while I wrote this book and keeping the noise down when I was losing my sanity. I love you, puppy.

To my P.A. - *Darcy Bennett*, you are a unique, supportive human being with the whip skills of Zorro. Thank you for putting up with me, keeping me organized, and preventing me from smashing my face on the ground.

To **Mia Fury** - Girl, I once again could not have done this without you. I love you and am so grateful to have found you on this journey.

Katelin - who beta-read this book when I was terrified it would cause readers to revolt and come for me with pitchforks. Thank you for all your support and all the chats.- I am honored and humbled by your support.

Sinner Street Team - Ladies, you are life! *I love you all*. Thank you for filling my days with smiles and laughter and for all your support. I am forever grateful.

Smutven Coven: You ladies are amazing. You make me laugh and forget all my stresses. I am privileged to call you my friends. Thank you for being but a click away.

My lovely members of the *Queen's Lair* on F.B. - You make me smile & keep me sane every day, and I am honored to have met you! Please keep up the naughtiness!

To my ARC Team - Thank you from the bottom of my heart for supporting me and helping me get the word out about my books! I appreciate everything that you do.

Bookish Girls - Thank you always for your kindness and support. You have my gratitude & heart forever.

Thank you to the other fantastic book community authors, PA, and readers who have been very supportive, inclusive, and patient with me.

To both my four-legged demon spawns, no, you cannot have another treat-o just because mom is having a breakdown. You both are the best doggies a momma could have.

Thank you, Cady Verdiramo of ***Cruel Ink Design***, for making this stunning cover. Thank you to J. Armstrong from **Furious Editing** for painstakingly helping me edit this book. I'm sorry, I'm still allergic to commas and proper spacing.

I have so many new worlds and books to be published. I hope you all stick with me and continue on this amazing journey.

I love ya, lovelies!

A.L. Maruga, xoxo

About the Author

Author A.L Maruga grew up in the big city of Toronto, Canada, reading romance and watching Buffy the Vampire Slayer. She always seemed to fall for the villain.

Her love of all things romance and paranormal has stayed with her over the years, and now she devours books at an alarming rate!

Drinker of gallons of coffee, a lover of all things chocolate, and a collector of broken souls. You can find her wandering around her small town in Southwestern Ontario with her trusty writing furbaby assistants '*Daisy and Rayo*' or spending time with her two grown kids and her soul mate.

2022 was her debut as a romance author with her first book, *Reign of the Queen* a dark enemy to lovers romance. In 2023, she released another four dark romance books, and she's just getting started.

She writes about demanding, unapologetic, possessive, dark alpha a-holes and the strong women who bring them to their knees.

www.ingramcontent.com/pod-product-compliance
Lightning Source LLC
Chambersburg PA
CBHW060936120726
47910CB00002B/357